TOO CLOSE TO HOME

ALSO BY LINWOOD BARCLAY

Bad Move
Bad Guys
Lone Wolf
Stone Rain
No Time for Goodbye

TOO CLOSE TO HOME

LINWOOD BARCLAY

DOUBLEDAY LARGE PRINT HOME LIBRARY EDITION

BANTAM BOOKS

This Large Print Edition, prepared especially for Doubleday Large Print Home Library, contains the complete, unabridged text of the original Publisher's Edition.

TOO CLOSE TO HOME
A Bantam Book / October 2008

Published by Bantam Dell
A Division of Random House, Inc.
New York, New York

Bantam Books is a registered trademark of Random House, Inc., and the colophon is a trademark of Random House, Inc.

ISBN 978-1-60751-027-7

Printed in the United States of America
Published simultaneously in Canada

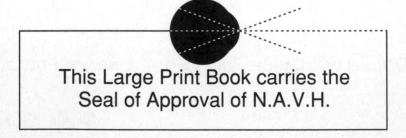

This Large Print Book carries the
Seal of Approval of N.A.V.H.

For Neetha

PROLOGUE

Derek figured, when the time came, the crawlspace would be the best place to hide. The only thing was, he hoped the Langleys wouldn't take that long, once he was in position, to get the hell out of their house and hit the road. The last time Derek had played with Adam in their crawlspace, they'd been eight, nine years old. They'd pretended it was a cave filled with treasure, or the cargo hold of a spaceship, and there was a monster hiding in there somewhere.

Well, that had been quite a few years ago. He was a lot bigger now; Adam, too. Pushing six feet, already taller at seventeen than his father, Derek wasn't looking forward to scrunching down in there for God knows how long.

He was hoping he could time it right.

When he saw the Langleys putting the last of their bags into the trunk but still doing last-minute things in the house, that's when Derek would say goodbye, make like he was going out the back door, let it slam, then tiptoe down the stairs, move aside the sliding door to the crawlspace, get in, pull the door back across. There wasn't anything in the crawlspace, which was right under the living room, that the Langleys would be needing for their week away. Just loads of boxes jammed with Christmas decorations, family mementos not worth displaying but too important to pitch, old paperback novels, and years' worth of legal papers belonging to Adam's dad, Albert Langley. There was an old tent down there, and a Coleman stove, but the Langleys weren't going camping.

Jesus, Derek thought, I'm getting a hard-on just thinking about it.

"I wish I didn't have to go," Adam said to Derek while his mother, Donna Langley, was taking some things from the refrigerator—a package of hot dogs, some beer—and putting them into a cooler.

She turned. It had been so busy around the house, getting ready to go away, it was the first she'd noticed Adam had his friend over. "Why, hello, Derek," she said, almost formally, as if they were meeting for the first time.

"Hello, Mrs. Langley," he replied.

"How are you today?" she asked.

"Very well, thank you," he said. "And you?" Jeez, he thought, he was sounding like Eddie Haskell, in that show his parents watched when they were kids.

Before she could reply, Adam whined, "There'll be nothing to do at this place. It's gonna suck, I just know it."

"Adam," his mother said tiredly, "it's a very highly recommended resort."

"Jeez, stop being such a hurtsack," Derek told him. "It'll be fun. Don't they have boats and shit? And horses or something?"

"Who cares about horses?" Adam said. "Do I look like somebody who cares about riding horses? Dirt bikes, if they had those, that'd be cool, but they don't. You sound like you want me to go, like you're on *her* side."

"I'm just saying, if your parents are going to make you go, you might as well make the best of it."

"Good advice," Donna Langley said, her back to the two boys.

Adam said to her, "I wouldn't do anything bad. I wouldn't have a party here."

"We've had this discussion," Donna Langley said, adding an ice pack from the freezer to the cooler. Adam's mother was pretty, especially for a mother. Brown hair down to her shoulders, a nice body, round in the right places, not like most of the girls at Derek's school. They were like sticks. But looking at her, thinking about her like that, made Derek uncomfortable now, especially with Adam present.

"But you can trust me," Adam said, a pleading tone to his voice. "Jesus, you don't give me any credit for anything."

"You know what happened at the Moffatts'," she said. "His parents went away and word got out and a hundred kids descended on his place."

"It wasn't a hundred. It was only like sixty."

"Okay," his mother said. "Sixty. A hundred. They still trashed the house."

"That wouldn't happen here."

Donna Langley leaned up against the kitchen counter, suddenly looking very tired. Derek thought at first she was just exhausted from arguing, but then it looked like maybe she didn't feel so hot.

"You all right, Mrs. Langley?" he asked.

"Just . . ." She gave her head a small shake. "Just felt a little woozy there for a second."

"You okay, Mom?" asked Adam, perhaps shamed into concern by his friend, taking a tentative step toward her.

"Yeah, yeah," she said, waving him away and pushing herself away from the counter. "Might be something I had for lunch. I've been feeling off all afternoon."

Or maybe it was some of her medicine, Derek thought. He knew she took pills, stuff to help her get through the day. She could be up and down. Some sort of bipolar shit or something, Adam had said.

She composed herself. "Adam, go see if your father needs any help."

But Albert Langley, a tall, broad-shouldered man in his early fifties with thinning gray hair, was already standing in the kitchen doorway. "What is it?" he asked his wife. Sounding slightly more annoyed than concerned. "Don't tell me you're coming down with something."

"No, no, really," she said. "It's probably something I ate."

"For God's sake," Albert said, "we've planned this thing for weeks. We cancel now, we're not going to get our deposit back on this place, you know that, don't you?"

Donna Langley turned her back to him, saying, "Yeah, well, thanks for your concern."

Albert Langley shook his head in disgust and left the kitchen.

"Listen," Derek whispered to Adam, "I gotta take off, you know?" He suddenly realized this was going to take a bit of choreography. He needed Adam to go off with his father, head out the front of the house, so he could pretend to slip out the back.

Part of him felt like a real shit, not telling his own best friend what he was up to, but it wasn't like it would be the first time he'd kept something from him. And it wasn't like anyone was going to get hurt or anything was going to be damaged. No one would even have to know. Not counting Penny, of course. Sure, the Langleys would wonder, when they got back, whether one of them forgot to lock one of the doors, to set the alarm system, but when they looked around and found nothing taken, they'd eventually forget about it. Next time they went away, they'd double-check things, that's all.

"I wish you could come with us," Adam said. "I'm gonna die without someone to hang with."

"I can't," Derek said. "My parents would freak if I ditched my summer job even for a week." The thing was, even if he hadn't already figured out how to make the Langleys' time away the best week of his life, spending seven days with them, that just wouldn't be cool.

They'd moved out of the kitchen, down the hall, around the midpoint of the house. All Derek had to do was keep heading to the back, go down half a flight of steps, and there was the door. Round the corner, take the other half flight, he'd be in the basement.

"I don't know if there'll be anybody there to hang out with," Adam said, still moaning, Jesus.

"Don't worry about it. It's only a week. You know what? When you get back, we'll read the rest of what's on that computer." He and Adam enjoyed collecting old, junked computers. Some of the stuff you found on them, man, you wouldn't believe it. Everything from school projects to kiddie porn. Some people, the stuff that went on in their heads. Looking through discarded computers, it was better than searching through somebody's medicine cabinet.

Adam looked down at the floor. "Yeah, well, there's a bit of a shitstorm about that."

That caught Derek by surprise. "What?"

"With my dad. He kind of found out what was on it. The thing we were reading."

"So what's it to him? He thinks you don't know about porn? And it's not like it's pictures. It's just written stuff. It's not even really porn. Not good porn, anyway."

"Look, I can't get into it now," Adam said quietly. "I'll tell you about it when I get back, or maybe I can give you a call about it during the week."

"Don't sweat it. If I want to read it, I've got the copy I made."

"Shit, don't let him find out about that," Adam said. "He seemed really pissed. I don't know why he got such a hair up his ass about it."

"What, you think I'm gonna go up to your dad, say 'Hey, Mr. Langley, I kept a copy'?"

"No, it's just—"

"Adam!" It was Mr. Langley, sounding pissed, calling for him from the front step.

"Listen, man, I gotta go," Adam said.

"He's already mad about my mom feeling sick."

"Okay, yeah, sure, see ya in a week," Derek said. Adam turned one way, Derek the other. Derek forced himself to call out, "Have a nice trip, Mrs. Langley!"

Everyone had to think he was leaving.

From the kitchen, a subdued "Bye, Derek."

He bounded down the stairs for effect, opened the back door, and closed it hard, making the usual racket he always did when he left and cut across the yard and headed into the woods that ran along the edge of the lane.

But this time he didn't leave the house. Once he'd closed the door with enough force for Mrs. Langley to hear in the kitchen, he was down into the basement in a second, heading to the far side and kneeling next to the couch in front of the sliding panel that led into the crawlspace.

Derek slid it to the left, crawled in on his hands and knees, the concrete floor hard and cold. He turned himself around, slid the door closed as quietly as possible, and held his breath for a moment as he became enveloped in darkness.

All he could hear was his heart pounding in his ears. Slowly, he exhaled, tried to compose himself. He knew there was a bulb on a pull chain in here somewhere, but he was afraid to turn it on. What if Mr. Langley happened to come downstairs for something at the last minute, saw light showing around the edges of the panel? He'd just have to sit in the dark here for as long as it took.

At least he could see what time it was. He reached into his pocket for his cell phone, made sure the ringer was off, and checked the time, the tiny screen the only source of light. Nearly eight o'clock. The Langleys *had* to be going soon.

He couldn't talk, but he could send a text message. He typed out "W8ING 4 LANGS 2 GO HIDING NOW." He pressed Send.

The idea of having his own little fuck palace for a week, it had to be the best thing he'd ever thought of. Okay, maybe not a "fuck" palace. Penny might be ready, but maybe not. But everything short of that, for sure.

He listened for house noises. Sitting cross-legged on the cement floor, jammed in between boxes of Christmas bulbs and a toboggan Adam probably hadn't used in five years, Derek could sense Donna Langley moving around in the kitchen. A house, it was like a living thing. You stepped on the floor in one room, and it was like a pulse went running along one of the studs underfoot, and then, when it met another beam, it kept on going, like that song Derek's mom used to sing to him when he was little, about the thigh bone connected to the hip bone, the hip bone connected to the—

"For Christ's sake, let's go!"

Adam's dad. Jesus, he could be a bit of a prick, Derek thought. His own dad could sure be a pain in the ass, but he wasn't the dick Adam's dad was.

He could hear a bit of shuffling upstairs. Someone walking to the back door, checking to see that it was locked. Then the sound of another door, opening and closing. The front door. Derek, not daring to breathe, thought he could even hear the turning of a key in a lock.

A couple of moments later, car doors opening and closing. The engine of the Langleys' Saab SUV coming on. Tires on gravel, perceptible at first, then receding.

And then nothing.

Derek swallowed, decided to stay in hiding a couple of minutes more to be sure. Long enough for the Langleys to get far enough away that if they realized they'd forgotten something, they'd figure it was easier to buy it along the way. His heart was starting to slow down now, things were looking good, all he had to do was—

Jesus Christ what the fuck was that crawling down his neck holy mother of God!

A spider! A goddamn spider had slipped below his collar. He went into a spasm of slapping at himself in the darkness, the side of his neck, the top of his shoulder, through his shirt. The spider had made him jump and he'd walloped his head on an overhead beam.

"Fuck!" he shouted. He threw back the crawlspace panel and practically tumbled out onto the carpeted basement floor. He reached under his collar, felt something small and mushy, pulled the shirt over his head and slapped away at his neck, desperate to get rid of the spider's remains.

His heart was ready to explode out of his chest.

Once the spider crisis had passed, he took another moment to pull himself together. The basement was almost dark. There was probably only a half hour of light left outside, but he didn't dare turn on any lamps. For the whole week, he wouldn't be able to turn on lights. Maybe, here in the basement, he could put the TV on. No one would notice that from the outside, especially with the house set back so far from the main road.

But really, who needed lights for what he planned to do? He could feel his way around in the dark.

He was surprised Penny hadn't responded to his text message. But it was time to get in touch again, let her know the house was empty. First, though, he should do a walk-through, make sure everything was okay.

He slipped his shirt back on, went up the basement stairs, saw that the deadbolt had been thrown on the back door. There was still enough light to see easily as he wandered the first floor. The front door was locked. On the wall in the front hall, the security system keypad. Derek had been in the house so many times with Adam, watched him engage and turn off the system, he knew the code. All he had to do was enter it, flip the deadbolt on the back door, and he could come and go as he pleased. It meant leaving the house unlocked, but around here, on the outskirts of town, hardly anyone ever had break-ins.

The house felt totally different, as he walked through it for the first time all alone, no one knowing he was here. He felt a charge, checking out the whole place, realized his heart was pumping overtime, his palms sweating.

He reassured himself he knew the layout well enough to manage it in the dark, even the places where he didn't plan to spend any time, like Adam's parents' bedroom, where he was standing now. Big king-size bed, thick white duvet, en-suite bathroom with a shower and one of those tubs that had the jets in it. He'd love to hang out in here with Penny—maybe she'd take a bath in there with him, with bubbles and everything, just like people in the movies—but no, that seemed a bit risky. The basement couch would more than do the trick. It wasn't so much where they did it in the house. The main thing was privacy, no interruptions.

A whole fucking week.

His phone buzzed. A message from Penny. It was about time. One word: "Well?"

Shit, he could just call her now. He punched in her number and she answered on the second ring.

"I'm in," he said.

"Oh my God," she said, her voice tinged with excitement.

"It's almost dark. Come on over. I'll let you in the back door."

"Okay, but, like, there might be a problem."

"Don't do this to me, Penny. I've got a woody the size of a fire log."

She made a shushing noise, even though there was no one to hear him. "Don't worry, it's just my parents are raging at me because I backed the Kia into that telephone pole at the end of the driveway. The one that's so close. It's like hardly a scratch, but my dad is shitting a brick over it because he says it's not worth putting through insurance, so he says I'm going to have—"

The call died. Derek looked at the screen on his phone, lost signal. How'd that happen?

He called her back. "What happened?" Penny asked.

"I don't know. Look, try to get here for ten, okay? Call me if there's a problem. I'm just going to hang out here for a while."

Penny said okay and hung up.

Derek stood in front of the Langleys' bedroom dresser, reached out, touched it, thinking about whether there was anything interesting in there. The thing was, part of him was feeling pretty guilty about this, even though everything was going to be okay and there was no way Mr. or Mrs. Langley, or Adam, was going to find out. Maybe he'd tell Adam, someday. No time soon. Like in a few years. When it wouldn't matter anymore.

Or maybe not.

He couldn't believe Penny's parents might not let her out for the evening. He was absolutely aching for her to come over. He thought, maybe take something from Mrs. Langley's lingerie drawer, whack off, take the edge off, be ready to go again by the time Penny got over.

Okay, Derek thought, maybe there are some lines that shouldn't be crossed. He could watch some TV, take his mind off things. So he returned to the basement, in pretty much total darkness now, and turned on the set. Flipped through some channels, hardly settling on anything for more than a second. He couldn't relax, even though he had this house to sneak into for the next seven days. It was a seventeen-year-old boy's dream. A place to bring his girl as often as he wanted.

Better than a car. Didn't have to worry about some cop tapping on a steamed-up window.

But it was starting to feel wrong. The Langleys had always been good to him. Well, Adam's mom, for sure. His dad always made you feel like you were intruding, like he wanted the house to himself when he wasn't at the office, defending people, getting them off, whatever the hell it was he did. Derek had known Adam, what, nearly ten years now? Been here for sleepovers, gone on short trips with the family.

What would they think of him if they ever found out? Jesus, Adam's dad was a lawyer. Could he sue him? Would he sue a kid he knew? Or worse, would he call the po—

His cell buzzed. He glanced at, recognized Penny's number. "Yeah?" he said. And before Penny could say a word, he lost the signal.

Sitting in the basement, he figured.

Too much interference or something. He reached over to the end table and grabbed the extension phone, punched in Penny's cell.

"I can't come," Penny said. She was whispering. "I'm grounded."

"Shit," Derek said. "Shit shit shit."

"Look, I gotta go. We can get together later in the week, maybe tomorrow, okay? I gotta go." And she ended the call.

Derek hung up the phone. The perfect plan, fucked. God, the blueballs he was going to have. The thing was, he didn't just want to mess around with Penny. He wanted to be with her. He wanted to hang out in that empty house and talk with her, for long stretches without anyone interrupting or walking in, about what he wanted to do with his life. His parents figured he was some lazy fuck without dreams or ambition, but that wasn't true. He could tell Penny. About wanting to be a software designer, maybe invent new games, shit like that. If he told his dad about wanting to design games, he'd tell him, "Hey, I wanted to turn my passion into a career too, but sometimes you have to be realistic."

Derek flipped through the channels, popped in Adam's Halo game for a while, watched some MTV, dozed off for a bit during Justin Timberlake. It was kind of cool, just hanging out here, even if he was alone. No one to bug him about anything.

But it was getting late. Time to get the hell out of here, he figured.

That was when he heard a noise from outside. Tires crunching on gravel.

He grabbed the remote, killed the TV. The basement had windows, the kind that came down about a foot from the ceiling. He jumped up on the couch so he could see outside.

It was the Saab. The Langleys' SUV.

"Shit!" he said under his breath. "Shit!"

He had to get out. He had to get out fast. He ran up the stairs to the back door, was about to open it when he realized that if he did, the house alarm would probably be set off. He'd have to enter the code first, but the keypad was by the front door.

He started running down the hall, thinking maybe he could get to the front hall and enter the code before anyone came through the door, then run back through the house and out the back door.

But then he saw shadows beyond the front door. It was Adam, with his mother right behind him.

Derek stopped, turned, ran back for the basement. He could hear the front door opening, voices, Donna Langley saying, "I said I was sorry. You think I wanted to ruin everyone's vacation?"

He dropped to the floor in front of the crawlspace opening and was about to slide the door open when the basement lights went on. He knew there was a switch at the top of the stairs, which meant someone was coming down. Derek scurried into the narrow space between the back of the couch and the wall, figuring he was pretty well covered, but Jesus, what if someone came down and decided to watch TV?

Someone did come down the stairs

right then. Derek heard the beer fridge open, a couple of things get put into it, then Adam, shouting upstairs, "Should I refreeze the ice packs?"

Derek wondered whether to get his attention, fess up, enlist Adam's help in getting him out of the house. Adam might be pissed, but there was no way he'd tell. His parents would find a way to blame him. But before he could make up his mind what to do, Adam was going back upstairs. But the light stayed on. Derek thought maybe he'd come back. Derek could make out some of the conversations upstairs.

Mr. Langley: "Honey, just go to bed. We'll unpack."

Mrs. Langley: "Maybe, in the morning, I'll feel better."

Mr. Langley: "Yeah, well, whatever. Maybe Adam and I will go up, you can join us when you're feeling better. Honestly, your timing."

Mrs. Langley: "For Christ's sake, you think I wanted to get sick?"

Mr. Langley: "I'll be up in a minute."

Okay, so if they went to bed, the only one to worry about was Adam. And if he went to bed, Derek would wait till they were all asleep, sneak upstairs, enter the code, get out the back door. So long as Penny didn't change her mind, sneak out of her own house and come over, Jesus, let's hope *that* didn't happen—

Mr. Langley: "Who the hell's that?"

Derek thought, *Shit, is he talking about me?* How could he know Derek was down here, how could he see—

No, someone outside, tires crunching on gravel, then stopping. The sound of a car door closing.

Christ, no. Not drop-in company this time of night.

Adam: "I don't know who it is, Dad."

Derek thought he could hear footsteps outside, then Albert Langley saying something, probably with the door open.

It sounded as though someone else, maybe two people, he wasn't sure, had come into the house.

Some muffled talk. Mr. Langley saying, "Who did you say you are?"

A new voice. Just snippets of sentences. Then one word, really clear: "Shame." And then: "Son of a bitch."

That was when Derek heard the first shot. Then Adam, screaming. "Dad! Dad!"

Mrs. Langley, sounded like from up on the second floor: "Albert! Albert! What's going on?"

And then Adam: "Mom! Don't come—"

That was when Derek heard the second shot. The sound of something— someone—falling down some stairs.

Then, footsteps running through the house. At least two sets, frantic running, from the front of the house to the back. Only lasting a second or two.

Derek heard a third shot, then someone tumbling down the half flight of stairs toward the back door.

After that, it was very quiet.

Derek realized he was trembling. His teeth were nearly chattering. He heard more footsteps going through the house, slower now, calm steps, measured steps. They came down the half flight of stairs, paused, turned, came all the way down to the basement.

Couldn't hear the person walking around that well now, not on the basement broadloom, which was laid over cement. But he could sense someone in the room. The person who had fired the shots. A killer. A few feet away, on the other side of the couch. Derek could hear shallow, rapid breathing.

He clamped his jaw tight together, determined to stop the chattering. He wondered if the killer could hear the blood pulsing in his temple.

Then the person went back up the stairs, turned out the light. The front door opened and closed, then a car door, same thing. Open, then slamming shut. A moment later, tires rolling away on gravel.

Derek waited about five minutes, slithered his way back out from behind the couch, crossed the rec room, and went up the stairs to the landing at the back door, just enough moonlight streaming through the window to show Adam lying there, his legs still splayed across the stairs, his head in a pool of black blood.

Derek delicately stepped over him, his hand shaking as he turned back the deadbolt, opened the door, and ran off into the night.

ONE

The night they killed our neighbors, the Langleys, we never heard a thing.

It was warm and humid that evening, so we'd closed all the windows and had the air conditioner cranked up as high as it would go. Even at that, we couldn't get the temperature in the house much below 76. This was late July, and we'd been suffering through a heat wave the last week, the thermometer hitting mid-90s pretty much every day, except for Wednesday, when it hit 100. Even some rain early in the week had failed to break it. It wasn't getting much below the mid-80s even after the sun went down.

Normally, it being a Friday night, I might have stayed up a little later, even have been up when it happened, but I had to work Saturday. That rain had set me back with all the customers I do yard work for. So Ellen and I had packed it in pretty early, nine-thirty or so. Even if we'd been up, we'd probably have been watching TV, so it's pretty unlikely we'd have heard anything.

It's not like the Langleys' place is right next door. It's the first house in off the highway along our shared driveway. Once you pass their place, it's still another fifty or sixty yards or so before you get to our house. You can't see our place from the highway. Homes out here on the outskirts of Promise Falls in upstate New York have some space between them. You can see the Langleys' house up the lane, through the trees, but we never heard their parties, and if the racket I make tuning up lawn mowers ever bothered them, they never said anything about it.

I was up around six-thirty Saturday morning. Ellen, who didn't have to go into her job up at the college, stirred as I moved into a sitting position on the side of the bed.

"Sleep in," I said. "You don't have to

get up." I stood up, wandered down to the foot of the bed, saw that the book Ellen had been reading before she'd turned out the light had fallen to the floor. It was just one of a stack of books on her bedside table. You have to do a lot of reading when you organize a college literary festival.

"It's okay," she mumbled resignedly, turning her face into the pillow and pulling the covers tighter. "I'll put some coffee on. You're just going to wake me up getting dressed anyway."

"Well," I said, "if you're already getting up, some eggs would be nice." Ellen said something into the pillow I couldn't hear, but it didn't sound friendly. I continued, "If I heard you correctly, that it's no trouble, does that mean you could fry up some bacon, too?"

She turned her head. "Is there a union for slaves? I want to sign up."

I got up and walked to the window, flipped open the blinds to let the early morning sun in.

"Oh God, make it go away," Ellen said. "Jesus, Jim, shut those."

"Looks like another hot one," I said, leaving the blinds open. "I was kind of hoping it might rain, then I'd have an excuse not to work today."

"Would it kill those people if their grass missed getting cut one week?" Ellen asked.

"They pay for a weekly service, hon," I said. "I'd rather work a Saturday than have to give them refunds."

Ellen had no comeback for that. We weren't quite living hand-to-mouth, but neither were we willing to throw money away. And a lawn service, especially in this part of the country, was definitely a seasonal business. You made your living from spring to fall, unless you diversified by putting a blade on the front of your pickup and clearing driveways in the winter. I'd been hunting for a used blade. The winters around here could be fierce. Couple of years back, over in Oswego, they had snow up to the first-floor roofs.

I'd only been running a lawn service for a couple of summers now, and I needed to find ways to make more money. It wasn't exactly my dream job, and it certainly wasn't what I wanted for myself when I was a young guy starting out, but it beat what I'd most recently left behind.

Ellen took a breath, let out a long sigh, and threw back the covers. She reached, reflexively, as she did occasionally, for where her pack of smokes used to be on the bedside table, but she'd quit the habit years ago, and there was nothing there. "Breakfast is coming, Your Majesty," she said. She reached down for the book on the floor and said, "I can't believe this was a bestseller. Hard to believe a novel about wheat isn't gripping. There's a reason they set a lot of books in cities, you know. There are people there. *Characters*."

I took a couple of steps toward the bathroom, winced, put my hand on my lower back.

"You okay?" Ellen asked.

"Yeah, I'm fine. I did something to myself yesterday, I was holding the weed whacker and turned funny or something."

"You're an old man in a young man's

game, Jim," Ellen said, putting on her slippers and throwing on a housecoat.

"Thanks for reminding me," I said.

"I don't have to remind you. You've got your aching back for that." She shuffled out of the bedroom as I went into the bathroom to shave.

I took a look at myself in the mirror. I had some sunburn on my whiskered face. I'd been trying to remember to use sunscreen, wear a hat with a visor, but the day before, it got so hot I threw the hat in the truck at one point, and must have sweated the sunscreen clean off. I still didn't look too bad for forty-two, and as tired as I felt, I was probably in better shape than two years ago, when I spent most of my day sitting in an air-conditioned Grand Marquis, driving around Promise Falls, opening doors for an asshole, being a glorified gofer without an ounce of self-respect. Since then, I'd lost thirty pounds, I was gaining back upper-body strength I'd lost over the last decade, and I'd never slept better in my entire life. Coming home every night dead tired had a lot to do with that.

Getting up in the morning, though, that could be a challenge. Like today.

By the time I came downstairs to the kitchen, the smell of bacon was wafting through the house and Ellen was pouring two cups of coffee. The Saturday edition of the *Promise Falls Standard* was on the kitchen table, rubber band already removed, so I could see the main headline.

"Your old friend's at it again," Ellen said, cracking some eggs into a bowl.

The headline read, "Mayor Rants at Single Moms' Home." And a drop headline, "Vows next time to 'bring cookies, not toss them.'"

"Oh Jesus," I said. "The guy never stops." I picked up the paper, read the first few paragraphs. Promise Falls's mayor, Randall Finley, had burst in unannounced Thursday night at a city-funded home where unwed moms can find support as they adjust to lives with newborns but no husbands. It was something the previous mayor fought for and got, and which Finley had always seen as a waste of taxpayer money. Although to be fair, Finley viewed almost everything as a waste of taxpayer money, except for his car and driver. And that was pretty much a necessity, given his talent for drinking to excess, and a DUI conviction a few years back.

Finley, the story suggested, had been touring around the city, dropping into a couple of bars after a city council meeting, and while passing the home ordered his driver—I was guessing that would be Lance Garrick, but the story didn't actually say—to stop. Finley walked up to the door and kept banging on it until the home supervisor, Gillian Metcalfe, opened up. She attempted to keep him out but the mayor forced his way in and started shouting, "Maybe if you girls had exercised a little restraint, you wouldn't be in the mess you are now!"

And then, according to reports from the young women living at the home, he threw up in the front hall.

"Even for Finley," I said to Ellen, "that's pretty impressive."

"You're feeling nostalgic," Ellen said. "You think he'd take you back?"

I was too tired to fire something back at her. I took a sip of my coffee and read further into the story. When reports began to circulate Friday morning about the mayor's behavior, he at first denied everything. It wasn't clear whether he was lying, or simply didn't remember. But by the afternoon, when presented with all the evidence against him, including the vomit-splattered front hall carpet runner that Gillian Metcalfe had taken down to city hall and left on the front steps, the mayor decided to revise his statement.

"I deeply regret," he said in a written release, not eager to face any media representatives in person, "my behavior last night at the Swanson House." It was named in honor of Helen Swanson, a late city councillor who had championed feminist causes. "I had had a particularly stressful session of council and may have had more refreshments afterwards than was prudent. I remain a strong supporter of Swanson House and offer my sincerest apologies. Next time I would hope to bring cookies rather than toss them."

"Pure Randy," I said. "Close with a joke. At least he didn't stick with trying to pretend it didn't happen. Must have been too many witnesses."

Ellen had three plates out, put three bacon strips and two fried eggs and a couple slices of toast on two of them, and brought them over to the kitchen table. I sat down and shoved some bacon into my mouth. It was salty and greasy and wonderfully delicious. "Mmmm," I said.

"This is why you keep me, isn't it?" she said. "For the breakfasts."

"Dinners are good, too," I said.

She reached over the paper, pulled out the lifestyles section. I took a sip of coffee, forkful of egg, bite of bacon, bite of toast. I had a good system going.

"You going to have to do a full day?" Ellen asked.

"I think we can be done a little after noon. The rain delayed everybody a day, but by the end of yesterday we were starting to catch up." We usually did seven to eight properties between eight in the morning and five in the af-

ternoon and squeezed in the odd landscaping job when one came along.
Ellen made more than I did with her job
at the college, but we wouldn't have
gotten by without my business. "Why?"
I asked. "You got something in mind?"

Ellen shrugged. "I saw you the other
day, looking at your paintings." There
were a number of canvases, in various
stages of completion, leaned up
against the wall in the shed, gathering
dust. When I didn't say anything, she
added, "I wondered if you were thinking of getting back into it."

I shook my head. "Ancient history," I
said. "I was just deciding whether to
throw them into the truck and take
them to the dump."

Ellen frowned. "Stop it," she said.

I used the last of my toast to mop up
some egg yolk, popped it into my
mouth, and dabbed at the corners of
my mouth with a napkin. "Thanks,
hon," I said, kissing the top of her head
as I got up. "What are you going to do
today?"

"Read," she said tiredly. "It's not like
I have to read every writer who comes

to the festival, but I at least need to know a bit about their work. You run into them at the cocktail parties, you have to be able to bluff your way through. Writers, honestly, a lot of them are really nice, but God they're needy. They need constant validation."

"No sign of my associate yet?" I asked as I took my plate to the sink.

"I think you'll have to wake him," Ellen said. "I thought the smell of bacon would do it. Tell him I saved him some and can do a couple eggs fast."

I went upstairs and stopped outside the door to my son's room. I rapped lightly on the closed door, then opened it about a foot, enough to see that he was under the covers, turned away from the door.

"Hey, Derek, wakey wakey, man," I said.

"I'm awake," Derek said.

TWO

Derek kept facing the wall. "I don't think I can go today," he said. "I think I'm sick."

I opened the door wide and stepped into his room. It looked as it always did, as though a bomb had gone off. Heaps of clothes on the floor, half a dozen different pairs of sneakers, none matched up, scattered hither and yon, countless empty software and game boxes, a desk along one wall with not one but three computer monitors, two keypads, half a dozen different computer towers underneath, wires—connected and disconnected—all over the place. He was going to set the house on fire one day.

"What's wrong?" I said. Derek was legendary for feigning illness to get out of school, but he was less likely to pull that kind of stunt working for his father.

"I just feel off," he said.

Ellen passed by the door, heard a snippet of conversation, came in. "What's up?"

"Says he's sick," I said.

She moved past me, sat on the edge of Derek's bed, and tried to get her hand on his forehead, but he turned away so she couldn't get near him.

"Come on," she said. "Let me see if you've got a fever."

"I don't have a fever," he said, his face still hidden. "Can't I just feel out of it one day? And besides, it's fucking Saturday."

"And you got last Monday and half of Tuesday off because of rain," I reminded him. "Win some, lose some. We should be done by noon. We've just got the Simpsons, the Westlake place, and what's-her-name, the one with the cat that looks like a furry pig, who gave you the computer."

Here's the thing about Derek. He's a good kid, and I love him more than I can say, but sometimes he can be a royal pain in the ass. Finding creative ways to get out of his obligations is one of his talents. He hates school, and he hasn't always made the best choices. A few that immediately come to mind: a couple of years back, he and his pal Adam were setting off firecrackers in the dry grass behind the house. It hadn't rained in a month and one spark could have started a fire that would have burned our place down. I nearly wrung his neck. There was the time he went joyriding with a fifteen-year-old buddy who took out his father's MG— without permission and without a driver's license—and wrapped it around a tree. Thank God no one was hurt, except for the MG, of course. And there was the time he and another friend decided to explore the rooftop of the high school, scaling gutters like they were goddamn ninjas or something. Maybe, if all they'd done was hang out there, no one would have noticed, but they'd chosen to do sprints across the roof, then leapt off the edge and over an eight-foot gap to another wing of the school. It was a wonder they hadn't killed themselves.

"We never even came close," Derek told me later, as if this constituted a defense.

They were doing so much thumping up there that the night janitor called the police. They got off with a warning, largely because they hadn't actually vandalized anything. I was furious when the cops brought him home.

"Another fucking stunt like this," I said, "and you can find some other place to live."

I regretted it later. I didn't mean it, that his next fuckup would be his last under our roof. Teenagers, honestly, sometimes they did some stupid shit, but you stood by them no matter what. It was all part of what you'd signed on for.

If Derek really was sick, I didn't want to drag him out to push a lawn mower through the heat and humidity. But it occurred to me that it might not be an actual illness he was suffering from.

"You hungover?" I asked. It was hardly an outrageous question. Only a month ago I'd found a six-pack of Coors hidden under some old storm windows that were leaned up against the back of the shed.

"No," he said. Then, abruptly, he threw off the covers, rolled over, and swung out of bed in one swift movement, bumping into his mother. "Fine," he said. I think Ellen and I were both surprised to see that he was still in jeans and T-shirt. He reached for his work boots, ignoring the sneakers right next to them. "I'll work. So I'm sick. No big deal."

Ellen looked at me expectantly, like she was wanted me to pick up on this, ask him what was the matter. But I just shrugged and said, "Good."

"There's some bacon already made," his mother said. "Would you like me to make some eggs for—"

"I'm not hungry," he said.

Ellen got up, leaned back, held up her palms in the universal backing-off gesture. "Okay, fine," she said and walked out of the room.

"I'll be out by the truck when you're

ready," I said, left, and closed his door behind me.

Ellen was standing there and said, "You think he's hungover?"

I shook my head. "I don't know. If he is, pushing a noisy lawn mower first thing in the morning is exactly what he deserves."

I brushed my teeth, took a baby aspirin because Ellen had heard some doctor on *Oprah* say it was a good idea, and went outside. There was hardly any breeze and you could tell it was going to be a scorcher.

We have a building behind the house, what I call the shed, but it's really a double garage with one big wide door on it, where I have a workbench and a place to keep all our stuff. I'd picked up half a dozen used lawn mowers for next to nothing and got them in decent running order so that if either of the two we took with us each day crapped out, I had a replacement set to go. Just the one lawn tractor, however, a John Deere, its green paint and yellow striping fading from constant sun exposure. It sat on the short trailer already hitched to the back of my Ford pickup, which has *Cutter's Lawn Service* and a phone number stenciled on the door, as well as my name, Jim Cutter.

I did a quick check to see that we had everything we needed. The hedge trimmer and extension cords, four small red plastic containers with plain gasoline for the lawn mowers and the tractor, and a fifth with a mix of gas and oil for the handheld trimmer and the leaf blower, which I hated for the racket it made, like a goddamn jet coming in for a landing, but it was a hell of a lot faster for clearing lawn clippings off driveways and sidewalks than a broom. When you wanted to pack up and move on to the next job, speed was everything. And after I'd already been pushing a mower or wielding the trimmer, the last thing I wanted to do was sweep by hand.

I glanced into the truck to make sure we each had our work gloves and our earmuff-like gadgets to keep the noise out of our ears. I opened the glove box, checked that I had a replacement spool of filament wire in case the weed whacker ran out.

Something was missing, though. I was trying to think what it was when I heard the back door of the house open and close and Ellen was standing there with the mini-cooler. The lunches I'd made the night before. I smiled, went over and took it from her.

"How's it going in there?" I asked her.

"I'm just staying out of his way," she said. "We should do something this afternoon if you've got any energy left. Maybe go down to Albany, do a bit of shopping."

"Shopping," I said. "That'd be fun." I wasn't using my sincere voice.

Ellen gave me a look. "We could go someplace for dinner. See a movie. There's that new Bruce Willis thing. *Die Really Really Really Hard* or something. I need a break from all this literary stuff."

I gave her a noncommittal shrug. "Let's see how the day goes. Going out for dinner sounds good. The shopping thing, not so much."

"You need to take at least one long

weekend this summer. You didn't even take the Fourth. Let Derek run things for a day. He's got his license, he can drive the truck. He could get as much done as he could on his own; the next day you could squeeze in a couple extra jobs. He needs to handle the extra responsibility. It would be good for him. We could drive up to Montreal. Go hear some jazz or something."

That was actually a pretty good idea, but all I said was, "We'll see."

"We'll see. We'll see. That's what they'll put on your tombstone."

She turned to go back in as Derek came out. He walked past her without a word, hair falling over his eyes, and headed for the truck.

"I guess we're off," I said to Ellen, and she rolled her eyes, a kind of "good luck" gesture.

As I got into the truck I said to Derek, "You wanna drive?" He shook his head. "I'm guessing you had no breakfast. You want me to stop along the way? A McMuffin or something? A doughnut? Coffee?"

Another shake of the head.

"Okay then," I said and turned the ignition. I had the windows down for now, would probably close them and turn on the air later. I pulled the column shift into drive and eased down on the accelerator. The trailer, weighed down with the Deere and other equipment, rattled as we picked up speed. As we headed down the lane, about halfway to the highway, the Langley house came into view. I noticed the Saab SUV parked out front of the house, as well as Donna Langley's Acura sedan.

"I thought they were going away," I said.

"Huh?" said Derek.

"The Saab's there. I thought they were going to some lodge or something. In Stowe? Somewhere that way?"

Derek glanced over. "I guess they didn't go."

"Didn't Adam say they were going up there for a week or something? Didn't you go over there to see them off last night?"

"They must have changed their mind after I left," Derek said, looking away from the Langleys' and out his own window.

"Just seems funny, is all," I said. "You book a place for a week and change your mind." Nothing from Derek. "Maybe Albert had something come up, some new case or something, they had to cancel at the last minute. I guess that kind of thing happens when you're a criminal lawyer." I glanced over at Derek. "Not that he's a criminal. Just that he *represents* criminals." An old joke. I'd probably only used it a hundred times or so.

When Derek said nothing, I raised my voice a notch and said, "Yeah, Dad, that's probably what happened." Dropped it a bit. "You think so, son? You think that's what happened?" Up again. "I'd say so, Dad, yeah. You're never wrong about these things."

Quietly, "Leave me alone, Dad."

We got up to the highway and I hung a right, heading north, which would take us into Promise Falls. It's an average-sized city, forty thousand or so, but we've got all the major fast-food joints and a Wal-Mart and a Home

Depot and a multiplex and most of the major car dealerships except the really high-end ones, like BMW. There's the college on the north side of town, so that accounts for the Volvo dealership.

Once you get past the newer subdivisions that surround the town, you reach the old part, which is big on charm with its hundred-year-old houses and large lots, like a lot of places in this part of the state and nearby Vermont. Big trees, a main street with lots of small businesses that have managed to hang on even after the Wal-Mart showed up. We had Mayor Randall Finley to thank for its arrival. He brushed off the local business association's concerns about the monster retailer, saying they could do with a little competition, that it wasn't enough to be quaint and charming, you had to give people value for their dollar.

Finley had managed to offend so many people in town, it amazed me he'd been reelected. But he had a constituency out there that loved it when he stuck it to unions and special interests and those who didn't live up to some moral code voters were under the impression Finley himself adhered to. There were probably more than a few residents of Promise Falls who loved it that he'd barged in on the un- wed mothers and given them a piece of his mind, and a little something extra.

"So what did you end up doing last night?" I asked, still attempting to draw Derek out. "I never heard you come in. I crashed early, went right into a coma. You see Penny?"

He'd been seeing Penny Tucker for a month or more now, and the few times she'd been by the house she struck me as a sweet kid. I could only imagine the limericks teenage boys might come up with that involved her last name.

"No," Derek said. "She was grounded."

"Why? What she do?"

"Banged up the car."

"Oh no. Bad?"

"No."

"What she hit?"

"The bumper."

"On what?"

"Telephone pole."

"She going to have to pay to have it fixed?"

"Don't know."

Jesus, it was like pulling teeth. And then, for the first time, I noticed something different about my son.

"When did you stop wearing that little stud thing in your ear?" I asked. "The peace sign."

He reached up and touched his left earlobe, where there was a tiny dimple from a piercing, but no jewelry. Derek shrugged. "I don't know. It fell out or something. I lost it a while ago."

We did the Simpson place first. A medium-sized property, no hills, nothing tricky. I assigned Derek to the tractor, since he likes riding it, thinking that if I started him with something he enjoyed, his disposition would improve. I did the trimming, then got out a mower for the spots the tractor couldn't easily reach.

Mrs. Simpson came out with a glass of water for each of us, which we gratefully accepted. I could see her husband standing back in the kitchen, looking our way slightly disapprovingly. I knew his type. We were the hired help, and if we needed water, we should know enough to bring it with us, or at least take it from the garden hose like we were a couple of golden retrievers. Mrs. Simpson, however, was not a shit like her husband.

Then all we had to do was blow the clippings off the drive, which Derek looked after. We were there barely an hour, and just as we were getting back into the truck, we were approached by a skinny kid about Derek's age, with thick black hair and skin so white you had to wonder if he'd been getting tanned by a refrigerator bulb, wearing a pair of shorts that had at least a dozen pockets all over them. He came up to my window.

"You hiring?" he asked. He handed me a slip of paper from a wad of flyers he was holding. I glanced at it and read, "Stuart Yost. Odd Jobs." And a phone number.

"Sorry," I said, handing the flyer to Derek, who jammed it into the glove box. "I got my son here working with me."

"I'm just looking for something for the rest of the summer," he said.

"Nearly the end of July, Stuart," I said. "Kinda late, isn't it? Another month and you'll be back in school."

"I had one but I lost it," he said. He shrugged. "Anyway, thanks."

As he walked off I said to Derek, "You know him from school or anything?"

He shook his head no, said nothing. Derek's disposition had not improved all morning, and I began to wonder what was eating at him. Was there another crumpled-MG incident? Had he and one of his friends been leaping from one tall building to another, maybe the police station this time, instead of the high school? Driven along the road after midnight, playing mailbox baseball, taking a bat to each mailbox they passed?

I could remember doing that. My later teen years weren't particularly well supervised.

Surely, if he'd gotten into any real trouble, and been caught at it, Ellen and I would have heard about it by now.

Next was the lady with the cat that looked like a furry pig. Agnes Stockwell. She'd been kind enough on our last visit to give Derek an old computer she'd had sitting in her garage for the better part of a decade. It had belonged to her son, Brett, a Thackeray College student who had, tragically, jumped to his death off Promise Falls— *the* Promise Falls, the one the city takes its name from—when he was in his last year. She didn't use a computer, and she'd never turned it on since his death.

"I'm not really a computer person," she'd told Derek. The garage was open the last time we were there, and Derek, who collects old hardware so he and his friend Adam can take apart and rebuild computers for their own amusement, spotted it on a shelf. Mrs. Stockwell, whose husband passed away the year before her son committed suicide, told him to take it.

Her place was a little more work because she has a lot of beds she tends, and it's hard to navigate the John Deere around them, so Derek and I each grabbed a lawn mower and went to work. But she rewarded us, even going beyond what Mrs. Simpson had done. She came out with lemonade as I was getting out the weed whacker to tidy up the edges, and we both gulped it down. Derek even managed a "Thank you."

The mercury had to be pushing 95 by now.

I was about to do the finishing touches on her yard when I heard my cell phone, which I'd left on the dash of the truck, ringing. I opened the door, sat on the edge of the seat, and grabbed the phone. It was home calling.

"Yeah?"

"You might want to come back," Ellen said. There was something in her voice, like she was keeping a lid on her emotions.

"What?"

"There's something going on at the Langley house. There's half a dozen cop cars, they're putting up police tape. And there's a cop walking up the lane headed this way right now."

"Holy shit," I said, and Derek, now in the truck, glanced my way. "What the hell's going on?"

"I don't know."

"Ask around, give me a call back."

"I went up there once but they wouldn't tell me anything. But I figured, with some of the contacts you made back when you were at city hall, you'll find out more than I will."

"Okay," I said. "We'll head back now." I flipped the phone shut and said to Derek, "There's cop cars all around the Langley house."

He just looked at me.

THREE

We could tell something was going on
even before we got there. A quarter
mile ahead, there were Promise Falls
police cars, marked and unmarked,
parked along both sides of the highway
out front of the lane that led first to the
Langley house, and then further on to
ours. I slowed the truck as I approached the phalanx of vehicles,
thinking, stupidly as it turned out, that
I'd be able to turn down my own drive.
But it was blocked with even more
cars, and I could see officers stringing
up more yellow police tape.

I drove on about a hundred yards
and pulled the truck and trailer over as
far onto the gravel shoulder as I could.
Because we were on the outskirts of
town, there were no curbs or side-

walks, but there were ditches that the Cutter's Lawn Service trailer could slide into if I didn't exercise caution.

Derek had his door open before I had the truck in park and was hoofing it back to the scene. I grabbed my keys and was out the door, running to catch up with my son, who hadn't said a word the whole way back.

I caught up to him as we reached the end of the drive. A cop raised his hand to us and said, "I'm sorry, you can't come onto this property."

I pointed down to the end of the lane, where you could just make out part of our house. "I live down there," I said. "I just got a call from my wife that—"

"Jim!"

I looked around the cop and could see Ellen, who'd been standing with a couple of officers, running my way. The cop who'd been blocking my path stepped back and let Derek and me pass. Ellen, in a pair of jeans, sneakers, and a T-shirt, her hair slightly askew, looked as though she'd had to face the world sooner than she'd planned, and if she'd had a chance to do her makeup, the tears running down her cheeks now would surely have made a mess of it.

She ran up, threw her arms around me, then reached out to grab Derek by the arm and pull him toward us.

"Ellen, what the hell's going on?" I asked.

She sniffed, looked at me first, then our son, her eyes lingering on Derek, as though the news she had to tell was going to be harder on him than me.

"The Langleys," she said. "Last night, someone, they came in, and . . ." Tears were welling up in her eyes again.

"Ellen," I said, keeping my voice calm. "Just get ahold of yourself."

She took a couple breaths, sniffed again, felt with both hands in her pockets for a tissue. Finding none, she ran her index finger across the bottom of her nose.

"They're all dead," she said. "Albert, Donna." She squeezed Derek's arm. "Sweetheart, I'm so sorry. Adam too."

I thought he would say something. Maybe a "What?" or an "Are you kidding?" or even a simple "No."

I know that I was about to ask, "What happened?"

But Derek said none of these things. Instead, his lip began to tremble, and almost instantly, tears welled up in both his eyes. He fell into his mother's arms and began to sob. The emotions over- whelmed him so quickly, it was like he'd been holding them in all morning.

"Hey, Cutter!"

I glanced away from my wife and son holding each other to see Barry Duck- worth, a detective with the Promise Falls Police Department, heading my way. Early forties, like me, we'd often crossed paths during the time that I'd worked for the mayor's office. I liked to think I was, at least in the last couple of years, in a little better shape than Barry, whose paunch was slightly visible where his white dress shirt pulled apart just above his belt, letting us in on a small triangle of hairy belly. There was more hair there than on his head, which was mostly bald save for a pitiful comb-over near his crown. He had his tie pulled down and his collar open, and his jacket must have been left behind in his car. It was too hot to wear one, but even without it, there were sweat stains under the pits.

I'd always thought he was an okay guy. A straight shooter. And while I couldn't claim he was a close friend, we'd spent more than a few nights sitting in a bar together, and that tends to count for something around these parts.

"Barry," I said solemnly. He extended his hand. We shook, both our palms sweaty. "What's going on, Barry?"

He ran his hand over his head, like he was squeegeeing off the perspiration. "You mind if I ask you a few questions first, Jim, before I fill you in?"

So we were going to be professional, at least at first. I could accept that. "Sure," I said as Ellen and Derek released their hold on each other and turned to see what they might learn.

"I've already asked Ellen some questions, but I'd like to go over some things with you," Barry Duckworth said. "You were home last night?"

"Yeah. Came home from work, never went out again. I was beat."

"Did you see the Langleys at all last night?"

"I didn't." I was about to say that Derek had, but I figured Barry would get to him.

"Hear anything at all last night, after ten o'clock or so?" he asked.

"Nothing," I said. "We had the house closed up pretty tight, the air on."

"See anything? Car headlights maybe?"

I shook my head again. "Sorry." I pointed to our place. "We're quite a ways down."

"How about you?" Barry said, turning to Derek.

"Huh?" he said. There was a small trail of clear snot running down to his upper lip. Derek turned and wiped his nose into the shoulder of his T-shirt, still flecked with grass clippings from our morning tour.

"Did you see or hear anything last night?"

"No," he said.

"But you saw the Langleys last night,

right? Before they left? Your mother was saying you went over there to say goodbye to Adam, before he and his parents went away for a week to some lodge?"

Derek nodded.

"What time was that?" Barry asked.

Derek half shrugged. "I think around eight? Maybe a little after? I left just before they got in the car and took off."

Eight? We hadn't seen Derek at all that evening. He must have done something else after leaving the Langleys. Hung out with Penny, probably.

I decided it was time to press for some information. "Barry," I said. "Come on. Tell us what's happened."

His cheeks puffed out as he blew out some air.

I persisted. "This place will be swarming with news crews in a minute. You're going to have to tell them something. You can practice on us."

He paused another moment, then said, "It was like an execution in there. Somebody, maybe two people, we don't know yet, came in last night and shot them. All three."

"Jesus Christ," I said.

Ellen gripped my arm. "Dear God," she said.

I looked up at the house, cops still going in and out, talking quietly, shaking their heads.

Barry continued, "Mr. Langley, he's by the front door, looks like his wife was shot coming down the stairs to see what was going on, and the boy— Adam?" He looked at Derek for confirmation, and my son nodded. "Adam, he was shot going down the stairs by the back door. Looks like he was trying to make a run for it, took a bullet right about here." Barry touched himself at the back of the neck, just under his left ear.

I was numb. And despite the kind of weather we were having, I felt chilled.

"I don't get it," I said. "I thought they'd gone away. They were taking a vacation or something." To Derek, I said, "Weren't they going away for a week?"

"Yeah," he said, his face still wet with tears.

"Wife got sick," Barry said. "They

were well on their way, but she was having stomach pains or something, it's a bit sketchy. But on the way back, around ten, Langley phoned one of the secretaries from his law firm, phoned her at home. Said his wife was sick, they were postponing their trip and coming back home, that if she got better by the morning they'd try heading off again, but in the meantime, there was a case he'd been thinking about, wanted her to bring a file out to him this morning so he could work on it, maybe take it with him if they managed to get away again."

"Okay," I said.

"So she drives in here about nine this morning to drop it off, knocks on the door, nobody answers. She tries a couple times, figures maybe they're sleeping in or something, so she phones the house from her cell, can hear the phone ringing in the house, but nobody's picking up, which seems pretty weird to her, right?"

We were all listening.

"So she happens to peer in through a window by the door." He pointed over to the house, the vertical windows flanking the door. "She can see Mr. Langley lying there, can just barely make out the wife on the stairs. That's when she called 911."

Ellen said, "The poor woman. How horrible. Imagine, finding something like that."

Barry continued, "When Langley phoned his secretary last night, he said he was only about ten miles from home, so they must have arrived back here not long after ten. So whoever did this, it was sometime after that, and probably not that much later. They were all still dressed. No one in their pajamas, not even the mother. You figure, she was the one not feeling well, she would have gotten ready for bed pretty soon after they got home. They still hadn't brought their stuff back into the house."

"They might not have unpacked," I said, "if they thought they were going to go back up this morning."

"True," Barry said. "It's very early in the investigation. We've got a lot to do.

Forensic guys are only just getting here."

Barry said to Derek, "Adam was a pretty good friend of yours, right?" My son nodded. "He ever say anything to you, you ever hear anything when you were over to the house visiting him, to suggest that someone might have it in for them? That his dad might have been worried about anything, anyone threatening him maybe? Some case he might have been working on?" He glanced at me. "He handled a lot of criminal cases."

"Yeah," I said. "There was that one I just read about in the paper. That gang fight or something? One kid beat up another kid, killed him, Langley got him off?"

Barry nodded. "That's right. The McKindrick case."

Ellen said, "I read about that, too. Tom McKindrick, that was the boy? The one that died? He was in his teens, right?"

Barry nodded again but said nothing, deciding to let Ellen do the work.

"He took a blow to the head, and Albert, Mr. Langley, he got the jury to believe that he'd more or less provoked it, that the other boy—what was his name?"

"Anthony Colapinto," Barry said hesitantly, as though he'd been forced to admit something that wasn't common knowledge.

"That's it," Ellen said. "Albert persuaded the jury that Anthony Colapinto was acting in self-defense when he went at the McKindrick boy with a baseball bat. When they read out the verdict, not guilty, the boy's father, Colin McKindrick, collapsed right there in the courtroom."

"Yeah," Barry said. "I was there."

"But then didn't he get up? And threaten Albert?"

Barry nodded. "He told Albert Langley he'd pay for getting the son of a bitch off."

I think my eyebrows must have shot up. "I hadn't heard about that," I said.

To Derek, Barry said, "You ever hear Albert Langley, or even his son, Adam, talking about that? Like maybe they were worried this Colin McKindrick might try to get even?"

"No," Derek said, almost dreamily. "I never heard anything like that at all." His words were trailing off, like he was getting woozy. Spending the morning cutting grass in these sizzling temperatures would be enough to send someone into heatstroke. Add to that the shock of what had happened at the Langleys', it was little wonder Derek looked as though he was about to collapse.

I grabbed him under the arms. Ellen said, "Derek? Derek?"

"Water," I said to Barry. "I've got some in a cooler in the truck."

Barry clearly had another plan and barked to a uniformed female officer, "I need some water here!" The woman bolted to one of the nearby cruisers, where evidently a few bottles were stashed. I eased Derek over to the closest Promise Falls police car and leaned him up against it. The cop was running back, cracking the plastic cap along the way, and handed the bottle to me. It was warm, but it was still water, and I brought it up to Derek's lips and tipped it.

He took a few swallows, breathed shallowly.

"We need to get him inside, where it's cooler," Ellen said. Our house was still a hundred yards away, and the female officer offered to drive him. "I'll go with him back to the house," Ellen said to me, figuring, I guessed, that if I stayed behind with Detective Duckworth I'd learn even more about what had transpired in the night.

"It's like he's in shock or something," Barry said as the car rolled up to our house.

"Wouldn't you be?" I said. "Your best friend gets killed along with the rest of his family?"

Barry nodded slowly in agreement.

"So's that your theory?" I asked. "That this is related to the case Albert was working on? Was there anything taken? The house torn apart?"

Barry appeared thoughtful. "I don't know why the fuck this happened, Jim. All I know is, three people dead? There's gonna be a shitstorm of interest around this one. Don't think we've had a triple murder around here in some time, if ever. A few single ones of late, but something like this . . ." He paused, then looked back to the highway. He seemed to be staring at our mailbox.

There was just the one, with the name Cutter on it. Last winter, I'd had to fix it after a snowplow took it down. The Langleys had their mail sent to a P.O. box in town. Albert didn't like the idea of his mail sitting in a box by the highway, available to anyone passing by.

"What you looking at?" I asked Barry.

"Huh?" he said, as though he'd been daydreaming. "Nothing."

FOUR

Before I could ask Barry anything else, our attention was caught by an approaching car. It was a big black vehicle, and it was slowing down at the end of the lane. Barry rolled his eyes and said, "Oh boy, we can all rest easy now, the big man is here."

It was a Mercury Grand Marquis with heavily tinted windows. I could only see the car in profile, but I knew that the license plates on it read "PF 1." What with all the other police vehicles up there, there was no room for the Mercury to pull over, so the driver opted to put on the flashers and block a lane of traffic.

Barry and I were standing side by side now, waiting for the great man's appearance. Barry said to me, "Tell me why you did it."

"Excuse me?" I was still thinking about the Langleys, and found Barry's question a bit jarring.

"Why'd you punch him in the nose? How many times you going to make me ask you?"

"That's just a rumor, Barry."

"There's not a civil servant in Promise Falls, or anybody else in town for that matter, who doesn't know you punched the mayor in the nose," Barry said. "It's like our own urban legend."

"You can't believe everything you hear," I said.

"Well, this is one of those stories I choose to believe," Barry said. "This, and the one about Elvis working as a short-order cook at that diner just north of town." He was watching the driver get out of the Grand Marquis. He was a tall man, lean, late thirties, with short blond hair except around back, where it hung down over his collar, mullet-style. "I mean, the mayor shows up at a council meeting, his nose the size of an orange, and guess who just happens to no longer be on the mayor's payroll? Just think, you could still be working with Lance there if you hadn't gone and fucked things up."

"I'm happy with the way things have worked out," I said.

The driver had his hand on the back door of the town car.

"What I heard is, even though you punched the mayor right in his fucking nose, you asked him for a letter of reference afterwards, and you got it," Barry said. "I guess that was before you decided to go into business for yourself. Anyway, that tells me that you've got something on him that's pretty fucking amazing. I mean, he never even pressed charges, and if there was ever a vindictive bastard out there, it's Randall Finley."

And with that, the door opened, and Mayor Finley emerged from the car.

He was a small man, a textbook case of the Napoleon complex. Carried himself like he was six-four instead of five-four. He'd opted to leave his jacket in the car, too, and gave his trousers a hitch as he stood on the hot pavement, gazing at the crime scene through a pair of Oakleys.

"Detective Duckworth!" he called out to Barry.

I whispered to him, "Show me how you scurry."

But Barry approached the mayor at a regular pace, like he was trying hard not to run, not wanting me to think he jumped every time the mayor asked him to, even if that was exactly what he did.

As Barry closed in on the mayor, his driver, wearing a pair of casual slacks and the kind of blue T that looked like it cost a couple of hundred bucks, walked in my direction.

"Cutter," he said. "My old man Cutter."

"Lance," I said. If ever there was a guy the name "Lance" was made for, it was Lance Garrick.

"Lots of excitement around here today," he said, forming a grin.

"My neighbors were murdered," I said. "My son just lost his best friend."

Lance shrugged. "Shit does happen. Especially around you." I didn't see the point in responding to that. I couldn't see where engaging in small talk with the guy who held the job I'd walked away from was going to make an already bad day any better.

"Mayor got the call," Lance said, recovering his dignity. "About Langley. Wanted to take a run by, see what was happening. He knew Langley pretty good, you know?"

I nodded.

"So," Lance said, looking up the road at my truck, chuckling under his breath. "How's the lawn-cutting business?"

"Good," I said.

"You're something else, Cutter," Lance said. "Quitting a good gig like this to go around mowing lawns. I used to do that when I was a kid. There were a few houses on my street." He shook his head in mock puzzlement. "Of course, I didn't have a little tractor to run around on. That must be fun. But even if I knew I could get myself a tractor, not sure it's the sort of thing I'd have dreamed of doing when I grew up. Is there like a course you take, some sort of degree you can get out at

Thackeray? Weed Eating 101? Hey, you ever thought of branching out? Maybe get a paper route?"

"You certainly made the right call, Lance," I said. "You get to wipe the mayor of Promise Falls's ass any time you want. I envy you."

Lance pretended to laugh at that one. "Yeah, well, if I got fired from a job, I'd want to put it down, too." If that was what Lance wanted to think, that I'd been fired, that was fine by me.

Barry was walking back from his chat with the mayor and said to me, "He wants to talk to you."

"So he can ask me," I said. "Since when do you deliver his messages?"

Barry looked embarrassed, but was spared from having to explain himself when Randall Finley shouted over to me, "Hey, Cutter! Gotta minute?"

I walked over. As I approached I realized the Grand Marquis was still running, belching out exhaust into the hot, humid air. Waves of heat rose off the hood, like if I looked into them long enough I'd see a mirage.

"Hell of a thing," he said.

I nodded. "Yeah," I said.

"I've told Barry to put everything he's got on this," Finley said.

"I'm sure he will."

"Albert, he was a good man. He did work for me over the years. Good guy. Horrible thing."

"Yep."

"And living next door to something like that, that would sure give me the willies," he said. When I said nothing, he continued, "Look, you should drop by the office sometime. I've hardly seen you since you left."

"I've been pretty busy," I told him.

"How's Ellen?" he asked. If you didn't know him better, you'd think he was actually interested. "Still working at the college under Conrad?" He caught himself. "That didn't sound right, did it?"

"Randall, is there anything I can do for you today, or did you just want to get caught up on old times?"

"I just wanted you to know that everything that can be done to find out what happened here will be done. This is a terrible crime. Promise Falls has never seen anything like this. A triple murder. One of the city's best-known citizens, a noted criminal lawyer, dead."

I wanted to go back and check on Derek. I began turning to walk away when Randall Finley said, "Cutter, you owe me more respect than that. I did you a favor. Assaulting a public official, a mayor for fuck's sake. You could have done time. I took a lot of things into consideration to let that slide."

I turned back, walked up to Finley until my nose was within a couple of inches of his, although that meant stooping just a tad. "You want to lay a charge, it's probably not too late. It's only been a couple of years. I'm sure Barry over there would take your statement."

Mayor Finley smiled and slapped me on the side of my shoulder. "Hey, listen, I'm just messin' with ya. Fact is, I still wish I had you working for me. Lance there, he's okay, but he spends a lot of time looking in the rearview mirror, always checking his hair, making sure he hasn't got something stuck in his teeth.

I liked you. You were always there to watch my back."

"There's a lot of people in this town who'd be happy to stick something in it," I said. "Pretty much everybody on the city payroll that you've accused of not doing their jobs, and most recently, a houseful of unwed mothers."

Finley waved his hand. "Oh that," he said. "Just a little misunderstanding. That never would have happened if you'd been working for me. You'd have never let me go in there and make a goddamn fool of myself."

"What else does Lance let you do that he shouldn't?" I asked.

Finley grinned nervously. "Nothing," he said. "He's actually not that bad. I just have to make sure he doesn't set me up on any bad blind dates, if you get my meaning." He flashed me a grin.

"I'm going to go see how my family is," I said, then turned my back on the mayor and walked away.

He shouted after me, loud enough for others to hear, "Will do, Jim! Anything you need, you let me know."

As I passed Barry he said to me,

"The nose thing? No jury would ever have convicted you."

I found Ellen and Derek sitting at the kitchen table. He had his head in his hands and she was turned toward him, reaching out and touching him tentatively.

"It's a shock, I know," Ellen said softly as I came into the room and stood just inside the doorway. Derek shook his head, not looking up, not taking his hands away. "We're all in shock. And it's not going to make any sense, not until we know why it happened. And it may not make any sense after that, either."

Ellen turned toward me, gave me a hopeless look. I noticed there was half a glass of white wine in a tall-stemmed glass on the counter. She caught me looking at it.

I went over to my son and rested my hands on his shoulders, not sure what words at this time could make things any better. He took his hands away from his face and, without turning to look at me, dragged one of my hands down around his neck, pulling me down close to him. Ellen moved closer, and we both held on to our son while he continued to weep.

FIVE

The police were in and out of the house so much that afternoon, Ellen made coffee for those who wanted it on such a hot day, and iced tea for those looking for something cold. I noticed Ellen offered wine to no one, and had finished off her glass and put it in the dishwasher before playing hostess. I wasn't sure whether Barry Duckworth and the other cops kept coming inside because they thought there was something we'd forgotten to mention, or they just wanted to get into the air-conditioning.

Derek finally settled down and retreated to his room, where he alternated between fiddling with his computers and lying facedown on his bed.

He seemed very tired, as though he'd had next to no sleep the night before.

When it appeared we were going to get a break from questioning, Ellen poured us each some iced tea, which we took out onto our back deck. It's well shaded out there, and there's usually at least a trace of a breeze.

We sat down in our wooden Adirondack chairs—what I still thought of as Muskoka chairs from when my parents would head up to a cottage in that region of Ontario every summer—and didn't say anything for a couple of minutes. Ellen took a sip of her tea and said, "You think he's going to be okay?"

"Eventually," I said. "How many kids lose a best friend that way?"

"I've always felt so safe here," she said. "Never again."

I let those two words hang out there for a while before I spoke. "What happened at the Langleys' doesn't have to mean we're any less safe than we've ever been."

Ellen glanced over at me. "What do you mean?"

"What happened there, there's no

reason it has to have anything to do with us."

"What the hell are you talking about?" She pointed. "It happened *right there.*"

"What I'm saying is," I said, "things like that don't happen for no reason at all. And whatever that reason was, it's got nothing to do with us."

"Unless it was some crazy psycho picking people at random," Ellen said.

"Even then," I said.

Ellen shook her head, dismissing me. "I don't get you. Is this you trying to put the best possible spin on a situation?"

"Bear with me for a second," I said. "Let's go through the various scenarios. Like murder-suicide."

"The police didn't say anything about it being a murder-suicide."

"I know. I'm just saying, if that's what it was. If it was a murder-suicide, it's this self-contained tragedy. Horrible, yes, but it doesn't impact on our safety one way or another."

"Okay," she said, so far unconvinced.

"Now, since it doesn't appear to be a

murder-suicide, let's move on to the next scenario, which is that the Langleys were killed for a specific reason. Or maybe just Langley himself, and Donna, and Adam, they were killed because they were witnesses, something like that. Maybe it's related to some case Langley's been working on, maybe the one where he got that kid off, the one who beat the other kid to death. I'm sure Barry'll be combing through all his files, interviewing others at the law firm, looking at all the things Langley's been up to, who might be pissed at him because he didn't keep them out of jail, and those who might be pissed that he kept others from going to jail they thought should have."

"Try to say that one again," Ellen said.

"Yeah, well, you get my drift. Regardless, there could have been a specific reason for what happened, which again means there's no reason for us to be worried for ourselves."

I watched Ellen for some kind of reaction. There wasn't much of one, but her skepticism was detectable. "This is what you do," she said. "You always find reasons for me not to be worried. Well, this is something to worry about. It could have been a robbery. Someone broke into the Langleys' and ended up killing them. You can't tell me something like that couldn't happen here, couldn't happen anyplace."

"Okay, point taken. Let's say it's a robbery, or some totally random, crazy act. A roaming serial killer. He happens upon the Langley house out of the blue. The odds of something like that happening to a family, even though there's a serial killer industry out there in the movies that makes everyone fucking paranoid, are absolutely a million to one. Probably a few hundred million to one. When you figure the odds are like that, what are the odds that something like that would also happen to the people who lived right next door?"

"That's your theory," Ellen said. "That we're somehow bulletproof"—and then she winced at her own analogy— "because it'd be like lightning striking twice. A crazed serial killer isn't going to hit two houses side by side."

I took a sip of my iced tea. "Yeah." Another argument had occurred to me. "Let's say it was the other way around, that something good had happened to the Langleys. Let's say they'd won the New York State lottery. Would you feel like you were next in line to win?"

"I'd probably at least go out and buy a ticket," Ellen said. She studied me for a moment, then said, "I think you're talking out of your ass. We should put the house on the market and get the hell out of here." Then she got out of her chair and went back inside.

To be honest, even as I was saying it, I knew I was talking out my ass, too.

We had several calls from reporters. A young woman from the *Promise Falls Standard* tried to get a quote out of Ellen when she answered the phone, and when I took two different calls from the *Times Union* and the *Democrat-Herald* in Albany, I said I had nothing to say. Something I'd learned while working for the mayor's office was that it was very rare someone's life got better after being quoted in a newspaper. I also spotted an assortment of TV news vans up on the highway at different times through the day, but the cops weren't letting anyone come down the lane. I figured Barry would be happy to answer questions for the cameras. He loved to be on TV, loved to see himself on the evening news. I just hoped he thought to tuck in his shirt beforehand. I wasn't sure viewers were ready for a shot of his hairy, perspiring gut.

When cops weren't actually questioning us, they were wandering all over the place. Guys in white Hazmat suits had been through the Langley home. Others were wandering through the backyard of the house, like they were examining each blade of grass. One time, looking out our front window, I caught glimpses of them taking baby steps through the woods, searching for what, I had no idea. Later in the day, a towing firm on contract with the Promise Falls Police Department hauled away Albert Langley's Saab SUV and Donna Langley's Acura.

Late afternoon, the phone rang yet again and I picked up.

"Jim."

There aren't that many people who can put so much into one word. Who can, in doing nothing more than speaking your own name to you, somehow assert their authority and sense of superiority. Conrad Chase packed arrogance and pretension and condescension into a single syllable like he was stuffing an overnight bag with a truckload of cow shit. Maybe he was entitled to. He was a former professor who'd become the president of Thackeray College, a onetime bestselling author, and on top of all that, he was Ellen's boss. He'd been involved in our lives, in one way or another, from the moment we'd moved to Promise Falls, and maybe by now I should have found a way to tolerate him. But some things don't come easily to me.

"Yeah," I said. "Conrad."

"Jim," Chase said, "I just heard about Albert. And Donna, and their boy, Adam, too? Good God, it's beyond imagining."

"That's right, Conrad."

"How are you folks doing? How's Derek? He and Adam were friends, weren't they? And Ellen? How's she bearing up?"

"I'll put her on."

"No, that's okay, I don't want to disturb her."

Of course he didn't.

"I just wanted to see how you all were doing. Illeana and I, we're terribly upset about all this, and while it's horribly tragic for the Langleys, it must be a shock for you, living right next door to something like this. Did you hear anything?"

"Not a thing."

"They were all shot, isn't that right?"

"That's my understanding."

"Three people, shot to death, Jesus, and you didn't hear anything?"

Like it was our fault. Or maybe just mine. If I'd heard something, if I'd heard the first shot, maybe I could have prevented it from being the total bloodbath it turned out to be.

"No," I said. "We didn't hear anything."

"Do the police know what happened?" Conrad asked. "Surely to God it wasn't a murder-suicide kind of thing."

"Doesn't appear to be that," I said. "But beyond that, I really don't know."

"Illeana and I, we'll drop by, see how you're doing," he said.

"We'll certainly look forward to that," I said.

"Okay then," he said. For an acclaimed author and former English professor who should know a thing or two about irony, Conrad seemed strangely oblivious to sarcasm.

"I'll tell Ellen you called," I said, and hung up.

By nightfall, things seemed to be settling down, but it would be a stretch to say things were back to normal. I wondered whether life around here would ever really be normal again. But Ellen and I did pull together a dinner—nothing too fancy, a salad and burgers on the barbecue—and the three of us did sit together at the table to eat.

There wasn't a lot of conversation, however.

Ellen told me to take it easy after dinner, go watch TV or read the paper, she'd clean up. I wondered if what she really wanted was for me to leave her alone in the kitchen. I left for a few minutes, then wandered back in on the pretext of making some coffee, and saw an almost empty wineglass next to the sink, where Ellen was standing. She was reaching for it when I said, "Hey."

She jumped, and as she turned knocked the glass into the sinkful of hot, soapy water.

"Jesus," she said. "Don't do that. Especially now."

"You okay?"

"I'm fine. Of course I'm fine. I mean, Jesus, no, I'm not fine. Who could be fucking fine?"

I took the long-stemmed glass from the water, set it on the counter. "It might get broken," I said, "in there with the regular stuff."

Ellen looked at me. "I was just taking the edge off."

"Sure," I said.

"It's been that kind of day," she said. "If there ever was a day I'm entitled to

a drink, this is it. At least I'm not smok-
ing again."

I nodded and went back to the living
room.

The police told us they'd be leaving
someone at the scene around the clock
for the next few days. There was a black
and white car parked up by the highway, and police tape still surrounded
the Langley house, as if pranksters had
toilet-papered the place, but neatly, and
with yellow tissue.

The police presence didn't make it
any easier for Ellen to get to sleep. She
went through the house several times,
checking doors and windows. She
asked me to do a check of the shed,
standing on the back-door step while I
went round the truck—the cops had finally let me bring my rig in from the
highway—and examined the building
where I kept my mowers and tools and
other incidentals, including my old art-
work.

"All clear," I said, stepping back into
the house, not mentioning that our
property was surrounded by trees, and
that if someone was watching us, he'd

hardly need to use the shed to hide himself. The number of places where one could hide seemed limitless.

We got into bed, and Ellen tried reading for a while but finally put her book aside. "I keep going through the same paragraph over and over again," she said, "and haven't the foggiest idea what I've just read."

I wanted to say something along the lines of "Rereading Conrad's book, are you?" but managed to hold my tongue. "Not easy to focus at the moment, is it?" I said.

She shook her head, placed the book by the base of her bedside lamp, reached up and twisted the knob to turn it off. I got under the covers and we both stared at the ceiling for a while. I don't know for how long, but I must have finally fallen asleep, because I was having that dream, where I'm on the lawn tractor, climbing a hill that's getting steeper and steeper, until the front end of the mower lifts off the ground and starts going over my head and—

Ellen jabbed me in the side, sometime around midnight, and I awoke with a start.

"What?" I said. "The smoke detector?"

"No, not that!" she whispered urgently.

"What?" I said, my heart instantly pounding.

"I heard something."

"What? Where?"

"A door. I heard a door downstairs."

"Maybe you dreamt it."

"No," she said. "I was already awake. I haven't been able to get to sleep yet."

I threw back the covers and, wearing only a pair of dark blue boxers, slipped out the bedroom door. "Be careful!" Ellen whispered.

I whispered back, "Call the police." If by some chance we were being visited by the same folks who'd gone to the Langleys' the night before—my theories of the afternoon seemed pretty pitiful all of a sudden—the time to call for help was now, not later. I didn't know what had happened to the cruiser up by the highway, whether it was still posted out there or not, and there was no way to tell, standing outside our bedroom door in the dark of night.

As I went by Derek's door I noticed it was closed, which suggested to me he was in there, asleep, although Derek didn't exactly keep us posted as to his comings and goings. I went down the stairs, feeling naked not so much because I was in nothing but a pair of shorts, but because I had nothing in my hands. We don't keep guns in the house, but right about then I'd have been happy for one. I'd have settled for a baseball bat, but we didn't have one of those either, at least not anyplace handy. Down in the basement, maybe, tucked away behind the furnace. Perhaps, if I could make it to the kitchen without running into anyone first, I could arm myself with a cast-iron frying pan, or the fire extinguisher that hung on the wall right next to the stove. You wouldn't want to get hit in the head with that sucker.

As I reached the first floor I could hear Ellen on the phone upstairs, whispering urgently. Across the living room I spotted a poker hanging among the tools next to the fireplace. That would do.

I crept over toward it, delicately slipping the pointed iron bar out of its holder. I liked the heft of it in my hand and felt, while not relieved, at least slightly better prepared.

I moved through the darkness into the kitchen, and my eyes went to the deadbolt latch. It was in the vertical position, unlocked. There was no way Ellen had forgotten to lock that door. If she checked it once, she checked it three times.

Was someone in the house? Or had someone already been here and gone back out?

I froze, held my breath, listening for anything. I thought I could hear some murmuring, voices, but not inside the house.

Outside, on the deck beyond the back kitchen door.

I moved up to it, put my hand around the knob ever so carefully, twisted it silently to the left until I could turn it no more, confident now that the latch had cleared, then swung it open as swiftly as I could. I wanted the element of surprise on my side.

And I had it.

There was a scream, a woman's scream, and that was followed by a man shouting, "Jesus!"

Upstairs, Ellen screamed, "Jim! Jim!"

My heart still pounding, I reached for the switch by the back door, casting light across Derek and his girlfriend, Penny Tucker. I'd met her enough times to recognize her, even in this limited light.

Evidently they'd both been sitting on the deck steps that led in the direction of the shed, just talking, but when I'd made my entrance they'd both jumped to their feet and Derek had reached out to steady Penny, who'd nearly stumbled over.

"Jesus, Dad, you scared us to fucking death!" Derek shouted at me.

Penny, who had enough sense not to use profanity with her boyfriend's father, caught her breath and said, "Mr. Cutter, hey. It's, like, just us."

That was when we started hearing the sirens coming down the highway.

And the car that had been parked up at the end of the lane was racing toward the house, then skidding on loose gravel as the driver hit the brakes.

"Shit," I said.

SIX

So, this little matter of the mayor's nose.

I think it was the kind of thing employ-ment consultants refer to as a "career-limiting" move. "Career-ending" would be more accurate, but the thing is, given the chance to do things over again, I can't see what I might have done differ-ently. Although it would have been nice to actually break the mayor's nose, in-stead of just bloodying it.

I got my job at the mayor's office a little over six years ago and spent four with Randall Finley before starting my own business. Working for the mayor wasn't all that bad a job. The money was reasonable enough. There wasn't a whole lot of heavy lifting, unless you counted getting the mayor into the back of his car when he was tanked. And being a bodyguard for Randall Finley wasn't exactly like a presidential assignment. You didn't walk around with a wire in your ear, whispering things like "Blowhard is on the move" to fellow agents. Just as well, too, or I'd have had to get myself a two-hundred-dollar pair of sunglasses, and I've always been the kind of guy who buys them from Rite Aid.

Sure, Finley had alienated most of the unions in town, mocked them, accused all of their members of sitting on their collective ass. Promise Falls, with a population of forty thousand, wasn't the biggest city in New York State, but you still needed a fair number of people to keep the water running through the pipes, staff the fire department, and collect the trash, and Finley had managed to get under the skin of all of them at one time or another. And there weren't many on the city council who'd piss on Finley's head if it were on fire, but still, the guy was an unlikely target for an assassin. You had to get him through the odd picket line, the occasional protest outside city hall, but nobody was scoping him out with a rifle from the top of the observatory (if we'd had an observatory). I got plenty of free meals out of it, all the banquets the boss had to go to, and he rubbed shoulders with the mildly rich and famous when they came to town on official business. Once, when Promise Falls had been chosen for a movie shoot, I got within five feet of Nicole Kidman. The mayor shook her hand and, even though I was standing right next to him, he neglected to introduce me. I was the hired help.

I'd known long before that my boss was a complete dick. I think that sunk in about an hour or so after he hired me to drive for him, when, while we were stopped at a light, a homeless man approached the mayor's window for some change. Finley buzzed down the window and, instead of tossing the guy a quarter, said, "Here's a tip, pal. Buy low, sell high."

The incident where he wandered into the unwed mothers' home and threw up all over the front hall carpet was a little more spectacular than his usual stunts, but still very much within his range of talents. Yet it wasn't that hard to account for his popularity. He had that "average guy" thing about him. He'd rather be duck hunting than attending the opera. One might have thought, in a town that supported a college and had its share of snooty intellectual and artsy-fartsy types, Finley would have limited appeal, but a majority of Promise Falls' regular residents, the ones unaffiliated with the college, saw him as their guy, and voting for him was a way to stick it to all those campus snobs who thought they were better than everybody else.

Yet Finley was politically savvy enough to know how to play to the university crowd as well. Thackeray College, while small, was highly regarded across the country. Over the years, the annual literary festival Ellen organized had attracted the likes of Margaret Atwood, Richard Russo, and Dave Eggers and drew several thousand tourists to town, and Finley wasn't about to mess with that. The local merchants—who'd managed to hold on in the face of Wal-Mart—depended too much on it. He was always there for the official opening, and it must have killed him to take second billing to Thackeray president Conrad Chase, whose ego gave Finley's a run for its money. Chase considered himself right up there with the stars the festival managed to score, having had a bestseller eight years ago, a critically acclaimed one-hit wonder he'd been unable to repeat. The one-time English prof hadn't simply failed to write another hit. He'd not written another book, at least not one for public consumption.

But I'd never punched Conrad in the nose, although I'd been tempted over the years to do much more than that.

So back to the mayor.

He had asked me to drop him at the Holiday Inn on the north side of Promise Falls. It was far enough from downtown that it had an air of anonymity about it, but it was hardly Vegas. What happened at the Promise Falls Holiday Inn did not necessarily stay at the Promise Falls Holiday Inn.

I learned early not to inquire too persistently about the mayor's purpose in any of his trips. Most I knew without having to ask. I was privy to Finley's meetings with his administrative assistant. I'd get a copy of his daily schedule, then hear him blathering away in the backseat into his cell phone.

But occasionally there were meetings that did not show up on his agenda, and this was one of those.

There was always a chance that these off-the-agenda meetings were arranged by Lance Garrick, the mayor's backup driver and all-around gofer. Lance was known by plenty of folks around Promise Falls as the go-to guy if you wanted an after-hours card game, booze when the stores had all closed, a hot tip on a horse at Saratoga, or even a girl.

I wasn't much interested in gambling or booze or hookers, and I felt the mayor's association with Lance was ill-advised and likely to bring him grief someday. But then, I was his driver, not his political strategist. He could do whatever the hell he wanted.

When Finley said he wanted to go to the Holiday Inn one night after the end of a council session, I said nothing, even though I hadn't seen any kind of hotel meeting listed on his itinerary. I put the Grand Marquis in drive and headed that way.

Mayor Finley was particularly upbeat. "So, Cutter," he said. "What's this I hear about you being a painter?"

I glanced in the mirror. "Where'd you hear that?"

"Just around. That true?"

"I paint," I said.

"Whaddya paint?"

"Landscapes, mostly. Some wildlife, portraits."

"Oh shit, *that* kind of painting," Finley said. "I was thinking of having you do my kitchen. Let me ask you this. You a good edger? I hate it when the wall color bleeds into the ceiling." He laughed. "But seriously, what are you doing driving my fat ass around if you're a painter?"

"Not all artists get to make a living from what they love," I said. "There reaches a point when you have to accept that you've either got it or you don't."

I'd never been inclined to open up to him, and this was as close as I'd ever gotten, and Finley must have realized it because he didn't have a quick comeback. "Yeah, well," he said, "seriously, you ever want to make a few extra bucks painting my kitchen, the offer's on the table."

I looked at him in the mirror. "Sure," I said.

Before we reached the Holiday Inn, Randall Finley let me know he wanted me to park around back. He didn't want the black Mercury seen up front. That gave me a hint about what sort of meeting he had planned.

I said fine.

"You talk to Lance today?" he asked.

"No," I replied.

"You and him, you don't get along so good," the mayor observed. It wasn't a question, so I didn't say anything. "You could learn a thing or two from him, you know? He's got terrific connections. Knows a lot of people. You need something, he can get it for you."

"He isn't offering anything I need," I said, putting on the blinker.

"Need's got nothing to do with it," the mayor said. "It's all about want."

It was ten o'clock, it had been a long day, and I wanted to go home and see Ellen before she fell asleep. I asked if he wanted me to wait or drive around awhile and come back in, say, an hour?

Finley glanced at his watch. "Forty-five minutes," he said. Then, hesitantly, "If you have to come and get me, should you happen to see Mrs. Finley drive into the parking lot, for example, I'm having a meeting in room 143. You might have to wait a bit after knocking. Or better yet, call my cell."

"Yeah," I said.

It didn't take Hercule Poirot to figure out what Finley was up to. What I didn't know was whether this rendezvous was with someone he actually had something going on with, or someone he was paying by the hour. Or by three-quarters of an hour. Chances were she wasn't some city hall employee. The mayor was mindful of sexual harassment suits. Maybe it was someone trying to get a contract with the city. Or, more likely, someone working on behalf of someone looking for a contract. There was no limit to what some of these consulting firms would do to get a multimillion-dollar deal, and few limits to what the mayor would accept in return.

I drove down the highway a mile to get a decaf coffee at Dunkin' Donuts, then drove back, taking a spot behind the Holiday Inn, in view of a Dumpster.

After about thirty minutes, my cell rang. I thought it might be Ellen calling to see whether I was ever going to get home. I wanted to talk to her, but at the same time was hoping it wasn't her. I wasn't proud to be cooling my heels while my boss got his ashes hauled, and I didn't want to talk to her about it.

I glanced at the number on the readout, saw that it was His Honor himself calling. "Yeah?" I said.

"Get in here! I'm hurt!"

"What's happened?" I asked.

"Just get in here! I'm bleeding."

I was no paramedic, so I said, "You want me to get an ambulance?"

"Jesus Christ no, just get the fuck in here!"

I drove to the front of the hotel, parked on the apron by the main doors, and ran inside. Finley had said he was in room 143, so I took that to mean the first floor. I found a hallway beyond the lobby, ran down it until I got to 143.

There was a girl leaning up against the wall a few feet down the hall. Mid to late teens, I guessed, frizzy blond hair, upturned nose, heavily rouged cheeks that failed to hide a pair of dimples. She was in a strapless top, short skirt, and heels, and gave me a once-over when I knocked on the door.

"Someone's in there," she said.

"That's why I'm knocking," I said.

"She's busy," the girl said. "But I'm available. I'm Linda."

From the other side of the door came a familiar, if somewhat muffled, voice. "Who is it?" Mayor Finley.

"It's me," I said.

He opened the door just enough to let me in, keeping himself hidden as he did so. Once I was inside the room I could see that he was in nothing but polka-dotted boxers, and there was blood soaked into the front of them.

"What the—"

"It's not my fault." Another voice, young and female.

The girl was on the floor beyond the foot of the bed, next to a toppled TV and stand. Short skirt, low-cut sweater, straight black hair down to her shoulders. Skinny legs, kind of gangly. Didn't fill out the sweater. She was working her jaw around, like she was trying to get the feeling back in it.

"I think I lost a tooth, you fucker," she said to Randall Finley.

"Serves you right," the mayor said. "You're not supposed to bite the goddamn thing off, you know."

"You jumped," she said, and sniffed. "It was an accident."

"I called Lance, too," the mayor told me. "He's coming."

"Terrific," I said. "Let me guess. He set this up."

The mayor said nothing. I turned my attention to the girl. What had struck me from the moment I'd seen her was how young she looked.

"How old are you?" I asked.

She was still rubbing her jaw, doing her best to ignore me.

"I asked you a question," I said.

"Nineteen," she snapped. I almost laughed. There was a purse on the bedside table and I grabbed it.

"Hey!" the girl said. "That's mine!"

I unzipped it, started rooting around inside. There were lipsticks, other makeup, half a dozen condoms, a cell phone, a small coil-topped notepad, and a wallet.

"Cutter, for Christ's sake," the mayor said, one hand pointed at the girl, the other pressed over his crotch. "Forget about her. You need to get me to a doctor or something."

The girl tried to grab her purse back but I swung it away. I looked in the wallet for a driver's license. When the only ID I could find was a Social Security card and a high school ID, I figured she wasn't yet old enough to drive. The name on the cards was Sherry Underwood.

"According to this, Sherry," I said,

putting emphasis on her name, "you're fifteen years old."

The same age as Derek at the time.

"Okay, so?" Sherry Underwood said.

The mayor had gone into the bathroom and was stuffing wads of toilet paper down the front of his shorts. He wasn't in an absolute panic now, not like he'd been when he phoned me, so I was guessing he was suffering from more of a superficial wound, as opposed to anything approaching an amputation.

I looked at him as he came back out of the bathroom. "You knew this?" I asked.

"Knew what?"

"That she's fifteen?"

The mayor feigned shock. "Fuck, no. She told me she was twenty-two."

No one could look at that girl and think she was twenty-two. "If she'd told you she was Hillary Clinton, would you have believed that too, Randy?"

"Randy?" he said, glaring at me. "Since when did you start calling me that?"

"Would you rather I said 'Your Worship'?"

"Jesus, you a minister?" the girl asked, her eyes wide.

Finley said nothing. Better to let her think that than tell her he was the mayor, if he hadn't already made that blunder.

Still holding on to Sherry's wallet and purse, I asked, "You okay?"

"He kicked me," she said. "Right in the face."

"How'd that happen?"

"He was, like, on his back on the bed and he jumped—"

"She caught me with her teeth," the mayor said.

"Shut up," I said to him.

The mayor opened his mouth to say something, but nothing came out.

"He jumped," I repeated for her. "Then what?"

"I took him out of my mouth and moved back and he brought up his leg and kicked me in the face." She looked at Finley. "That's what you did, you asshole."

"Sherry," I said, "you should go to the hospital, see a doctor."

"Christ's sake!" the mayor said, throwing some bloodied paper into the wastebasket. "I'm the one who needs medical attention. What the fuck are you doing, asking her if she needs to go to a hospital?"

I gave the mayor my best stare. "I'd be happy to take you to the ER right now if you'd like, but first I have to make a call to the *Standard*."

The mayor blinked. That was all he needed, to have the press show up asking about his bit dick. He mumbled something under his breath and went back into the bathroom.

I turned my attention back to Sherry Underwood. "Whaddya say?"

She was getting to her feet. "My shoes," she said. "I have to find my shoes."

I saw a pair of high-heeled sandals half tucked under the bed. "Over here," I said, pointing. Sherry slipped her feet into them, teetered on them precariously, an amateur. She'd need a couple more years to master them.

"I guess I'm okay," she said.

"You got parents?" I asked.

"Not really," she said.

"What's that mean?"

"They're dead," she said. "More or less."

"Who looks after you?" I asked.

"Linda."

"Who's Linda?" Then I thought, the girl in the hall?

"She's my friend. We look after each other."

"Sherry, you're a kid, this is no way to live. There are people, agencies, folks who can help you out."

"I'm okay," she insisted.

"No, you are not okay." I looked into her purse again, pulled out the notebook. I flipped through the pages. It was part diary, part address book, part accounting ledger. One page would have a date followed by a column of numbers, presumably how much she'd made that day. Another page would have a couple of phone numbers next to names or initials, like J., Ed, P., and L.R. I didn't, at a glance, see Randy's name in there. I flipped past more pages of shopping lists, license plate numbers, the phone number for something called "Willows," until I finally reached a blank page.

"That's personal stuff," Sherry said.

I took a pen from inside my jacket and wrote "Jim Cutter." And wrote down my phone number.

I said, "You have any problems, you call me, okay? If you decide to take this further, you'll need a witness to back up your story." I didn't have much hope that Sherry would make a complaint to the police, but you never knew about these things.

She didn't even look in the notebook when I handed it, along with her wallet and purse, back to her. "Whatever," she said.

"You need to get your shit together," I said. "You're a kid. Jesus, you're too young to be on your own like this. How long you been doing this? Stop now while you've still got a chance." She wouldn't look at me. "Are you listening to me? Getting kicked in the jaw, that could be the best thing that ever happens to you if it knocks some sense into your head."

She shrugged.

As she started to head for the hotel room door, the mayor came out of the bathroom and said, "You forgettin' something, honey?"

She looked at him, cocked her head. "Huh?"

"My money," he said. "I want it back. I might have to pay for some fucking rabies shots."

Sherry shot him the finger. The gesture so enraged Finley that he started moving across the carpet for her, pretty quickly for a middle-aged guy with a wounded pecker. He grabbed the girl by the elbow, hard enough to make her yelp. Her purse slid off her shoulder and down her arm as she tried to wrest herself away from him.

"Hey," I said.

"I want my money back right now, all of it." He had his hand locked on that elbow, and he was shaking the girl.

"Randy," I said for the second time, figuring further disrespect from me would make him direct his anger my way, and he'd let the girl go.

No such luck. With his free hand, the mayor reached for the girl's neck. That was when I did it.

I made a fist and ran it right into the mayor's nose.

Finley released Sherry, screamed, threw both hands to his face, tenting them over his nose.

"Jesus!" he screamed, blood trickling out between his fingers. "My nose! You broke my fucking nose!"

I hadn't, as it turned out. I'd only bloodied it. But at that moment, I knew, regardless of whether his nose was broken, I was going to be looking for a new job the next day. As the mayor returned to the bathroom for more tissue, I thought about the best-paying job—something that didn't involve putting a brush to canvas—I'd ever had.

It would have been when I was eighteen, cutting grass all summer for a landscaping outfit in Albany. I think I liked it so much because it was a job where you could see what you'd done. You cut a front yard, every pass with the lawn mower, back and forth, you could see the progress. You knew how much you'd accomplished, you knew how much you still had to do. Pushing the Lawn-Boy, watching the perimeter shrink with every trip, the sense of job satisfaction grew. How many jobs could you say that about?

That was more than twenty years ago, and I hadn't had that sense of accomplishment since. Certainly not during my stint trying to make it as a welfare investigator. I'd felt like shit every day in that job. And the time I'd spent working for a large security firm hadn't been much better. I already had a pickup truck. Buy a trailer, a second-hand lawn tractor, some mowers, I'd be in business. Get some kids working for me, maybe Derek could help out during the summer. Good hours, might even lose a bit of weight.

I wasn't sure how Ellen would respond, but I had a feeling she'd be okay with it. "You're still not pursuing your dream," she'd say, "but it's no worse than what you're doing."

All that went through my mind in a

couple of seconds. Then, back to reality, as the mayor tended to his wounds in the bathroom, I said to Sherry, "Take off."

She slipped out the door. "Jesus," I heard Linda say, probably looking at Sherry's face. "What the fuck?"

When the mayor came out of the bathroom, I took hold of his hand and with my other slapped the Grand Marquis keys into his palm. "Take it easy around the corners," I said. "It turns wide."

I ran into Lance in the lobby.

"What happened?" he asked, breathless. "What's going on?"

"He's in there. If he asks you to bandage his dick, get a raise first."

"Jesus, what the hell happened?"

I didn't have the energy to explain. Instead, I phoned Ellen and asked her to come pick me up.

SEVEN

A typical Sunday morning, we might have slept in. It's the one day of the week where I don't feel guilty sleeping late. If it weren't for the goddamn work ethic drilled into me by my father, I think I might be happy to stay under the covers until noon most days, but I generally wake up before six, thinking about the things I have to get done. Not just work stuff, but things around the house. If there aren't clients' yards to mow, there's a screen door that needs new screening, a slow drain that needs to be unclogged, a busted lawn mower that needs to be fixed.

But Sundays, screw it.

There's certainly no church to get up and dressed for. I'm not a big fan of organized religion. Ellen's parents raised her as a Presbyterian, but sometime in her late teens she simply didn't buy it anymore and couldn't be persuaded to go. I was never sure whether being a lapsed Presbyterian was that big a deal. It wasn't like being a lapsed Catholic. My parents, on the other hand, had raised me to be nothing, other than a decent, I hoped, and responsible individual who could figure out what was the right and moral thing to do in any given situation, and then do it.

My track record in that regard, however, had not always been exemplary. Working for as long as I did for Mayor Finley is a case in point.

While for Derek, a standard sleep-in means getting up in time for supper, for me and Ellen, it's somewhere between eight and nine in the morning. But this was hardly a typical Sunday morning, not even twenty-four hours since we'd learned about the Langleys.

And even though our scare in the night—Derek's rendezvous with Penny— had turned out to be nothing, it took us a long time to get back to sleep after that. Around six, lying on my side and staring at the clock radio's digital display, I sensed Ellen was awake as well. We had our backs to each other, and no one was moving, but there's a way she breathes when she's sleeping, deeper, that I wasn't hearing, so I reached over and lightly touched her back.

"Hey," I said.

Ellen turned over without saying anything, looked into my eyes without so much as a smile, then reached out and pulled me close to her, pressing her body up against mine. I responded as she knew I would, and she rolled me on top of her. We engaged in an act of wordless lovemaking that was born not out of any kind of sexual frenzy, but a need to reassure ourselves that we were still alive, that we had each other, that we could connect in this most intimate of ways, aware that at any moment, without any warning whatsoever, it could all end.

Ellen was putting a plate of French toast in front of me when she looked out the window and said, "Barry's coming around the side of the house."

A moment later, Barry Duckworth was on the deck, rapping lightly at the back door. It was nearly eight in the morning by now, and Ellen and I had been up a couple of hours but only just now gotten to breakfast.

I stayed in my seat at the kitchen table while Ellen opened the screen door. "Hi, Barry," she said.

Barry nodded, almost apologetically. "Sorry to disturb you folks so early," he said.

"Come on in," I said.

"Coffee?" Ellen said.

"That'd be nice," Barry said. "Black." He stepped into the kitchen, moving tentatively toward the table and me. Only eight in the morning and already his white shirt was starting to stick to his ample stomach. Ellen handed him a mug of black coffee as he glanced at my breakfast, drenched in maple syrup. Ellen noticed, and said, "A slice of French toast, Barry?"

"I really shouldn't," he said.

"It's no trouble."

"Well, if you insist," he said. "All I had before I left home was a tiny bowl of bran with some strawberries on it."

"Sounds healthy," I said.

"Maureen's trying to get me to lose some weight," he said. "So I eat healthy at home, then get something else later."

I smiled and motioned to the chair across from me. Barry took a load off. I saw Ellen dipping two slices of bread into some eggs, turn the heat back on under the frying pan.

"How's it going?" I asked.

Barry ran his hand over his nearly bald pate. "Well, we're following a number of enquiries," he said. "Isn't that how the Brits say it?"

"I think so," I said.

"You can't have been a lawyer as long as Albert was and not made a few enemies over the years. I'm sure he knew plenty of folks who might be capable of this sort of thing."

Ellen said, "I can't imagine anyone being capable of what happened over there."

"Yeah, well," Barry said. "I know what

you mean. I was gonna say, when you're in my line of work, you start accepting that people are capable of all sorts of horrible things, but the God's honest truth is, I've never seen anything like this. Not a whole family. Not like that. Not in Promise Falls."

"This is America," Ellen said, putting the two slices of bread into the frying plan. "These kinds of things can happen anywhere."

"We've had more than our share the last little while," he said.

I perked up at that. "You have?"

"Well, a couple anyway," Barry Duckworth said. "There was that one out back of the Trenton, three weeks ago." A bar on the north side of town. Not an area where I get many calls to cut people's lawns. "Guy named Edgar Winsome. Forty-two, married, couple of kids, cement worker. Shot in the chest."

"Jesus," I said. "A bar fight?"

Barry shook his head. "Maybe. But it didn't spill out of the bar. No one saw him having it out with anybody. Nobody remembers him getting into an argument or anything. Came in, had half a dozen beers, talked with a few of his buddies, leaves, they find him later, out back. Loud music, no one heard a thing."

"He must have pissed off somebody," I said.

Barry nodded at that. "Seems a reasonable assumption. He wasn't robbed. Still had his wallet, cash, and charge cards."

"Well," said Ellen, flipping the toast.

"And we haven't gotten anywhere with it," Barry said.

"A couple," I said.

"Huh?" said Barry, taking a sip of his black coffee.

"You said there were a couple."

"Yeah. The other one, older guy, fifty, last name of Knight, has a machine shop about five miles west of town, on 29. He was locking up one evening, everyone else had already left, still light out, someone comes along and pops him in the head. This was about a week before the Trenton guy bought it, a Friday night."

Ellen put the French toast on a plate.

"Powdered sugar and syrup?" she asked.

"Oh, yes, please," Barry said. Ellen dressed his toast and set the plate in front of him. "Good God, this looks magnificent," he said.

"How come I don't know about this?" I asked him.

He was about to put the first forkful of toast and egg and syrup into his mouth, and he looked at me. "I can't help it you're uninformed." He savored his mouthful, swallowed, raised the mug to his lips, had some more coffee. "To be fair, the Trenton thing, papers only gave it a couple of inches, guy gets killed behind a bar, how weird is that, really? The Knight guy, at the machine shop, that one got a bit of attention, but not all that much, I suppose."

Ellen said, "That's when we were away, remember?"

I thought a moment. We'd driven to Vermont, taken the ferry across to Burlington for a couple of nights, an anniversary getaway, leaving Derek on his own, but not quite. We'd arranged for Ellen's sister Carol to drop by periodically, make him some dinner, pop by unannounced in the evening. We weren't going to give him the opportunity to have a party at the house, and it's fair to say he hated us for it. "Add it to the list," I'd told him at the time.

"By the time you got back, it was out of the paper," Barry said. "Honest to God, Ellen, this is delicious. I shouldn't even be having this. What I'm going to do is, I'm going to skip lunch. This should carry me through the whole day."

Ellen smiled, but it looked forced. She had to be wondering, as was I, why Barry was here so early on a Sunday morning. It was a given that he was working on the Langley murders, but I didn't believe he'd dropped in just to be friendly, or score a breakfast out of us. I had the feeling Barry was working up to something.

"So, Barry," I said, "these various leads you have, how're they coming?"

He waited to swallow another bite. He was making fast work of Ellen's French toast. It's one of the things she does best. He glanced into his mug, saw that it was empty, and said to Ellen, "You got another half a cup there?"

"Oh, sure," Ellen said, and brought the pot over to the table and poured him another full cup.

"Oh, that's great." He used his napkin to dab some syrup from the corner of his mouth. "We have some idea of the order of things, that Albert answered the door, that he was probably shot first, that his wife was shot next, and that Adam, he was shot trying to get away."

Imagining it, I couldn't think of anything to say.

"Right there at the back door," Barry said. "He almost made it. Maybe, in a weird kind of way, it's a good thing he didn't. If he'd made it, he'd probably have run straight here. And then whoever was coming after him would have been led right to your door."

Ellen gave me a look. This wasn't the sort of thing she needed to hear.

"Barry," I said, "you and I, we're friends, but I'm guessing you didn't drop by just to shoot the shit. What's on your mind?"

He shoved the last bite of French toast into his mouth, washed it down with coffee, and said, "It's about your boy."

EIGHT

I went upstairs to Derek's room while Ellen stayed down in the kitchen with Barry. I eased open his door, and unlike the morning before, he was sound asleep. I didn't know how much longer he'd been up with Penny in the night. After I'd discovered it was them on the back step and not some insane serial killer, and once we'd explained to the police that everything was okay and offered our apologies, Ellen and I had gone back to bed.

I'd been inclined to tell Derek to go to bed as well, but what had happened to the Langleys was as troubling to him as it was to us, perhaps even more so, and if he needed to spend time with his girlfriend to get through this, I wasn't going to be a pain in the ass about it.

I sat on the edge of his bed and lightly touched his shoulder. He woke with a start.

"What?" he said, turning over and opening his eyes.

"It's okay," I said. "Sorry to wake you."

He blinked a couple of times. "What's going on? We're not working today, are we?"

"No," I said. "Barry Duckworth is here." Derek, who didn't instantly recognize the name, looked blank. "The cops. He's the detective in charge. The one who talked to us yesterday. He wants to have a word with you."

Derek swallowed, blinked again. "What does he want me for? I didn't do anything."

"Nobody's saying you did. He's just got a lot of questions for a lot of people. He'll explain it to you when you come down."

"Should I get dressed?"

"That'd be a good idea," I said. "But don't worry about a tie."

"A tie?"

"A joke. Just throw something on and come down."

I returned to the kitchen and Derek showed up two minutes later. He'd pulled on a New York Islanders T-shirt and some torn jean shorts, and his black hair was still going every which way.

"Hey, Derek," Barry said.

Derek nodded without saying anything.

His mother said, "You want some French toast?"

"I'm not even awake, Mom," he said.

"Have a seat," Barry said, and Derek pulled out a chair and sat down at the table. "How you doing this morning?"

"Tired," Derek said.

"Yeah, sorry about rousting you out of bed so early, but I'd like your help with something."

Derek eyed him, warily I thought.

"You were with the Langleys until shortly before they left, right?"

Derek nodded very slowly, like he had to think about the answer. The question seemed pretty straightforward to me.

"That was around eight?"

Derek nodded again.

"So that means you're the last person who may have seen the Langleys alive, unless they stopped for gas or something after they headed off, but you're also the last person to see their place, the inside of their house, before they got killed."

Derek swallowed. "I guess," he said.

"So what I'd like you to do is, the reason I came by is, I'd like you to come over to the Langley house with me, see if anything looks out of the ordinary."

Ellen took in a sharp breath. "You can't be serious," she said. "You can't be thinking of dragging our son through that house, where all those . . . things happened." I could almost imagine her saying to herself, *You son of a bitch, you eat my French toast, and then come up with this?*

Barry looked unapologetic, even though he said he was sorry. "I need Derek's help. He's a very important part of this investigation, Ellen. He might see something out of the ordinary.

Something missing. Maybe a painting, or—"

"A painting?" Ellen said. "You think the Langleys were killed because someone wanted to steal a painting?" She looked at me, supposedly the art expert. "Did the Langleys have valuable art?"

"Not that I know of," I said.

"It's just a for instance," Barry said, trying not to sound impatient. "I don't know that they have any expensive paintings at all. Maybe someone came into the house, I don't know, to steal Mrs. Langley's jewelry or—"

"What on earth would Derek know about Donna's jewelry?" Ellen said. "Why would you even think—"

"Ellen," I said.

"—he'd know anything about that?"

"Again," Barry said, still very patiently, but it seemed to be a strain, "it was just an example. There might have been things in full view in the house, things I don't know about, but Derek here might notice if they were gone. That's all I'm talking about."

"Well," Ellen said, "I absolutely forbid it. There's no way—"

"I'll do it," Derek said.

"That's great," Barry said.

"No you won't," Ellen said. "You're not going over there."

"I'll do it," Derek said again, still looking at Barry. "If you need me to do it, I'll do it."

Ellen's mouth opened. She was ready to voice her objections again, then stopped. Derek said to her, "It's okay, Mom. If there's anything I can do to help catch whoever killed Adam, I want to do it."

Barry reached his hand out to Derek to shake it. Derek, awkwardly, extended his in return and they shook. "Good man," Barry said. "You want some breakfast first? That's okay. Get something in your stomach. I don't mind waiting. Your mom's French toast, it's pretty goddamn amazing. Although, I don't know, maybe it's better to go over on an empty stomach, you know what I'm saying? Just a bit of advice from a guy who's been there."

Ellen was giving me an imploring

look, indicating that she wanted me to ask Barry something. I took a shot at what it must be. "Barry," I said, "you mind if I come along with Derek?"

I could see the relief in Ellen's face. I'd guessed right. Barry said, "Sure, that would be fine, Jim. That's a real good idea."

Then no one said anything for a couple of seconds, until Derek said, "Well?"

As the three of us headed out the door, me trailing behind Barry and Derek, Ellen touched my arm to hold me back and whispered, "I'm sorry. I can't go over there. I just, I can't do it."

"I understand."

"Be there for him."

I touched her on the shoulder and went out the door, taking a few steps at a gallop to catch up.

"So you're working for your dad for the summer?" Barry was saying.

"Yeah," Derek said. And I thought, *Even under the circumstances, could he not say "Yes"?* You're always a parent.

"Pretty hot week to be doing yard work, huh?"

"Yeah, it's been kinda brutal," Derek

said. "We had that rain early in the week, gave us a bit of a break, although then we got behind, you know?"

"I hear ya," Barry said, like he and my son were suddenly best friends. I couldn't pinpoint exactly why, but that gave me an uncomfortable feeling.

The conversation died out as we neared the Langley house. I felt that I was seeing the place for the first time. There wasn't anything structurally different about it from a week or a month ago, aside from the decorative yellow police tape surrounding it, but now it had this ominous presence. I wondered, momentarily, what would happen to the house, now that the Langleys were all dead. Relatives would have to come in, sell the place. I'd hate to be the real estate agent brought in to find a buyer for a house where three people had been slain.

We were coming up to the back of the house, but Barry said, "We'll be going in around the front. Still a bit of a mess around the back door there."

My son was very quiet. But then,

"They're, like, they aren't still there, are they?"

Barry smiled. "No. The bodies have been removed, Derek."

Derek nodded quickly, as if to suggest he knew that, he was just kidding, as if anyone was in the mood for jokes.

We came around the front of the house, where there was a patrol car in addition to Barry's unmarked cruiser, an officer parked behind the wheel. Barry sidled over, talked to the cop through the open window, said we were all going in for a tour. Barry hardly had to ask the guy for permission, but he was being extremely polite today.

"Okay," he said, leading the way to the front door. "Let's go in."

As we entered the house he said, "Don't touch anything." He held the door for us. "In fact, you might want to put your hands in your pockets just to be sure."

We complied. Derek went in ahead of me, and once the three of us were just inside the door, we all stopped, like we were on some sort of historic house tour and Barry was our guide.

It didn't take long for us to realize we weren't on that kind of tour.

The carpet immediately in front of us, and at the base of the stairs, was nearly black with blood. And even though the bodies of the Langleys had been removed, the stench in the house took our breath away. A hand came out of my pocket and went instinctively to my mouth.

"Yeah, sorry about that," Barry said as I slipped my hand back into my pocket.

I took a look at Derek to see how he was coping. Trying to breathe through his mouth, eyes darting around. I could make out his fists clenching in the front pockets of his jean shorts.

"Right here," Barry said, pointing to the blood closest to us, "is where Albert Langley died, where his body was found. We think he went to the door, that one or more persons had knocked on it and he was shot very shortly after opening the door. And then over here," he said, guiding us around the blood and over toward the stairs, "was where Donna Langley's body was discovered." There seemed as much blood there as by the front door. "She must have come downstairs when she heard the commotion, and that's where it happened."

"Dear God," I said, and took another look at my son, who was stone-faced. Hesitantly, I said, "And Adam?"

"Down the end of the hall here, at the bottom of a half flight of stairs, by the back door."

Before we could proceed any further into the house, Barry wanted us to slip on some booties in a bid not to contaminate the crime scene any further. He pulled three pairs of them from his pocket, and we all took a moment to get them on. This, of course, necessitated taking our hands out of our pockets, and Derek and I leaned against each other, taking turns, to slip them over our shoes. They were crinkly, a bit like paper, but much stronger.

Once that was done, Barry motioned for us to follow him along the hallway, which we both walked down as though we were tightrope walkers, hands back in our pockets, careful not to let our shoulders brush the walls. I noticed light-colored powder on many surfaces within the house. On doorknobs, stair railings, the corners of walls.

Barry, who'd been watching me, said, "Fingerprinting."

"Of course," I said.

To Derek he said, "We'll be wanting to get a set of your prints."

"Huh?" said Derek.

"Not to worry," Barry said. "We already know you've been over. But if the killer, or killers, left any prints behind, we have to be able to weed out the ones that don't matter."

"Right," said Derek.

We'd reached the end of the hall, where the steps came up from the back door. We looked down onto a third puddle of dried blood. I felt myself getting woozy.

"Derek," Barry said, "have you noticed anything? Something that seems out of place? Something missing? Something that's there that wasn't there before?"

I'd been inside this house several times over the years, and to my eye everything looked in order, aside from the obvious signs. The place had not been ransacked. Cushions hadn't been tossed. It didn't look, for example, as though someone had been searching for drugs after murdering the occupants.

Unless, of course, they knew exactly where to look for whatever it was they'd come to get.

"I just . . . I don't notice anything," Derek said.

"Let's do a slow walk-through," Barry said, directing us to turn around and head back down the hallway. "We'll start in the kitchen."

It was a relief to go in there. So long as you didn't actually breathe, there wasn't anything to tip you to what had transpired on the other side of the wall. Donna, who'd had more than her share of quirks, was also something of a neat freak, and the kitchen showed it. Nothing out of place, no dishes in the sink, everything in perfect order in the fridge, which Barry opened by pulling on the side of the door itself, and not the han-

dle, which had also been dusted for fingerprints.

"Mrs. Langley was here, packing
stuff for the trip," Derek said. "She was
feeling kind of woozy."

"Right," Barry said. "That's what
Langley's secretary said was the reason they'd come back. The cooler with
the food in it, some other groceries,
they were all still in the SUV, they hadn't
had a chance to bring it back in yet before they were killed. So nothing here,
nothing looks out of the ordinary?"

"No."

"Okay, let's head upstairs."

Stepping over Donna Langley's
blood at the bottom of the stairs was
like trying to straddle a puddle at the
edge of a curb after a rainstorm.
Thankfully, once we were up the carpeted stairs, there were no more blood
pools.

"Again," Barry said, "try not to touch
anything." We'd kept our hands in our
pockets, except for when we navigated
the blood and needed our arms to
maintain our balance.

"Okay," said Barry, easing himself

into the first door on the left. "This is Adam's room, but you probably already know that, right, Derek?"

Derek nodded.

"Just have a look, see if you notice anything out of place, out of the ordinary."

I figured Barry Duckworth, who had kids of his own, realized the fact that this room looked as though it had been tossed was not necessarily evidence that some bad guy or bad guys had been here searching for something. It was a teenage boy's room, and at a glance, it could have been Derek's. There were heaps of clothes on the floor here and there, the bed was unmade, magazines about computers and skateboarding and girls littered the top of his desk. Posters adorned the walls, including one that was drawn in the style of a World War II recruiting ad, showing a smiling soldier holding up a mug of coffee and saying, "How about a cup of shut the fuck up?"

Also like Derek's room, there were computer parts everywhere. Three monitors, half a dozen keyboards, countless wires and cables, boxes from computer games, an old-generation Nintendo system shoved under a desk, three computer towers.

Barry sighed. "I don't know how you'd tell, exactly, whether something was missing from here, but what do you think?"

Derek studied the room from where he stood, didn't say anything for about half a minute, then, "It looks fine."

"You're sure?"

"Yeah."

Barry moved us back into the hall. The next room was a guest bedroom and looked as pristine as a hotel suite, not much to spot in there. We all poked our heads into the bathroom, and it looked as though Donna had left it ready should company drop by.

Well, somebody dropped by.

All that was left on this floor was the master bedroom. "I don't know whether you've ever seen this room or not," Barry said to Derek, "but go ahead and have a look."

I was relieved he hadn't said the same thing to me. I looked in over

Derek's shoulder, and the bedroom looked pretty much the same as it had the only other time I had seen it, except maybe for the fingerprint dust all over the dresser.

"Nothing," Derek said.

"Okay, that's okay," Barry said. "If you don't see something, that probably means that there's nothing much to see. So we've got just one thing left to check out."

"What?" Derek said, surprised.

"The basement."

"Oh," he said. "You think anyone was in the basement?"

"Well, we need to check out everything," he said.

And so we went back down the stairs, over the puddle of Donna Langley's blood, then down the hall, and down the half flight of stairs to the landing at the back door, where Adam Langley had died. Barry maneuvered himself around the bloodstains and went down the last few steps into the basement, but Derek, who had been behind him, stood breathless on the last step before the landing.

"You okay?" I asked him. Maybe Ellen had been right. This was too much to put our son through. Barry shouldn't have made him do this. And so far, dragging our boy through this hadn't provided any new insights.

"I can just . . . I can just picture him there," Derek said.

"I know," I said.

"If he could have just gotten out the door. If only he'd run a little faster," Derek said.

Barry poked his head around the wall. "What do you mean, Derek?"

"Just that, if he'd been quicker, he might have gotten away."

"He was shot in the back of the head," Barry said, "so he was probably already running, trying to get out, but it's hard to outrun a bullet."

Derek's breathing was quick and shallow. "If he could have made it out the door, he could have hidden in the woods."

"I think Derek's had enough," I told Barry.

"We're almost done," he said. "Just

try to get around without stepping in anything and come downstairs."

"You need a drink of water or anything?" I asked my son.

"We'll be out of here in no time," Barry said. "And I don't want us using any glasses from the Langleys' cupboard, you know?"

We got around the blood and walked down into the rec room. The lights were already on. It looked like a million other basements. Wood paneling on the walls. A couch that had seen better days, had probably belonged upstairs at one point. A TV, about a thirty-six-inch screen, I figured, but not a flat screen that hangs on a wall.

To my eye, the room looked pretty undisturbed.

"What do you think?" Barry asked. "You and Adam must have hung out down here a lot."

"Yeah, we did," he said quietly.

"Anything look out of place?"

Derek shook his head slowly.

"You're sure?"

A slow nod.

"What about over here?" Barry said, pointing to the far end of the room.

"What?" I said. I didn't know what he was getting at.

Barry walked across the room and pointed to a panel, about three feet wide, that ran from the floor up to a chair rail molding that ran around the perimeter of the room. The panel was open about an inch or so.

"What do you make of this?" he asked Derek.

"What do you mean?"

"This panel, to the crawlspace. It's open an inch or two. You see that?"

"Sure," Derek said.

"You think that means anything? I mean, you look around this house, and there's not a thing out of place, except for maybe in Adam's room. Donna Langley, she kept this place like a home out of *House Beautiful* or something. A place for everything and everything in its place. I just thought this panel, partly open like this, looked a bit odd."

"I don't know," Derek said.

"Maybe," I offered, "since they were going away for a few days, maybe Albert got some stuff out of there, like a cooler or something. The kind of stuff you only take out when you're going for a trip."

"That might be," Barry said. "I'm sure it's nothing. It's just, when I looked at it, I thought, what a perfect place for someone to hide."

"When we were little," Derek offered, "Adam and I used to play in there all the time. Like it was a cave. We'd pretend we were explorers or something, or Indiana Jones, you know? But now, I don't think I could even fit in there."

"Too big now?" Barry said. "You know what? Why don't you try it on for size?"

"Huh?"

Barry slid the panel back. The space was filled with boxes, most with Magic-Markered labels like "Xmas bulbs" and "Yearbooks." He said, "Someone must have been in here. The dust is pretty thick on the cement floor in here, except just inside the opening, where it's kind of been rubbed away. Come on in, have a look."

"I don't really want to," Derek said. "I just want to get out of here."

"I'll do it then," Barry said, taking his hands out of his pockets, getting down on his hands and knees, and back-crawling into the space. "Now, I'm a big fat fucker compared to either one of you guys, but I can squeeze in here, so I guess just about anybody could."

"But, Barry," I said, "you already figured the killer, or killers, came in through the front door. So what's this prove, that someone could fit in the crawlspace?"

He crawled back out, huffing and puffing when he got back on his feet. I hoped he wasn't going to have a heart attack. "Damned if I really know," he said. "You just want to keep your mind open to everything."

"Are we done?" I asked Barry.

"I guess we are." He let out a long sigh, still recovering from his crawl-space adventure. "So, Derek."

"Yeah?"

"You said you left here around eight, right?"

"That's right."

"So what did you do then?"

"I don't know. I thought maybe I'd hook up with Penny."

I spoke without thinking. "I thought you said she was grounded or something. She hit her dad's car or something like that?"

"Well, yeah, she was. What I meant was, I was going to see her, but then we couldn't get together, so I just kind of hung out a bit, and then I went home."

"Hung out where?" Barry asked.

Derek sniffed, took a hand out of his pocket and rubbed his nose, then slipped it back in. It almost seemed like he was buying time.

"Just walked around, was in town a bit, went by the video-game place. Just stuff."

Barry didn't say anything for a moment. Then, "What time did you get home?"

"I guess, I don't know. Nine or nine-thirty, I think."

I tried to recall whether I'd heard Derek come in that night. Ellen and I had gone to bed pretty early. By half past nine, I thought. I didn't remember hearing him come in. We certainly hadn't spoken to him.

"That sound right to you?" Barry asked me.

I opened my mouth, thought for half a second, and said, "Yeah, that sounds about right."

"You heard him come in?" Barry asked, wanting to be sure.

"Yeah," I lied.

NINE

After Barry gave me one of his cards and got in his unmarked car to drive back into Promise Falls, and as Derek and I were walking slowly back down the lane toward our house, he said to me, "Why'd you do that?"

"Why'd I do what?"

"Tell that cop you heard me come in?"

"Was I wrong about that? Didn't I hear you come in around nine-thirty?"

Derek hesitated.

"You saying that if I thought I heard you come in then, I'd be wrong?"

He still didn't know how to respond. "I don't think you heard me come in, is all I'm saying."

"Is that because you didn't come in,

or you snuck in so quietly you don't think we could have heard you?"

Derek shook his head in frustration. "Either way, I just don't understand why you lied to him."

It was my turn to figure out how to respond. "I was just trying to help. Like, I don't know, if you really were with Penny or something, if she'd snuck out even though she was supposed to be grounded, and you don't want to have to drag her into this. It's just easier for me to say I heard you come in."

Derek thought about that. "Okay."

I stopped walking and put my hand on my son's arm. "Is there something you want to tell me?" I asked, looking him in the eye.

"No." He looked down at the gravel.

"Look at me," I said. "I understand what a shock this has been to you, losing your best friend, what something like that must do to your head. So I get it, you acting funny. It'd be weird if you weren't acting this way. But sometimes I think there's something more going on. That there's something you're holding back, something you should be telling us. If not Barry, certainly me and your mother. We can't help you if you don't level with us. This is serious shit here, Derek."

"I know. You don't have to tell me that. I'm not stupid."

"So, is there something you want to tell me? About when you got home?"

He paused. "It was sort of around when I said. I don't know the exact time. I think you guys were asleep is all. I know how you are on a Friday night. You're beat, so I came in real quiet because I figured you and Mom would have gone to bed early. Maybe not nine-thirty, maybe a little later."

I waited.

"So that's all."

"What about what Barry asked you?" I said. "What were you up to between eight and when you got home?"

"Nothing," he said defensively. "Nothing really."

"Where were you?"

"Jesus, what the fuck is this, anyway? You think I killed our fucking neighbors?"

I didn't flinch or back down. "No," I

said evenly. "Of course not. But I *am* starting to wonder whether you know something about what happened there. Answer my question. Where were you between the time you left the Langleys and the time you came home? I'm figuring you weren't with Penny, that she wasn't allowed to leave the house."

"I went for a walk," he said.

"To Penny's house? She's all the way into town. That'd take you thirty, forty minutes."

"No. Just around. Is that a crime? That I took a walk?"

"Where?"

"Huh?"

"Where did you walk?"

"Around. Down the highway, to the creek. I sat down there, called Penny on my cell, we talked for a while, I guess for an hour or something, and then I walked back home. I guess I was feeling kind of down. We're kind of going through a rough patch right now."

That was either the truth or bullshit designed to garner sympathy, get me to back off. I was inclined to believe the latter.

"Things looked okay between you two in the middle of the night."

"Yeah. It's mostly her parents, you know. They don't like me."

"What do you mean? Why?"

"I don't know."

"You must have some idea."

"Well, it might have something to do with her dad kind of finding us, you know, making out. In her room."

"You think?" I said.

"He's a real tight-ass," Derek said.

"You don't have to be much of a tight-ass to get upset finding some guy making out with your daughter in her bedroom. Under your roof."

"Yeah, well, that was sort of why she had to sneak out here to see me."

"For Christ sake, Derek, you're just going to make things even worse with her dad, you start letting her do things like that."

"Jesus," he said, adopting a tone I didn't much care for, "you gonna start getting all tight-ass on me too?"

I squeezed his arm and shook him. "Don't you ever speak to me like that. I don't care how much shit you might be in, you talk to me like that and I'll knock your fucking block off."

If I'd actually struck him he couldn't have looked any more stunned. I kept my grip on him for another second, then let go.

"I'm sorry," he said.

"We clear?"

"Yeah."

"So you were saying."

"Uh . . ." Derek had lost the thread of his story. Then, "Okay, what I was trying to say is, please don't say anything about her being here, because she snuck out of the house after her dad fell asleep. One of her friends picked her up and dropped her off on the highway and she came in. She got right past that cop parked up at the end of the drive."

That was a comforting thought, but hardly surprising. There was so much tree cover out here, it would take a team of cops to keep watch in all directions at all times.

"Whatever's going on between us didn't really matter when she found out what happened to Adam. She came over to see how I was doing."

I thought there were enough things to worry about having a seventeen-year-old son. I couldn't imagine being Penny's parents and finding out she'd slipped away in the night to visit her boyfriend where three people had been murdered only a few hours earlier.

"You shouldn't have even let her come out here," I said. "It's not safe, a girl going out in the middle of the night. Anywhere. Let alone out here, after what happened to the Langleys."

"So now I'm in shit for what she does, too?"

This was invariably what happened in parent-teen discussions. You started off getting mad about one thing, and before you knew it you were getting mad about something else. Focus, I told myself.

"You're leveling with me?" I said.

Derek nodded slowly.

"Honestly?"

He nodded again, but then looked ready to say something.

"What is it?"

"It's just . . ." he said. "It's just, well, I mean, it might not be anything. Because Adam said something, I think, before he left, before he got in the car with his parents, but the thing is, it might not mean anything at all."

"What are you talking about?" I felt my pulse quicken.

"I think I noticed something missing in the house. Something that was there the other day, but wasn't there just now."

"Jesus Christ," I said. "What did you—"

"Hello!" It was Ellen, standing at the front door. "You coming inside, or what?"

Back in the kitchen, Derek was finally persuaded to have some breakfast. For a boy who half an hour ago claimed to have no appetite, he downed four slices of French toast drowning in butter and syrup like he'd just been released from prison.

"You want some coffee with that?"

Ellen asked. Derek's mouth was so full all he could do was nod.

When Ellen had called out to us from the house, Derek had whispered quickly, "I'll tell you later."

And I had said, "Okay."

It wasn't that I wanted to keep secrets from Ellen. But if there was a chance Derek was willing to tell me something I needed to know, then I was willing not to make a fuss about his not being open with both of his parents until I knew what it was.

Ellen threw her arms around him when he came into the house, fearing he might have been somehow traumatized by having to tour the Langley house with Barry Duckworth.

"It was fine," he said. "No big deal."

Ellen looked at me, trying to read in my face whether Derek was really okay, or putting up a front. I shook my head, unable to give her a definitive answer. Then she talked him into downing an enormous breakfast.

I could tell Ellen wanted to ask him about his experience in the Langley home, not to find out what he'd seen—

she could find that out from me later— but to determine what kind of effect it had had on him. But I think she concluded that if he was able to eat like this, perhaps there was no permanent damage to his psyche. I was less sure. If there was one thing I knew about teenage boys, it was that you could turn off the outside world long enough to stuff yourself.

"I was thinking," Derek said, looking at me, his mouth still full, "that we should try to fix that one mower today. Since we've got the time."

"Sure," I said. "I think it might be as simple as a gummed-up spark plug."

"I got a theory," Derek said, "it could be the fuel filter. Maybe it's all gummed up with crap."

Ellen had a choice, listening to this. She could figure that Derek was reaching out to his father, looking for comfort in his company in the wake of tragedy, or he was up to something.

Not being quite the cynic I am, she said, "That sounds great. You two could get a few things done today." She smiled at me. She'd bought it.

When Derek finished the last of his toast, he got up and went to take his plate to the sink, but his mother stopped him and said, "I'll look after that. Why don't you help your father."

"Okay," he said, and went out the back door.

"I'll be right there," I called out after him. Ellen looked to me and I knew she wanted to hear something about our tour through the Langley house. "He was okay," I told her. "It was awful over there, but he was okay."

"Barry never should have—"

"Don't worry about it. He's just doing his job. You'd have been proud of Derek, holding it together over there."

"What was it like—" Ellen started to ask. "No, don't tell me. I don't want to know."

I found Derek in the shed, fiddling about, wielding an oversized electric hedge trimmer. I was not surprised to see that he was not paying the slightest bit of attention to our ailing lawn mower.

"So," I said. "What did you want to tell me? What was missing?"

"Like I said, it might not be anything. But you remember when we went to Mrs. Stockwell's house?"

"Agnes? The one with the cat that looks like a pig?"

"Yeah."

"What do you mean, when we went there? We go there pretty much every week."

"This was like, two times ago," Derek said. "She gave me the computer."

"Right," I said, nodding. "Some old piece of crap. From her garage."

I hardly needed to say "some old piece of crap." It was all Derek and Adam liked to collect. They loved—well, had loved—tearing them apart, messing around with the hard drives, comparing the guts of old computers to the guts of new ones. Derek hadn't left with the whole computer, just the tower. The keyboard and the monitor weren't of much interest to him, although we did take them off Agnes's hands and dropped them off at the dump on one of our occasional trips up there. I had a soft spot in my heart for Agnes Stockwell, living alone in her bungalow on Ridgeway Drive. She loses a husband, then a year later son Brett, a Thackeray College student, kills himself by jumping off Promise Falls. It's not the highest waterfall in the world by any means, but when there's nothing but jagged rocks at the bottom, how high does it have to be?

"So, Adam and me," Derek said, "we'd been messing around with it. Seeing what kind of processor it had, that kind of shit, but we were also looking at what was on it."

That, I'd learned, was half the fun. It probably never would have occurred to Agnes that her son's computer was a repository of information about him. Old e-mails, stories, maybe saved porn images. Agnes, not exactly computer literate, probably figured all that stuff had evaporated by this time. How could all those things survive in a metal and plastic box all these years? But a tower like that was the ultimate shoebox of memories.

"Okay," I said.

"Anyway, when we were in the

house, with Barry? The cop? It wasn't in Adam's room."

"How could you tell?" I asked. The image of Adam's room hadn't quite burned itself into my memory like the three enormous bloodstains, but I remembered it was a mess.

"I could tell, Dad. It had been right on top of his desk. I know what it looked like. It was like a beigy color; most of the other ones Adam had in there were black. And it wasn't there."

I thought about that for a moment.

"Was it there when you last saw Adam? Before he left with his parents?"

"I didn't go up to his room. We were hanging out in the kitchen mostly. Last time I'd been up in his room was, like, the day before. Thursday? It was there then."

"Did anything else in the room look out of place? Did it look like anything else was taken?"

"Not that I could tell, but, like, I only looked in there for a second. But I saw right away that it was gone."

"Why didn't you tell Barry?" I asked

him. "That's the kind of thing he wanted to know."

"It's just, like I said, it might not mean anything. Adam said to me, one of the last things he said to me, was that his dad was kind of pissed about it."

"What do you mean? Mr. Langley was pissed because you had an old computer from Agnes Stockwell's house? Why would he give a shit about that? You two were always collecting old computers and messing around with them."

"I think Adam must have mentioned to him what we found on it."

"What the hell did you find on it?" I asked.

Derek let out a long sigh. "Like, all kinds of shit was on the hard drive. Bunch of school essays, some really lame game based on the first *Star Trek* series. You know, the one with Kirk and Spock and those guys. Really sad graphics, but kind of cool at the same time, you know."

"Okay," I said a bit impatiently, trying to move him along.

"And there was a résumé, and letters

he wrote when he was applying to Thackeray and other schools, you know, and some letters to a teacher he had back in high school, but the main thing is, there was a story."

"A story? What, a short story? Something Agnes's son wrote?"

"Not a short story. It's, like, a novel. A whole bunch of chapters. Twenty of them, at least."

I was shaking my head, trying to understand. "Okay, so there's a book or something in that computer. Why didn't you mention it to Barry?"

"I don't know. I guess because it was kind of embarrassing."

"Why?"

Derek showed me the closest thing to a grin that I'd seen from him in a couple of days. "It's pretty dirty."

I leaned up against the workbench. "Jesus, Derek. So why would Adam's dad be pissed that you found a computer with some porno on it? I mean, it's not your fault what's on somebody else's computer, and besides, Albert didn't strike me as someone who'd have a fit about that kind of thing."

Derek shrugged. "I don't know. Adam never said. I mean, it wasn't even like it had pictures with it or anything. Maybe if it was really obvious porn, he might be upset, but when it's all written out, it doesn't seem like it's that big a deal. The thing is, the book was actually pretty cool. Even though it was dirty, it was pretty well written."

"So Agnes's son wrote high-class porno," I mused, raising an eyebrow. "Maybe he just wanted to write his own stuff to whack off to."

Derek blushed. He couldn't have been shocked to learn that his father might know about such things. But I suppose my frankness had taken him by surprise. It must have made it easier for him to say, "I don't know. It was all about sex and stuff, but it was written like an actual novel, so it really wasn't high-class jackoff stuff, if, you know, if you get what I mean."

I smiled at him. "I get what you mean. But really, I can't imagine that someone would come into the Langleys' house and kill them all over some porn story that some kid wrote more than ten years ago. That just doesn't make any sense."

"That was kind of why I didn't mention it," Derek said. "I figured I'd look like some kind of idiot."

"And something else might have happened to that computer between the time you last saw it," I said, "and the time the Langleys were killed."

"I suppose."

"Well," I said, coming off the workbench, "since there's no computer there now, there's no way to read the story, or guess whether there was anything in it that would make somebody want to kill three people."

Derek looked at the floor. "That's not exactly true," he said.

I waited for him to continue. "What?" I said.

"I kind of made a copy."

TEN

Derek said he had a copy of the entire book on a floppy disc, instead of a CD, up in his bedroom. The computer was so old, he said, it didn't have a CD-ROM drive. This was all supposed to mean something to me, evidently. This certainly wasn't like when I was a kid, where you had to wait for someone else to finish a book before you could start it. He and Adam were reading this thing at the same time, and comparing notes the next day.

I suggested we go up to his room so I could read some of it on his screen, but Derek didn't care much for that idea.

"Then Mom's going to know," he said.

"Is that a problem?" I asked him.

He looked uncomfortable. "The book's all about, like . . . pussies. You know. Vaginas?"

I stared at him. "I'm aware," I said. I poked the inside of my cheek with my tongue for a moment, then said, "Go up to your room, print off the first ten pages or so for me and bring them back, and if your mom asks what you're up to, tell her you're on the Lawn-Boy website or something printing off tips on how to fix the mower. And bring the disc, too."

Derek ran off, kicking up gravel with his sneakers once he was out of the shed.

His departure gave me a moment to think. It didn't seem even remotely possible that the Langleys could have been killed over something that was on some student's ten-year-old computer. I was almost glad Derek hadn't bothered to mention it to Barry. It seemed too out there.

But even if you accepted the premise that the computer did have something to do with their deaths, which struck me as pretty unlikely, how the hell would anyone know it was there? Okay, it sounded as though, at some point, shortly before someone killed the Langleys, Adam's father learned about it, maybe even what was on it. But why would he have become quite so upset? Albert had never struck me as a prude. I could remember once, at a barbecue, Albert telling me dirty jokes.

Were Albert to learn his son had uncovered an aspiring—and now deceased—author's dirty book on an old computer, did it make any sense for him to have cared? And even if he had, how could learning about the novel's existence have triggered a series of events that culminated with someone killing him and his family?

That didn't make any sense at all.

So I thought about it some more, that if you still accepted the premise that the missing computer had something to do with the murders, but ruled out Albert's involvement as having anything to do with them, where did that leave you?

How would anyone have even known Adam had the computer? After all, it hadn't even been given to him in the first place. Agnes Stockwell had given it to my son, who in turn had shared his discovery with Adam. So if someone had learned from Agnes, say, what had happened to the computer, they wouldn't have even been looking for it at the Langley house in the first place, but then again—

"Got it!" Derek said, breathless, running back into the shed, clutching some pages fresh from his printer. He handed them to me.

"I think that's the whole first chapter," he said. "Seven pages. You'll see, when you get into it, why it's not really your basic porn story, you know? It's, like, Agnes's son, what was his name again?"

"Brett," I said.

"Yeah, Brett. It was like he was trying to take a porn novel or something, but make fun of it. Like, whaddya call it, like satire or something. Like a send-up. Or maybe even like—you remember that stupid movie you showed me one time, when I was little, where Arnold Schwarzenegger, the Terminator guy, he gets pregnant? *Junior,* that's what it was called."

I held up my hand for Derek to stop. I riffled through the pages quickly. Seven, like he'd said. Double-spaced, medium-sized paragraphs. No title page, nothing in the headers of each page with a title or the author's name. Just a page number, tucked in the upper right corner.

I sat on the stool by the workbench and held the sheaf of papers in my hands and started to read.

Nicholas Dickless: Chapter One

Nicholas didn't realize when he first woke up on this Tuesday morning that anything was particularly amiss. He swung his legs out of bed, rubbed the sleep out of his eyes, and padded into the bathroom just as he did every morning. Standing at the toilet to empty his full bladder was the first part of his morning bathroom ritual, and this Tuesday morning was no different than any of the other thousands of

*mornings that had preceded it,
with the possible exception that
when Nicholas rooted around
through the fly of his pajamas to
pull out his penis, he was unable to
locate it.*

My eyebrows went up.

"You see?" Derek said, able to tell
where I was in the story. "It's kind of different. But go on."

I went on:

*"What the fuck?" Nicholas said,
to no one in particular since he
was all alone, reaching somewhat
frantically through the fly, still unable to locate his member. But it
was worse than that. He was unable to find his testicles, as well.
His genitalia were not there. He felt
his pubic hair—that remained—but
what in God's name had happened
to the rest of him?*

*He told himself that he must be
dreaming. He was having a night-
mare. In a moment he would wake
up. He stepped away from the toi-*

let, looked through the bathroom
door back to his own bed, expecting to see himself there, still under
the covers, thrashing about perhaps, on the verge of waking.

But Nicholas was not in the bed.
The covers were turned back, just
as he'd left them a moment ago.
He approached the bed, tentatively, fearfully, and pulled the covers further down, expecting to find
his cock and balls in a pool of
blood, but the sheets were white
and clean.

He was afraid to inspect himself,
terrified to see what kind of damage had been done to him. Slowly,
he pulled down his pajama bot-
toms. He did not appear to have
been wounded in any way. There
was no blood, no cuts, no obvious
signs of amputation of any kind.
He looked untouched and undisturbed, except for the fact that
those parts of him that constituted
his manhood were missing.

Delicately, he reached down to
touch himself, to see if somehow

his eyes were deceiving him, that perhaps that which did not appear to be there actually was. And Nicholas discovered something that was even more unimaginable than what had already transpired.

There was an opening.

I looked up from the pages.

Derek said, "Pretty warped, right? So he finds out that somehow, in the middle of the night, like magic or something, he loses his, you know, his dick, and instead, he's got a vagina."

I glanced through the remaining pages, then set them on the workbench.

"You're not going to read all of it?" Derek said.

"I've got the general idea," I said.

"Because it does get better. Even though it's weird, in a way, he makes it believable, all the shit that's happening."

"I've read enough," I said.

"It's actually more funny than porno, you know? It's like how his life completely changes when he's got, like, no dick anymore. How he starts to see life from the point of view of a woman, how the only way he's going to be sexually satisfied is to make out with guys, even though he's not gay or anything, and shit, you can see why I didn't want to talk about this with Mom around."

"Sure," I said, not really listening all that closely to what Derek was saying.

"I can go print out more of it if you want, or I could just make a copy of it and e-mail it to you and you could read it on your own computer, although maybe that's not a good idea because then Mom will see it and she might freak out or something, right?"

"You don't have to do any of that," I said. "I've already read this book."

ELEVEN

It was not actually published as *Nicholas Dickless.* It was released as *A Missing Part.* It was a major bestseller about eight years ago. Hit the *New York Times* list. It didn't hurt in the slightest that some of the major non-bookstore chains, like Costco and Wal-Mart, refused to carry it out of fear of offending their more conservative customers. It was the best thing that could happen to *A Missing Part.* Once it got labeled as forbidden, Borders and Barnes & Noble and independent bookstores could barely keep it in stock.

I don't know how many copies it actually sold. A hundred thousand, half a million, a million, did it really matter after a certain point? There was talk at one point of making it into a movie, but that never happened. If it had, I think I would have waited for the DVD. Actually, reading the book was enough, and I hadn't particularly wanted to do that. But I couldn't stop myself. I thought maybe reading it would provide some insights into the author, would help me understand why my wife had chosen to sleep with him. But I have to say, once I'd finished it, I was none the wiser.

What I do know is that the book made Conrad Chase a literary star. It catapulted the Thackeray College English professor to national fame and paved the way for him to become that institution's president. It's unlikely a guy could write a book like *A Missing Part* and be made principal of an elementary school, but a college with a fairly left-of-center point of view was a different thing altogether. Granted, someone who'd written a book about a man losing his penis and testicles and ending up with a vagina instead, if he was going to become a college president, you might have at least expected it to be a college in California, and not upstate New York.

But Conrad Chase had brought fame not only upon himself, but Thackeray as well. And while at first the college administration and fellow faculty had responded uncomfortably to Chase's outrageous novel and were inclined to distance themselves from it, as it soared up the bestseller list, and as critics embraced it as a work of satirical genius and brilliant social commentary, the general feeling on campus was, what the hell, let's see how we can use this to our advantage.

Chase, who taught early American literature and a course on the plays of Eugene O'Neill, became the college darling. Thackeray had never had a bestselling author before. Chase wasn't the first professor to get published—everyone who taught there felt tremendous pressure to publish something, at some point, during their careers, even if no one would ever actually read it, which was generally the fate of most of the academic treatises that Thackeray professors produced. He wasn't the first to publish a work of fiction, but he was the first to receive international recognition.

The administration decided to use Chase's notoriety to fashion a new reputation for the college. They had already been running a literary festival for a couple of years that they wanted to continue as an annual event. It's why they had hired Ellen. Now they had their own headliner in Conrad Chase. It made it easier to attract famous authors to Promise Falls. And that's what the college had been doing for several years, running the thing over four days, setting up lots of different venues where authors could read or talk about their works, bringing in the public. They got Mayor Finley on board, who saw this not only as a way to get Promise Falls more recognition, but also as a way to give his profile a boost.

But Conrad was still a fairly anonymous professor when Ellen was hired to help set up that literary festival.

We'd been living in Albany. Ellen had been working for a company that planned and organized major events. They did concerts, corporate functions, speaking series. When Thackeray started advertising for someone full-time to look after an annual literary event, Ellen applied and, to her own amazement, got the job. I was working for an Albany security firm at the time, going through, to be honest, a bit of depression because I wasn't getting anywhere with my art.

It was something I was struggling to come to terms with. As a young adult with no parents, I'd managed to scrape up enough money to attend a single year of art college, and I'd tell myself I'd be the one to beat the odds, the one in a hundred who could actually make a living with his talent. I'd had a buddy that year, Teddy, a brilliant sculptor who could find a leopard hiding in a block of wood, and I figured if any graduate would make it, it'd be him. A few years later I ran into him driving a truck weighed down with hot asphalt.

We grabbed a beer, the smell of tar sticking to him, and I got around to asking him about the dreams he'd had in college.

"They got overtaken by fucking life, man," he said.

I knew the feeling. How else to explain working for a security firm that was sucking a little bit more of life out of me every day? So when Ellen was offered her job in Promise Falls, I had no qualms walking away from mine and looking for something else. Even another job that had no meaning would at least be a change.

On top of all that, Derek was seven and not having the greatest time in elementary school. Didn't pay attention, the teacher said. Wouldn't focus on his studies, she said. Wouldn't settle down, she said.

We chose to do what a lot of parents do. We blamed the teacher. Maybe it even was her fault, who knows. So we figured a move to Promise Falls would be a new start for all of us. Ellen would begin her new, terrific job, I'd find something better, and Derek would start afresh in a new school.

So we bought a place a couple of miles south of Promise Falls, a modest but charming two-story tucked down a lane, just beyond the Langley house. Ellen started her new job. Derek started with a clean slate at a new school, where his teacher, in about a month, asked us in for an interview to discuss the problems Derek was having paying attention, focusing on his studies, and settling down.

I found work at another security firm, spent my evenings and weekends painting, even persuaded a gallery in town to put together a show of my work. Did the whole wine-and-cheese-party thing, invited everyone we could think of, sold one painting, a small one that went for under a hundred bucks, to a friend. Ellen tried to keep my spirits up, insisted I had talent, told me stories she'd heard about great writers who'd taken a long time to be recognized. None of that helped. I fell into a deep funk that lasted several months. Ellen, either discouraged or fed up, or a bit of both, gave up trying to boost my spirits. I think Ellen had been attracted to me in the first place because I was an artist, and as I seemed to be giving up on it, I wondered if there was a part of her that was giving up on me.

I quickly came to hate my new security job. No surprise there. So when I saw an ad in the *Standard* that the mayor's office was looking for a driver, I thought, what the hell, why not apply. Ellen ended up working very closely with Conrad to get the first festival organized. He'd offered to be an adviser for the event, given his background in English literature, particularly as practiced by those who were still alive and could accept invitations. This was a heady experience for Ellen, working with someone as charismatic and sophisticated as Conrad, and this was even a couple of years before he ended up on the cover of *Newsweek,* when it did a story on a new crop of writers who were supposedly pushing the envelope. As it turned out, Conrad mostly wanted to push himself onto Ellen, and maybe, if I had been more attentive at the time, hadn't been so wrapped up in my own problems, dragged down by not being able to make a career through my own creative outlets, he wouldn't have been successful.

It didn't last long. I don't even know whether you could call it an out-and-out affair. A misstep, perhaps, on Ellen's part. Getting caught up in the moment. That doesn't mean it didn't hurt, and it doesn't mean I didn't think about responding in ways that would only have made the situation worse.

But it was nearly ten years ago, and the whole thing was, for the most part, behind us. It was a rough patch, I'm not glossing it over. For a while there, Ellen tried to assuage her guilt with drink. I don't think she was ever a bona fide alcoholic, but she certainly was in a fog for several months there, and how she managed to do her job during that time, I have no idea. It was as though a small, slow-moving hurricane had settled on our house for several months. The turbulence was always there, but then Ellen, on her own, came to some kind of inner realization that she could not continue on the way she was going, and she stopped drinking. Just like that. That's one thing I have to say about Ellen. When she decides it's time to pull herself together, she does it. I remember, when her mother died, she was torn up pretty bad for a couple of weeks there, then one morning got up and said aloud, "Time to move on."

But sometimes, while you were waiting for that moment, it could be a rough ride.

Once the storm had passed, and Ellen and I had found a way to forgive each other, life improved. We were both smart enough to know that what we had together was too good to throw away. We had a son. We weren't going to ruin Derek's life by splitting up.

Ellen still had regular dealings with Conrad Chase after the affair, but those became less of a worry once his book was bought by a big New York publisher, and he started moving in circles very far removed from ours. And then, while out in Hollywood for exploratory meetings about turning *A Missing Part* into a movie, he met Illeana Tiff, a B-movie actress. She had the big hair and the tits to match, but to dismiss her as an airhead was a mistake. She wasn't a great actress and was smart enough to know she had a limited future in Hollywood. But hooking up with a famous writer was almost as good, so she came back to Promise Falls with Chase, and about a year later they were married.

Chase had so wormed his way into the college's board that when President Kane Mortimer had a heart attack while snorkeling in Fiji, he made a strong push for the job and got it. By this time, Illeana had learned to tone down the hair and lower the winch on the boobs, and she fell comfortably into the role of the college president's wife.

It seemed odd to many that Chase took that route. Being a college president had some cachet, no doubt about it, but not nearly as much as a famous writer. Upstate New York college presidents didn't do talk shows, didn't get invited to celebrity-filled parties, weren't written about in *The New Yorker.*

But Conrad Chase had no follow-up to *A Missing Part.* For the first few years, when people asked, he claimed to be working on a new novel—supposedly his deal for *A Missing Part* included a follow-up book—but if he ever wrote it, it had yet to be published.

Eventually, most people stopped asking, and when the rare one did, Conrad replied, "I've a college to run."

The simple truth was, as far as I could tell, he was done with writing. But unlike me and my art, he'd managed to make a name for himself before packing it in.

I took the disc and the pages Derek had printed out for me and started walking back to the house. I hadn't said anything to him when he asked me what I'd meant when I said I'd already read the book, and I didn't say anything when he protested my showing the pages to Ellen, which it was clear, by the direction I was headed, I had every intention of doing.

Ellen was upstairs, stripping our bed. Even though it was Sunday, it wasn't the kind of Sunday where you could sit down and relax and read the paper. We were all agitated, and Ellen's way of dealing with that was to keep busy.

I extended the printed pages across the bed to her. She dropped the bedsheets she was holding and took them. She glanced at them without reading so much as a word and said, "What's this?"

"Just have a read and see if it rings a bell," I said.

"Can you just tell me what it's—"

"Just read it."

So she dropped her eyes to the pages and read. She got as far as the bottom of the first page and stopped.

"What's the point of this?" she asked, looking up.

"You recognize it."

"Of course I recognize it." She was keeping her voice very even. I realized I was already going about this the wrong way. Ellen was going to think this was something personal about Conrad Chase, about what had happened so many years ago. She was going to think I'd chosen, after all this time, to open old wounds. That wasn't the plan, although sometimes things turn out in ways you did not intend.

"It's Chase's book," I said. I hardly needed to tell her which one. "Not word for word, I think. More like an unedited version, you know? But the same story, different title."

"I already told you I recognize it," she said. "How many other people have written about a guy who loses his cock and ends up with a pussy?"

Get to the point, I told myself.

"That just got printed off. It was on the hard drive of a computer that Agnes Stockwell gave Derek, which he gave to Adam to keep over at his house, and now it's missing."

Ellen stared at me. "I have no idea what you're talking about. Agnes Stockwell gave Derek a computer? That's where he got that one he brought home a couple of weeks ago? If somebody told me that, I don't re-member."

"We probably didn't. It wasn't a big deal, then."

"Is it a big deal now?"

I took a breath. "You remember Brett Stockwell?"

Ellen nodded.

"Agnes saved all his stuff after he committed suicide, but it's been so long, she's finally clearing it out, at least

the stuff that doesn't hold any senti-
mental value. She had his old computer
in her garage, and when she found out
Derek's into that kind of thing, she gave
it to him. The novel, Conrad's novel,
what looks to be Conrad's novel, is on
the computer. And now that computer's
missing from the Langley house." I
paused, then added, "Doesn't that
seem odd to you?"

Again with the stare. Then, "Which
part? That it was on the kid's computer,
or that the computer is missing?"

"All of it."

"What kind of computer? A desktop?
Not a laptop?"

"No, not a laptop," I said. "The tower
part."

"And how the hell do you have a
printout of it if the computer's missing?"

"Derek had made a copy."

Ellen sat down on the edge of the
bed. "What are you suggesting? I can't
get my head around this. You must be
suggesting something."

"I don't know what I'm suggesting," I
said. "I'm trying to get my head around

it, too. But I can't help but wonder, maybe Conrad isn't the great literary genius everyone thinks he is. Maybe *A Missing Part* isn't his."

Ellen was speechless for a moment. It was, I had to admit, a somewhat stunning hypothesis, to be all professorial about it.

"Jesus, what are you saying?" she said. "That some kid wrote it? That's ridiculous. That book was on the *New York Times* bestseller list."

"I'm just putting it out there," I said. "I'm just saying, it's kind of a strange thing for it to be on that computer."

"Maybe," Ellen said, "he had a student who was such a fan, he typed it out, word for word. Or had a copy of it, a Word file or something. Did they offer books back then as e-books? Maybe Brett Stockwell downloaded it. Did you ever think of that?"

"When did Conrad's book come out?" I asked. "When was it published?"

Ellen tried to think. "Was it nine, ten years ago? Hang on." She got up, walked out of the room, went downstairs. I followed her down to the living room, where she was scanning the wall that's lined with bookshelves. They're pretty much overflowing, books tucked in sideways on top of other books, so it took Ellen a moment, cocking her head so that she could read the spines, before she could put her hands on our copy of *A Missing Part*.

She flipped it open to the copyright page. "It was in 2000," she said. "The hardcover. Trade paperback a year later."

"Brett Stockwell killed himself ten years ago," I pointed out. "Two years before the book came out."

"There must be a simple explanation," Ellen said.

"Sure," I said. "Maybe so. It's just funny, is all. And there's the fact that the computer's gone missing."

"Someone stole it?"

I shrugged. "It was in the Langley house as recently as Thursday, Derek says, and now it's gone."

"Did Barry say it was stolen when the Langleys were killed?"

"No. Derek noticed that it was missing when Barry took us through the house."

She looked away from me and shook her head. "This is crazy. What did Barry say when Derek noticed that it was gone?"

"He didn't tell Barry. He told me afterwards. He wanted to talk to me about it first, because he was too embarrassed to talk to you about a book with that kind of content. He didn't know it was a published novel. I mean, he was what, nine when it came out? I think maybe he was reading the Hardy Boys then, and Frank and Joe weren't exactly waking up in the morning with their dicks missing. Derek just thought it was some student's attempt at porn, although as porn goes, Derek said it kind of missed the mark."

Ellen almost smiled, but then it faded away. "What are you going to do about this?"

"I guess I should tell Barry, don't you think?" I said. "It may not actually mean anything. And the fact that the computer's missing doesn't mean it has to have anything to do with what happened at the Langleys'. It might have disappeared between the last time Derek was in Adam's room, which was Thursday, when he saw the computer there, and the murders, which were Friday night. Maybe it's someplace else in the house where Barry didn't take us."

Ellen paced about the room, then said, "You should let Conrad know."

"What?"

"Before going to Barry. Conrad deserves to know, because there really may be a simple explanation. If there is, we'll be glad we went to him directly instead of involving the police."

"We?"

Ellen looked at me. "Don't be like that."

"I'm not being anything. I'm just saying, you may be interested in sparing Conrad from trouble and embarrassment, but that's not really a priority for me." Even as I said it I knew I wasn't being totally honest. The guy did sign my wife's paychecks.

"This isn't about that," Ellen said. "This is about fairness. Particularly when this is probably a big fuss about nothing." She shook her head in frustration. "Maybe it would be better if I talked to him. If you do it, he may think you've got some other agenda." She met my look. "You know that's true."

I nodded very slowly. "I have another idea," I said. "Why don't I talk to Agnes. Without telling her everything, maybe I can get an idea why her son might have had that book on his computer." There was something else I'd be wanting to ask Agnes, too. "And if there's a simple explanation, I can just tell Barry that Derek noticed the computer was missing, and leave it at that."

Ellen nodded. "Yeah. Okay. Do that. Talk to Agnes."

Neither of us said anything for a moment. I took a deep breath and exhaled slowly. Something that I'd been thinking about, out in the shed, just before Derek returned with the pages from his printer, was still nagging at me.

Ellen had turned away and was looking out the window toward the Langley house. "I hadn't even talked to any of them in days. Hardly even saw them."

"Me neither," I said.

"I guess the last time I saw Donna was that day she came to the door," Ellen said.

"When was that?" I asked. I had no memory of this.

"That publisher in New York, they sent me some advance copies of books by writers I was going to ask about coming to the festival."

"What was Donna doing bringing them over?"

"The courier delivered the package to their place instead."

She stood for another moment, looking out the window, then turned, and it seemed as though a bit of the color had drained from her face.

"Donna said he got the house wrong—he saw the mailbox, with our name on it, and he just assumed their house was ours."

TWELVE

Derek and I hadn't quite finished up at Agnes Stockwell's house the day before. That was when Ellen had phoned my cell to tell me that something was up at the Langley house.

So I had an excuse to go back. I didn't need to hook up the trailer to the pickup. Her yard was cut and there was no need for the lawn tractor. I put the weed trimmer in the bed of the truck. All I had to do was a bit of tidying.

"Where are you going?" asked Derek, who'd remained outside when I went into the house to talk to Ellen, and had been passing the time trying to jump from one side of the driveway to the other without touching gravel.

"Look after your mom," I said. "I'll be back in a bit."

I drove slowly up the lane, nodded to the cop still babysitting the Langley house, turned onto the highway, and pointed the truck in the direction of Promise Falls. I parked at the curb out front of Agnes Stockwell's house, stepped up onto the wide, old-fashioned porch, and rapped lightly on the door. It was still Sunday morning, although it was nearly noon.

When she pushed on the screen door, she smiled. "What are you doing here today?" she asked, her cat slinking around her leg to see who'd come to call. It was, without a doubt, one of the ugliest cats I'd ever seen, looking as though it'd be more at home in a pigpen, wallowing in the mud, than curled up on a couch.

Agnes had no doubt been an attractive woman at one time, but a lingering sadness had worn away at her over the years. She'd lost a husband—to a heart attack, if I remembered correctly—and then a year later her son, for no apparent reason, had taken his own life. I didn't know how someone ever recovered from something like that. Perhaps you never did. She'd continued to live on in this house, making it, as far as I knew, her only project. Working on her garden when the weather allowed, keeping pretty much to herself.

"We had to take off early yesterday," I told her. "I didn't finish up the trimming."

"Oh, I hadn't even noticed," she said, although she probably had been too polite to mention it. "Isn't your boy with you today?"

"No," I said. "There's just a bit to do, so I thought I'd look after it myself. Give him the day off." I was about to say, *You know how teenagers are, how they like to sleep in,* but caught myself before doing it.

"When you're done, I'll have some lemonade for you," she said.

That was what I'd hoped she'd say.

It took barely fifteen minutes to do what had to be done. I put on safety goggles, got out the weed whacker, and ran the filament line along the edges of the sidewalk and driveway and by her flower beds, making sure there was no stray piece of long grass sticking up anyplace. I liked this kind of work. I got a sense of satisfaction from it that I got from little else, except perhaps when I used to paint.

As I was putting the trimmer back into the truck, I heard the front door open and there was Agnes with a tall glass of lemonade, beads of moisture dripping down the side. I walked up the drive and took the glass from her.

"Do you mind if I sit down?" I asked her.

She had a couple of garden-type chairs flanking the front door. "Of course not, Mr. Cutter," she said. I was going to invite her to sit down, too, but she was in the other chair before I had a chance. I suppose, when you lived alone, it was nice to have someone to talk to once in a while, even if it was just the guy who cut the grass.

"Call me Jim," I said.

"Jim," she said quietly.

"This lemonade really hits the spot," I said, and that was the truth. Her cat brushed up against my leg. "What's his—her?—name?"

"That's Boots," Agnes Stockwell said.

"I don't believe I've ever seen a cat like her," I said.

"She's pretty hideous," Agnes said, "but I love her."

I took another drink of lemonade, nearly polished off the glass. I wiped my mouth with the back of my hand. If I looked like a sweaty mess to her, she didn't seem to mind.

"Did you hear about that lawyer?" Agnes asked me. "The one who was killed? Along with his wife and his son?"

"Yes," I said.

"That's sort of out where you live, isn't it?"

"It is out our way," I admitted. "A terrible thing."

Agnes was shaking her head. "Oh yes, just awful. It makes you think. You know, things like that just don't happen around here."

I nodded. "Pretty rare event. Like you say, makes you think." We both took a moment to do just that. And then I said,

"My son wanted me to pass on his thanks again for the computer."

"Oh, that was my pleasure," Agnes said. "I'm just glad to see someone else get some use out of it. I wasn't sure it would be good to anyone, being so old and all. I was surprised he'd even want it."

"The older the better," I said. "He's a tinkerer with that kind of stuff. He's lucky you hadn't already given it to anybody else. You'll have all the boys in the neighborhood coming here to see if you've got any other computers to give away."

"I don't really know that many. I'm just glad I found someone who could take it."

"You didn't happen to mention to anyone that you gave Derek that computer, did you?"

Agnes appeared puzzled by the question. "Why no, I don't think I did. Why?"

Had to think fast. "I was just thinking, if you had, you might get others coming by, seeing what else you had to give away."

She nodded. That made sense to her. "Oh no, no troubles like that. Maybe, someday, I'll have a little garage sale. Every summer, I think about doing that but never get around to it. What did you say your boy's name is again?"

"Derek."

"He seems like a good boy."

"He is," I said. "He has his moments, but he's a great kid."

"They all have their moments," Agnes said. "Brett certainly did. I felt a little guilty, giving away his computer, but what can you do? You can't hang on to these things forever. He had one of those other computers, those little ones that fold up, but I must have gotten rid of that a long time ago. I don't even remember what happened to it. His clothes, I didn't hang on too long to those. Gave them to the poor. I think that's what he would have wanted."

"I'll bet he was a good son," I said.

That sad smile again. "Oh yes. There's not a day . . ."

She let the sentence hang there a moment. "Not a day?" I said.

She sighed. "There's not a day I

don't wonder. Wonder why he did what he did. You know what happened to Brett, don't you, Mr.—Jim?"

"I had heard," I said, "that he took his own life."

She nodded. "I can't even go downtown. I can't go near the falls. I could pop into town and drop off my property tax payment, but I just mail it in. I can't look at the falls, don't even want to hear it."

"Sure," I said.

"I try not to blame myself. But even now, it's hard not to. I should have been able to read the signs. But I swear, I never noticed anything. I didn't see it coming. Just that last day or so, just before he killed himself. He seemed just fine right up to that point, but that last day, he seemed so troubled, so upset about something, but he wouldn't talk to me about it. That's why I have such a hard time forgiving myself. I didn't appreciate just how unhappy he was then. And yet, he was my whole life after my husband died. There must have been signs in the weeks leading up to that day, but I didn't spot them.

How could a mother not see that her son was that troubled, before it was too late?"

I shook my head slowly in sympathy. "We never know everything about our own children," I said. "There're always things they keep from us. I'm sure Derek's no different." I tried a light chuckle. "Sometimes there are things you don't want to know."

Agnes stared out into her yard, saying nothing.

I said, "Tell me about Brett. What was he interested in? What did he like to do?"

"He wasn't like the other boys," she said. "He was—" She stopped suddenly. "Would you like to see a picture of him?"

"Of course."

She excused herself, was gone no more than half a minute, and returned with a framed high school photo. "That was his graduating year, it would have been four years before he, well, it's pretty much how I remember him."

Brett Stockwell was a good-looking young man. Sandy-colored hair that came down over his ears, brown eyes, fairly unblemished skin for a boy his age. He had a sensitive, artistic look about him. Not jock material.

"I think I can see your eyes in him," I said.

She took the picture back and studied it, as though looking at it for the first time. "He looked a lot like his father. Took after him, I think. Borden was a small man, only five-five, and Brett had that same kind of build."

"You were saying he wasn't like the other boys."

"He didn't care much about sports. Never went out for football, didn't care much about that stuff. He liked to read. And he loved movies. But not the ones everyone else liked. He liked the ones with the words at the bottom."

"Subtitles."

"That's right. Movies in different languages. He liked to watch those. He had an appreciation for things that other people didn't care much about."

"That's nice," I said. "We don't need everyone to be the same. What kind of world would that be?" I had another drink of my lemonade.

"And he loved to write," Agnes Stockwell said. "He was always writing things."

"What sort of things?" I asked.

"Oh, you name it. When he was little, he liked to write stories about going to other planets. People traveling through time, things like that. And poems. He wrote hundreds and hundreds of poems. Not the kind that rhyme, though. Poetry's not like it was when I was a girl. It doesn't have to rhyme anymore. Doesn't even seem like poetry if it doesn't rhyme. It's just a bunch of sentences otherwise."

"I can't say as I know a lot about poetry. Ellen, she likes to read poetry sometimes."

"Is that your wife?"

"Yes."

"You should bring her around sometime. I'd love to meet her."

"I should do that. I think she'd like to meet you, too. She knows you as the one who gives us lemonade."

She smiled, then, "Sometimes, on

my birthday, Brett would write me a poem. He'd try to make those ones rhyme because he knew I didn't understand the other ones as well. They were a bit more like the ones you find in greeting cards, you know?"

"Did he show you all the things he wrote?" I asked.

"Oh, some he did, some he didn't. He liked to have something done, all polished up the way he liked it, before he showed it to me. And some things, as he got older, I think some of those things were a bit more private. A boy doesn't want to show his mother everything, you know." She blinked at me, and her eyes seemed to twinkle.

"Yeah, well, I know what you mean," I said. "Do you think that's what he wanted to do with his life? Become a writer?"

"Oh, without a doubt. That was his dream, to be some famous novelist. He talked about writers he admired, like that Truman Capote, and James Kirkwood, and lots of others. And I really believe, if he hadn't . . . if he'd made different choices, I think that's what would have happened. Because he was good, you know. He had tremendous talent. And I'm not just saying that because I'm his mother." She paused. "Was his mother."

"Others thought he had talent?" I asked.

She nodded. "His teachers, they said he was very good. Some said he was actually quite brilliant."

"Really?"

"When he was in high school, he had this one teacher, what was his name?" She closed her eyes for a moment, searching. "Mr. Burgess. That's who it was. I remember what he wrote on one of Brett's short stories. He wrote, 'John Irving, watch out.' How about that?"

"Wow."

"You know who John Irving is?"

"I do," I said.

"Brett got in trouble once, his senior year it was. Wrote something that upset some of the staff. The subject matter was a bit, it was a bit mature. Do you know what I mean? And the language, it was not totally appropriate for high school."

"What was it about?"

"It was about other students. Not actual students, but a story about boys and girls his age, and the things they did that their parents didn't know about. A kind of sexual awakening story." She said the words as if there were quotation marks around them. "A little too out there for the folks at Promise Falls High School."

"Did Brett get in trouble?"

"He might have, if it hadn't been for Mr. Burgess. He defended Brett from the administration, said that his work, while dealing with controversial material, was honest and a fair representation of what was actually going on. He said Brett didn't deserve to be suspended or punished in any way for pointing out things that everyone else knew was going on but didn't have the courage to admit."

"Well. He sounds like quite a teacher."

"Brett never showed me that story. He'd have known that I'd have tried to talk him out of handing it in or showing it to anyone. I'm not the sort of person who likes to make a fuss."

"Not many of us are," I said. "How about when he got to Thackeray? Did he have mentors there? Professors who encouraged his writing?"

"Oh yes. Although, once you get to college, there's often less opportunity for the kind of creative writing that appealed to Brett. It's all very academic stuff, you know, and I don't think that ever interested Brett quite as much. Although he did very well with essays, and he was a voracious reader. He had so many books. I haven't decided what to do with all those yet. Do you think the library would want them?"

"Maybe," I said. "So once he got to college, he stopped writing stories and poems?"

"He kept writing them. He was always writing them. And showing them to his professors. Some of them were more interested than others, of course."

"Sure," I said.

"Mostly his teachers who taught English, or literature, I guess that's what they call it when you get to college. If he tried to get his political science teacher or history professor interested, well, they didn't care so much. They're all so busy, you know, not all of them want to take the time to read something that's really not part of the course. But he also had professors who'd actually let him submit a poem or a story as an assignment, instead of having to write an actual essay with footnotes and a bibliography."

"I hated doing bibliographies," I said, thinking back. "Sometimes I'd just make them up."

Agnes slapped my shoulder playfully. "I'll bet you didn't fool anyone."

"No," I said.

"Some of the professors," Agnes said, "were writers themselves, and they didn't mind bending the rules a bit. They were the ones who'd let Brett hand in a story instead of something he had to go to the library to research."

"Do you remember who they were?"

Agnes shook her head. "It's been so long. I wouldn't know them if they stood up in my soup naked. Except

maybe for that one who runs the college now. I see his name in the *Standard* now and then and recognize it."

It felt as though a minor tremor had
gone off beneath me. "You mean Conrad Chase?" I asked.

"That's right. That's the one. When
he was still a professor, he took an interest in Brett's stuff. Brett talked about
him all the time. Probably his favorite
professor the whole time he was at
Thackeray. He even came by to see me
a couple of times after Brett died. He
brought flowers the first time, and he
even sent me some concert tickets
once. He was very thoughtful."

And then, suddenly, she teared up.
She dug a tissue out from under her
sleeve and dabbed at her eyes. "I'm
sorry," she said. "It's been so long,
you'd think I could hold it together
when I talk about him now."

"That's okay," I said. "These things
are always with us." I gave her a moment to compose herself, then asked,
"So did Brett ever show Professor
Chase his writings?"

"I know he did. He was very encouraging. Brett even got invited to Professor Chase's home a couple of times, I think. This was back before he became famous, and before he met that actress and married her. I think Brett would have been very excited to see what happened to Professor Chase after that book of his came out. Imagine, if his future hadn't been cut short the way it was, trying to go on as a writer, being able to count someone like Conrad Chase among your friends. I bet that would have opened some doors."

"I bet it would have."

But then she shrugged and dabbed away a couple more tears.

I said, "Did you ever read it?"

"Hmm?" she said, not sure what I was referring to.

"A Missing Part," I said.

Agnes Stockwell shook her head as though I'd asked her if she did table dancing in her spare time. "Oh no. Well, I tried. I got about fifty pages into it and thought it was so . . . well, it wasn't my cup of tea, if you know what I mean. I'm not saying it was a bad book, just not the kind of thing I want to read. There are so many wonderful words in the English language, so many nice things to write about, but some writers, they don't like those words and those things. I like to pick up the latest Danielle Steel, but reading about a man's privates getting changed into a woman's? I don't care how brilliant the critics say it is. It's not for me."

I smiled. "I totally understand."

"But I'll tell you this," she said, softening. "Brett was always a lot more open-minded than me about these things. He was what I guess you'd call a more experimental writer, willing to take chances. I think he would have loved that Professor Chase's book."

THIRTEEN

I asked Agnes whether I could borrow her phone book before I left. She went in and fetched it for me, leaving me with Boots. She rubbed her ugly pug-nosed face up against my pant leg.

Agnes Stockwell returned with not only the phone book but a small notepad and a pencil.

"What are you looking up?" she asked, and then, quickly, "Forgive me. That's none of my business."

"That's okay," I said. "There's another stop I have to make on the way home, but I needed to double-check an address."

I found three listings for Burgess in the Promise Falls directory and wrote down the number and address for each. "Thank you," I said, handing the book back to Agnes. "And for the lemonade, too. So long, Boots."

As I walked down the driveway, I dug my cell phone out of my pocket. I thought a quick call to Barry was in order, to tell him that it had occurred to Derek, after he'd been through the Langley house, that the computer tower was missing. It either meant something or it didn't, but he might as well know.

I realized I'd not turned the phone on when I left home, and hit the button to bring it to life. While I waited for it to come on, I happened to glance up the street and saw a black car sitting there, a block or more away. As I took a couple of steps toward my truck, the car, a Grand Marquis, started moving, and rather than get in I decided to wait and see whether this had anything to do with me.

The car pulled up alongside the truck, and before it had come to a full stop the back window powered down.

"Hello, Randall," I said, slipping the phone back into my pocket.

Mayor Finley flashed me his big shit-eating grin. "Cutter, you son of a bitch, would it kill you to say 'Your Worship'?"

"It might," I said.

"Listen, Jim, have you got a minute? I'd really like to talk to you."

"I'm kind of working," I said. "How did you find me here?"

"I asked Ellen," he said. "She tried to call you."

"My cell was off," I said.

Finley said, "I told her it was really important, and when she couldn't raise you, she told me where we might find you. Come on. Take a minute. Get out of that heat." He opened the door, his version of an official invitation.

"Randy, really—"

"Please, Cutter, come on. I'm asking real nice here."

So I opened the back door wide enough to get in. Finley shifted over to the other side of the seat. It was wonderful and cool back there. As I pulled the door shut, Lance Garrick turned around in the driver's seat and sneered, "Hey, Cutter, how goes the weed whacking?"

I pretended he wasn't there.

"Lance," said the mayor, "instead of sitting around wasting gas, why don't we drive around a bit? That okay with you?" Finley asked me.

"Whatever," I said. "I'll sit back and enjoy the A/C."

"Pretty fucking hot week to be cutting grass, and on a Sunday, too," Lance said, shaking his head, making a "tsk-tsk" noise, as if I were in violation of some Promise Falls bylaw. He looked ahead, steered, and said, "Mighty cool in here, though."

"Lucky you," I said, unable to ignore him completely.

"Yeah, I sure wouldn't want to be cutting grass in this heat, no sirree Bob."

"I get it, Lance," I said.

"If I was, like, fourteen, then it'd be a different story."

"Lance," Finley said, "would you just shut the fuck up?" To me, he said, "I gotta see if there's money in the next budget for one of those pieces of glass between the seats." Up front, Lance twitched. "I want to have a talk here,

Lance. Can you put in your fucking iPod or something?"

"I didn't bring it," he said, sounding hurt.

"Then just watch the fucking road," Finley said. "I'm conducting business back here."

Not so far, I thought. I was just looking out the window, enjoying the ride. I wondered whether Randall would get Lance to wipe my sweat off the gray leather seat after I got dropped off back at my truck.

"Jim," Mayor Finley said, "you're looking good. You really are."

I didn't say anything.

"How y'all managing, after this thing at the Langleys'? You must be shook up. How's your wife and boy?"

"What can I do for you, Randy?" I said.

"That's the Jim Cutter I know. Cut to the chase, no pun intended. That's something I always liked about you. Langley, he acted for me on a number of occasions, did you know that? His office, not him personally, even handled my divorce from my first wife." He paused a moment. "Or my second. Or maybe it was both of them."

I rubbed my hand over the leather seat between us. I wondered how many times Finley had gotten laid back here.

"Yeah," I said. "Albert did work for a lot of the movers and shakers around Promise Falls. That is, if Promise Falls is big enough to have movers and shakers."

Finley laughed. "True enough. We're not Albany. We're a smaller pond. But even one of those has a few big fish, am I right?"

I waited.

"The thing is," Randall Finley said, his voice growing more quiet, "I'm thinking of making a move."

"A move?" I said. "Jane finally kicking you out of the house?" A reference to his third wife, who'd stood by him for longer than anyone would have expected. She must have been expecting a payoff at some point to stay with Randall Finley, or was just a hell of a lot more forgiving than the two wives who'd gone before her.

"Funny one," he said. "I'm taking a run at Congress."

I had no reaction.

"What?" Finley said. "No smart-ass comment?"

"Knock yourself out, Randy. Run for Congress. Run for president. It doesn't matter to me. I won't be voting for you."

Another laugh. "You're a straight shooter, Jimmy boy. I'm not counting on your vote, but I was wondering if I could count on your discretion."

"Discretion?"

"When you're mayor, well, you can make an ass of yourself the odd time and get away with it. Believe me, I know. But on the national scene, particularly when you're from a state like New York, not some bumfuck state no one's ever heard of, like North Dakota—"

"My mother was from North Dakota," I said. She wasn't, but what the hell.

"You know what I mean," Finley said, not offering to apologize. "My point is, when you're on the national scene, that's a hearse of a different color." He looked at me to see if I liked his spin on a shopworn cliché. I gave him nothing. "Anyway, you start running for Congress, people start digging into your past, start asking questions. They start talking about *character*."

"You should be okay there, Randy. You're quite a character. Ask anybody. Ask those unwed mothers whose rug you puked on. I'm sure they'd back you up on that."

"Yeah, well." Finley almost blushed. "That was unfortunate. I'm gonna drop by and see Gillian in the very near future and give that home a big fat fucking grant. May not shut up their whining babies, but it ought to shut up their mothers."

"There should be some sort of award, Randy, for the good works you do," I said.

"So anyway, what I wanted to know was, could I count on you to be discreet should anyone come sniffing around asking things about me?"

"Discreet about what?"

Finley did half an eye roll. "Look, there were times, while you worked for me, when I was not on my best behavior. But I'm not that person anymore. I'm a different guy. That guy you worked for, that guy, he doesn't even exist anymore."

"Good to know," I said.

"So all I'm saying is, if someone was to come asking what kind of guy I was to work for, could I count on you to say the right thing?" When I didn't say anything, he continued, "I mean, we're square, right? You kept things to yourself, and I didn't go charging you with assault. A lot of guys, they'd have had your ass thrown in jail for what you did."

Lance interrupted. "You never should have called him at all that night, boss. You should have just called me. Then nothing woulda happened."

"Maybe," I said to Lance, "if you hadn't set up Randy here with jailbait, nothing would have happened then either." I turned to Randall Finley. "And as for you, you can't be serious, thinking you were doing *me* a favor when you didn't press charges? Think of the witnesses you'd have had to call. How old was that girl? And her friend in the hallway? They'd have had to get permission slips to skip class so they could testify."

"Here's the thing," Finley said. "I could find you a job, Cutter. Working for me, on my campaign."

"Hey," said Lance, "you're not giving him his old job back, are you?"

"Jesus fucking Christ, Lance, would you just fucking drive?"

"What? I'm supposed to pretend I can't hear?"

"Jim, ignore him. What I'm proposing to you is some other kind of job in my campaign. There's plenty of work to go around. And you'd be paid well. A lot more than I'm sure you're getting cutting people's lawns, for Christ's sake. What the hell's happened to you? Have you no pride?"

I wanted to tell him that if I had no pride, I'd still be working for him, but I didn't have to justify my life to him or anyone else.

He wasn't done. "Driving around in a silly truck, doing that kind of work, it's totally beneath you, Cutter. You're a capable man with a lot of skills. You know how to deal with people. You have great instincts. You're not easily flustered. I like that. And that business, punching me in the nose, water under the bridge. It's like it never happened."

To Lance, I said, "Can you take me back to my truck?" To Randall Finley, "Look, I don't care what you do. Run for whatever you want. I don't have anything to say to anybody."

"You're a stand-up guy, Jim."

"Because if I told people what sorts of things I'd witnessed, I'd have to explain why I worked for you as long as I did. And I don't know how I'd do that. So you don't have a thing to worry about. And as for the job offer, I'll pass. I like what I do. I like working with my son. I can look myself in the mirror at the end of the day."

Finley nodded thoughtfully. "I can't ask for anything else," he said. "You don't want to work for me, I accept that. And I'm grateful for your discretion."

"That girl," I said. "The one in the room. What ever happened to her?"

"I don't know," Finley said. "Never

saw her again. I cleaned up my act after that night, Cutter. Swear to God."

I could see my truck up ahead. The town car slowed and pulled over to the curb.

Finley extended a hand. Shaking it seemed to take less effort than refusing it, so I gave him mine. I tried to tell myself I wouldn't be compromising my principles if I didn't squeeze too hard. While he was pumping my hand, Finley said to Lance, "Go around and get the door for Mr. Cutter here."

"Huh?" said Lance. "You kidding?"

"You heard me."

Lance got out and started walking around the car. For a second I thought, fuck it, I can open my own goddamn door, then figured, why not let Lance do what he's paid to do?

The door opened and I got out. As Lance closed it, he leaned in close to me from behind, his chin over my shoulder, and whispered in my ear, "That's a first. Don't think I ever opened the door for a fucking lawn boy before."

I drove my elbow back, fast and hard, taking him just below the rib cage. The air went out of him and he dropped.

"Sorry," I said. "That's my weed-whacking arm. It gets twitchy."

FOURTEEN

Once Lance had gotten himself off the pavement and driven away with Finley, I got out my phone again, ready to dial the number on Barry's card. Then I stopped myself.

What did I actually intend to tell him?

There was the short version of the story, of course. That it had occurred to Derek, after our tour of the Langley house, that he hadn't seen one of the computers that had been in Adam's room a couple of days earlier. "For what it's worth," I could say to Barry.

And he could do what he pleased with the information.

The truth was, I didn't know that the computer had anything to do with the Langleys' deaths. For all we knew,

Adam had put it in his closet. Barry hadn't opened it up for us to examine.

And if the computer didn't have a damn thing to do with this, was there any point in getting into this can of worms of what Derek and Adam had found on it? Other than to cause some possible grief for Conrad Chase? I might enjoy seeing him squirm, but at the same time, I wasn't vindictive enough to drag an innocent man into a murder investigation purely for my own entertainment. Almost, but not quite.

I decided the best course of action was to know a little more before calling Barry Duckworth. That's why, for now, going to see Mr. Burgess, Brent Stockwell's high school teacher, seemed like a plan.

Mothers always think their sons are brilliant. Sometimes they even turn out to be right, but Burgess could supply an unbiased assessment. He could tell me whether Brett really was the gifted writer his mother believed him to be. If he didn't share that opinion, then there had to be some other explanation for Conrad's book being on the boy's computer. I'd realize my rush to judgment, my conclusion that Conrad had stolen his bestseller from a student, was totally off base.

And then, holding off on calling Barry would look like a wise move.

I found the Burgess I was looking for when I called the second of the three numbers I'd taken down from Agnes Stockwell's phone book. He wasn't much more than a ten-minute drive from her house, and I didn't need a map to find it. I'd lived and worked in Promise Falls long enough to know my way around.

I didn't know what exactly to tell him when I got him on the phone. Once I'd told him my name, and determined that he was an English teacher from Promise Falls High School, I said I needed to talk to him about one of his former pupils. When he'd asked for more information, I'd said it would be a lot easier if I could talk to him about this in person.

"Fine, come on over," he said. But I could hear the suspicion and distrust in his voice.

Along the way, I was feeling a buzz about what had happened with Lance. It wasn't exactly a buzz of excitement. Mostly it was a feeling of agitation, with dollops of anxiety and regret thrown into the mix.

It was a stupid thing to have done, to have sucker punched him with my elbow. Briefly satisfying, yes, but I should have been above that kind of behavior. The thing was, he'd pushed my buttons once too often. I guess, when you're driving around an asshole mayor, there aren't that many occupations you can feel superior to. So sticking it to a guy who cuts grass for a living, well, that's an opportunity too sweet to pass up.

I wasn't particularly worried that Lance would press charges. He'd have a much better chance seeing me convicted of assault with a solid witness in his corner, and I knew he didn't have one in Mayor Finley. He wasn't going to jeopardize my pledge to keep my mouth shut by testifying against me for the likes of mullet-headed Lance.

Lance had to know that. But the thing was, a guy like Lance Garrick no doubt had plenty of other ways to seek justice that were outside the court system. Now, because I'd felt the need to show I had some balls, I was going to have to be watching my back for the indefinite future.

It was an aggravation I really could have done without at the moment.

I pulled up out front of the Burgess house—I had yet to learn the man's first name—and killed the engine. It was a simple, one-story home with a carport at the side, sitting about ten yards back from the street on a small lot. The treeless yard was well kept, not a dandelion or blade of crabgrass in sight. An older model Toyota and a new Civic sat in the driveway. Before I could knock on the glass-and-aluminum storm door, a man appeared there. In his early sixties, I guessed, thin, with hair to match. If he weren't slightly round shouldered, he might have been six feet.

He opened the door a crack. "You're Mr. Cutter?" he said.

"That's right."

He glanced at the truck and back again. "Kind of a good name for your line of work." I smiled. He was the first to notice, today. "I'm not in the market for a lawn service, if that's what this is about."

"No, it's not about that," I said.

"Well, come in, then," he said, but his tone was not welcoming.

He led me to a small kitchen and directed me to take a seat at an old Formica-topped table. "I'd offer you some coffee but it's just so hot." There was no air-conditioning on in the house, and it was bordering on stifling, even with the windows open.

"That's okay, Mr. Burgess," I said. "Thanks for taking the time to see me."

"My name's Walter," he said.

"Walter," I repeated. "So you teach English at Promise Falls High." Derek went to one of Promise Falls's other high schools, closer to where we lived, so I wouldn't have heard of this guy.

"Well, I did. I'm retired."

"I didn't realize," I said. "Been retired long?"

"Four years now," he said.

"Well," I said, giving him an obvious once-over, "it seems to agree with you." I was about to ask whether there was a Mrs. Burgess, but some sixth sense told me not to.

As if on cue, I heard someone coming up a set of steps from the basement. Another man, about the same age as Burgess and as neatly dressed, but heavier, and with slightly more hair, appeared at the kitchen door. He, too, gave me the kind of warm look you might reserve for someone with the IRS.

"Trey," Walter said, "this is Mr. Cutter. Mr. Cutter, Trey Watson."

"Hello," I said. Trey barely nodded.

I didn't know what Trey's relationship to Walter was, and wasn't about to ask. But then Walter said, "Trey and I share this house."

"Great," I said.

"What's this about?" Trey asked. It was the first he'd spoken.

"Mr. Cutter hasn't quite gotten to that yet, but I'm given to understand it involves one of my former students."

"For Christ's sake, Walter, get him the fuck out of here." Trey turned on me. "He's been through enough. What trumped-up story you here to peddle?"

I looked from Trey to Walter. "I'm afraid I don't know what he's talking about. I came here to ask you about a student you once had named Brett Stockwell. Do you remember him?"

"Of course," he said cautiously.

"He was one of yours, right?"

"Yes, I remember him."

"He committed suicide ten years ago," I said.

"Yes, I know," he said.

"You see?" said Trey. "He's going to find a way to blame you for that."

"Trey," Walter said gently, "why don't you give me and Mr. Cutter a minute and afterwards I'll make us some lunch."

"Just not tuna," Trey said. "You made that yesterday."

"I was thinking maybe chicken salad."

Trey grumbled something neither of us could hear, meandered through the kitchen, disappeared into another part of the house, and then we both heard a back door open and close.

"Sorry about that," Walter said.

"That's okay. Brett Stockwell," I reminded him.

"Jumped off Promise Falls. I remember. Very tragic." Walter Burgess looked genuinely saddened.

"Brett's mother said you were very supportive of his writing."

"Look," Burgess said, "we don't get a lot of drop-in company here, Trey and I, what with both our families pretty much disowning us, so it's quite lovely and all to have someone drop by who wants to chat, but I don't understand what you're doing here. Are you related to Brett? I know you're not his father. I remember meeting his father, back at parent-teacher nights. Besides, I think he died before Brett did."

"No, I'm not his father. I'm not a relative."

Burgess's eyebrows soared for a moment. "So?" he said. "A stranger, no offense, drops by, asking about a student I had more than a decade ago. I don't get it. It's no wonder Trey thinks you're here to do me harm."

I said, "I don't mean to do you any harm whatsoever."

"I have my reasons for being cautious."

"Okay then," I said. "My son, Derek, he likes to collect old computers. Tinkers with them, fixes them up. He was given an old computer that Agnes Stockwell, Brett's mother, had tucked away in her garage. She was probably going to throw it out eventually, but when Derek expressed an interest in it, she let him take it. When he was looking through what was on the hard drive, I guess it was, he found something kind of interesting."

Burgess leaned forward a little. He looked more than curious. He looked apprehensive. "What was that?" he asked.

"A book. A novel. There was a novel on the computer."

"Well," Burgess said, "that's not all that surprising. Brett was a prolific writer. By any standard, not just that of a high school student."

"The book, at least what I've read of

it, it's, well, it's quite unique. I'm certainly no judge of its literary merits, but as a person who does read books, it strikes me as being written by someone mature beyond his years. It has a very interesting central character."

"And you're here," Burgess said, "because you want to know whether the book is based on me."

I must have done some sort of double take. I wasn't expecting that. Surely the man sitting at this table with me had not awoken one morning to find his genitals had gone missing. It wasn't the sort of thing I thought I could ask.

"No," I said. "That's not what I was wondering. What I wanted to know is, was Brett capable of something like that? Was he, as a high school student, and later, as a young college student, someone who could write a book that would possibly be publishable?"

"Well," said Walter Burgess, "I don't have in front of me the piece of work you say your son found on that computer. All I have to go on are the writings Brett showed me when I had him as a student, and based on those, my answer would be yes." He paused. "He was an extraordinarily gifted young man. I never had any other student whose talents even began to approach those of Brett Stockwell's."

"That's saying something," I said. "That's definitely saying something." For a moment, neither of us said anything. Then I asked the question I wanted to ask. "Why did you think the book might have been about you?"

Now Burgess looked embarrassed. "I feel a bit foolish. I don't know why I said that."

"I think you do," I said, trying not to make it sound like an accusation.

"Brett was a very intuitive young man," he said carefully. "Very insightful."

I leaned back in my chair. "About you?"

"At . . . times. Brett showed his stories to me for a couple of reasons, I think. First of all, I was his English teacher. I was, of all his teachers, probably the best equipped to offer him some guidance, although I don't claim to be any writer myself. But I tried to be encouraging to students who showed promise."

He stopped.

"And second?" I prompted.

"And I was probably the only teacher he had who was gay," he said. "Or that he at least knew to be gay."

"Why would that be an issue?" I asked slowly.

"Because I was someone Brett felt he could talk to. He was struggling with those kinds of issues himself."

"Brett was gay?"

Walter Burgess nodded. "His parents didn't know. I don't think he'd actually come out and told anyone, aside from me. Although I think the other kids suspected it. You think everyone's so open about it now, you think they were even a decade ago. But it's not always that way. Certainly not where parents are concerned."

"But he could talk to you."

"Yes. We talked."

I tried to keep my expression as even as possible, but Burgess was able to read my mind.

"No," he said. "He and I did not have a relationship. It was always professional. But I did counsel him, just as many teachers find themselves counseling troubled students. Sometimes young people need to talk to an adult they're not related to. Lots of high school girls who find themselves pregnant have told a teacher before they've told their parents."

"Sure," I said. "I remember telling my teachers stuff I never told my folks."

The way Burgess was looking at me suggested he did not think I was being sincere. "I know what you're thinking." He shook his head tiredly. "You already know about me, don't you?"

"Excuse me?" I said.

"Why I left teaching. Most people, they know. It's an open secret."

"I'm afraid I don't." And I wasn't asking. All I'd come for was some insight into Brett's skills as a writer. This other stuff was of no concern to me. I wasn't a cop. I wasn't Barry Duckworth. Whatever had happened in Walter Burgess's past was none of my business.

Burgess laughed softly to himself. "Well, aren't I crafty. The one person left in Promise Falls who doesn't know my business, and I have to open my yap."

"I don't care," I said. "Keep your secret."

Burgess waved his hand at me. "Doesn't really matter now anyway. It's been five years." He cleared his throat. "I met a young man at Whistle's." A downtown bar, known to appeal to a gay clientele. "It wasn't anything important. Just a connection. But we met a few times, were seen together, people talked. He'd just graduated from Spring Park." The same high school Derek went to. "So I'd been seen in the company of someone fresh out of high school. Didn't matter that it wasn't my school. That I'd never been this young man's teacher. But just the same, it drew the attention of the morality police. My behavior was deemed unprofessional, inappropriate. I could let them fire me, fight it, or I could take them up on their offer of early retirement. I was only a couple of years

away from being eligible anyway. So I
took it. I got out. And I never could
have gotten through it without Trey's
support." He paused. "He's not always
that grumpy."

I just nodded.

"But I never, ever, took advantage of
Brett," Walter Burgess insisted. "And
that's the God's honest truth."

"I want to thank you for your time," I
said. I got up from the table and turned
in the direction of the front door.

Once we were both outside, Burgess
glanced at my truck and asked, "What
do you charge?"

"Huh?"

"Your lawn service, how much to do
a house like this, once a week?"

I gave him a price.

He nodded, considering it. "My knee
gives me a lot of trouble, and I hate
nagging Trey to do it. Be a lot more
peaceful around here, I just hired
someone to do it, you know?"

"Sure," I said. "I can add you to the
list if you like."

He thought about it once more, nodded. "Deal. Trey'll say we don't have

money for it in the budget, but he says that about everything. He's cheap, but more than cheap, he's lazy, so he'll go for it."

I shook his hand, and as I headed for the truck, Burgess said, "Brett's book. Would it be possible to get a copy of it? I'd very much like to read it."

I turned and asked him, "You ever read *A Missing Part*?" He blinked, and nodded. "If you've read that, you've basically read Brett's book."

Burgess appeared thoughtful. "What, similar themes?"

"You could say that."

Burgess nodded. "I can see where Brett might have been interested in the kind of material that Chase explored in that book. The thing I could never figure out was why Chase wrote it."

"What do you mean?" I asked.

"Well, it's not the kind of book I think a heterosexual man would be able to write," Burgess said. "Unless Conrad Chase is possessed of insights I'd never have thought him capable of."

"You know him?"

"I've met him socially a few times over the years. He's not gay."

"No," I said. "That's true."

Ellen was proof of that.

FIFTEEN

As I was driving home, my cell, now on, rang.

"Did His Worship find you?" Ellen asked.

"He did."

"I tried your cell but—"

"I forgot to turn it on when I left."

Ellen said, "Randy said he just had to talk to you and I couldn't bring myself to lie and say I didn't know where you were."

"It's okay."

"What did he want?"

"He's going to run for Congress."

"Get out," Ellen said. "On what platform? That there's not enough corruption in politics, and he can change that?"

I needed the laugh. "I like that. You

should suggest it. 'Vote Finley: Keep Government Slimy.' Not a bad bumper sticker."

"What did he want from you?"

"My silence, basically."

"And what do you get in return?"

"I don't have to vote for him."

"Well, that's something," Ellen said.

"He offered me a job," I said. "Not my old one, not as a driver. He's got Lance for that. But other stuff, with the campaign, I guess."

"And you said?"

"I said no."

"Did he mention anything about salary?"

"Ellen, there's not enough money in the world."

"I know. I was only asking. Every day you came home after driving him around, you were just so fed up."

"No kidding." I couldn't bring myself to tell Ellen how I'd left Lance, doubled over, the wind knocked out of him.

"Listen," Ellen said. "I've been thinking about what we were talking about, before you went out, about Donna coming to the house with the package from the courier. How he mistook the Langleys' house for ours, because of the mailbox. Unless you know our house is down the lane here, it's pretty easy for people to assume the Langleys' house is our place."

"Yeah," I said.

"Tell me what you're thinking," Ellen said.

"I don't know," I said. "I don't know that I'm thinking anything, at least about that. But this whole computer thing is bothering me. The fact that it wasn't there, that it had the book Conrad wrote on it. The fact that the computer was given to Derek, not Adam. I saw Agnes, asked her whether she'd told anybody that she'd given that computer to Derek."

"What did Agnes say?"

"She said she hadn't."

Then I thought, what about Derek? What about Adam? Had either of them told any of their friends? Had Derek told Penny? And had Penny passed that information on to anyone? Had any of them gone online and blabbed to all their friends at once about the discovery?

"Listen, Jim, where are you going with this?" Ellen asked. "I mean, if there were anything to any of this, that this missing computer has something to do with what happened to the Langleys, what are you suggesting? Because some book that bears a strong resemblance to Conrad's is on it, the Langleys were all killed? Can't you see where that sort of thinking is going to lead someone?"

I'd already connected those dots.

"Jim?" Ellen said. "You there?"

"Yeah, I'm here."

"I thought I'd lost you."

"No, I'm here. I was just driving, that's all."

"You heard what I said? What that would mean?"

"I'm not sure what it would mean," I lied, waiting to see whether Ellen was thinking along the same lines I was.

"Don't play dumb with me, Jim. You know what it would mean. That somehow Conrad's connected to what happened to the Langleys."

"I guess that's one way of looking at it," I said.

"Well, that's ridiculous," Ellen said. "No matter what you might think of him, he's not capable of being involved with that."

I said, "There has to be some reason why *someone* killed the Langleys."

"It's not the one you're hinting at. This is over the top, Jim."

"I'm not hinting at anything," I said, my skin prickling under my collar. "But it was kind of interesting, talking to Agnes, about her son. And then I talked to his high school English teacher."

"You called his high school teacher?"

"I went by and saw him. Walter Burgess."

"Christ, you get around," Ellen said. "You're a regular Sam Spade."

I didn't detect any admiration beneath the sarcasm. "The kid was some kind of boy wonder. A genius. And that wasn't just his mother talking. It was his teacher, too. He was a brilliant writer. Mature beyond his years, as they say."

"I see."

"So I think, even if it may not mean

anything, I have to let Barry know that computer may be missing, and that one of the things on it was that book, which appears to have been written long before Conrad's book came out."

There was silence at the other end of the line.

"Ellen?" I said.

"I'm here. Here's what I think, whether you like it or not. Conrad's entitled to know about this, to offer some theory as to how this might have happened, before we talk to Barry. Telling Barry about this could do tremendous damage to Conrad's reputation. Spark all sorts of rumors and innuendo."

"I'm not trying to spark rumor or innuendo."

"Bullshit," Ellen snapped. "You've never let it go. You think there's a chance now, after all these years, to get back at Conrad."

"That's not true," I said, and almost even believed it.

"You're suggesting he ripped off this boy's novel."

"I just think Barry should know everything there is to know, that's all."

"You have no idea what else the police may have already uncovered. They may already have a suspect, for all you know. Look at the kind of work Albert did. Representing all sorts of lowlifes. Lots of people could have had a grudge against him. He pissed off a lot of people when he got criminals off. Maybe somebody Albert didn't get off was holding a grudge. Or somebody mad about someone Albert *did* get off."

I thought about everything Ellen had said. There was a lot of truth in it. I had no idea what else the police investigation was turning up. Barry wasn't exactly updating me.

"Okay," I conceded. "Everything you say is true. And it may well be that Barry won't give two shits about this information. But I think he should have it just the same."

"It's just that," Ellen said, her voice softening, "whatever Conrad might have been years ago, all he is now is my boss. I have a good job. A job that means a lot to me."

"I know."

"On top of that, Conrad's Thackeray's literary darling. The whole festival's built around him."

"I know that, too."

"It'd be bad enough for my job if his reputation were unfairly smeared. Imagine how bad it'd be if we're the ones doing the smearing."

"I hear you."

"We need my job," Ellen said. "It pays the bills."

So there it was.

"And mine doesn't," I said.

"I never said that," Ellen said quickly. "That came out wrong. I didn't mean that the way it sounded."

"Sure," I said.

"For fuck's sake," Ellen said, "I take it back. I was an asshole. I'm sorry."

I said nothing.

"Listen, all I'm saying is, let's know what we're dealing with before we talk to Barry. Let's talk to Conrad first."

"What would you have me do?" I asked, ending my silence. "Stroll into his big office and say, 'Hey, did you plagiarize from one of your students years ago?'"

"The thing is, this is why I called you

in the first place. He's here. With Illeana. They stopped by. You know that thing he does, walking into houses without knocking? He just about gave me a heart attack."

"You hadn't locked the door? After what happened?"

"I thought *you'd* locked the door when you left. Anyway, I'm in the kitchen, he walks in, and I guess I screamed."

Conrad had always thought he was too important to knock.

"They're out back now, on the deck."

"I'm pulling into the drive now," I said.

As I drove down our lane, past the Langley house and the cop car still posted there, I noticed a couple of people proceeding, very slowly and with their heads down, across the backyard of the Langley house, heading toward the wooded area that separated their house from ours. Forensic cops, I figured.

I drove my pickup past our back

deck and parked out front of the shed next to Conrad's Audi TT, one of the new redesigned ones. Conrad and Illeana were sitting on the deck, bottles of beer on the arms of their chairs. Ellen's Mazda sedan was nowhere to be seen, which must have meant Derek was out. Too bad, because I had some new questions for him.

Conrad was on his feet and walking over to the truck as I got out, arm and hand extended, his other hand wrapped around the brown bottle. I didn't have much choice but to take it. He had a grip that was stronger than it needed to be, like he was out to prove something. He was already a big guy—250 pounds I was betting—and a good six feet tall. Full of swagger and confidence. I wondered if, where I was concerned, he laid on the ol' buddy routine a bit too hard. He knew he had wronged me in the past, and seemed desperate, even after all these years, to be able to show that we could be friends.

I wasn't interested.

"Jim," he said, smiling.

"Excuse the mess," I said, holding up the grimy hand he'd already gripped, then gesturing to myself and my work clothes. "I had to go out this morning and finish up a yard or two."

"Don't apologize," he said, then, tipping his head in the direction of the Langley place, said, "Can you believe it?"

I just shook my head, walking back to the house, Conrad keeping pace with me.

"And to be right next door," Conrad said, lightly patting me a couple of times between the shoulder blades, demonstrating that you can fuck a guy's wife and still be pals. "I can't imagine what that must be like. And you didn't hear anything?"

We'd already been through this on the phone. "No," I said.

Conrad said, "I'd known Albert for years, you know. He was more than just my lawyer. He was a good friend. Known him since high school. He and Donna, they'd been to the house a number of times. Albert was on a couple of college committees over the years. Got involved in his community, a terrific guy, at least for someone who managed to get a lot of scumbags off over the years. But hey, that's the job description."

We'd reached the deck. Conrad's wife, Illeana, in a white blouse and white shorts, blond hair cascading down to her shoulders, smiled as I mounted the steps, but didn't get up. She extended a hand and I shook it lightly.

"Illeana," I said.

"Hello, Jim," she said. "Conrad felt we should come over." As if she were apologizing, justifying their presence. "This is a tragedy for all of us."

In the years since she'd moved here from Hollywood, Illeana had gotten the small-town-college-president's-wife thing down pretty well. Expensive but tasteful clothes, heels that were high but not towering and no longer made of clear plastic, a blouse unbuttoned far enough to draw your eye in, but not enough to give you any real kind of a show. But under all that upstate New York respectability, there was still something of the tart about her. Like she was chewing invisible gum, making high-frequency snapping noises detectable only by the true hound dogs of my gender.

Ellen handed me an Amstel and I sat down. Ellen was drinking her new drink of choice, white wine, her glass poured almost to the top. Conrad dropped back into his seat next to Illeana and said, "We just wanted to be sure you folks were okay. You're part of the Thackeray family, and when something like this happens—not that anything like this has happened before—we need to be sure you're managing okay." He looked at Ellen. "We figured that was why you called?"

"Called?" I said.

Conrad said, "I noticed your number was on my cell this morning. Illeana and I were out driving around in the new Audi. You see that? Pretty sharp, huh? Illeana's getting used to the stick. We must have missed the call."

Ellen, glancing at me and then to Conrad, said, "That was me. I was actually going to suggest you drop by, and then what do you know, you did."

I gave Ellen a look. So she'd tried to give Conrad a heads-up on her own. She'd probably tried his home first, and when she couldn't get him there, tried his cell.

"Next time," Conrad said, grinning, "leave a message and I'll get back to you as quickly as I can." Sounding like a voicemail recording.

"Well," I said, "it looks as though it all worked out, you coming by anyway. Here we all are."

"So, Barry Duckworth," Conrad said, "he's heading the investigation, is he?"

I nodded.

"Good man," Conrad said, "although you have to wonder whether he'll be in over his head. I can't imagine he has the background to deal with something like this."

"I'm sure he'll give it his best," I said, taking a big swig from the Amstel bottle. "I think Barry worked for a while in Albany."

"Well, it's still not New York or L.A., is it?" Conrad observed. "Albany," he said dismissively. "When's the last time anything big happened in Albany? And I'm not just talking about politics. Anything, really."

I said nothing.

I wasn't very good at this small-talk thing, at least not with Conrad. Several times a year, Thackeray social engagements where I was obliged to accompany Ellen brought me into contact with Conrad and Illeana. Given that he was Ellen's boss, bumping into him and the occasional conversation over the phone were impossible to avoid. Conrad had always struck me as someone who wanted to be liked and admired by everyone, and would go to great lengths to achieve that goal, even so far as to pretend the two of us did not have a history.

But then, it was easier for him. He wasn't the cuckold. (Jesus, there was a word you didn't hear every day.)

"I'm inclined to give the chief a call," Conrad said, referring to the Promise Falls chief of police, no doubt a close personal friend. Conrad was well connected. "I'll remind him he needs to put all available resources into solving this. And if that means calling in the state police or the FBI or whoever to give Barry a helping hand, then that's what he'll have to do. This is no time for false pride. If Barry needs assistance from someone with a little more experience, then he should be goddamn smart enough to accept it. Wouldn't you say, love?"

He was looking at Illeana. "Absolutely, Conrad," she said softly, and touched him on the arm. "You should make a call. At least they'll know you're watching their progress with interest."

"I wouldn't be surprised if Randy will be doing the same," I said.

"Randy, yes," said Conrad. "I'm sure he will. When he's not tossing his cookies in a home for unwed mothers!" He slapped his own knee and cackled. "I tell you, he never ceases to amaze."

"For sure," I said. As much as I hated chitchat, I couldn't keep myself from asking, "Have you heard what he's up to?"

Conrad eyed me warily. "The Congress thing."

I nodded.

"Yeah, he's had an exploratory committee working on this for a while. I think the bastard might actually have a shot at it. You don't have to be an angel to get elected, you know."

"That should be good news for Randy," I said. "I think he intends to announce in the next few days."

"Where did you hear about this?" Conrad asked. I guess he was surprised that I'd be up to speed on the comings and goings of the town's socially prominent, given my current status.

"He told me," I said.

Conrad blinked. Then, "Well, anyway, we don't want to take up your whole afternoon here. Ellen, if anything should come up, if you need a day or two off to deal with what's happened next door, don't hesitate to call."

"Sure, Conrad," Ellen said, finishing off the last of the wine in her glass. "That's very thoughtful."

"So we'll just be on our—"

"Conrad," I said, "there's something I'd like to talk to you about before you go."

Ellen looked at me. I could see in her face that she didn't want me to do this, that she wanted to handle it herself.

Fuck that.

"Sure," Conrad said. "What's up?"

I stood up. "Take a walk with me."

Conrad got to his feet and came in step beside me as I wandered over toward the shed. The double-wide garage door was open.

"Ellen," he said to me, "is she holding up okay?"

I hated it when he said her name. "We're all a little on edge," I said.

"Of course," he said. "I just noticed she knocked back that wine pretty fast."

"Like I said, we're all a bit stressed out. Three people getting shot next door, it can have that kind of an effect on you."

Conrad Chase walked straight into the shed, started looking around, checking out the lawn mowers, picked up a hedge trimmer, felt the heft of it in his hand. Then he spotted, in the far corner, my stack of canvases—there were about a dozen of them gathering dust—leaned up against the wall. He walked over to them, pulled the first one forward, then the second, and so on.

"This is no way to treat your paintings," he said. "Out here, subject to all the changes in temperature, the dust."

I didn't say anything.

"These are not bad, you know," he said, managing to be flattering and patronizing at the same time. He flipped back to the first one, an Adirondacks landscape. "I like this. I think, the farther back you get, the better it is. Very impressionistic. Lots of paint, heavy, you get too close and all you see are these globs, but you stand back"— he took three steps back—"and it really comes together. You had a show a few years ago, right?"

"Yes."

He went back to the stack, found the third one, lifted it out. "This is . . . let me guess. That's Promise Falls."

"Yes," I said again.

"You have an interesting way with color. Very muted, almost as though every color is filtered through gray. I don't think I've ever seen anyone who can bring sadness to a landscape the way you can." He shook his head in a way that almost seemed to be admiring. "You're a complex guy, Cutter," he said.

I couldn't help myself. "How?" I asked.

"Well, you're not particularly talkative, you drive around in a truck these days cutting people's grass, you used to spend your days driving Randy around, but there's a lot more going on inside there," and he pointed at my head, "than anyone would give you credit for."

"Really."

"You're a very insightful guy. I'm betting you were a serious kid. You don't talk much about growing up."

"No," I said. "I don't."

"Interesting thing about the brain, though. People like you, there's a large part of it that can be tapped for creativity. But you've decided not to tap into it anymore."

"I need to make a living," I said.

Conrad nodded, as though he understood. "I feel I've done that a bit myself. Running Thackeray, all this administrative shit, when I should be tapping into that creative side. That's the kind of thing that fulfills us, that nurtures us."

Or maybe tapping into someone else's creativity, I thought.

"Anyway, what's on your mind?" he asked, putting the Promise Falls painting at the front of the pile.

"I had something I think should be passed on to Barry Duckworth," I said, "but Ellen felt you were entitled to know about it first."

"Really?" His eyebrows rose a notch. "And what might this be about?"

"You remember a student you had, about ten years ago, by the name of Brett Stockwell?"

"Of course," he said without hesitation. I guess I was hoping he'd briefly pretend to forget, say the boy's name a couple of times like he was struggling to remember. "Brilliant student, absolutely brilliant," he offered. "A terrible tragedy. He committed suicide, you know."

"Yeah," I said. "I know."

"I was stunned. Although, at the same time, I wasn't totally shocked."

"Really? Why was that?"

"Sometimes, very creative people are very troubled as well. Creativity's more than a gift, Jim. It can be a curse. I don't have to tell you." He gestured again at my paintings. "You've had your downslopes, am I right? Times with the black dog? You have all these thoughts you want to get out, but if there's not an avenue, no outlet, that can be terribly damaging."

"So you're saying you saw signs. With Brett."

Conrad shrugged. "Well, Brett was moody. I remember that. Hard on himself. Like whatever he did, it wasn't good enough. That line, that idea in your head, it never seems quite as good when you get it down on paper." He paused. "So what makes you bring up Brett Stockwell?"

"Did you ever know his mother, Agnes?"

"I met her at the funeral, of course. I went to the service for Brett, and I can still see her there, standing over his

coffin, crying. And so alone. Her husband was already dead."

"She's one of our customers," I said.
"Derek and I look after her yard."

"Isn't that nice," Conrad said.

God, I just wanted to kill him right
then and there. Get my lawn tractor out
and run right over the smug fuck.

"She says you were very kind to her
after her son died. Sent her flowers,
even some concert tickets."

He nodded, remembering, but there
was something in his look that told me
he was unnerved that I knew this.

"Agnes, she's hung on to a lot of
Brett's things over the years," I continued, "couldn't bear to part with them,
but a few weeks ago, she gave his old
computer to Derek. Derek and Adam,
the Langley boy, they liked to mess
around with old computers."

"Is that so," Conrad said. He was
running his hand again over the hedge
trimmer, looping his finger over the trigger, squeezing, nothing happening because it wasn't plugged in.

"Brett, he was evidently quite the
writer, as you already know, having

taught him. And on this computer, there's an entire book."

Slowly, Conrad said, "That's not too surprising. I'd be surprised if there weren't a book, or two or three, on his computer. He had ambitions to become a novelist."

"All the boys found was the one, as far as I know. It's about a man named Nicholas who wakes up one day to find his plumbing a bit rearranged."

Conrad's eyebrows floated upward. "No shit? Seriously?"

"He wakes up with a pussy instead of a dick."

"I'm familiar with the story," Conrad said. "I'm afraid I don't understand."

"The computer that this was on, it was in the Langley house as recently as a couple of days ago. But it's not there now."

Conrad remained stone-faced. "I still don't understand."

"Frankly, neither do I. How does your book end up on a dead kid's computer? How does it end up there a couple of years before your book even comes out? So I was thinking, it would make sense to bring this to Barry's attention. Let him figure it out. But Ellen said I should talk to you about it first. That there might be a very simple explanation." I paused. "As a courtesy."

Conrad's cheeks looked flushed, but his voice remained very even. "I don't want to seem incredibly thick here, Jim, but I'm still having a little trouble understanding this. If this so-called computer you say your son was given is missing, how can you be so informed about what's on it?"

I swallowed. "Because my son made a—" And then I stopped myself. I was overplaying my hand.

"Made a copy?" Conrad said.

I didn't say anything. But I didn't have to. I had a lousy poker face. Conrad understood correctly what I had been about to say.

Conrad said, "You know what I think, Jim? I think this is complete and total horseshit, that's what I think. And I'm surprised at you. I thought you'd moved on. I thought you were enough of a man to leave the past in the past. Ellen, she's a wonderful woman, but she means nothing to me now and she hasn't for years. It was a fleeting relationship, a triviality. We have a completely professional relationship now. She's a valuable member of the Thackeray staff. She puts together an annual literary event that makes this town proud. But I am not having an affair with her. I have a wife. A *beautiful* wife."

Funny, how you could hate a guy for screwing your wife, but at the same time be enraged by his insinuation that she wasn't as desirable as the woman he had now.

"Jim, I've tried with you, I've really tried, to let bygones be bygones, to be a friend to you, to consider you a friend—"

"Don't put yourself out," I said.

"As I was saying, I've tried to make things civil between us, not just for the sake of my working relationship with Ellen, but for all of us, as reasonable human beings. So why you'd choose, at this time, years later, to concoct some scheme to discredit me, well, it's completely beyond me. I am astonished. I'm flabbergasted. And let me make something perfectly clear to you. If you attempt some feeble scheme to try to damage my reputation, I will come back at you with everything I have. I will crush you. I will destroy you. It'll be fucking shock and awe, my friend. And although I'll feel terrible about this, there's no way Ellen won't be dragged down with you when it happens. And that'll be a terrible shame. But at least now you know where things stand. I will not be ruined by some petty, lawn-cutting cuckold."

There it was again. Was it because it almost sounded like "cock" that the word packed such a punch?

I held his gaze through the entire speech. When he was done, I said, "Why'd you only write the one book, Conrad? Your ghostwriter take a fall?"

I thought he'd get angry, but he grinned. "Is that what you think? Oh, Jim, I'd have thought you were above all this. The fact is, I'm just completing a book, something I've been working on for years. My New York agent's up at her place on Saratoga Lake and she's dropping by this week to fill me in on all the publishers who are fighting to see who gets to read it first. Want me to find out, while she's up here, if she represents failed artists who get by doing people's lawns?"

"What's going on?" It was Illeana, standing just outside the garage door. "What are you two fighting about?"

SIXTEEN

What the hell did you say to him?" Ellen asked me as Conrad and Illeana sped up the lane in his shiny new Audi. "He looked like thunder after you were done talking to him."

"Maybe I should have found a more polite way to suggest that he ripped off some dead kid's novel," I said.

"This is terrific," Ellen said, shaking her head. "Just fucking terrific. I guess I can start looking for a new job tomorrow."

"Hey, I was only doing what you suggested," I said. "I talked to him before going to Barry."

"You should have let me do it."

"You already tried, didn't you? While I was out this morning. You called but didn't get him."

"All right, so I wanted to talk to him before you did. Without all the added baggage that you'd bring to things. And if he hadn't shown up with Illeana, I'd probably have done it before you got back."

"I gave him a chance to explain," I said. "I'd call that doing him a favor."

"And?" Ellen asked. "What'd he say?"

"A lot of things. But none of them included any kind of explanation."

"What do you mean, a lot of things? If he didn't explain, what did he say?"

"He thinks this is personal. He thinks I'm going after him because of what happened between you two."

Ellen started to say something and then stopped.

"I know that's what you're thinking, too," I said. "But what do you think I did? That somehow I came up with this elaborate plan? That I arranged for Agnes Stockwell to have this computer that she could give to Derek, and then somehow I managed to get a copy of Conrad's novel onto it, knowing Derek and Adam would eventually find it and

Derek would show it to me, and then I could use it to start asking questions that would end up destroying Conrad's reputation? Is that what you think I did? And I did it all because I was still bent out of shape because you fell into bed with that fucking great literary genius years ago? All these years, I've been putting this plan together? And if I planned all that, just how did the Langleys figure into it? Did I know they were going to be murdered, so I timed it just right to make the computer disappear when it happened, so somehow Conrad would be implicated? Because I'll tell you, if I was able to pull all that off, I should be running the fucking CIA."

"Enough!" Ellen screamed at me, grabbing her empty wineglass and shattering it against the side of the house. "Enough!"

I stopped.

We stood there on the back deck, a foot apart, facing each other but unable to look each other in the eye, the gulf between us as big as a football field.

"Look," I said, "maybe it's true that—"

But then there was the sound of a

car racing down the driveway. We both turned our heads to see Derek driving Ellen's Mazda up to the house. He hit the brakes a bit too hard and the car did a short slide in the gravel. Before he was out from behind the wheel, I could see his face was flushed with anger. He looked as red as Conrad had when he'd left.

"Those bastards!" he said.

He got out of the car and slammed the door and stormed toward the house. He tried to get past us as he crossed the deck, but I got in front of him and gently put my hand on his chest. His lips were held tightly together and I could hear the air whistling through his nostrils.

"Whoa," I said. "Slow down, pardner. What's going on?"

"Penny's parents," he said. "Fucking assholes."

"What happened?" Ellen said. "The Tuckers? What did they say? What happened?"

Derek shook his head angrily. "I couldn't believe them."

"Just tell us what happened," I said.

I hoped to God there hadn't been some kind of fight, that Derek hadn't slugged Penny's father or something. That was all we needed right about now.

"They wouldn't let me see her," he said. "I couldn't get her on the phone, she wouldn't answer her cell, and when I called the house her parents wouldn't put her on, so I drove over there."

"Why?" Ellen asked. "Why wouldn't they let you see her?"

"They think—fuck, I don't know what they think. It's, like, I don't know, I guess it's not safe to know me because I live next door to a house where every-body got offed."

"That's ridiculous," I said.

"Yeah, well, tell them."

"So you got there," Ellen said. "Then what happened?"

"I knocked on the door and Mrs. Tucker opened it and I asked for Penny and she said Penny couldn't see me."

"She say why?" I asked.

"I asked her. I said, 'Why can't Penny talk to me?' And all she'd say is, 'This isn't a good time.'"

"I don't get it," Ellen said. "Because

of what happened next door? They think she shouldn't see you?"

I thought about that, tried to see it from the point of view of Penny's parents. "If it were our daughter," I said to Ellen, "maybe we'd be scared for her to come over here, to be this close to a place where something that bad happened."

"What?" Ellen said. "You're taking their side? They don't want our son to see their daughter and you think that's fine?"

I couldn't win with Ellen today. "I'm not taking sides. I'm just trying to figure it out."

"I don't even know if it was that," Derek said. "They were really weird. Then Mr. Tucker comes to the door and tells me to move along."

"'Move along'?" I said. "That's what he said? 'Move along'?"

"And I'm leaving and I see Penny up in her bedroom window, you know? And I look up there and give her this shrug, right?" He demonstrated. "Figuring she'd do that, too, like she was sorry her parents were being such assholes, but she doesn't do anything, she just looks at me, and then her mom shows up at the window and pulls her away."

"I'm going to call them," Ellen said.

Almost in unison, Derek and I said, "No." Derek added, "Jesus, no, don't do that."

"Let's let it go for now," I said. "We've got enough on our plates. We hardly need to get into a fight with Penny's family."

"They have no right to treat Derek that way," Ellen said, looking as though she wanted to hit something. If there'd been another wineglass handy, I think she'd have thrown it against the house, too. Suddenly, she threw up her hands. "I can't deal with this," she said, and went back into the house.

I stood out there with Derek, put a hand on his shoulder. He shook it off.

"What?" I said. "What are you pissed with me for?"

"I don't know," he said. "I'm sorry. I'm just, fuck, I'm just so mad."

I waited a few seconds. "Okay," I said. "I can understand that. But every-

one, not just us, but everyone even remotely connected to this, everyone's
feeling it. People are scared. Somebody killed the Langleys, and people
are scared about what's going to happen next. The Tuckers, they're probably
scared, you're scared, your mom is
scared, I'm scared."

He took a few breaths. "I know," he
said. "I know."

"You okay?" I asked. "Because I
need to ask you something."

"What about?"

"The computer."

He looked at me, as though he'd already forgotten about the computer,
even though it had only been a few
hours since he'd filled me in on what
he'd found on it. "What about it?"

"After Agnes gave it to you, did you
tell anyone you had it? Or what you'd
found on it?"

He didn't need time to think. "No.
Nobody. Well, nobody other than
Adam."

"Okay," I said. "What about Penny?
Did you tell her?"

"No, I . . . I don't think I told her."

"Are you sure?"

"I mean, I might have told her we found some book on it. But not much more than that."

"Would she have told anyone?"

"I don't see why. I mean, she probably didn't care. I'm always talking about shit Adam and I find on old computers, and I don't think she's ever listened before."

"What about Adam?" I asked him. "Who might he have told?"

"Why? What's the deal?"

"Derek, figure it out. If—and it's still a big if—but if someone went into that house for that computer, they had to know it was there. So do you think Adam told anybody about it?"

"I don't think so. Except for his dad. Like I told you, he said his dad was upset about it."

Albert Langley. Lawyer for, among others, Conrad Chase.

"Would he have done that, you think? I mean, did Adam talk about things with his dad? Does it make sense that he might have said, 'Hey, you wouldn't believe what Derek and I found on this computer he got from Agnes Stockwell'? Would he have done something like that?"

Derek gave it some thought. "He might have. I guess. I don't think he would have told his mom, though. For the same reason I didn't want to talk to my mom about it. Because of what the book was about."

I settled into one of the chairs on the deck. My beer was still sitting there, but the bottle was now warm to the touch. Derek took a seat opposite me.

"What?" he asked.

"I don't know," I said. "I just don't know." I drank some of the warm beer. "I'm so goddamn tired I can't think."

Something caught Derek's eye. I turned and saw him looking at the forensic cops I'd noticed earlier, still examining every blade of grass behind the Langley house. "Why are those guys searching around in the woods like that?" Derek asked. "What are they looking for?"

SEVENTEEN

It seemed as though all of Promise Falls showed up for the funeral two days later. St. Peter's must have easily been able to hold five hundred people, and it was a standing-room-only affair. Albert Langley ran one of the town's biggest law firms, his wife, Donna, was one of Promise Falls's most recognized power spouses, and their son, Adam, if not the most popular kid at his high school, was at least well liked. That produced a pretty big pool of friends, acquaintances, and associates to draw from.

Not to mention family.

There was Donna's sister Heather, and her husband and two children, who'd flown in from Iowa. Albert's mother, an elderly woman who had moved down to St. Petersburg, had come, accompanied by Albert's brother Seth, from South Carolina. There were cousins and nephews from across the country, an uncle of Albert's from Manitoba.

A whole lot of crying.

It was the first funeral Derek had ever been to. In a perfect world, we would have started him out with something smaller, a little less overwhelming than a combined funeral for three people, all taken much too soon in an act of horrific violence.

A funeral for a grandparent, that would have been a good place to start. Ellen's mother had passed away when he was six, but we'd decided he was too little to attend, that the ceremony would be too upsetting.

We sat together, Ellen and Derek and I, around the middle of the church, off to one side. As close as we were, geographically, to the Langleys, a great many of the people attending the service were more connected to them, and we weren't interested in sitting up near the front anyway.

Mayor Randall Finley said a few words, and he performed true to form, with an abundance of platitudes and almost convincing expressions of sincerity. "Albert Langley," he opined, "exemplified what made this community special, through his commitment to his fellow citizens, his pursuit of equality and fairness, his dedication to making Promise Falls a better place."

No mention of the fact that he often treated his wife like shit, but you couldn't expect Randy to say something like that in a speech that was clearly a warm-up for his imminent announcement that he was seeking a congressional seat.

There was an unusual amount of whispering going through the church about three-quarters of the way through the service, and not just because Finley had gone on too long. Some story, a rumor, we didn't know what, at least not until it spread to our row.

A woman sitting to my right whom I did not know had just been told something by a man I took to be her husband sitting on the other side of her.

"No," she whispered. "Oh my."

I leaned in a bit closer to her and whispered, "What's happened?"

"A man took his own life," she said. "Someone the police wanted to question."

"Who?"

"The police came to the house to interview him and he killed himself."

"Who was it?"

"I don't know the name. He had something to do with that case of Albert's, where he got the boy off."

Now Ellen was nudging me in the ribs. I whispered to her what I'd heard. "Who?" she asked. I shook my head. We'd have to wait for the service to end to learn anything more.

Once it was concluded, and mourners started spilling out of the church, the women dabbing their eyes with tissues, the men trying to be stoic, everyone started quizzing one another, trying to learn more.

I saw Donna's sister Heather, whom I recognized from the times she and her family had come to Promise Falls to visit.

She was standing with her husband, Edward, when I approached, with Ellen and Derek flanking me. It took her a second to realize who I was.

Ellen said, "We're so sorry."

Heather nodded, and said, "Have you heard?"

"We've heard something," I said. "But just bits and pieces."

"I was speaking with Detective Duckworth," she said. I had spotted him in the crowd earlier. "They went to speak with a man, his name was Colin McKindrick."

Of course, I thought. The man whose son had been beaten to death with a baseball bat by Anthony Colapinto.

"Yes?" I said.

"And when they were knocking on the door, saying they wanted to talk to him about the threats he'd made to Albert, he told them to go away, told them he'd shoot if they came in. And then, a minute later, a gun went off in the house, and when they went in, Mr. McKindrick was dead." Heather put her hand over her mouth, overcome. "He'd shot himself in the head." Edward put his arm around her and held her close.

"Dear God," I said.

Edward asked me, "Who's this McKindrick?"

"McKindrick had said something to Albert, that he'd get even with him, or something along those lines, when the boy who'd been charged in his son's death was acquitted. Albert persuaded the jury that the Colapinto boy had acted in self-defense."

Heather shook her head, overwhelmed by the enormity of it all.

Ellen reached out and touched Heather's arm. "Again, we're so sorry. We'll let you go." Our signal to move on.

Once we had moved away, Ellen said, "What do you make of that?"

"I don't know," I said. "Has to make you wonder."

"Maybe it's over."

"Could be," I said.

"They come to the man's house, want to ask him about Albert, and then he kills himself?"

"What?" asked Derek. "So they think

he must have killed Adam and his parents?"

"Police come to your door, want to ask you about these murders, you take your own life, looks kind of incriminating," Ellen said. "He must have been so torn apart. Losing a son, then, if he did kill the Langleys, dealing with the guilt."

I still didn't know what to think. Ellen continued, "Bad enough you kill the lawyer for keeping the guy who killed your kid out of jail, but why his wife and son? Maybe that was part of the deal. He lost his son, he figured he'd take away Albert's, and his wife, too."

As tragic as the news was, it had the effect of a weight being lifted off our shoulders. If there was any truth to the conclusions we were jumping to, it meant maybe I'd be able to let this business of Conrad and the computer go.

Ellen shook her head sadly. Derek, looking very uncomfortable in his suit and tie on this very warm day, said, "I just want to go home."

I did, too. We turned to head for the parking lot, and standing there in front of us were Conrad Chase, his wife, Illeana, and a woman I did not recognize. Thin, silver hair, early sixties, makeup that struck me as a bit overdone, understated but expensive-looking earrings and a large rock on one of her fingers. Her cream slacks and red silk blouse were casually elegant. A little too nice for everyday wear, but not quite subdued enough for a funeral service.

"Jim, Ellen," Conrad said, a little more pleasantly than I might have expected, given the exchange we'd had the last time we'd seen each other. He gave a nod to our son, and added, "Derek."

"Conrad, Illeana," I said. I turned to the silver-haired woman. "I don't believe we've met."

"Elizabeth Hunt," she said.

"Jim Cutter," I said. "And this is my wife, Ellen, and our son, Derek."

"Pleased," she said. "I understand that was quite a moving service they just had in there."

"Elizabeth is just meeting us for lunch," Conrad explained. "She drove in from her place on the lake." He paused, then, "Elizabeth is my literary agent." He said this like he was telling me he had a new car.

"Well," I said. "That's great."

"It was just so sad in there," Conrad commented, nodding in the direction of the church. "So, so sad." Conrad's sorrow, like so many of his emotional expressions, seemed designed for show. "But we all have to move forward in our own ways, isn't that right?"

There were some general murmurings about how that was true, although not from me.

"Jim," Conrad said, "Elizabeth here might be able to put you onto some agents who handle artists. What I said the other day, it may not have come out right, but I was sincere."

"What?" Ellen said. I hadn't repeated for her, word for word, what Conrad had said to me when we'd had our talk.

"Actually," said Elizabeth, "I'm afraid I don't really have that much involvement with—"

"That's all right," I said. I had some sympathy for her, getting dragged into

Conrad's shenanigans. "That won't be necessary."

Illeana spoke up. "Elizabeth has enough to deal with, prying Conrad's latest book out of his hands."

Ellen's eyes widened. "You've finished a book? A new book?"

Conrad feigned modesty. "Well, just about. Elizabeth says there are a number of houses that want to see it."

"Conrad," said Elizabeth cautiously. She was clearly uncomfortable having a discussion about this with all of us present.

"That's wonderful news," Ellen said in an understated way. "About the book."

"We should get back," I said, eager to extricate all of us from this.

But Conrad wasn't quite ready to let us go. "You heard what happened?" he asked. "What everyone was talking about as we came out?"

"McKindrick," I said, and Conrad nodded, almost eagerly.

"That's right," he said. "News like that, it spreads like wildfire. You can already see what the take on this is going to be. Distraught father sees the boy who killed his son get off, goes after Albert, then takes his own life when he realizes the police are closing in on him."

"That's certainly one way it could play out," I said.

Conrad looked at me. "A minute?" he said.

The two of us stepped away from the others. Quietly, Conrad said to me, "Surely this new development, if it pans out the way I think we all expect it will, puts an end to all your speculation about some damned computer with a copy of my book on it having anything to do with all this."

I couldn't think of anything to say. That was okay, because Conrad was always ready to fill the silences.

"You should know that you got Illeana terribly upset. She heard the tail end of those accusations. I've told her to put them out of her mind, they're not worth talking about. But I'm willing to put this behind us, Jim. I'd like to apologize for my outburst at your place. That was uncalled for. But you can understand, a man of my reputation doesn't take kindly to attempts to cast aspersions upon it."

"Yeah. Whatever you say, Conrad."

He smiled and patted me on the shoulder. "Glad we see eye to eye on this, Jim. And to show there's no hard feelings, I want you and Ellen to be the first, after my agent, to have a copy of my new manuscript."

"Well, what a gesture."

"I'd value your opinion. Very much. And I think it may figure largely into Ellen's handling of the next festival. A new book from me is going to make it a more meaningful celebration."

"I'm going to rejoin my family, Conrad," I said, and excused myself.

Maybe Conrad was right. Maybe this whole thing was over. Since I'd had that argument with Conrad and a subsequent one with Ellen, I'd done nothing about the missing computer. A couple of times I'd been about to phone Barry, then held off. I didn't know that my information meant anything, and I was second-guessing my motives, second-guessing everything. Any action I took could have a lasting impact on Ellen's job and, no less important, my marriage.

I'd decided to let things cool down for a while, at least until the funeral for the Langleys was over.

There was still a good part of the day left, and Derek and I decided that once we were home, we'd change out of our suits, get into our work clothes, and cut a few clients' yards.

We were doing a house on the town's west side when I noticed Barry's unmarked car trolling down the street, stopping at the end of the driveway.

Derek had on earmuffs while he used the noisy leaf blower to clear the sidewalk of grass clippings. I tapped him on the shoulder, pointed to Barry when he whirled around. "I'm over there," I mouthed.

He nodded and kept working.

Barry powered down the passenger window and said, "Hey, Jim, take a ride with me."

I opened the door, got in, the air-conditioning blasting me in the face. Before I could find the button to power the window back up, Barry had done it.

He let his foot off the brake, took us down the street, slowly, like he had no real destination in mind. "Where we going?" I asked.

"Nowhere in particular," he said. "I just wanted to be able to talk to you."

"About what?"

"About you puttin' it to Donna Langley. You never mentioned that you'd slept with her."

EIGHTEEN

She'd come over because the power had gone off in their house. Donna Langley wanted to know whether we'd lost electricity, too.

I was on a day off from the security firm I'd been working for, for about the last six months, and was using my time to paint some windows—as opposed to actual landscapes—on the side of the house that faced the highway and the Langley house. Derek was at school, in the second grade, and Ellen was at her relatively new job at Thackeray, organizing their first annual literary festival.

I had been toying with the idea of killing myself.

When I was on the ladder, doing a second-story window frame, I thought about whether I'd be able to break my neck, fatally, falling from that distance. It seemed unlikely. An arm or leg, perhaps. A wrist, probably. Even if I could break my neck or back, I'd probably just end up paralyzing rather than killing myself, and what fun would that be? What were the odds I'd get another chance at this if I needed someone to feed me and wipe my ass?

While I was feeling pretty down, it was not a particularly good time for either Ellen or me. Ellen was in the thick of her dalliance with the bottle, and I was weighing the pros and cons of sticking my head in the oven.

I had found a note, about a month earlier, that Conrad Chase had written to my wife. Given that he was supposed to be some brilliant English professor—this was almost a couple of years before he managed to scale the *New York Times* bestseller list—I guess I was expecting something slightly more metaphorical than "I can't wait to have you on my face again."

He hadn't actually signed it, but there were enough other things around the house in Conrad's handwriting with which to make a comparison, and conclude that he was the author. And the fact that he hadn't actually started it with "Dear Ellen" didn't matter all that much, considering that I found the note in her purse.

I hadn't gone searching for it. I'm not even sure I had any suspicions at that point. Some resentment, maybe. Ellen's new job took up a lot of her time. She wanted to make a good impression with the Thackeray administration and was under a tremendous amount of pressure. She'd organized plenty of events at the Albany public relations firm, but she'd always had plenty of help with those. And nothing she'd done for them was as ambitious as what she was pulling together for the Promise Falls college.

I was just looking for a five-dollar bill. It was a school morning, Ellen was still upstairs getting ready for work. I was down in the kitchen with Derek, who was already running late and taking forever to eat his peanut butter toast. It wasn't the easiest breakfast choice to chow down in a hurry, but if he didn't get his seven-year-old butt out to the end of the lane in the next three minutes, the bus was going to go right on by and get to school without him.

"Come on, pardner, you gotta move it," I said.

There was still half a piece of peanut butter–slathered toast on his plate, and he must have realized he didn't have a chance of finishing it, so he said, "I gotta go brush my teeth."

"There's no time, man."

"I gotta brush—"

"Where's your backpack? Is everything in your backpack?"

"Where's my lunch?"

"Lunch?"

"Remember Mom asked you to make me a lunch?"

"Buy a lunch at school," I said.

"Mom's been making me a lunch so I won't go to—"

"Derek, chill out. Tomorrow, we'll all be a little better organized. Today, you can buy a lunch. Hang on." I reached into my back pocket for my wallet, but there was nothing in it but a twenty.

There was no way I was giving him a twenty. The odds I'd ever see my change at the end of the day were too long to calculate.

Ellen's purse was on the bench by the front door.

"Hang on," I said, and grabbed the purse. She had her wallet in there, but you could find cash in it almost any-place. In the wallet, any one of the three or four inside pouches, or loose in the bottom. I could feel change down there, but counting out nickels and dimes and quarters was going to take too long. I glanced in the wallet and saw that Ellen was well equipped with twenties, but nothing smaller. Welcome to the ATM world.

I reached into a pouch, felt some-thing papery, and pulled out two pieces of paper. One of them was a ten, which I immediately handed to Derek and shoved him out the door.

The other piece of paper was a note.

One moment you're trying to get a kid to eat his peanut butter toast, and the next you're seeing your whole world fall apart.

It was like I was seeing everything around me for the first time. That house, the furniture, the lane out to the road. It was as if, suddenly, none of it existed. All this had been some sort of mirage, a dream. My life, as I'd thought I'd known it, was nothing more than a piece of performance art.

"Hey!" Ellen shouted from the up-stairs bathroom. "Did Derek make the bus?"

"Yeah," I said.

"What?"

"I said yeah!"

As I heard Ellen's footsteps at the top of the stairs I slipped the note into my pocket. For a moment, I thought of stuffing it back into the purse, pretend-ing I'd never seen it. But that really wasn't an option. I'd opened a door and had to know what was on the other side.

"Gotta go," Ellen said, kissing me on the cheek. "You okay?"

"Yeah," I said.

"You seem funny. You sick?"

"I'm okay," I said.

"Don't you have to be going soon, too?"

"I don't have to be in till ten today," I told her.

"Okay, well, look, I'm off. I'll figure out something for dinner tonight since I'm going to be home before you."

"Sure," I said, and saw her to the door. Once she was in her car, I went upstairs to the room she used as an office.

It didn't take long to find a sample of Conrad Chase's handwriting. There were notes from him all over Ellen's desk, suggestions about who to get for the festival, phone numbers, a listing of public relations people for various publishing houses. I took the note from my pocket and compared it to the samples in front of me.

There was no doubt.

And then I got ready and went to work. What else do you do? Phone in, tell the boss you're feeling too betrayed to come in today?

That night, Ellen had some lasagna ready when I came in the door.

"Hey," she said. "How was your—"

I handed her Conrad's note. Didn't even take off my jacket. Ellen looked at it and burst into tears.

It was over, she told me between sobs. It was over before it really even started. They'd been working so closely together, she got carried away, she did a stupid thing, but she'd ended it herself. I had to believe her, she said. And I'd been so distant, she said, I—

So it was my fault.

No, she said. She slipped, she said. It was a slip. I had to know, she said, that she was telling the truth.

I had no idea what to believe, but I had some idea what might have drawn her to Conrad. I recalled the times she'd come home from work and talk about how creative he was, how inspiring it was to see someone so committed to harnessing the talents he'd been blessed with. He was everything I was not. He'd thrown himself into his art and I'd given up on mine, despite Ellen's repeated encouragement.

I thought I'd be furious. But I felt too crushed to generate any anger. I left that night and didn't come back for a couple of days. Stayed in a motel, still went in to my security job. One day, Derek phoned me at work and said, "I cleaned up my room, Daddy. Now will you come home?"

I did come back to pick up some more clothes, and Ellen was there, like she'd been waiting for me since the moment I'd left.

"I'll do anything," she said, but her words were slightly slurred. I could smell the booze on her breath. "Whatever it takes, just tell me."

I decided to come back. Not so much because I was ready to move forward with this, to find a way through our problems, but if Ellen was starting to drink heavily, there needed to be someone else there to look after Derek.

I went through the next few weeks on autopilot. Went to work, came home, got Derek ready for bed, slept in the spare room, got up the next day and did it all over again, trying to keep my conversations with Ellen to an absolute minimum.

"Talk to me," she said.

I felt myself falling into depression.

That was my mood the day I chose to paint some windows. When Donna Langley walked over to ask if our power was out, too.

"I don't think so," I said. "Let me go in and check."

I went inside, flicked a light switch in the kitchen, came back out. "We're okay," I said. "We're on the same line, so it must just be your house."

"Okay, well, I guess I'll call an electrician," she said. Then, "Sorry for interrupting you there. That's a lot of windows you've got to do."

"Before you call an electrician," I said, "you might want to check the breakers."

She was a good-looking woman. Not stunning, but attractive. Tall, with a generous bosom and rounded hips. Brown hair down to her shoulders. Every once in a while, I'd see her, in shorts and a top, jogging along the highway into Promise Falls. She'd do the odd fund-raising marathon, hit us up for a pledge.

"There's a box on the wall in the basement," she said. "I never even thought to look there. It's probably just one of those switches. All you have to do is flip them back, right?"

"Unless it's the main one, for the whole house," I said. "But it's more likely just a single switch."

"I'll try to figure it out," she said, and laughed.

I was starting to come down the ladder. I'd put aside, for now, any thoughts of coming down headfirst. "I can check it out if you'd like," I said.

She nodded. We walked back to her house. It was empty, of course. Albert was at work, Adam at school. He and Derek had the same teacher that year, Mrs. Fare, who, according to the kids, looked like a rabbit. "You should see the way she eats a sandwich," Adam said one time when he was over.

Donna and I entered her house through the back door. "Are the lights out all over the house?" I asked.

"I don't know," she said. "I was in the kitchen, making something, when the Cuisinart died and the light went out. I thought I'd actually try to make something for dinner tonight. Most nights, we're so busy, we end up ordering in or going out, you know?"

I didn't. Ellen and I didn't have enough in our budget to eat out every night. Subs once in a while, maybe a pizza. But I said, "Oh yeah." I went to the kitchen and tried a light switch. Nothing. Then I went to the living room and tried a lamp on one of the sofa tables. It came on.

"Well, you've got power to the house," I said. "Looks like it's just the kitchen, so like I said, it's probably just a breaker. Show me where the box is."

She led me downstairs to the furnace room, pulled a chain to turn on a bare bulb. "Over there, I think," she said, pointing to a gray metal box above a worktable. She followed me across the room. "That's it, right?"

"Sure looks like it," I said. I opened the panel door and looked at the two columns of black switches. The light was so poor in the room, I could barely make out the masking-tape labels by the switches that told what parts of the house they controlled.

I turned and said, "Have you got a

flashlight or anything, Donna?" She was standing close enough that I could feel the warmth of her body.

We had socialized occasionally with the Langleys. A couple of barbecues. When they had a party that wasn't strictly for the folks from his law firm, they'd invite us over, a neighborly thing. If you're going to make some noise, invite the neighbors so they're not pissed off. If we were the type to hold parties, we'd have returned the favor. They seemed like your typical professional couple. Reasonably happy, upwardly mobile, one kid.

She found a flashlight tucked in behind a toolbox on the worktable, and when she handed it to me she held on to it for half a second, and my hand overlapped with hers.

I clicked on the light. "There you go," I said, finding the one switch that had flipped out of alignment with the others, labeled "Kitchen." I forced it over. "I'll bet things are back on now."

"That didn't take any time at all," she said, a hint of disappointment in her voice.

She was standing so close that when I turned to hand her the flashlight, my thigh brushed up against hers. She didn't move back at all, and as I continued to turn she put a hand on my side, just above my waist.

"Donna," I said.

"I've noticed something about you," she said. "The last few weeks. When I see you. Driving in and out, walking. Something's different about you."

"I don't know what you mean," I said.

"It's like you've lost your spirit," she said, slipping her thumb inside my belt. "I know what that's like."

I swallowed. It was like that moment when I found the note in Ellen's purse, how everything could change at once. One minute you're up on a ladder, painting windows, wondering about the most efficient way to kill yourself, and the next you're in a basement with a woman holding on to your belt.

I found myself putting a hand on her shoulder and she turned her head toward it, as though inviting it to touch her face. Softly, I caressed her cheek.

"Donna," I said again. "I'm . . . I . . ."

"You don't have to say anything," she said. "I just wanted you to know that if you're sad, you're not alone."

"Look," I said. "I'm married." It seemed a dumb, obvious thing to say.

"So am I." She paused. "If your marriage is perfect, then I apologize for my forwardness, and you can leave right now."

That was when I should have walked, but that would have been akin to speaking a lie, because things between Ellen and me, at that time, were far from perfect.

"What about you?" I asked. "And Albert?"

"Why don't you just kiss me?"

So I did. Her arms slipped around me, and there seemed to be only one way this was going to end. And not there, in the basement, next to the breaker panel, but upstairs in her and Albert's bed.

She led me upstairs to the bedroom she shared with her husband. We were sitting on the edge of the bed. I was about to do something I felt entitled to do. I'd been wronged. Wasn't I allowed to get even?

But I pulled back and said to Donna, "I can't do this."

"Yes you can," she said, reaching up to touch my face. I gently took hold of her wrist and brought it down.

"No," I said. "I can't." Her eyes were moist with tears about to spill onto her cheeks. "I'm sorry," I said. "I have to go."

As I got up she said, "This never happened."

I nodded. "That's because nothing did happen," I said.

It's even possible that things actually got better between me and Ellen from that day forward. I didn't get even, but I'd had my opportunity. And I knew just how close I'd come. Maybe when Ellen had come that close to the edge, she had tried to stop, but teetered in the wrong direction.

And even though nothing happened, I guessed Donna felt we'd come close enough that it was worth telling someone about. I wasn't sure I wanted to know who.

NINETEEN

Her sister," Barry said as we drove into Promise Falls, past car dealerships, the town's Wal-Mart, a KFC, a doughnut joint.

"Heather," I said. "From Iowa."

"Sisters tell each other everything," Barry said. "Had a chance to talk to her before the funeral. She and her husband came in last night."

"We saw them at the service," I said. "And she's wrong."

Barry ignored that. "We talked for a bit, and she couldn't think of anyone who'd want to do harm to her sister, or her brother-in-law for that matter, or their son. But she did mention to me that her sister had told her that she'd slept with the neighbor, that it had been the wrong thing to do, but it happened."

"If Donna really told her sister that, she was exaggerating."

"Why would her sister lie about something like that?"

"Barry," I said patiently, "I'm not particularly interested in discussing this, but I'm telling you this much. It didn't happen. I didn't have an affair with Donna Langley. I didn't sleep with her. I had an opportunity, but I didn't take it. I know you're doing your job, but for the life of me I don't know what this has to do with anything, even if I had slept with her, which, I repeat, I did not. And, if the rumor mill is to be believed, your investigation into this whole thing must be about over."

"Where'd you hear that?" Barry asked.

"It's all anyone was talking about after the service. Colin McKindrick. The one who made threats against Albert after the kid who killed his son was acquitted."

"What'd you hear?"

"That when you went to talk to him about this, he blew his brains out."

"Well, that part's certainly true,"

Barry said. "Happened early this morning. Hell of a thing."

"And that doesn't tell you something?"

"What, suddenly you're a psychiatrist, Jim?"

"Is it a stretch to think Colin McKindrick was feeling guilty about something? That he'd kill himself when you came asking about the Langleys?"

"Yeah, well, he might just have been depressed, Jim."

"But you don't know for sure."

Barry bristled. "You seem to think you know everything. Well, wise one, here's what I do know. I went to see him, identified myself through the intercom thing at the door, said I was with the police, looking into the Langley thing, and he told me to get the hell off his property or he'd start shooting right through the door. So I put in a call for backup, but before you could say 'Bob's your uncle' the bastard shot himself. Front door was locked but I found my way in through the garage, found him in the hall, but some of his brains found their way to the kitchen."

"Barry," I said, not impressed by his attempt to shock me.

"But here's what you don't know," Barry said. "Colin McKindrick spent from Friday night to Saturday morning in the drunk tank."

I just looked at him.

"He was in the Promise Falls lockup. He'd been drinking downtown at Casey's, apparently he'd been doing a lot of that since his son died, and even more since Albert got the guy off who did it. Got in his car, went weaving down Charlton Street, cop pulled him over, he blew off the scale, he got hauled in. His car, too."

"He was in jail," I said, more to myself than Barry. "When the Langleys were murdered."

"The whole time. As alibis go, being in jail's one of the better ones."

I shook my head slowly. "Maybe he hired someone. McKindrick hired somebody to kill Albert Langley, ended up killing the bunch of them."

Barry Duckworth made a face. "Hired killers. In Promise Falls. What do you think this is, Jim, *Fargo*?"

I leaned my head back against the headrest. I was feeling exhausted.

"So," Barry said, getting back on track, "the case is open, and I'm still asking questions, which is why I'm asking you about this not-an-affair you had with Donna Langley."

"Why don't you tell me what her sister said, and I'll see what I have to say," I said.

One corner of Barry's mouth went up a notch. "That's good, Jim. That's really good. But I don't think you understand how this whole criminal investigation thing works. I don't tell you the other person's story first so that you can get yours to line up with it. That was one of the first things they taught me back in detective school."

I looked straight ahead and said nothing.

"Look, Jim, we've known each other a pretty long time. Ever since you went to work for Finley. I think you're a pretty good guy. I'm trying to be straight with you. I didn't sit down at your kitchen table and ask you this question with

Ellen there. I'm trying to cut you some slack. So play ball with me here."

"You could have asked me this in front of Ellen," I said. "Because nothing ever happened." I paused. "Not really."

"There's a couple of weasel words if I ever heard them," Barry said.

"It was a long time ago. Not long after Ellen got her job at Thackeray. I was working outside, Donna came over because her power was out, I went over, flipped a breaker—"

Barry snickered. "Is that what they're calling it now?"

I shook my head. "She kissed me. I mean, we kissed each other. She wanted me to have sex with her, but I didn't go through with it."

"Okay," said Barry skeptically.

"It's the truth. She . . . Donna seemed like a very unhappy person. There was a sadness in her. I think trying to get me into her bed was a way of dealing with that." I thought about that for a moment. "Maybe there were other men, other than me, that she was a little more successful with."

"Yeah, maybe," Barry said.

"I'm telling you the truth. After it happened—almost happened—I decided to try to fix what was wrong in my marriage, to put things back together."

"There was trouble between you and Ellen?" Barry asked.

Shit. I hadn't intended to open that door. Especially now that, with the news that Colin McKindrick couldn't have killed the Langleys, I was again considering telling Barry about the missing computer with Conrad's book on it. I didn't want him thinking I was acting out of malice, that I was trying to get Conrad in trouble to settle an old score.

"Just . . . it was a bit rocky," I said. "I was, I don't know, kind of distant. A bit depressed, unhappy with where I was in life. Ellen had thrown herself into her job, and maybe I was a bit jealous of that."

Barry, one hand on the wheel, pointed at a doughnut shop with the other. "Want a coffee or something?"

"Too hot," I said. "Maybe you could turn around and take me back. Derek's probably done and waiting for me."

Barry pulled off at the doughnut shop and got in the drive-through line. "Medium coffee, black, and a chocolate dip doughnut," he said into the speaker.

When he had the window back up, I said, "So now that you've ruled out McKindrick, do you have any other leads?"

"Oh yeah," he said, inching the car forward to the delivery window.

"Like what?" I asked.

"This and that."

"What about other clients Albert had? Somebody at the law firm?"

"You bet, we're looking into all of that."

I decided the time was right. "I might have something for you."

He turned, raised his eyebrows. "That so?"

"Yeah. You know when you took Derek through the house Sunday morning?"

"Yeah."

"Afterwards, he was talking to me, and he realized he'd noticed something. He wasn't even sure it was a big deal, which is why he didn't mention it to you, but it was kind of bugging him."

"Hang on," Barry said. We were at the window. Barry gave the clerk a five, got some change and his coffee and doughnut. "You're sure you don't want anything?" he asked me. "Maybe something cold for Derek? One of these frosty things?"

"We're good."

Once he had his coffee in the holder and we were back on the road to my job site, he said, "So, go on."

"Derek says there was a computer in Adam's room, one of those bulky tower things, that was there as recently as Thursday, the day before the murders, but he didn't see it there Sunday when we did the walk-through."

"A computer?"

"Yeah."

Barry shrugged. "Derek said this." There was something, I don't know, dismissive in his voice.

"That's right," I said.

"How's Derek know about this computer?"

I told him about Agnes Stockwell giving it to him, that it was old, that it had belonged to her son, Brett.

"Jumped off Promise Falls," Barry said. "I remember that." He reached into the bag with one hand and worked out his chocolate dip doughnut. "So this was Derek's computer in Adam's room, then."

"Yeah. They both tinkered around with old computers."

"Well, I'll keep that in mind, Jim. It might be important and it might not be—"

"There was a book on the computer. A novel. Brett Stockwell was a writer."

"That's great, Jim," he said between bites. "You mind prying that little cap back on the coffee for me? I can't do it while I'm driving."

I peeled back the lid and gently put the cup back in the holder. It was filled right to the top and a sharp turn would see it spilling all over the place.

"The book was virtually identical to *A Missing Part,*" I said.

"*A Missing* who?"

"You don't know that book? By Conrad Chase?"

"What the fuck did you call it?"

"*A Missing Part.* It's a novel."

"Guess I missed that one. If it isn't written by Tom Clancy or Clive Cussler, I don't know about it," Barry said.

"What I'm trying to tell you, Barry, is that a book supposedly written by Conrad Chase was on that dead kid's computer, two years before the book came out."

Barry was struggling to get the coffee to his lips without spilling it. Once he got it there, he said, "Shit, that's fucking hot."

"You don't find this interesting?" I asked him. "You're not the least bit curious?"

"I don't know, Jim. I guess what I find most curious is that Derek's your source for all this."

I must have looked puzzled when he said that. "What are you getting at?"

"I'm just saying, he might have some of his information wrong. But thanks for telling me about this, and I'll keep it in mind."

I could see my truck and trailer up ahead. Derek had already put the lawn tractor back on the trailer and was sitting in the cab of the truck.

"All right then, fine," I said. "I was just trying to help. If you don't want me telling you stuff that might turn out to be important, that's fine. If you don't want to solve this, that's your business."

"Oh, I want to solve this," Barry said. "And you want to know something? I've got a feeling there's going to be a break in this case very soon."

That surprised me. "Seriously?"

He pulled the car over to the curb near my truck, stopped, and looked at me. "I think we might have an arrest any time now."

You'd have thought, if he was close to solving this, he would have looked happier about it.

I didn't bother to watch him drive off as I got into the truck. "Sorry I took so long," I said to Derek, who'd finished up and was waiting for me to return. I noticed some tears had made tracks through the dust and debris that was stuck to Derek's face.

"Hey man, you okay?" I noticed his cell phone was in his hand.

He shook his head, not wanting to talk.

"Come on, what is it?"

Derek sniffed, said, "Penny called me."

"Okay. What's going on?"

Another sniff. "Nothing."

"Come on," I said, reaching over and patting his knee. "We're all in this together."

"She just . . . she said that since she'd got me on the phone, it must not have happened yet."

"What?" I asked. "What hasn't happened yet?"

Derek wiped his nose on the back of his hand. Without looking at me, he said, "I just want you to know that no matter what anyone says, I'm a good kid."

I didn't like the sound of that at all.

TWENTY

As we neared our house, I spotted a familiar car parked on the shoulder at the end of our lane. It was a silver Audi TT. Great. Just what I needed to make this a perfect day. More Conrad.

Once I put my blinker on, the Audi's driver-side door opened and Illeana got out. She was dressed in white slacks and a top, and she seemed to shimmer in the late-afternoon sunlight.

"Isn't that Mrs. Chase?" Derek asked.

"Yeah," I said.

"What's she want?"

"Hard to say."

As I pulled into the drive, I put down the window and Illeana approached. "Jim," she said, then peered around me to Derek and said, "Hi, Derek." He barely nodded.

"Hello, Illeana," I said. "You been waiting for us?"

"For you," she said. "Do you have a minute?"

"You want to come on down to the house?"

"No, we can talk here," she said. "I don't want to be a bother."

Given what time it was, Ellen probably wasn't home from work yet. I asked Derek to scoot behind the wheel and take the truck in.

Illeana was rubbing her right wrist, almost unaware she was doing it.

"Have you hurt yourself?" I asked.

"Oh," she said, glancing down at her hands. "I'm getting used to this shifter. Conrad wanted to get one of these stick things and I'm still getting the hang of it."

"Well," I said, looking at the new car, "we all have our problems."

"About the other day," she said. "I'm sorry how things went. We kind of left in a hurry. After you and Conrad had your little disagreement."

I shrugged. What was there to say? Especially to Illeana.

"If I hadn't heard the tail end of what you were talking about," she said, "I'm not sure he would have told me what got him so agitated."

I didn't want to talk to her. I was talked out. It had been a draining day. A funeral, a ride with Barry, my son in tears fearing I had no idea what. "So he filled you in on our discussion," I said.

"He did." She leaned up against the Audi. "I think you were out of line, Jim."

"Illeana, I'm not sure I should be getting into this with you."

"You accused him of something. Of plagiarism. Of stealing the work of someone else. A student."

"All I did was ask him to explain something for me."

"What makes you think he answers to you?" She managed to ask the question in a way that still sounded very polite.

"If there was a simple explanation, I don't know why he didn't just offer it."

"You clearly caught him off guard," Illeana said. "You blindsided him. You didn't even give him a chance to explain."

I didn't say anything. I figured if she had something to say, she'd say it.

"Conrad didn't want to discuss this with me, said it was nothing, that he didn't want to trouble me, but he did say that this student, this Brett Stockwell, was an extraordinary young man," she said. "Absolutely brilliant."

"So everyone says."

"He'd never had a kid like him. A sensitive young man, whose insights were that of a much older person."

I waited.

"But he was not brilliant enough to have written *A Missing Part*," she said. "A boy like him, smart as he was, wasn't capable of that."

"Whatever you say, Illeana," I said. I was about to say that it was in Barry's hands now, but didn't. Barry had seemed strangely uninterested in what I'd had to tell him, as though he'd already made his mind up about something and didn't need the story about the missing computer clouding his vision.

"What happened was, Conrad had already written that book," Illeana said.

"He'd finished it about three years before it was published, but he hadn't shown it to anyone. He kept tinkering with it, rewriting it, but he just wasn't sure whether it worked or not. He wanted an opinion on it, so he gave it to Brett to read. On a disc, not a printed-out version. That explains why it was on the boy's computer."

I moved my tongue around the insides of my cheeks, thinking about it. "This is what Conrad told you," I said.

Illeana nodded confidently.

"So before Conrad gave it to a colleague, or a literary agent, or some other published author, he decided to give it to one of his students," I said.

"Exactly," Illeana said.

"Well," I said. "So it's as simple as that."

"Simple as that," she said, smiling, showing off her perfect teeth.

I said, "Well, there are clearly sides to Conrad I'd never have guessed. A professor of his experience and reputation, and he gives the book to a kid to read."

"I think what he was looking for was an honest, unvarnished opinion," she said, still smiling, like she thought I'd buy it. I think she'd bought it herself. Maybe she had to believe it. The alternative would be unthinkable. "I know Conrad comes across sometimes as a bit full of himself, but he's no different from anyone else. Once you've created something, there's a certain amount of fear, handing it over to someone else to be judged. He wanted to take a smaller step before giving it to anyone in the publishing industry."

"I see."

"So I'm here to ask you a small favor. I understood from what Conrad revealed to me about your conversation that there exists a copy of this book, presumably on a disc? I can understand how you might have reached a conclusion that might reflect negatively on Conrad, and if someone as insightful as yourself could do that, others might as well. So I'd be grateful if you could give that disc to me to prevent any further misunderstandings."

Not a bad speech for someone who had taken her top off in, among other things, *Scream Fever.*

I said, "You should have stayed in Hollywood, Illeana. That was a terrific performance. You learned your lines well, delivered them absolutely convincingly. Did Conrad write them out for you?"

She didn't flinch. "Conrad doesn't even know that I'm here." The way she said it, I was inclined to believe her. "You're only going to make a fool of yourself if you pursue this, suggest somehow that my husband didn't write *A Missing Part*. Because his new novel is going to blow people away. It's even more brilliant than his first book. There'll be no question as to his talents and abilities. Not that there are now, except from you, Jim."

"I wish him good luck with it," I said.

She smiled. "You really do have it in for him, don't you? Why don't you grow the fuck up?" This didn't sound like the college president's wife talking. "Where I come from, people fall into each other's beds all the time and they get over it. Bruce Willis, he goes on trips with Demi and Ashton."

"I bet that's fun," I said. "Maybe they'd let you go with them sometime."

For the first time, she looked wounded. "What have I ever done to hurt you, Jim? We hardly even know each other."

And for the first time, I thought maybe I'd gone too far. "You're right, Illeana. Any quarrels I might have are with Conrad, not you. But I'm not going to give you the disc."

She nodded, as though she accepted that my decision was final. But she still had more to say. "Conrad and Ellen had their thing a very long time ago. We're all adults." She came off the car and stood less than a foot away from me. Even on a day like this, you could feel the heat her body threw off. "A bigger man might find it in his heart to let bygones be bygones, to forgive and move on."

I started to say something but stopped. I had no comeback for that, maybe because I recognized the truth in it.

Illeana turned away, opened the door to the Audi. "Nice talking to you, Jim," she said, then slid into the car and put it into first, kicking gravel up against my jeans as she turned the car around and sped off. She went through the gears just fine, didn't stall it once.

Ellen showed up not long after that, and around six we threw some burgers onto the grill. After Derek had eaten and gone up to his room, I filled her in on my encounters with Barry and Illeana. I made my visit from Barry sound like we'd just bumped into each other, since I didn't want to tell Ellen that he wanted to know about me and Donna Langley. While it was true that nothing had happened between me and Donna, I didn't want to reveal how close we'd come.

But I told her that Colin McKindrick, while dead, was not a suspect in the Langleys' murders. I also told her that I had told Barry about the book on Brett Stockwell's missing computer, and whose work it bore a remarkable resemblance to.

Ellen stared at me a moment before

saying, "And what was his reaction to that?"

"He didn't give a rat's ass," I told her.

"Really?"

"Really. It was like he already had a better lead to follow."

And then I told her about Illeana's visit, and her explanation on Conrad's behalf. That he had given an early draft of the book to Brett for feedback.

She thought about that for a moment. "I suppose it's possible," she said.

"You think?" I said. "Everything you've ever told me about him suggests that he's always viewed even the smart kids with contempt. To him, they're still a bunch of babies."

"Yes, but . . ."

"But what?"

"Maybe—"

There was a sharp knock at the front door that made us both jump. We hadn't heard a car come down the lane, but we had the house shut up tight and the air-conditioning on.

We both got up from the table, went from the kitchen and through the living room to the front door. Through the sheer curtain at the window I could make out Barry, and it looked as though he was holding something in his hand.

I opened the door. Standing behind Barry were three other police officers, all wearing those surgical-type gloves. "What is it, Barry? What the hell is going on?"

He held up the paper. "It's a warrant, Jim. To search the house."

"What?" said Ellen. "What are you talking about?"

"Get Derek," Barry said, his voice no-nonsense.

"What do you want Derek for?" I asked.

"Jim, please, don't make this any harder than it has to be," Barry said. "Just call him down here."

I hesitated a moment, then shouted, so that I could be heard upstairs: "Derek!"

"What?" Muffled, from behind his bedroom door a flight up.

"Down here! Now!"

A moment later, his footsteps thundering down the stairs. When he got to the bottom, he met the cops, heading up. "Oh shit," he said, with less surprise than I might have expected.

I thought of the phone call he'd received from Penny. Maybe now it was happening.

"Kitchen," Barry said, leading the rest of us out of the living room. Once we were in the kitchen, no one sat down.

"Derek," Barry said, "I wonder if you'd like to change your story any about what happened on Friday night."

He looked baffled, but there was something in his eyes, the way they danced.

"No," he said. "Nothing."

"So you want to stick with what you told us. That you left the Langleys about eight, wandered about, went to see Penny, came back here around nine-thirty."

"Yeah," Derek said hesitantly. "Although I didn't really see her, just talked on the phone, walked around some on my own."

Then Barry turned to me. "How

about you? You want to stick with what you told me? About hearing Derek come in around that time, before ten?"

"Barry," I said, "why don't you just tell us what the hell's going on here."

Upstairs, we could hear things getting tossed about. It sounded like it was all happening in Derek's room.

"I want to know if anyone wants to rethink what happened that night," Barry said.

"I'm pretty sure that's what happened," Derek said, but his voice lacked conviction.

"Then maybe you can explain something to me," Barry said to Derek.

"What?"

"You talked to your girlfriend, Penelope Tucker, a couple of times that night on the phone."

"Penny, yeah," he said. "Sure, I talk to her all the time. Well, until, like, lately. Her parents are being all weird."

"You can blame me for that," Barry said. "I was speaking to them early Sunday. I advised them not to allow any communication between you and their daughter."

"That's fucking great. So you're the reason—"

"Derek," I cautioned, trying to stay calm, "just take it easy."

"Take it easy?" To Barry, he said, "You had no right to do that. Why did you have to—"

"Derek," Barry said, getting close to him, almost in his face, "tell me about the calls you made to Penny that night."

"I don't know. I called her a couple of times, I guess."

"From your cell?"

"Sure."

"Always from your cell?"

It was like something clicked in Derek's brain at that point. Some sort of realization dawned on him. "I think," he said.

"Penny says you called her from the Langley house."

"Uh, sure, maybe. I mean, I was there, earlier."

"No," Barry said. "Later."

"She must be wrong," Derek said.

"Derek," Ellen said, "what's going on here?"

Upstairs, more rummaging.

"If you don't mind," Barry said to my wife, as politely as the circumstances allowed, "I'd like to ask the questions for the moment. Derek, I don't think she's wrong. The phone, in the basement of the Langley house, it's one of those phones that keeps a record of numbers dialed out. Saves the police a lot of time asking the phone company to give us a list of calls."

This didn't sound good.

"And what's interesting is, just before ten, that phone was used to call Penny Tucker. How do you explain that? A couple of hours after you supposedly left, nearly an hour and a half after the Langleys had left, someone makes a call from inside that house to your girl-friend. And you know what she told me? She told me she was talking to you."

Derek said nothing.

"And Albert Langley, he phoned his secretary on his cell just around that time, said they were nearly home. So guess what? It looks like you were in that house, after the Langleys left, and very likely still in that house when they got home."

Derek shook his head.

I said, "Barry, what you're suggesting here, this is crazy. You know me, you know Derek. I mean, you know him well enough to know that he wouldn't, that he couldn't . . ."

"Maybe," Derek said, his voice weak, "maybe the phone was wrong or something."

"You think Penny's phone was wrong, too? Because it shows a call coming in at the exact same time as the Langley phone shows a call going out. She said your cell was breaking up, so you had to use a land line."

"You don't understand," Derek said. "Okay, maybe I was there but—"

"Derek," I said, "don't say anything."

"What do you mean," Ellen snapped at me, "telling him not to say anything? He didn't have anything to do with this!"

"That's right," he said, his eyes beginning to water. "I didn't. I swear."

"But you were in the house, weren't you, Derek?" Barry said, his voice taking a more conciliatory tone. "It started out innocently enough, am I right? Go ahead and tell us. Penny filled me in a bit."

"It was just, it was . . ." A look of hopelessness came over his face. "Okay, the thing was, I had this idea, because the Langleys were going to be away for a week, if the house was empty, it would be this great spot for me and Penny, you know, a place for us . . ."

"Oh for Christ's sake," Ellen said. "What the hell were you thinking? What did you do? Did Adam give you a key?"

The tears were coming down his face now. "We just wanted a place we could go. When I was leaving, I said goodbye to Adam, I made like I was going out the back door, but then I snuck downstairs and hid in the crawlspace until they were gone. That's all. And after they left, I came out, and I called Penny a couple of times, but she had been grounded. She was in trouble with her dad because she dented their car, you know? That's all."

"Okay," Barry said, almost friendly,

like he understood. "I can see all that. It sort of makes sense. So that's where you were the whole time, hiding in the basement?"

"That's right."

"You weren't anyplace else in the house?"

"Well, I wandered through. The kitchen and stuff. And I was in Adam's room before they went away."

"Anyplace else?" Barry persisted.

Derek shook his head in frustration. "No!"

Barry nodded, then, almost offhand-edly, pointed to Derek's left ear and said, "Did you used to have a stud or an earring there? I can see the little hole."

Derek held his ear briefly between his thumb and forefinger, just as he had in the truck a few days earlier when I'd noticed the peace sign stud he used to wear was gone.

"I don't know what happened to it," he said.

"Okay," said Barry, again adopting a softer tone, "but then, when the Lang-leys came home, unexpectedly, be-

cause Mrs. Langley got sick, they must
have been pretty pissed to find you in
the house. More than pissed, I'll bet.
Pretty goddamn furious, is my guess.
And then something happened, I can
totally see how a situation like that
could spiral out of control. Did Mr.
Langley threaten you, come at you or
something? He had a bit of a temper,
am I right?"

"No," Derek said. "No."

"It'd be pretty embarrassing, getting
caught hiding out in your best friend's
house. They must have felt pretty betrayed, Mr. and Mrs. Langley. Maybe
even Adam. Or was Adam in on the
idea? Did he know what you were going to do?"

"No, Jesus, no, he didn't know."

"So he must have felt pretty pissed,
too," Barry surmised. "You didn't just
go behind his parents' backs, you went
behind his, too."

"Okay! Fuck! I know!" Derek said, his
cheeks flushed. "It was a stupid, shitty
thing to do. I'm really, really sorry."

You dumb kid, I was thinking, *you
dumbass kid.*

But I said, to Barry, "There, you see? He did a stupid thing, and he's admitted it, but that's where it ends."

"No," said Barry, still looking at Derek, ignoring me, "there's more, right? They came home, found you, and you panicked. You had access to a gun, maybe a gun that was in the house—"

"No!" Derek shouted. "No! I didn't do anything! Someone else did it! Not me!"

"Then who was it, Derek?" Barry said. "You know who it was?"

"No!"

"Barry," I said, "can't you see he's upset? Ease off a little."

He turned and looked at me. "I don't like this any more than you do, Jim."

Derek was almost sobbing now and Ellen had taken him into her arms. "Look what you've done," she said to Barry.

The detective ignored her. "Okay, Derek, you say you didn't do it, but we've got you placed at the house right around the time the whole thing went down. But you didn't see who did it. You can't have it both ways."

"I never saw anybody," he said. "I was hiding."

Barry was shaking his head sadly when one of the tech guys who'd been upstairs appeared in the kitchen. He was using just a finger and a thumb to hold a shoe. One of Derek's many pairs of sneakers.

"Detective Duckworth," the cop said, and turned the shoe around, displaying the sole. He pointed to a dark smudge near the heel. "Bingo," he said.

Barry leaned in for a closer look. "You sure it's blood?" he asked.

"Pretty sure," said the cop. "And once we get a DNA test done, we'll know a hell of a lot more."

Neither Ellen nor I seemed to be breathing at that moment. But Derek was sobbing, muttering under his breath, "No, no, no . . ."

"Barry," I said.

Then Derek said, "I didn't see any-thing. But I heard it! I heard them come in! I heard the shots! I heard all of them die! I swear to God!"

Barry appeared unmoved.

He said, "Derek Cutter, I'm arresting

you for the murders of Albert Langley, Donna Langley, and Adam Langley. You—"

"Barry, Jesus," I said. "He admits he was there. Listen to him for Christ's—"

"Jim, please," Barry said, holding up his hand. He continued. "You have the right to remain silent. Anything you say can and will be used against you in a court of law. You have the right to speak to an attorney, and you can have that attorney present during any questioning. If you can't afford a lawyer, one will be provided for you."

He took a set of handcuffs from his belt, turned our son around, and cuffed him.

It seemed to me that our world, at that moment, more or less ended.

TWENTY-ONE

Derek was arraigned the following morning.

Ellen and I had been up all night, first just dealing with the shock of his arrest, then scrambling to find our son legal representation. Under other circumstances, of course, we would have gone straight to Albert Langley. We knew him, we trusted his reputation, we knew he knew his stuff.

Not exactly an option at the moment.

Nor did we feel we could call on anyone else in Langley's firm. Who would want to defend the person charged with the murder of a colleague and his family? And besides, even if someone Langley had worked with agreed to represent Derek, we didn't want to take any chances there might be underlying animosity. So Ellen put in a call to some people she knew from Thackeray, asking for recommendations, and came up with the name Natalie Bondurant. Eight years working as a criminal defense lawyer in Promise Falls, and according to at least one person Ellen talked to, a "smart cookie." We put in a call to her service sometime around nine, and she called us back before ten.

I laid it out for her over the phone, my voice shaking at times. Then she had a number of questions for me, which I tried to answer as succinctly as possible. Her questions were clear and direct. She managed to cut through the emotions that were overwhelming us, got us to focus on the facts, to try as best we could to view the situation rationally, even if it was impossible for us to see it very objectively.

"So the police have no weapon," she said. "That's a problem for them. Unless they find it, in which case that could change things."

"They won't find it," I said. "He didn't do it."

Natalie Bondurant chose not to argue.

"It weakens their case. Your son had opportunity, he was there, that's bad, but he has no record of violence—"

"He was in a bit of trouble once. He went joyriding with a friend, who'd taken his dad's car without permission, and the car got smashed up. Another time, he was caught with some friends playing on the roof of the school and—"

"I wouldn't worry too much about those things. They're a far cry from killing three people in cold blood. But I think there's more to this than meets the eye. The police are saying your son killed the Langleys because they discovered he'd hidden out in their house, but I don't know. That doesn't strike me as much of a motive. I'm worried they haven't played all their cards yet. We'll have to see. I'm going to want to talk to this Penny Tucker, find out exactly what Derek's state of mind was when he talked to her on the phone from the house. I'll have a chance to speak with him tomorrow morning before he goes before the judge, but I don't think you should expect he's going to get bail. He's a suspect in a triple homicide. The state's case may seem weak, but until we knock it down, I don't think he's going to be allowed out."

Ellen, on the bedroom extension, said, "What's going to happen to him? In jail? Is he going to be safe there?"

"I'll talk to some people. Given the nature of the charges, I think it's more likely he'll be put in a separate cell, rather than with the general population."

I knew Ellen was thinking what I was thinking. Our seventeen-year-old boy sharing a cell with grown men being held for God knows what. I didn't want to think about it, but all I could do was think about it.

"There's going to be a lot of media attention, too," Natalie warned us.

"What do you mean?" Ellen asked.

"An arrest in a case this big, it'll be a mini-circus outside the court. All the Albany media will be here. Probably a contingent from New York, as well. It's going to be bad."

"Oh God," Ellen said.

"You have cell phones?" We gave her the numbers. "Because if I need to get in touch, I'll call one of those. Your house phone, you're going to reach a point where you're not going to want to answer it. You may want to unplug it altogether. Media, crank calls, threats, the whole gamut. Don't watch the news. The cops still have someone on the Langley house, it's still a crime scene, they may keep the media from your door. I'll talk to Barry and see if that's possible."

Barry. Like he was going to do us any favors.

As though reading my mind through the phone line, Natalie said, "He's an okay guy. I'll see what I can do. Also, there's the matter of money. I don't come cheap." She outlined her fees. "It could go on for a while."

Ellen, who looked after the finances in our house, said, "Okay. We've got some IRAs we could cash in, but not that much." I could feel her desperation and hopelessness coming through the line from our upstairs bedroom. "I'll start looking into that tomorrow."

"Okay," said Natalie. "We'll talk then."

* * *

Natalie Bondurant was right. Derek didn't get bail. She gave it her best shot, said Derek had no prior charges or convictions, came from a good home, was not a flight risk, but the judge would have none of it. He acceded to the prosecution's request that Derek be held without bail. He was charged, said prosecutor Dwayne Hillman with much fanfare, in the most horrific murder case in the history of Promise Falls. Surely, if ever there was a case where bail should be denied, this was it.

In court, Ellen wept. I did my best to be stoic.

Derek, standing next to Natalie in the high-ceilinged prestigious courtroom, seemed smaller, almost childlike compared to the day before. In beltless jeans and a T-shirt, his hair an oily mess, he stared down at the floor, his shoulders hunched forward, as though he'd caved in on himself. If this was how he looked after only a few hours in jail, how would he look after a week or, God forbid, after—

I couldn't let my mind go there.

He tried to give us a small wave, with his wrists cuffed together in front of him, as he was led to a door near the front of the courtroom.

"Derek . . ." Ellen said. "Derek . . ."

Neither Ellen nor I had slept, and we looked it. Ellen had aged ten years since Friday, before any of this madness had begun. And I was running on empty.

Natalie met us in the courthouse hallway. It was our first face-to-face meeting. She was black, mid to late thirties, tall, maybe six feet, short black hair, dressed in a conservative blue suit. Her solemn expression gave us no reason for optimism.

"Okay," she said. "There was no way they were going to let him post bond, no matter what the amount was. No surprise there. They've got him in a cell of his own so he's away from the other prisoners most of the time."

I looked at Ellen. She was dying inside.

"We don't have anything back yet on the blood on your son's shoe, but we're assuming it's going to be Adam Langley's. Your son admits he had to step over him to get out of the house, and must have stepped in some blood. He left a small trail of it, heading in the direction of your house. They've also taken a DNA sample from Derek, which isn't exactly surprising."

She gave us a more detailed account of Derek's version of the events. How he'd hid out in the Langley home in the hopes that he and Penny could rendezvous there all week. How Derek was trapped inside the house when the Langleys returned unexpectedly, how he hid in the basement, how not long after that someone else came to the house and shot Albert and Donna Langley, and then Adam as he tried to escape by way of the back door.

Derek told his lawyer that someone came down to the basement while he hid behind a couch, holding his breath, fearing for his life. Derek slipped out once he was confident the killer or killers were gone.

"I can't believe he kept all this to himself," Ellen said.

"He's a teenager," Natalie said.

"Scared of whoever murdered the Langleys, maybe even more scared of you two, and the trouble he'd get into by admitting he was in the house, how he came to be there. He said you'd told him"—she was looking at me now— "that after the incident at the school, when he was jumping from roof to roof, that the next time he did something dumb, you'd throw him out on his ass."

I remembered that.

"Still," said Ellen, "for something like this, he should have known he could come to us."

Natalie paused, then said, "There's something else that might be a problem." Neither Ellen nor I said anything. We weren't up for even more bad news. "The police are looking at links between the Langley killings and two others in the Promise Falls area in recent weeks."

"How?" Ellen asked. "What do you mean?"

"The police say the gun used to kill the Langleys is the same one that was used to kill a man named Edgar Winsome out back of the Trenton bar, nearly a month ago, and another man, Peter Knight, about a week before that."

"I don't know either of those people," I said. I did have a vague recollection, however, of Barry Duckworth mentioning these cases to me on Sunday.

"But you said the police don't have the gun," Ellen said. "How can they know the same gun was used?"

"You're right, they don't have the weapon," Natalie Bondurant said. "But they have the bullets. And the ones taken from the Langleys match these other two cases. Do you know of any connection between your son and these two men?"

"Nothing," I said, at almost the same moment Ellen did. "They want to blame those murders on Derek, too?"

"They're not saying that. But the cases are linked by the ballistics reports. It's a part of the investigation and you need to be aware of it. I want to keep you informed. That's the way I do things." She must have judged, by the looks on our faces, that we needed a pep talk. "Look," she said. "The whole rah-rah thing is not my specialty. I'm not going to tell you there's nothing to worry about. There is. But the case against your son is far from perfect. It has holes, and I think Barry knows it. The motive, as it's been laid out so far, is weak. And as far as how you're bearing up, you have to know that this is the worst time. You're still in shock. Your world feels as though it's falling apart. But hold it together. Your son needs you. And believe it or not, there's actually some good news."

Ellen and I both blinked. "What?" I asked.

"Well, if we accept Derek's story as gospel, that he was in the house at the time of the murders, that he actually heard these executions take place, and that he slipped out of the house without being seen by the perpetrator or perpetrators, the good news is, your son is alive."

Ellen and I exchanged looks and held each other. I'm sure neither of us had looked at it that way yet, that Derek was fortunate not to have ended up like the Langleys. I said, "And *do* you accept Derek's story?"

Natalie Bondurant waited a moment, looked me in the eye, and said, "I was going to say it doesn't matter. My clients don't have to be innocent for me to defend them. But I think Derek's giving it to me straight."

"Shouldn't Derek be telling all this to Barry?" I said. "What he heard? I mean, maybe Derek heard something, anything, that might help Barry find out who really did this. Because there's still someone out there, someone who killed the Langleys."

"Barry's aware of all of this," Natalie said. "But right now he figures he's nailed this one." She paused. "Derek did say he heard one thing."

"What?" Ellen asked.

" 'Shame,' " Natalie said. "He heard a man say 'shame.' "

Ellen and I looked at each other, not knowing what to make of that.

I reached into my pocket for something I'd brought along with me from home. I handed the disc, the one Derek had used to make a copy of *A Missing*

Part, or as Brett Stockwell had called it, *Nicholas Dickless,* to Natalie Bondurant.

"What's this?" she asked, Ellen watching as I placed the disc in her hand.

"Just hang on to it for me," I said. "For safekeeping."

TWENTY-TWO

I asked Natalie Bondurant whether she could join us for a coffee to talk about things, but she had another pressing court appearance. So I suggested to Ellen we hit a diner a block down from the courthouse for something to eat. We'd not had breakfast. It was nearly noon, and as bad as I felt, emotionally and physically, I was hungry.

"I can't eat," Ellen said.

"I feel the same," I said. "But we need to keep our strength up if we're going to help Derek."

But I abandoned the plan when we came out of the building and found half a dozen photographers and three camera crews waiting for us. They shouted their questions all at once, so they became a jumble of "Did we believe our son was innocent why would he do this was a guilty plea forthcoming." I held on to Ellen's arm and kept us moving forward, looking straight ahead, not responding to anything anyone asked us.

Not even "How does it feel to have a son who's a murderer?"

I felt Ellen stiffen, and thought maybe she was going to stop and answer that, but I whispered to her, "Come on."

We got to her Mazda, and once we were closeted inside, the photographers swarmed the car. They had the good sense to step out of the way as I eased it forward. Try not to run anyone down, I told myself. We had enough on our plate without adding a vehicular manslaughter charge. And engaging the services of a lawyer for just one case was likely to bankrupt us, not that financial worries were our primary concern at the moment.

Once we were away from the courthouse and back on the road out of town to our place, I thought we'd escaped them. But as our lane came into view, we could also see a couple of TV news vans and some other cars parked along the shoulder.

"Motherfuckers," I said.

I hit the blinker and turned, slowly, into our lane, edging past more people shouting out questions to us. There was still yellow tape around the Langley property, and once we passed the cop who was babysitting the house, he got out of his cruiser and stood in the path of the reporters, preventing them from getting any closer to our home.

We'd bring him some lemonade later.

Once home, Ellen put on some coffee and took out some bread slices and peanut butter. As she began to spread the peanut butter onto the bread, she stopped and began to sob. Loud, wracking sobs that shook her entire body.

I took her in my arms, held on to her, thought if I held her tighter the shaking and the sobbing would stop. And I was right. Except it took half an hour.

Ellen stepped off the deck, where we'd both sat down for a few minutes, and walked out onto our gravel drive, near the shed. From there, you could see past the Langley home and get a pretty good view of the highway.

"It looks like they finally gave up," she said, coming back onto the deck. "They're gone. The reporters are gone."

I was still in my chair, wondering if I had the energy to get up. We'd been home a couple of hours. Although the coast looked clear, I suspected a few hangers-on might be camped just down the road a ways, waiting to see if we'd show ourselves.

"We don't have anywhere to go right now," I said. "Let's not reward any who might still be hiding."

Ellen sat down, took a long breath, and looked at me. "I want to tell you something," she said.

"Okay," I said slowly.

"I couldn't do this without you. There's no way I could get through something like this if I didn't have you by my side."

It seemed dumb to say thank you. And I could have thrown the same kind of comment back at her, but given the

timing, it might not have seemed genuine. So I nodded.

"I know, sometimes, I accuse you of
not getting over it," she said. "That it's
been ten years. That it's time you for-
gave me for the mistake I made, time
you buried the hatchet with Conrad.
But the truth of the matter is, I still
haven't forgiven myself. I wasn't thinking about anyone but me when I did
what I did. I wasn't thinking about you,
or Derek. Not about us, as a family. And
there's not a day goes by when I don't
think about what I nearly threw away,
and how lucky I am that you stayed by
me, even though I wasn't worthy."

"Ellen."

"When something as terrible as
this—this thing with Derek—happens, I
think, how would I ever be able to handle all of this on my own? I wouldn't be
able to. You're my rock, Jim. You're my
rock. And I nearly let you slip out of my
hands, right to the bottom of the
ocean. I love you, you know."

"I love you, too," I said.

"It's not the only mistake I've made,"

she said. "Maybe more than you have the capacity to forgive."

"Ellen, what—"

But she got up and went into the house. "I have stuff to do," she said. "Like figure out how we're going to pay for Derek's lawyer."

I wandered over to the shed.

I checked the gas levels in the lawn mowers and the tractor and the weed trimmer, oiled the hedge trimmer, which had been squeaking a bit last time we'd used it, cleaned out the truck, tidied the shed, stared at my stack of canvases and debated whether to cut them to shreds.

There were half a dozen properties that Derek and I would typically do this day of the week. I hadn't exactly had a chance to call anyone and tell them we wouldn't be making it. If they watched or listened to the news, they might be able to figure out we had more pressing matters than their overgrown lawns and dandelions.

My son was in jail. My son was in jail, charged with three murders.

I picked up the closest thing that was handy. A lawn edger, with a small semi-circular blade at the end of a three-foot-long handle. I held it in my hand, then swung it, like an ax, into the shed wall. It whipped through the air and lodged itself in the wood. I pried it free, swung again wildly, took a chip out of the wall, swung again, and this time when the blade hit the wall it snapped off and flew back, right at me, right for my face. I spun out of the way, just in time, figured if I'd been a millisecond slower, I'd have lost an eye.

I needed to get a grip. I needed to work. I needed to do something with all this pent-up anger.

I leaned up against the workbench, took in the tools and lawn mower parts scattered about. It was time to clean the place up.

There was a cutting blade on the bench, an older one that came from the housing under the John Deere lawn tractor. It was so badly battered it wasn't worth the effort to sharpen it, so

I took it with me for reference as I went back to the house, thinking I could look up the part online and order a new one.

I thought I'd find Ellen at the kitchen table reviewing bank statements and retirement forms, figuring out what we'd have to cash in to pay Natalie Bondurant, but instead she was standing at the living room window, by the bookcase, looking up the lane. Just staring.

I came up behind her, set the blade on top of a row of books, and said, "You okay?"

"Yeah," she said as I rested my hands on her shoulders. "I just . . . need some space."

I took my hands away and said, "Sure, okay." I could give her what she wanted, and get what I needed, at the same time. "You know what? I'm going to go to work," I said, then slipped out of the house and got into my truck.

I started with the Fleming house. Normally, our first stop on a Wednesday. Average-sized yard, not a lot of fiddly tidying around flower beds, but you had to be sure not to leave any grass clippings on the driveway or Ned Fleming would have a shit fit. There usually was no one home when we came in the morning, and there was no one here in the afternoon, which was fine. The fewer people I had to talk to, the better.

The job took a lot longer than usual, of course. And not just because there was only one of us to do the work.

As a team, Derek and I could knock off a place like the Flemings' in half an hour. One of us on the tractor doing the big, easy-to-reach areas, the other with the lawn mower doing the narrow spots. Then one of us would grab the weed whacker and trim up along the sides of the house and next to the driveway and along the sidewalk while the other got the blower and swept all the clippings to the street.

The gods, who'd already been fucking me over of late, decided to keep it up at the Flemings'. First, the belt that drives the three blades under the Deere slipped off, and it took me ten minutes of lying on my side to get it back onto the pulleys, and not without jamming my fingers in there twice.

Then, the weed whacker ran out of line, and when I had the sucker up-ended and the housing off to take out the old spool and put in a new spool, the little spring that sits under there fell out and disappeared into the uncut lawn. Lost another five minutes finding it.

If I'd had Derek with me, either one of us could have been dealing with these setbacks while the other kept on with the job.

The gods weren't finished. I was using the mower in the backyard when the blade caught the edge of a piece of sod Derek and I had laid in a couple of weeks earlier to fix up some dead patches. I thought the grass had stitched its way into its new home, but it came up like a bad rug off a bald guy. The mower chewed up the sod and sprayed it across the rest of the yard.

"Jesus Christ!" I shouted. Sweat was trickling down my forehead and into my eyes and stinging like all get-out.

I went back to the truck, opened the

passenger door, then the glove box, and found the crumpled flyer Derek had shoved in there a few days earlier. I dialed the number on it with my cell.

A woman answered. "Hello?"

"Is Stuart Yost there?" I asked. The kid who'd asked if we were hiring.

"May I ask who's calling?"

"It's about a job," I said.

"Oh!" she said, and shouted, "Stuart! Telephone! It's about a job!"

I waited twenty seconds or more, then heard an extension pick up. "Yeah?"

"Stuart?"

"Yeah?"

"This is Jim Cutter. You came up to our truck the other day, looking for work. We cut grass."

"Yeah?"

"If you're interested, I've got work." I paused. "My son's not able to help me at the moment. Ten bucks an hour."

"I guess," Stuart said.

"Great," I said. "You just aced the interview." I found out where he lived and said I'd pick him up at eight the following morning.

"Could you make it eight-thirty?" he asked. "I usually sleep till eight."

In the background, the woman who'd answered, presumably his mother, said sharply, "Stuart!"

He said, "Eight's okay."

We were in kind of a holding pattern for the next day. Ellen was going to see if she could get in to see Derek in jail, check in with Natalie Bondurant, deal with our financial situation, even make a couple of calls to Thackeray concerning the literary festival, even though Conrad had already indicated to her that she could take whatever time she needed to deal with the events of the past week. "I might as well have something else to take my mind off things, if only for a little while," she said.

I left the house about a quarter to eight, found Stuart Yost's place in a subdivision built sometime in the sixties, when developers, influenced by *The Jetsons,* thought carports with slanted roofs looked cutting edge. He wasn't out front when I got there, so I sat at the curb a moment, waiting for him to appear. When it got to be 8:05, I got out of the truck and was heading up the walk when he blew out the front door like there'd been an explosion inside the house.

"Sorry," he said, and got into the truck.

I laid it out for him. I'd take the tractor, he could do the hand-mowing and trimming.

"Can't I do the tractor?" he asked. "I like riding around on stuff."

"Maybe later," I said. I wanted an idea of how bright he was before I turned him loose on a piece of machinery that could lay waste to someone's garden in three seconds if you weren't careful. So far, I wasn't particularly hopeful.

We were on our second house of the morning, and I was doing loops in the backyard with the Deere when it occurred to me that I'd not caught any recent glimpses of Stuart with the mower or weed trimmer. He hadn't exactly distinguished himself at the first house, telling me when we got into the truck that he was getting a heat rash on the insides of his elbows.

I drove the tractor back around the house and into the front yard and still didn't see him anyplace, then noticed someone sitting in the truck.

Stuart was in the front seat, with the windows up. When I killed the Deere, I could hear that the truck was running. I walked over to Stuart's window and rapped on it lightly with my knuckle. His fingers were busy with a Game Boy or something, and I'd startled him.

He powered down the window and a blast of A/C came out. "Yeah?" he said.

"What are you doing?"

"I was just taking a break," he said.

I got out my wallet, peeled off a twenty and a ten, put the money into his hand, and said, "That's all your pay, severance included. You got a cell, or do you want to borrow mine so you can call your mom to pick you up?"

It would have been wrong to make generalizations about kids today, that they don't know how to put in a good day's work, that they think they're entitled to something for nothing. Derek certainly wasn't like that. He always kept pace with me, pulled his weight.

But Jesus Christ, kids today.

I must have muttered it under my breath a hundred times through the rest of that day as I handled the rest of my clients solo. By the time I got to the Blenheims, on Stonywood Drive, I thought I was going to plant myself facedown into the lush, green front yard.

Stonywood's a quaint old street in Promise Falls, and the Blenheim place is on a corner, situated across the street from a two-story century-old house with hedges so tall you can hardly see the first floor. If it were me, I'd cut them down to show the place off, but at least the place was well tended.

There was a gap in the hedge where the walk led up to the front porch, and I'd seen a man poke his head out from behind the bushes a couple of times, watching what I was up to. Maybe he'd spotted my name on the side of the truck parked at the curb out front of the Blenheim house, recognized it from the news. *There's the guy,* he was probably thinking, *whose kid whacked that family.*

Although I'd only caught a glimpse of him, I put him in his mid-thirties or so. Hair cut short, military-style, round head, thick neck, broad shoulders. About my height, maybe not quite as tall, but built, as they say, like a brick shit house. Probably played football in his younger days. Maybe he still did, for all I knew.

As I was finishing up with the Blenheim house, feeling a bit groggy and disoriented from the heat, I drove the lawn tractor around to the back of the trailer, where the ramp was already extended and in position. I was about to drive up it when something huge and red seemed to come out of nowhere, only inches away from me.

I swung my head around to see what it was, and I guess my arms, and the steering wheel, must have moved a bit with the rest of me. A shiny van, with four big letters on the side followed by two more: "TV." A local news crew. The van screeched to a halt, its entrance so jarring and dramatic that I allowed the tractor to veer a bit too far to the left, and the front wheel slipped over the edge of the metal ramp.

The tractor tipped about forty-five degrees and I lost my grip on the steering wheel. Maybe, if I hadn't been feeling so logy from lack of sleep, I'd have been ready. But I wasn't, and I tumbled off the machine and landed on the pavement. The tractor was still roaring, the right back wheel spinning in the air, looking for purchase, and then there was a man in a nicely tailored suit, shouting, "Oh fuck!" He'd come running out of the van and was attempting to grab the steering wheel, but the dumb shit ended up nudging the tractor further, so it fell right off. The housing that enclosed the blades landed on my leg, halfway between my knee and ankle.

"Jesus!" I shouted, and as I writhed I caught sight of my football player, looking out from between the hedges, a stunned expression on his face. "Help me out here!"

He bolted across the street and had to more or less step over me to get to the tractor. He got his left hand on the steering wheel and gripped the sheet metal of the rear fender and lifted.

The tractor might as well have been a toy to him, he lifted it so effortlessly. I crawled far enough away so that if the machine fell again, it wouldn't land on me.

The man gently let the tractor back down, half of it touching the pavement, the other half still on the ramp. He reached over and turned the key, and the tractor went silent. The guy in the suit, whom I now recognized as an on-air reporter for the local news, now had a young, long-haired man in jeans at his side. His driver and cameraman, I presumed.

"You okay?" the reporter asked.

"Fucking hell!" I said. "You just about cost me a leg there!"

"I was just trying to help," he said.

"That's what you were doing, when you drove up and scared the living shit out of me?" I shook my head and then looked at the man who'd lifted the mower off me. "Thanks," I said.

"Can you walk?" he asked. For a tough-looking guy, his voice was very quiet.

"I don't know yet," I said. He got on one side of me, the van driver on the other. My leg was sore, but it didn't feel as though anything was broken.

I let the two of them back off to see if I could stand unaided. I was okay. I bent down, pulled up the leg of my jeans, and while I had a bruise forming, the skin hadn't been broken.

"Hey, that's great," said the reporter. "Listen, we'd like to ask you a couple of questions about your son."

I said, "If you leave right now, maybe my first stop on the way home won't be to a lawyer to sue your fucking station's ass off for nearly putting me in the hospital."

The reporter glanced at his cameraman, then back at me and said, "Sorry. Maybe we can catch you later." He extended a business card to me between two fingers, but I didn't reach for it.

Then the two of them got back in the van and drove off.

"Assholes," said the football guy.

I extended a hand. "Jim Cutter," I said. "Thanks very much. Jesus, you've got arms like a bear."

"Drew," he said, taking my hand and giving it a firm squeeze. "Drew Lockus."

"Well, thanks, Drew."

Drew looked a bit sheepish. "I didn't mean to be spying on you there before."

"No problem."

"It must have looked funny, me peering at you from behind the bushes. It's just, I saw the name on the truck and wondered if you were related to that boy, the one that got charged." Drew spoke slowly, deliberately, like he was thinking everything out before he said it. "It was on the news."

I nodded. "I am," I said. "That's my son."

Drew let out a noiseless whistle. "That must be tough."

"He didn't do it," I said, wanting to make the point right away, whether Drew got around to asking or not.

"Sure," said Drew, nodding. "I'm sure he didn't. Cops, you know, they're always railroading people."

He sounded as though he was speaking from experience, but I had enough problems without inquiring about someone else's.

"Your tractor," he said, pointing. "It's still off the track here, if you want a hand."

I said I'd be grateful, and he got on one side and I on the other, and we got it back on the ramp. I could see muscles bulging under his shirtsleeves. When I lifted, putting weight on my leg, I could feel pain shoot through it.

"Shit," I said. "That smarts." I felt the need to explain why I was even out here, considering my circumstances. "It's been quite a day so far. My son, he normally helps me," I added. "We're a team."

"That's a nice tractor," Drew said. "I used to fix these."

"Really?" I said. "What kind of work do you do now?"

Drew shrugged. "I'm sort of between jobs." Then, as if he'd just remembered where he was, he nodded back at the house surrounded by the high hedges and said, "I look after my mom here at the moment. Big house for her to live all alone in."

I glanced over at it. "Beautiful house."

Drew nodded. "Well, if you're okay . . ."

I nodded, took a couple of breaths. I had a thought, then shut it down. Then it came back.

"You looking for work?" I asked.

He shrugged. "I don't know. Sort of. But not that much. Why?"

"I had someone else working for me today. Kind of a short-term thing. A kid. Didn't work out."

"Oh. I don't know," he said slowly. "I'd have to bounce it off my mom, see if she'd be okay with me being gone some through the day."

"Your call," I said. If Drew didn't want a job, no big deal. I was sure I could find someone else. There was some kind of unemployment office down at city hall. I could probably luck into someone there.

But I gave him one of my business

cards, wrote my cell phone number on the back. "If you're interested, try that number. We're not answering the house phone much these days."

"Hope your leg feels better," he said, his voice quiet, like he was afraid if he spoke too loud out here on the street, he'd wake his mother.

"Thanks again," I said, and got back in the truck. In the mirror, I saw him standing in the street, watching me drive away until I turned the corner, and then we lost sight of each other.

TWENTY-THREE

Any other day, it would have been time to pack it in and head home. Ellen called my cell and said she'd thrown a small chicken into the oven an hour ago, and dinner would probably be ready by the time I got back.

"I'm going to try to get one more job in," I said. I was only a few blocks from the Putnam house, which was a property of almost two acres, but I thought, cranking up the speed a bit on the Deere, I could finish it off before it started getting dark, even without help.

"Jim," Ellen said, "come home."

"Just set a plate aside for me," I said. "We need money now more than ever. I don't make a lot, but it's better than nothing. You figure out the finances,

how we're going to pay Natalie Bondurant?"

"Yes," Ellen said. She sounded de-
feated. "We're going to have to cash in
a few things."

"Sounds like I better keep cutting
grass," I said. "I'll be home when I'm
home."

"I'll see ya," she said tiredly.

I pulled up to the curb in front of the
Putnam home. A big, two-story affair,
double garage, a Porsche parked on
one side of the drive, a Lexus on the
other. Leonard Putnam was some
hotshot financial adviser, far as I knew,
and his wife was a much-respected
psychiatrist.

I rarely ran into either one of them.
The last time was probably when they
hired me to look after their property for
the season. I'd come out on a Saturday
to meet with them, summer before last.
I didn't need to see them if all I did was
cut their grass. I did the job—or Derek
and I did the job—and once a month a
check showed up in the mail. A hefty
one, too, given the size of their property.

But because I was running behind, and getting to the Putnam house at an hour when they were likely to be home, I wasn't surprised to see Leonard Putnam coming out the front door as I walked around to the back of the flatbed trailer to unload the Deere.

"Mr. Cutter," he said. Not really a friendly greeting. There was a tone to it that suggested an imminent scolding. He had silver hair and was dressed in a creamy yellow sweater and white slacks. He dressed rich, looked rich. If he got a grass stain on those pants, it'd never come out.

"Evening," I said.

"May I have a word?" he said.

This was different. Leonard Putnam wasn't the type to talk to the hired help. Maybe he was pissed I'd come so late in the day. The noise of the mower was going to interfere with his predinner cocktail.

"Sure," I said, walking up the drive. He met me halfway, by the back end of the Porsche.

"Mr. Cutter," he said, "I'm afraid

we're going to be going with someone else."

"Excuse me?" I said.

"Another lawn company."

"Is there a problem? If there's something you're unhappy with, I'm sure I can address your concerns. I wasn't aware that you or Dr. Putnam have been anything but satisfied."

"Oh no, nothing like that. You've always done a good job."

"My rate's competitive. Look around if you don't believe me," I said.

"It's not that, either, Mr. Cutter." He paused. "You see, Albert Langley, he was my lawyer."

I studied him a moment, then nodded slowly. "I see. And what does that have to do with whether I look after your yard or not?"

He almost laughed. "Is that a serious question, Mr. Cutter?"

"Yes," I said. "It is."

"I cannot, in good conscience, maintain our relationship, given what your son has done. My wife is very troubled, to think that he has been here, with you, week after week, that there were even times when she was home when you and your boy were here, that he could have had access to our house. God knows what could have happened. My wife is most distraught. Otherwise, she'd be out here with me to deliver this news. She also knew Donna Langley quite well, personally and professionally, in fact, although I'm certainly not at liberty to discuss what that involved. She's quite destroyed by this tragedy, as am I."

"My son is innocent," I said, feeling the hairs on the back of my neck standing up.

"Well, I certainly don't blame him for pleading not guilty," Leonard Putnam said. "That's how the game is played. Albert Langley knew that better than anyone, I suppose. I wouldn't have expected anything different, and that's not a reflection on you or your boy. I suppose, were I to somehow lose control of my impulses and commit an act of violence, I'd no doubt proclaim my innocence, too."

"I didn't say he was pleading not guilty. I said he was innocent."

Putnam half chuckled again. "Look at *me,* actually having a debate with *you* about this. It's quite extraordinary, really. We won't be needing you anymore, it's as simple as that. I'll send you a check to cover the entire month, however. I'm a reasonable person."

I wanted to kill him. But even more than that, I wanted to throw him to the ground and drag his white-panted ass across his lush green yard. Once I'd made a sufficient mess of him, maybe then I'd kill him.

But I didn't knock him down, or drag him across the yard, or grab him by the neck. I turned around and walked back to my truck, nearly blind with rage. Maybe that's why I didn't see Lance Garrick in time.

As I was rounding the back of the trailer, I caught a momentary glimpse of something down there, hiding behind it, but there wasn't time to react as this shadow leapt up and came at me.

I only had time to dodge slightly to the right, which meant the fist coming at me didn't connect squarely with my nose, but caught the side of my cheek.

Even though its path was slightly deflected, it still hurt like hell and kept me from seeing the other fist, coming a fraction of a second later and at the same rate of speed. That one caught me just under the ribs and completely took my breath away.

I collapsed to the pavement, clutching my side, writhing and moaning. I looked up at Randall Finley's driver, standing over me and grinning.

"Not fun to get sucker punched, is it?" Lance asked. "Who's laughing now, dickwad?"

I was gasping, still trying to get my breath.

Lance had knelt down, and I could feel his hot breath on my ear as he continued, "Tough break about your kid, huh, motherfucker? Guess he's got some of the same problems you got. Maybe, if they don't actually give him the chair, when he gets out in twenty years, the two of you can go to anger management classes together."

And then he spit in my ear.

From the pavement, the world at right angles, I watched him walk up the street, whistling, then get in a blue Mustang and drive off.

Driving home, feeling the pain in my gut more than the blow to my face, I phoned Natalie Bondurant. Not to get some sort of restraining order against Lance, but to ask her a question. I got her voicemail, so I left my question with her and asked her to call me when she had a chance.

Ellen met me at the door and said, "Hey, I'll just warm up your din—"

And then she saw my face. I told her what had happened. Not just my encounter with Lance, but my discussion with Leonard Putnam. I wasn't sure which made her angrier. Putnam, I think. She knew I had to take some of the blame for what had happened with Lance. I'd sucker punched him days earlier, and he'd returned the favor.

She got an ice pack, wrapped in a towel, for my face. I tried holding it there while I ate my dinner. It hurt to chew, but I was hungry enough to put up with the aggravation. Ellen was pouring me some coffee when there came a soft rapping on the kitchen door.

We looked at each other warily. At least we knew it wasn't Conrad. He'd have tried to walk straight in.

"Stay," I said to Ellen, and got up from the table. I pulled the curtain back an inch and saw Penny Tucker standing on the deck. I unlocked the door that was so rarely locked before, and opened it. "Penny. Come in."

She did. She was a pretty girl, petite, with slightly olive colored skin, indicating, I thought, a Mediterranean background. "Thanks," she said. "How's Derek?"

"Not so good," I said. "He's in jail. The judge wouldn't allow him to post bond."

"How did you get past the police?" Ellen asked.

I figured she'd snuck past, just like last time, but she said, "I talked to him. He let me come down."

Ellen and I exchanged glances. I said, "He's really there to protect a crime scene, not run interference for us."

"What can we do for you, Penny?" Ellen asked, her voice slightly icy. She hadn't forgotten, and neither had I, how our son had been treated by her parents the last time he'd gone to see her.

"Look," she said. "I'm not even supposed to be here, and my parents are going to kill me"—she paused a moment, maybe second-guessing her choice of word—"when they find out I've snuck out of the house."

"You should call them," I said, pointing to the phone. "They'll be worried sick about you."

"Derek, he must have told you, what happened when he came to my house."

"Yes," I said.

"I just felt awful about that. But the policeman, Mr. Duckworth?"

We nodded.

"He'd been to the house earlier that day, about the phone calls. He figured out Derek had phoned me from the Langleys' house, and then he came to see us, to see *me,* and, like, he made me tell him everything, because my parents were there, and they said I had to tell, so I told him he'd been in the house right before they all got killed." She was talking so quickly she was starting to run out of breath.

"It's okay, Penny," I said. "Just take your time."

"But he didn't do it!" she said.

"We know that," Ellen said. "We know Derek couldn't do that."

"The detective, he just thinks I'm covering up for Derek so he won't get in trouble, and my parents are all like, 'You better tell the truth or you'll be in trouble, too.' But I am telling the truth. Derek called me later, in the middle of the night, from your house, from the kitchen, right here, he was totally freaked out. He told me about hearing the shots and someone walking around and then having to step over Adam to get out and then I came over the next night, remember?"

"Yes," I said. When we heard noises in the night, at the back door, and called the police. "You told this to the police?"

She nodded. "Derek told me he wanted to tell you guys, but he was scared. He was scared about the killer finding out he was there, because he thought that might end up getting in the papers or on the news, you know? And he was worried about what you'd do if you found out about this plan he had, to use the house while the Langleys were away." She looked away, embarrassed. I could have told her stories about when Ellen and I were dating, to make her feel less mortified, but this didn't seem like the time. "I didn't want to have to tell Mr. Duckworth all this, not in front of my parents, but I figured, if he knew the truth, even if it was, like, totally embarrassing for me and Derek, he'd understand why Derek hadn't come forward, and he'd see that Derek didn't kill the Langleys."

"That's not how it's worked out," I said.

Penny looked frustrated enough to stomp her foot. "That policeman, he just won't listen."

That nearly brought a smile to my sore and wounded face. "Yeah, well, we know how you feel," I said.

"What if I talked to the judge?"

Penny said. "What if I told him I was with him after, that the things he told me, I could tell he didn't do it?"

"You can't talk to the judge, but you can talk to Derek's lawyer," I said. "She'll be more interested in hearing what you have to say in Derek's defense than Barry is. He thinks he has this thing all figured out."

"What if my parents won't let me talk to her?" Penny asked.

"They can't do that," Ellen said, then, looking at me, "Can they?"

"Why would your parents want to stop you?" I asked.

"They've never really approved of me going out with Derek anyway, you know?" she said.

"No," Ellen said, trying to keep her voice even. "We didn't know. Why would that be?"

"I guess they thought we were spending too much time together, that I wasn't paying attention to school, which is totally not true, because my marks are as good as they've ever—"

I held up a hand. "It's okay," I said. "I think most boys are viewed with suspicion by the parents of their girlfriends. It's been that way for a thousand years."

"But then, after the detective came to the house, they wouldn't even let me talk to him. Because he was, you know, a suspect."

"Penny," I said, "you should call your folks, tell them where you are. We can drive you home, or they can come and get you."

"I took my mom's car," she said. "It's parked on the side of the road, down a ways."

"Let me ask you something," I said, "before you go."

"Okay."

"Did Derek tell you about the computer he got from Agnes Stockwell, the one with the novel on it? That he and Adam had been reading?"

"Yeah," she said. "He said it was really weird."

"Did you read it?"

"No. I wasn't really interested, you know?"

"Did you tell anyone about the book,

that Derek and Adam had found it? Any of your own friends, your parents?"

She thought a moment. "I'm not sure. I mean, I've told them about Derek's hobby. My dad one time, he even got Derek to restart his computer, when it was all frozen? I thought that would make my dad like him better, but it didn't really last."

"So you're saying you might have told them?"

"Well, if I did, I sure didn't tell them what it was about."

"Sure," I said. "I understand. Okay. Thanks. It was good of you to come by. We'll tell Derek you were asking about him."

Penny nodded, sniffed, wiped a tear from her cheek, and said goodbye. As Ellen walked her to the door my cell phone went off.

"Yeah?" I said.

"Hey," a man's voice said. "It's Drew? Drew Lockus?"

It took me a moment. The man who'd pulled my tractor off me. "Yeah, Drew, how's it going?"

"Look," he said, "I talked it over with

my mom, and she said if I want to earn a few extra bucks cutting grass, it's okay with her, so yeah, if you still want me."

"Sure," I said. As long as I didn't have more clients cancel like the Putnams, I thought. "Why don't I pick you up out front of your place tomorrow morning, eight o'clock?"

"Okay," he said. He sounded more resigned than pleased by the prospect. "See you then."

I'd barely set the phone down on the counter when it rang again. I flipped it open. "Yeah?"

"Mr. Cutter, Natalie Bondurant, returning your call."

I took a second to collect my thoughts. "Thanks for calling. Hey, Derek's girlfriend, Penny Tucker, was just here. I think she's got things to say that could help Derek."

"She's already on my list. I'll set something up. As for your question, the one you left on my voicemail, the answer is yes."

My heart sank.

"Officially, yes, New York State has

the death penalty, but in 2004 the courts ruled it unconstitutional, so even if it's on the books, it's not being used."

"I see." Ever since Lance had raised the likelihood of my son facing the death penalty, I hadn't been able to put it out of my mind. But I'd not shared my thoughts with Ellen.

"So, on that score," Natalie said, "you can rest easy."

"What do you mean, 'on that score'? Is there something else?"

"The police found an earring. Very small, a peace sign."

"Go on."

"Did Derek lose one recently?"

"Yes. That's right."

Ellen was mouthing, "What?" I held up my hand to her.

"The police found one in the Langley house."

"Okay," I said, trying not to panic. "He's already admitted he was there. How does a found earring make things any worse?"

"First of all, it's not yet confirmed that it's his. They're doing DNA analysis on it."

"They can get that?" I asked. "Off an earring?"

"They're working on it."

"But I still don't understand. So what if they prove it's his? He's admitted he was in the house."

Natalie Bondurant paused. "It's where they found it in the house."

I felt my heart skip a beat. "Go on."

"In Donna and Albert Langley's bedroom. In the folds of the bed skirt. And Derek's fingerprints are on the bedroom dresser."

I felt numb.

Natalie said, "If the DNA test comes back and says that's Derek's earring, the prosecutor's going to wonder just how it got there. And before you know it, they're going to have a whole lot more interesting motive than what they've got now."

TWENTY-FOUR

What the hell does it mean?" Ellen asked when I'd filled her in on what Natalie Bondurant had said.

"I don't know."

"It doesn't make any sense. The earring probably isn't even his."

"It looked like his," I said.

"But what would it be doing in Albert and Donna's bedroom?" she asked. "Maybe Derek lost it someplace in the house, Donna found it and took it into her room, dropped it or misplaced it."

"It was right in with the sheets or something, the bed skirt," I said.

"The bed skirt?" Ellen said. "How's that possible? Someone must have put it there."

"I don't know," I said, and I could hear the sense of defeat in my voice.

What I kept wanting to do, instinctively, was go to the bottom of the stairs and call Derek down to offer up some sort of explanation. But we'd have to wait until we were next able to visit Derek and ask him questions, or his lawyer had more information for us.

"What if this DNA test proves it's Derek's?" Ellen asked. "What then?"

"Let's not get ahead of ourselves," I said.

"You know what they'll say?" Ellen said. "Barry? And that prosecutor? They'll probably say Mrs. Langley dragged our son into bed or something crazy like that. That *that* was what Derek got in a fight with the Langleys about, not his hiding in their house."

I felt despair overtaking me. But I was supposed to be the rock.

Ellen said, "They wouldn't think that, would they? No one would seriously think Donna would have gone to bed with our son?"

I recalled what Barry had told me, what Donna had supposedly confessed to her sister. That she'd slept with the neighbor.

Maybe she hadn't been exaggerating after all.

Ellen opened the fridge, took out two bottles of white wine, set them on the counter. She got the corkscrew out of the drawer and opened both of them. Christ almighty, I thought, how much is she planning to drink?

She unwound the corks from the corkscrew, tossed them across the counter, then turned both bottles upside down over the sink and drained them. "I need my mind clear to get myself through this," she said.

If she wanted to be the rock from here on, that was okay by me.

She stood the empty bottles back on the counter, turned to me, and said, "I think we're being punished."

"What?"

"For things we've done, or not done, in the past. What's happened to us now, it's some kind of retribution. We're being made to pay."

I asked, "I don't get you. For things we've done in this life, or past ones?"

She walked out of the kitchen without answering.

*   *   *

It was another sleepless night, at least for me. For most of it, I stared at the ceiling, unable to see anything but my son in a cell. This was his third night behind bars, away from us, and it still didn't seem possible that all of this was happening to our family.

I was only able to stop worrying about one thing when I moved on to worry about another. I couldn't seem to focus on any one aspect of our troubles because there seemed to be so many of them.

Derek, of course, was my primary concern. But because I remained convinced he was not responsible for the Langleys' deaths, my thoughts kept returning to what might have actually happened there that night, and who pulled the trigger.

One thought that kept coming back to me was whether the murder of the Langleys was a mistake. Not in the obvious sense. Of course it was a mistake; a tragedy, a horrific event.

I was thinking a different kind of mistake.

And about our mailbox. With our name on it. And no mailbox with the name "Langley" on it.

What if the Langleys' killer, or killers, had gone to the wrong door? Was it possible our house had been the target? And if so, why?

That computer. I always kept coming back to that computer. It had been given to Derek, and now it was missing. Maybe, whoever killed the Langleys assumed they'd found the right house, because what they were looking for was there.

And maybe it was all bullshit. I wished I were confident that if I went to Barry and laid this all out for him, he'd at least consider it. But the chances of that happening now were somewhere between nil and zilch.

After we turned out the lights, Ellen put her head on her pillow, and moments later, I could hear her taking tissues out of the box on her bedside table. She cried herself to sleep, and I held her until she stopped. I rolled over and pushed my face into the pillow. I figured if I could muffle my own crying, I would not wake her.

The priority, as we both saw it the next morning, was seeing Derek and his lawyer and finding out what the hell was going on. But setting that as a goal, and actually being able to do anything about it, were two entirely different things. We divvied up duties in the morning. Ellen was on the phone first thing, trying to set up a visit to the jail, checking in with Natalie Bondurant.

She couldn't reach anyone at the jail with the authority to set up a visit, and Natalie wasn't available to take her call.

So we could spin our wheels all day, or try to get some other things done.

I decided to go to work. Ellen could reach me on my cell if something happened. She'd make a trip to the bank and start going through the process of cashing in some, or possibly all, of our retirement savings. It wasn't as though we had hundreds of thousands of dollars set aside. Like most people, we often found ourselves struggling with our week-to-week obligations, and figured we'd deal with the financial needs of our golden years by purchasing a winning lottery ticket.

"It's going to be okay," I said to her as I prepared to go outside.

Before I got in my truck, I checked that I had everything I needed. The gas cans were full, the mowers and weed trimmers were in the back, my cell was turned on. I had my cooler with a sandwich, a piece of fruit, and several bottles of water. Not fancy, store-bought, bottled water, but tap water in bottles that once held the fancy stuff. Finally, I threw a metal watering can into the pickup bed, not something I usually brought along with me, but I thought it might come in handy today.

I'd promised my new employee to pick him up by eight, so one other stop I wanted to make that morning, one I hadn't mentioned to Ellen, would have to come after. But I wanted to make it before I got sweaty and had tiny bits of grass stuck to my neck.

Drew Lockus was right where I expected him to be, standing on the corner out front of his mother's house, paper bag in hand. Had he been a hitchhiker, I might not have been inclined to pick him up. Short and solid, those thick arms straining at his shirtsleeves, eyes set deep under a heavy brow, he had a bit of a Cro-Magnon thing going on.

I hoped I wasn't making a mistake here. It was an impulsive decision, asking him whether he wanted some work. But what were the odds he'd turn out to be a worse employee than Stuart Yost, Heat Rash Boy?

Drew had been in the right place at the right time, as far as I was concerned. I don't subscribe much to the belief that things happen for a reason, that there's some higher power at the controls, directing all of us like we're in some cosmic summer-stock production. Shit just happens is more or less my philosophy. I'm more a cause-and-effect guy. I believe one thing leads to another.

I didn't believe in destiny, but I was grateful that the gods, who'd been so angry with me lately, had decided to cut me some slack and place Drew in my vicinity when the tractor had landed on my leg. I certainly wouldn't have been rescued by that dipshit idiot of a reporter, or his driver.

Ellen, when I told her the night before how I'd met Drew, suggested fate had played a hand. Maybe we'd been drawn together so that he could save me from losing a leg when the tractor came down on me. Or maybe, she speculated, our paths had crossed so he could save us from a greater peril.

This time, I told her, you're the one talking out of your ass.

I was feeling pretty sore this morning. My leg had throbbed all night, and my face and gut were still sore from Lance's pounding. But there wasn't much I could do about that. I couldn't phone in to myself and say I was sick. I had to make a living. I had to help my son.

Drew opened the passenger door and got in. "Hey," he said.

"Morning," I said. "I see you brought a lunch. If you want, you can tuck it in

my cooler, behind the seat there."
Drew, who didn't yet have his seatbelt
on, looked around, found the cooler,
opened it up, and dropped his lunch in.
"You're welcome to share my water,
too," I said.

"Thanks," Drew said. "I guess I
should have thought of that."

"Not a problem. Most houses have a
hose hooked up to the side anyway, if
we need a drink. And some people, at
least the ones who aren't miserable
pricks, if they're home, they offer you a
drink, especially on a hot day like this."

"That's good," Drew said. He studied
me. "What happened to your face?"

"Oh," I said, reaching up to it without
actually touching it. "I had a little run-in
with a former associate." I hung a right,
aimed the truck toward the downtown.

"That's some shiner you got there,"
he said.

"I kind of wasn't ready."

I thought Drew might ask for details,
but instead he said, "Where's our first
place?"

"Up on Culver. But I've got one stop
before that. Down at city hall."

"Forget to pay your property taxes?" he asked.

"Not exactly," I said.

Promise Falls is too large to be called quaint, but it's a pretty city, lots of historic architecture, a river running down from the falls it's named for through the center of town, and the closer you get to that center, the better it looks, with old-fashioned-looking streetlamps and signs, brick sidewalks, most of the shops having a colonial look about them. City hall is a bit of a mixed bag. It's fronted by several sets of doors and three-story columns that have a Faneuil Hall kind of look, but with modern additions flanking them.

I parked out front and said to Drew, "I'll only be a couple of minutes. If someone wants the truck moved, just circle the block."

"Got it," he said.

I went around to the back of the truck, grabbed the watering can, and walked briskly to the front doors and through the rotunda and up the long flight of marble stairs to the second floor. I knew where I was going.

The mayor's office is actually several rooms. There's the reception area, with the main desk, and the deputy mayor's office to the left, several smaller offices for administrative aides to the right. But the door to Mayor Finley's office was straight ahead, and when the woman behind the main desk saw me heading for it, a smile broke out across her face and she said, "Christ on a cracker as I live and breathe, Jim Cutter."

"Hey, Delia," I said, flashing back a smile, but not breaking my stride.

"What's with the can?" she asked. "Don't tell me you're working for Building Services, keeping the office plants from getting thirsty?" She winked. "It's still a better gig than driving His Worship around, I'll bet." I just smiled. "Jesus, Jim, what happened to you? You walk into a mountain?"

"It's nothing," I said.

"If you want to see the mayor, he's in his office, but he's kind of busy right now with this lady he's got helping him map out his campaign for Congress. You've heard about that, I guess."

"Oh yeah."

"Can you believe it?"

I just shrugged. "The voters always get who they deserve, Delia," I said.

"You want me to let him know you're here?"

"No, that's okay. I just wanted to know if he was in. If he is, I figure that means Lance must be around."

"I saw him a few minutes ago. I think he's down the hall in the coffee room." Delia was reaching for the phone. "Want me to let him know you're here?"

"No no," I said quickly. "I'm heading down that way anyway." I held up the can.

Delia reached out and grabbed my arm as I started to slip away. "I'm sorry about your boy. About Derek." I nodded, grateful for her concern. "I don't believe it for a minute," she said, and let go of me.

As I strolled down the hallway I practiced my grip on the handle of the galvanized steel can. It was important that I have a good hold on it.

I pushed open the door to the coffee room. It was big enough for half a dozen tables, with some vending machines along one wall, a coffee machine on a counter next to a sink and refrigerator.

The room was empty but for one man. Lance was seated at one of the tables, his right hand around a paper cup of coffee, his left turning the pages of the sports section.

"Hey," I said.

As Lance turned to look I brought the watering can back over my shoulder, then swung it full force across his face. There was a loud, hollow bang as it connected. He tumbled back across the table and collapsed in a heap onto the floor.

"You shouldn't have spit in my ear," I said, then turned around and went back out to the truck.

Drew didn't need much instruction. Not that yard maintenance is, as they say, rocket surgery. But he knew what to do without being asked. At each of our stops, I took the Deere and Drew fired up one of the push mowers and went into the places I couldn't reach with the lawn tractor. When he was done with that, he used the edger, then took the blower and cleared the walkways and driveways of grass debris.

I tossed him a bottle of water after our third house, and he downed it in one gulp. "Why don't we break for lunch," I said. There was a park along the river, just down from the falls, where we could find plenty of shade and, with any luck, some breeze. I drove down to it, found a spot along the curb long enough for the truck and the trailer, and invited Drew to follow me to one of the picnic tables.

"When you came out of city hall," he said, "you looked kind of, I don't know, funny. A kind of shit-eatin' grin. Smug."

"Yeah," I said. "Smug sounds right." I gave my head a scratch, tousled my hair to get rid of some lawn debris. "I've been under a bit of stress lately and was looking for an outlet."

"Okay," Drew said, and pursued it no further.

"So," I said. "Your mother. You're looking after her?"

Drew nodded, took a bite of his peanut butter sandwich.

"I got the sense she's not well."

He took another couple of bites and nodded. He waited until his mouth wasn't too gummed up, then said, "She's old. She's got cancer." Then another bite of sandwich.

"I'm sorry," I said.

Drew Lockus had already finished one sandwich, and reached into his bag for a second. "I guess we all have to die of something." He bit hurriedly into his second sandwich.

"Take your time," I said. "We don't have to rush. It's good to recharge the batteries a bit, especially in this heat."

"Sorry," Drew said, chewing steadily. "I guess I eat kind of fast."

"So what kind of work have you been doing?"

"Small engine repair, machine shop work, that kind of thing," Drew said. "But like I said, I haven't been working all that much lately. When my mom took sick, I came up here to look after her."

"Your father, he still alive?"

"No, he died a long time ago. Heart attack."

"That's too bad. Brothers, sisters?"

"Just me."

"That's tough, when there's no one else to share the load." I drank some water. "Married?"

"Not anymore," Drew said. "Long time ago. And we lived together. Not actually married."

"Kids?"

Drew hesitated before answering. "Same deal. Not anymore."

"Sorry," I said again. "I don't mean to pry. It's none of my business."

"That's okay," Drew said. "Fact is, I haven't had a very happy life. And I don't see it going in a direction where it's going to get any better."

At first I thought, great, I've found the perfect guy to cheer me up. But then I saw it from his point of view. With all the troubles he seemed to have, he had to go and get hired by the one person who might actually have, at least for the moment, even more.

Maybe my dilemmas would give him something to be thankful for. It could be worse. Or, I could end up bringing him down even further.

We both enjoyed the breeze for a moment without talking. Then Drew said, "How are things with your son?"

I took a sip of water. "They could be better," I said. "I'm just hoping that, once we start gathering some more information, the police will realize they've made a mistake, drop the charges."

"Prison," he said, shaking his head. "It's not a good place to be."

"No," I said, weighing the meaning behind his comment. "You sound as though you're speaking from some experience."

"Like I said," Drew reminded me, "I haven't had a very happy life. Sometime, maybe I'll tell you about it, when you feel like being bored." He paused, then said, "I notice you looking upriver a lot."

"I was just looking at Promise Falls," I said. Watching the water come down, the white foam and mist rising up from the bottom, bordered on hypnotic.

"Pretty," Drew said.

"Yeah," I said, picturing Brett Stockwell going over the railing that spanned the falls.

I could see it. The boy falling, his body hitting the rocks below.

That wasn't all I saw. Back up there, on the bridge, I imagined Conrad Chase looking down, waving goodbye, a smile on his face, all his problems solved.

Driving out of the downtown, we passed by the Clover Restaurant, an upscale place where you could get a nice dinner for two if you had an extra hundred bucks, maybe lunch for half that. What caught my eye as we drove past the parking lot was a Mazda sedan, just like Ellen's.

"Looks like my wife's car," I said, slowing. I glanced at the license plate, saw that it was indeed her car. "Maybe she's having a meeting with Derek's lawyer, maybe I should—"

I spotted another familiar car just as I was about to turn into the lot. A silver Audi TT, parked half a dozen cars down from Ellen's.

I wrenched the wheel back, kept on going.

"What?" said Drew. "You want to pop in, I don't mind waiting in the truck."

"I was wrong," I said. "Not her car."

A couple of hours later, standing by the truck, getting ready to unload the Deere, my cell rang. I put it to my ear so quickly I didn't have a chance to look at the readout and see who it was from.

"Hello?"

"Hey, Jimmy, I hear you were in the building. You should have dropped by and said hello."

Mayor Randall Finley.

"Sorry," I said. "Delia said you were in a meeting with your campaign strategist."

"Yeah, Maxine Woodrow. She's a real looker, plus she's got brains. Not the sort of combination I'm typically attracted to." He laughed.

"What can I do for you, Randy?"

"Listen," he said, "Lance had to take a sick day because you knocked half his face off. It wasn't that bad, I'm sure he'll be back tomorrow, but Jesus, I really wish you wouldn't do that kind of thing. Fucks things up for me."

"I had a score to settle," I said.

"I don't doubt it. There's days I wouldn't mind taking a frying pan to his head myself. What did you use, anyway? Delia said you had a watering can with you."

"That's right."

"Fucking hell. Now the lefties will want everyone to register their watering cans. All I wanted to say is, if you're in a pissing match with Lance, don't do it in my sandbox. Understand what I'm saying?"

"I hear ya," I said.

"You ever think maybe you have a bit of a problem? You keep things all bottled up, you talk in monosyllables, then every once in a while you just explode." A chortling noise. "Nobody knows better than me."

"I'll join a group."

"There's the spirit." Then, adopting a softer tone, "Hey, Cutter, about your kid."

"Yeah."

"That's a damn shame. I see you got Bondurant. Good lawyer, and a pretty nice piece of ass, too, from what I hear, not that that's particularly relevant to you."

"Not really."

"Listen, you hang in there. There's no way a kid of yours could have done that."

Randall caught me off guard in a way he never had before. It took me a moment to find the words, but I managed to say "Thank you."

"Okay. Later." And the mayor hung up.

"Who was that?" asked Drew, who'd been adding gas from a red plastic container to one of the lawn mowers, and had been in earshot the whole time.

"The mayor," I said.

"We supposed to cut his grass, too?" Drew asked.

Before I could answer, the cell phone, still in my hand, went off again. This time I glanced at the tiny screen and saw that it was Ellen.

"We can see Derek," she said. "Half an hour, three-thirty."

"Have you talked to Natalie? Does she know any more about the earring?"

"I saw her briefly, but I don't have any news. She's going to meet us when we go in to see Derek."

"Anything else?" I asked. I was wondering whether she'd mention her lunch at the Clover.

"No, except that there's going to be about eight hundred and fifty bucks left in our retirement fund."

I glanced at my watch. "I'll be there in about fifteen minutes," I said, and closed the phone.

Drew said he could look after this property while I left with the truck for the Promise Falls jail. I looked a fright, but no one seemed to mind when I got there. Ellen and Natalie Bondurant were already waiting for me. We were taken to a small meeting room and told to wait while a guard went and fetched Derek.

It was all I could do not to weep when he walked in. He was pale, there were circles under his eyes, his shoulders sagged, and he had a bandage on his chin.

Ellen threw her arms around him first, and then I got a hug in before we were both reprimanded by a jail official standing over by the door. No personal contact allowed, he told us.

"What happened to you?" Ellen asked, reaching out to his bandage without actually touching it.

"Some guy shoved me into a wall," he said.

"A guard?" Natalie asked.

"No," Derek said. "One of the prisoners. I didn't move out of his way fast enough."

To Natalie, I said, "What can we do about that? Can't we get him into some sort of protective—"

She put up her hand to stop me. "I'll look into it. I want to get started. We've got a lot to cover. Derek," she said, leaning over the narrow table toward our son, "there are a few things we need to work out here."

"Like what?"

"The police found an earring. A peace

sign. They're testing it for DNA, but tell me now. Is it yours?"

He nodded. "Probably."

"When did you lose it?"

He seemed a bit bewildered. "I don't know. Two, three weeks ago or so, I think."

"Not the night you were hiding in the basement? When the Langleys were killed?"

He shook his head. Of this he seemed sure. "No, before then. Where'd they find it?"

Natalie, Ellen, and I exchanged glances before Natalie said, "In the Langleys' bedroom. Caught down in the dust ruffle."

Derek's eyes darted back and forth.

"Plus," Natalie Bondurant said, "they found your prints on the dresser."

"Okay, wait a minute. I might have touched the dresser the night they got killed."

I broke in. "You didn't tell Barry you were in there."

Derek sighed, looked briefly up to the ceiling tiles. "Shit, I just went in there for a second. I just walked around, and I think I touched it."

"You sure you didn't lose the earring then?" Ellen asked.

He was silent a moment. "No, not then."

"Then how do you think it got into that room?" Natalie asked.

Derek's eyes began to well up with tears. He looked at his mother and said, "Do we really have to get into this?"

"We really have to get into this," Natalie said.

"It's just . . . really hard to talk about."

Ellen did her best to give him a reassuring smile. "Ms. Bondurant can't help you if you aren't completely honest with her. I know it may be hard to tell her some things with us here, and if you need us to leave—"

"No," he said. "I guess not. I mean, shit, you'll find out sooner or later anyway, the way things have been going lately."

Fasten your seatbelts, I thought.

"I kind of, I guess I kind of had sex with Mrs. Langley," Derek said.

If it had been left to me and Ellen, there might have been a long, stunned silence, but Natalie dove right in with her questions. "When was this, Derek?"

"Like, three weeks ago or so."

"One occasion, or several?"

"Just once."

"Tell us how this happened."

Derek took a long breath. "I'd gone over there to see Adam, but it turned out he was out with his dad, they'd gone to a movie or something. But Mrs. Langley invited me in anyway. She did that a lot, like she wanted to have someone to talk to, you know? She was always kind of nice to me. So I came in, and she made me a sandwich and opened a bag of chips, and she sat down at the table with me, just talking about all kinds of stuff, and then she was asking me about my girlfriend, you know, Penny?"

We nodded.

"And Mrs. Langley started talking about how kids nowadays, how, you know, they're more sexually active, and she started asking me whether I was careful, about getting a girl pregnant, and about diseases and stuff, and I told her that, technically speaking, I really hadn't, you know, hadn't actually done it yet." He flashed me a look, like maybe I'd be disappointed, I don't know. "I said I'd just done some stuff, you know, but not the actual thing."

"Okay," said Natalie.

"She asked me if I was nervous about that, about what it would be like the first time, and I guess I said maybe a little, and she said that she might be able to help me out with that nervousness." He paused, working up to it. "She said, like, if I never told anyone, she could give me kind of a lesson, that it would be our secret."

We'd been living next door to Mrs. Robinson.

"So you went up to her bedroom," Natalie Bondurant said.

Derek nodded. "She . . . showed me."

Ellen said, "She raped you."

Derek screwed up his face. "Not . . . really, Mom."

Natalie again: "Derek, did you ever

tell anyone about this? Before now? Before this very moment?"

"No. Not anybody. Nobody."

"Do you think Mrs. Langley told anyone? Do you think it's possible that Mr. Langley could have found out about this somehow?"

He shook his head. "I kind of think he might have said something to me."

"But it's not something we can prove," Natalie said. "And now we know how the DNA test is going to come back on that earring. We might have been able to come up with some sort of story of how it got there, but with your fingerprints on the dresser, you're placed in that room. The prosecution's probably already working up a theory, that somehow Albert Langley found out you'd slept with his wife, that there was some kind of confrontation that night, one that ended with all of them dead." She paused. "The good news is—"

"There's good news?" I said.

"It's still circumstantial, and a whole lot of conjecture. But it gives the prosecution a much better motive than we thought they had."

"I'm screwed," Derek said.

"No," Natalie Bondurant said. "We just have our work cut out for us."

Derek looked at his mother, his eyes red. "I'm sorry."

"We all make mistakes," Ellen said.

Ditto, I thought.

"I'm never going to get out of here," he said.

"You can't think that way," I said. "Ms. Bondurant, she knows what she's doing. We're all doing everything we can. I need you out of here. I can't cut all those yards without you." I hoped I could make him smile, but it wasn't to be.

"I'm sorry I'm such a fuckup."

"You're not a fuckup," I told him.

He shook his head slowly, looked off into space. "I've always been a fuckup. I got myself into this by being a fuckup. Even if, somehow, you and Mom manage to get me out of here, I'll just end up doing something else, because that's just what I always do. I always fuck up. It's like the only thing I'm good at."

Behind us, a door rattled. "It's time," said the guard.

Natalie Bondurant was on her feet, telling all of us she'd be in touch, and heading for the door. Ellen and I snuck in some quick hugs and headed for the door. Ellen had slipped out ahead of me when Derek said, "Dad?" I turned.

His eyes met mine. "You know your paintings?"

I thought, *Huh?* But I said, "Yeah?"

"I know you've been thinking about getting rid of them, but I don't want you to."

"Okay," I said.

"I think they're really good," Derek said. "I don't know whether I've ever mentioned that."

I didn't know what to say.

"If I have to stay here, like, if they keep me in jail a whole long time, like for a few years or forever, would they let me hang one of them in my cell?"

I managed to hold it together long enough to get back in my truck, out of Ellen's sight.

TWENTY-FIVE

That night, they came for us.

The day itself wound down uneventfully after I got back from seeing Derek. Drew asked me how it went, but I couldn't bring myself to talk about it.

At our last house, Drew was having some trouble getting one of the hand mowers to start. He yanked and yanked on the pull cord, pumped the primer button several times, yanked again, then wondered if he might have flooded the damn thing, then decided to give it one last pull.

He pulled so hard, he did something to the mechanism that retracts the cord, and suddenly he had four feet of it dangling over the mower.

"Well, shit," he said when I walked over to see what had happened.

"No big deal," I said.

"Sorry," he said, holding the grip at the end of the cord, spinning the line around like it was a skipping rope. "It just came out."

"Don't worry about it," I said.

"I could fix it. I could take it apart, see what I've done, rewind the cord—well, if I had the right tools."

"I've got everything I need in my shed," I said. "I can do it."

"If you want, I could come over later tonight, after . . . after I make my mom's dinner. You've got enough on your plate, Jim, without having to clean up after my mistakes."

"All right then," I said, and told Drew where I lived. But I felt he was entitled to a bit of a heads-up. "There's a cop car out front, standing guard over the Langley house. They might have a couple of questions for you before they let you come up to our place." Not that they'd been able to intercept Penny when she'd come by—twice.

"That's okay," said Drew.

"If you can make it, fine," I said. "But if you can't, don't worry about it."

Later, as I was dropping him off out front of his mother's house, he reminded me of his intentions. "I'll come round, if my mom doesn't need me. Might be well after dinner."

"Drew, either way, it's cool," I said.

He stood by the curb, watching me drive away, and in the rearview mirror I spotted him giving me a small salute as I rounded the corner.

When I pulled into our lane at 5:50, the police tape was gone from around the Langley house, and the police car that had been there for so many days was pulling out.

I put down the window so I could talk to the cop. It was the same young man who'd been covering most of the day shifts here since the murders.

"All done?" I said.

"I don't have to babysit the place anymore," he said. "They're done with it as a crime scene. It's kind of wrapped up. What with there being an arrest and all." He cast his eyes down so he wouldn't have to look into mine.

"Okay then," I said, and took my foot

off the brake and continued down to our house.

I had to unlock the door to get in. Ellen was still on guard, as was I. She'd arrived a few minutes earlier with a pepperoni and double-cheese pizza, still hot in the box. I dropped into one of the kitchen chairs, all the energy drained from me.

"You disappeared pretty fast after we left Derek," she said.

I couldn't tell her that I was about to fall apart and didn't want her to see me when it happened. "I had to get back to Drew," I said.

Ellen got out some plates. It didn't matter how much of a shambles our lives had become these last few days, we weren't going to eat pizza out of a box.

She said, "I heard you dropped by city hall today."

I glanced up at her. "What'd you hear, exactly?"

"That you put a huge dent in our watering can."

"I can bang it out."

"Jim, honestly, doing that, trying to

get even with Lance, that's not going to help things."

"That's probably true," I said. "But I felt better, briefly."

"What if he decides to press charges?"

I shook my head. "He won't. Not after what he did to me." I swallowed. "But he might try getting back at me again."

"Terrific," Ellen said, picking at a stray piece of green pepper that had somehow gotten onto our pizza by mistake.

"What about you?" I asked. "What did you do, before we saw Derek?" I wanted to ask where she'd had lunch, whether she'd met with anyone.

"Mostly here and at the bank," she said. "Then just a couple of errands after we saw Derek, and then grabbed the pizza on the way home. I couldn't think about dinner."

Besides, I thought, she'd had a good lunch, with Conrad. Most likely Conrad, anyway. Sometimes Illeana drove his Audi.

I decided, at least for now, to let it go. Maybe part of me didn't want to know. I couldn't deal with any more complications. She did, after all, still work for the man, and if she was entitled to meet with him at Thackeray, I supposed she had the right to meet with him at the Clover.

Ellen was ignoring her pizza. "It's all I can do to eat," she said. "I can't stop thinking about Donna Langley. I can't believe what she did."

And even though Donna had once, many years ago, tried to get me into bed, I too found what she had done with my son hard to comprehend.

"I feel . . . I feel so angry with her," Ellen said. "I wish I could go over there now, tell her what I think of her."

"Whatever sins she may have committed," I said, "she's paid for all of them now."

I sat down on the couch after dinner, turned on the news, and before I realized it, I was asleep. Out cold. Three nights with almost no sleep could do that to you.

I woke up around eight, Ellen sitting across from me. She smiled, first time I'd seen her do that in several days.

"You've been snoring your head off," she said.

Slowly, I worked myself off the couch. "Boy, I was out like a light."

"I nodded off for a while, too. We should both go to bed, get a good night's sleep."

I agreed. "First, I'm going to go outside, check the shed, lock things up. We don't have cops up the road anymore, you know."

"We don't?" Ellen sounded concerned.

"They've packed it in," I said.

"The guy was there when I got home with the pizza," Ellen said.

"He left just after. They've wrapped it all up, you see."

"No," Ellen said defiantly. "They haven't."

I gave her an upturned thumb and went outside by way of the kitchen, locking the door behind me so that Ellen would be safe. There wasn't much spring in my step as I walked across the gravel to the shed. My feet were dragging. It was dusk, and would be dark in another half hour or so.

There were things I could do, equipment to tend, bills to prepare, but all I had the strength for was to lock things up.

They got me as I came through the open garage door. Coming from my right, a shadow, then the blow.

Followed by darkness.

I couldn't have been out that long, because when I woke up, there was still some light outside. The world beyond the shed was gray, verging on black. Maybe only a couple of minutes. But it had been long enough to secure me into an old wooden chair from the shed.

Even before I began to assess my situation, I was aware that the fingers of my right hand were very sore. Other parts of my body hurt, of course. My head was pounding. But the four fingers of my right hand felt pinched and uncomfortable.

I moved my head around, started to say something, and realized my mouth was secured with tape. I looked down at my body and saw duct tape wrapped around me just below my shoulders, more down around my waist. I couldn't move my legs, and while I couldn't see them below my knees, I assumed they'd been tied to the chair with more tape.

Tape held my left hand to one of the rungs of the seatback. I had to blink a couple of times, however, to comprehend what had been done to my right hand.

It wasn't tied to the chair. It was taped to my hedge trimmer, which was sitting in my lap. I couldn't see my fingers or hand at all, there was so much tape wrapped around them.

I understood now what had been done to me. And what I was facing.

My fingers had been jammed into the open slots of the trimmer, the ones the blades went through at lightning speed when the trigger on the handle was squeezed. Then my fingers had been wrapped with tape to keep them there. Squeezing the trigger, only for a fraction of a second, would cut all four fingers, probably down to about the first knuckles. The blades might not have been designed to go through bone, but I had little doubt they could do it. I'd cut plenty of bushes with this machine, hacking through small wooden branches under half an inch thick.

And these blades, they'd go through flesh like butter.

Once I'd figured out my situation, my eyes moved to the back of the trimmer, and the yellow extension cord attached to it. I followed the cord down to the floor, where it came up from a huge coil, like a snake before a charmer. From the bottom of the coil, a single line of cord emerged, leading toward the wall. I couldn't see, from my position, whether it was plugged in or not.

"Hey, Sleeping Beauty's awake," someone said.

"Oooh, goody," said someone else.

The voices came from behind me, and I turned my head to one side, then the other, trying to get a look at them. But I needn't have bothered. They both came around in front of me.

They were wearing stocking masks. My guess was they hadn't been wearing them until they'd seen me stir, because they were both tugging them down around their necks. Their faces were mashed and distorted behind the hose, but I could tell that one man's hair was dark, brown or black, while the other man had almost no hair at all.

"Fuck," said the dark-haired one. "It's too fucking hot for these."

"Try to cope," said the bald one. He looked at me. "So, how ya feeling, asshole? You weren't asleep all that long."

I raised my head to look into their shrouded eyes. I wondered if they could see the fear in mine.

Where, I thought suddenly, feeling the panic well up in me, *is Ellen?* I wasn't sure, if my mouth hadn't been taped, whether I'd even ask what they'd done with her, on the off chance they didn't know she was in the house.

But then, as if he were able to translate my darting eyes into words, the bald one said, "Your wifey is just fine, Cutter. She's in the house, tied up like you, except she doesn't have her hand attached to a hedge trimmer."

"Woulda been easier, though," said the dark-haired one. "Her fingers'd be smaller, easier to jam in."

The bald one shrugged. "Not to worry. We should be able to get what we need from this one."

They must have taken my keys off me, or somehow tricked Ellen to come to the door. I tried to place the voices, wondered if I had ever heard them before, didn't think I recognized them. They were both in pretty good shape. Lean, close to six feet, dressed casually but not cheaply. Expensive-looking jeans, the bald one had on a Lacoste T-shirt, the little green alligator emblem on his left chest. The other guy had on a simple black T, cut high enough on the arms to reveal well-toned biceps and part of a tattoo on his right arm, what looked like the end of a knife blade.

I tried to recall whether I'd ever seen Lance without a shirt on—it seemed unlikely—and if I had, whether he'd had a tattoo like that. Surely, if I'd ever seen it, I'd have remembered. This guy was about the same height and build as Lance, and if his face was damaged from a run-in with a watering can, I couldn't tell through the dark stocking.

The few words he'd uttered didn't put me immediately in mind of the mayor's driver, but for obvious reasons, I had him on my mind.

"You've noticed that we have you at our advantage," the bald one said. He reached down and picked up the hedge trimmer, which dragged my hand up with it. I started to pull my arm back, but all that did was take the trimmer with it. "Tut-tut, you better behave," he said.

He grabbed hold of the handle, floated his finger just beyond the trigger.

"So you see what's happening here," he said. "I touch this button, just even for like a fucking fraction of a second, and all the tips of your fingers are going to come off."

I could feel droplets of sweat rolling down my forehead. One of them found its way into my right eye, and the saltiness of it stung like hell. I blinked several times.

"It's going to be messy as hell," he said. "And I have to be honest with you. I don't really like the sight of blood. The good thing is, there's so much tape wrapped around your hand here, I won't have to see it squirting around all over the place."

"Jesus," said the dark-haired one, who'd been looking at my hand but then looked away. "That's going to fucking hurt." He reached under the nylon and scratched his neck. "Man, this is so goddamn hot. Couldn't we just tape his eyes so we wouldn't have to wear these things?"

"I think we'll have an easier time persuading Mr. Cutter here to help us out if he can see what it is we plan to do with him."

I made some noises behind the tape.

"Say what?" said the bald one. "You don't even know what I'm going to ask you yet, and already you're ready to talk?"

I slowly nodded my head. The bald one took his hand off the hedge trimmer handle and ripped the tape off my mouth. It hurt like all get-out but I held back a scream through gritted teeth.

"You son of a bitch," I said. "If you've

hurt my wife, I swear to God I'll fucking kill you."

The bald one's misshapen mouth appeared to turn into a grin. "Uh, hello? Do you understand your situation at the moment? Do you think you're in any position to be making threats? Maybe I need to make that clear to you right this fucking minute."

And he gripped the handle again, held his finger over the trigger, and squeezed.

"Shit, Mortie!" said the dark-haired one with the knife tattoo.

"No!" I shouted. This time, I couldn't hold back the scream.

I reflexively tried to jerk my hand away, but that only dragged the hedge trimmer closer to me. The bald one still had a firm hold of the machine, his finger still gripped about the trigger.

Nothing happened.

The trimmer made no noise. My fingers, beyond the pain they were already in by being jammed into the teeth of the machine, felt nothing.

The bald one dropped the trimmer into my lap and began to laugh. "Oh fuck!" he said, taking a step back, bending over, putting his hands atop his knees, laughing the entire time. "That was priceless! You should have seen the expression on your face!"

"Jesus, you scared the shit out of me, too!" his partner said.

The bald one managed to pull himself together, let out a couple of enthusiastic hoots, then walked over to the wall, where the yellow extension cord disappeared behind some cardboard boxes. He kicked them aside, exposing the wall outlet, and I could see that the cord had not been plugged in.

He knelt down, grabbed the end of the cord, and shoved it firmly into the receptacle.

He walked back over to me, rubbing his hands together, still smiling inside his mask. He grabbed the trimmer, lifted it, and my hand, up to the level of his waist, and said, "The next time, it'll be the real deal."

TWENTY-SIX

Now, to get to the business at hand, so to speak," said the bald one, the one I knew went by the name Mortie, if his associate was to be believed. "There's some things I'd like to ask you."

"What?" I said. My fingers, still held in the teeth of the hedge trimmer, were sweating inside the tape.

"You have a copy of a certain book," he said. "On a disc? Am I right?"

I said nothing.

"I don't know if you've got a printout of it, too, or it's just on a disc, or two discs, or what the fuck, but we want it."

"Okay," I said, my mind racing. "You can have it. But I want to see that my wife is okay. I'm not telling you where it is until I see that my wife is unharmed."

Mortie laughed. "I don't think so, pal, because—"

I cut him off mid-sentence. "I want. To see. My wife."

"What I was trying to tell you, asshole," he said, moving around the hedge trimmer, "is that you're not in a position to negotiate."

I mustered as much courage as I could, given my circumstances. "I don't care if you cut off all my fingers and all my toes. You can cut off my dick and suck on it if you want, but I'm not telling you anything until I see that my wife is okay."

Mortie thought, weighed his options, then glanced over at the dark-haired one with the tattoo. "Go get his fucking wife."

"I gotta take this thing off my head," he said. "Just for a couple of minutes. Then I'll go get her."

As he left the shed and my field of vision, he was peeling the stocking off his head. "Jesus," I heard him say. It didn't sound like Lance to me. And besides, why would Lance want that disc?

"You must be getting a bit warm, too," I said to Mortie.

"The heat doesn't bother me," he said.

"So Conrad sent you," I said.

"Shut the fuck up."

"I'd never have thought that a college president would know where to find people who do your kind of work."

"I said shut the fuck up. You want me to squeeze this?" He waved his index finger playfully about the trigger of the hedge trimmer. "Let me ask you a question," he said. "You want me to put all your fingertips in a sandwich bag or something, you can take them to the hospital later?"

I had nothing to say. And for the better part of a couple of minutes, we said nothing to each other. Finally, Mortie said, "Jesus, I *am* starting to get hot." He walked out the shed door and stepped around the side of the building, presumably to slip off the mask where I couldn't see him.

I looked around the room I was in, my own shed, looking for some sort of inspiration, some idea of how to get loose. But they had me well tied into the chair, and even though my right arm was not secured to it, with my hand taped to the trimmer, it was useless to me.

When it became clear to me I couldn't actually escape, I started thinking about other plans. Assuming they brought Ellen in, and she was okay, what was I going to do then?

Because I did not have the disc. I had given it to Natalie Bondurant for safekeeping.

Which was the better way to play this? Tell them I didn't have the disc, but could get it for them? Would that buy me time, or would they just kill both of us? The Langleys certainly hadn't found a way out of this alive, and, as far as I'd been able to determine, they'd handed over the computer.

The thing that really worried me was, we knew, and I was sure Mortie and his buddy knew that we knew, what was on the disc. Because I'd run my mouth off to Conrad. So, even if these two were able to leave with the disc, there was the problem of what we still might say. We could still do a lot of damage to Conrad's reputation, telling people he'd ripped off his bestseller from one of his students.

But how credible would we be without proof?

I could tell them the disc was on Derek's desk, next to his computer. There were probably dozens of discs there. They could leave with all of them, be tricked into thinking they had what they wanted. But there was no guarantee they still wouldn't kill us.

Mortie came back in, mask pulled down over his face.

I said, "I guess, when you got the computer from the Langleys, you figured your problems were over. But you don't have to kill us like you did them. We're not going to say anything. We don't care. Honest to God, we just don't give a shit anymore."

Mortie appeared to be squinting at me, as though puzzled. "Shut up. Your wife'll be along in a minute."

Outside, I heard our kitchen door slam shut, then steps shuffling across the gravel lane. Seconds later, the dark-haired one, mask in place, appeared at the door, dragging Ellen along with him.

She was alive. That was some relief. But it didn't last long, not when I saw how frightened she was.

They'd taped her wrists in front of her, then run tape around her body at the elbows, and tape around her head over her mouth. There were torn pieces of tape stuck to her jeans down around her ankles, which had clearly been removed so she could be led over here.

Her eyes were wide with terror, and I could tell she'd been crying.

"It's okay, honey," I said. "Have they hurt you?" She shook her head nervously from side to side. "That's good." I could see her looking at my hand, how it was attached to the hedge trimmer, and her eyes seemed to open even wider. They followed the cord from the trimmer itself to the wall outlet.

"Okay," Mortie said. "Your wifey's here, and as you can see, she's perfectly all right. So, where's the disc?"

"First of all," I said, "there's some pages printed out of the thing I think you're looking for. I'm pretty sure it's up in our bedroom, next to the bed. On the table. It should be there." Looking at Ellen, I said, "Isn't that where it is, honey?"

She nodded.

"Okay," Mortie said. To the dark-haired one, he said, "Go check it out."

"Okay!" he said, clearly relieved that if he wasn't in our presence, he wouldn't have to wear the hot nylon on his head. "What about her?"

"She's okay here with me," Mortie said. He motioned for Ellen to come farther into the shed, to go over by the wall. "You stay over there. You move and I'll be after you in a second."

I could hear a door open and close. The dark-haired one was in our house now.

Ellen positioned herself over by the wall. Mortie stood about halfway between the two of us.

"Now what about the disc?" he asked.

"I don't have it," I said.

Mortie cocked his sheathed head to one side. "Excuse me?"

"I don't have it. Not here."

"Don't fucking tell me this."

"But I can get it," I added hurriedly. "It's in a safe place. I gave it to someone else to hold on to."

"A safe place where?"

Outside, in the darkness, I thought I saw a shadow moving somewhere between the shed and the house. If Mortie's friend was in our house, who was this?

"I gave it to someone," I said.

"Who?" Mortie was sounding very pissed.

"I gave it to my son's lawyer," I said, figuring the truth was as good as anything at this point. "But only for safekeeping. I don't think she looked at it. I didn't tell her to. If I asked her to give it back to me, she would."

Mortie patted the top of his nylonclad head with the palm of his hand, thinking. "How the fuck are we supposed to accomplish that?"

I said, "Let my wife go. You hold me here. She can go see our lawyer, get the disc back, and when she gets back here with it, we give it to you, and you're on your way."

"That's your plan," Mortie said derisively. "We let your wife go, send her on an errand. And while she's gone, she calls the police."

And I was thinking, *I sure hope so*. But I looked over at her and said, "You wouldn't do that, would you, honey?"

She shook her head.

"Oh, now I'm convinced," Mortie said. "How about this? We keep her, let you go get the disc. I'm pretty sure you don't want anything to happen to her. We could tape her hand to the hedge trimmer every bit as easy as we did it to you."

Outside, I saw the shadow again. Hanging around my truck. And then it was gone. I felt my pulse racing.

"What?" Mortie said, looking over his shoulder. "Is he back already?" At least Mortie was smart enough not to use his partner's name, and didn't seem to have noticed that his had been uttered before.

Mortie walked over to the door and peered outside, shrugged, and came

back in. This time, instead of position-
ing himself between me and Ellen, he
was much closer to me. I, after all, was
the one he wanted answers from.

"Uh, I think your plan's not, what do
they say? Viable," Mortie said. "Once I
let your wife go, no matter what she
says, she's going to call the cops. Unless she's the stupidest bitch who ever
walked the earth. I got a better idea.
Tell me the name of the lawyer."

I didn't want to do that. And I realized
I'd already made a mistake telling him
my son's lawyer had it. Even though it
wouldn't take long for him to find out
her name—it had been all over the
news in the last couple of days—I
feared that if I gave it to him now, he'd
go straight to Natalie Bondurant's
house in the dead of night and kill her,
if he had to, to get the disc from her.

Out of the corner of my eye, I noticed
that Ellen was inching her way along
the side of the shed. So slowly, it was
almost imperceptible. She was standing, with her back to the wall, her eyes
on us the whole time. Every few seconds, Mortie would glance her way, but

she wasn't making any fast moves, and he'd failed to notice that in the last couple of minutes she'd moved about two feet.

"I asked you a question, shithead," Mortie said to me.

"I'm telling you we can get the disc. It doesn't matter who the lawyer is."

Mortie shook his head. "I've had enough." He took hold of the hedge trimmer sitting on my lap, one hand on the bar across the top, the other on the handle where the trigger was located.

"The tricky thing for you," Mortie said, "is going to be getting gloves. You're going to be needing pairs with one hand about an inch shorter than the other. I guess you could just put the glove on, put your hand back in this thing, turn it on, and you've got 'em custom made."

"Wait!" I shouted, squirming my fingers beneath the tape, trying to wriggle them out of the grooves so the blades wouldn't get them. "Listen to me!"

"Fuck it," Mortie said, and squeezed.

I held my breath, hoping Ellen would get to the plug in time. Just as his finger went to tighten on the trigger, out of the corner of my eye, I saw her drop. If her hands had been bound behind her, she'd have had to hunt blindly for the plug, or tried to knock it out of the wall outlet with her feet, but they were tied in front. Once she'd dropped to her knees, she leaned in close to the wall, got her fingers on the plug, and yanked.

She cut the power at the very instant the trimmer blades were getting the message. I felt them start to move, but before the blades could begin their back-and-forth cycle, they stopped. The ends of my fingers were now pinched even more than they'd been before, but I was pretty sure they were still connected to the rest of me.

"What the—" said Mortie. He clicked on the trigger a couple of times, then whirled around and saw the source of the problem.

"You bitch!" he said, his voice full of rage. He dropped the trimmer back onto my lap and moved in on Ellen, who was still down on her knees by the wall, looking terrified.

"Leave her alone!" I shouted. "Stop!"

That was when Drew Lockus ran into the shed.

He was wielding a shovel in his hands, one of the tools I kept in the back of the pickup, and as he closed in on Mortie he swung it like a baseball bat into the side of his head.

The shovel blade rang out like a tuning fork.

Mortie went down in an instant, collapsing over the lawn mower that had had the cord ripped out of it that afternoon.

"Drew!" I said. "God, Drew!"

I thought maybe Mortie would try to get up, at the very least twitch a bit. But he wasn't doing anything. From where I sat, he didn't even appear to be breathing.

Drew stood over him, looking a bit dumbfounded, like maybe he couldn't believe what he'd just done, that Mortie wasn't making any sort of objection to what had just happened to him.

"Jesus," Drew said slowly, not taking his eyes off Mortie.

"Drew!" I said. "There's another one, in the house!"

That woke him up. As he took his eyes off Mortie, the dark-haired one appeared at the shed door, a handful of pages in his hand. Although he had the stocking pulled down over his face, he was able to see instantly that things had taken, from his perspective, a turn for the worse.

He dropped the pages and bolted. Drew grabbed for the shovel he'd used to whack Mortie in the head, but as he turned, the blade of the shovel caught in the handle of the lawn mower and was yanked out of his hand. He stumbled, then reached down to grab for it again, but by that time the other guy had disappeared into the night.

Drew ran after him anyway.

I started squirming frantically. I twisted and wriggled my trapped fingers and managed to get them out of the teeth of the trimmer. Now I had to try to free myself from the tape.

At the same time, I was trying to free my left hand from the chair. Whichever one I could free first, I'd use to release the other.

But now Ellen was on her feet and moved into position in front of me. The fingers of her duct-taped hands were free, and she used them to pick away at the tape on the hedge trimmer. Even though it was now unplugged from the wall, she seemed afraid it would somehow magically start up. I felt possessed by the same illogical fear.

Drew reappeared a few seconds later. "I couldn't catch him," he said, out of breath. "He got in his car and took off."

Ellen freed my hand from the trimmer and I reached up to gently peel the tape away from her mouth. "Oh, Jim, oh my God," she said.

Drew helped both of us get freed of the tape. I threw my arms around Ellen, held her a moment, and with one hand reached over and patted Drew on the shoulder.

"I came to fix the mower," he said.

TWENTY-SEVEN

The first thing I did was make sure Ellen wasn't hurt. When I told her I was going to phone for an ambulance, she said she didn't need one. She was shaken up, yes, but not physically injured. She was more concerned for me. My hand was unhurt, but I'd taken a blow to the head. Not something I was going to trouble 911 with.

"I was going to pull down the lane," Drew explained, "but there was a car blocking the end of it. I thought maybe that was the cop you said would be there, but it didn't look like a cop car to me. So I just left my car on the shoulder up there, walked in, and I saw that other guy, the one that got away, he was walking this lady here across the yard, all tied up, and I knew something funny was going on."

"This is Drew," I said to Ellen, realizing there hadn't actually been a moment for formal introductions. "The new guy, who worked with me today. Drew, this is my wife, Ellen."

They shook hands, then Ellen simply threw her arms around him. "Thank you," she said, trembling.

Drew, his head on Ellen's shoulder, looked down at Mortie. Blood from his head had soaked through his stocking mask and was dripping all over the lawn mower.

He said, "I think I killed him."

Ellen took her arms from around Drew and looked at the man. "God, I hope so," she said.

"No," Drew said slowly. "That wouldn't be good."

I knelt down next to Mortie, tentatively worked my finger under the bottom of the blood-soaked stocking pulled down over his head, and peeled it off. I let it drop on the mower, put my head closer to Mortie's. His eyes were open but vacant, and I couldn't detect any breathing.

"Honey," I said, "you still better call an ambulance. I think he's dead, but we need to make the call."

Drew said, "I have to get out of here."

"Drew," I said, "you don't have to worry. You saved our lives. You did the right thing."

"You don't understand," he said quietly. "I just got out."

"Excuse me?" Ellen said.

"I just got out of prison. Something like this, they'll send me back for sure."

"Not when I tell the police what happened," I said. "You've got two witnesses. Me and Ellen, we can tell the police what you did. Drew, you're a hero. You took this one out of the picture, you chased the other one off."

Drew was listening, but didn't look persuaded. "The cops won't care, not when you've got a record."

Ellen reached out and touched his arm. "Drew, you did the right thing. We'll back you up a hundred percent."

Still unconvinced, he said, "You don't

know cops. If they've got an excuse to put you back in, they'll do it." He looked at me. "Couldn't you say you did it? That you got free, and when he was attacking your wife here, you grabbed the shovel and hit him? They'd understand that. And your wife is your witness. And you don't have a record, so they won't give you a hard time like they'll give me."

He'd saved our lives. That made this doubly hard. "Drew, the police, they'd figure it out eventually. They'd find a hole in our story somewhere, and then, when they pieced it together, and knew you were involved, and that we'd tried to cover it up, it'd be even worse for you. For all of us, but especially for you, having a record and all."

He nodded solemnly, but I knew we hadn't persuaded him. "I don't know about that."

"And, Drew," I said, "there's more. It's pretty obvious to me that these two are the ones who killed the Langleys. I mean, it just makes sense. They were looking for the same thing. You haven't just saved us. You've helped nail a murderer, and now the cops have a pretty good chance of finding his partner."

A light seemed to go on for Drew. "I guess."

"And on top of all that," I said, "you may have helped us get our son out of jail."

I glanced over at Ellen. I could tell she was already thinking the same thing, but was afraid to express the hope out loud for fear of jinxing it. She said, "I'll go call 911," and ran back to the house, like every second wasted was another second Derek would have to spend in his cell.

"Thank you, Drew," I said again.

He shook his head. "I don't know," he said. "I just don't know." He started moving toward the door.

"Drew, where are you going?"

"I don't know," he said. He was walking up the lane, toward his car.

I called out after him. "Drew, you should stay. The police, they won't have any reason to arrest you. You're not violating your parole by saving someone's life. They'll understand why you did what you did."

But he kept walking in the direction of the road and his car, and soon he was swallowed up by the night.

I wasn't going to run after him and drag him back. He had to know that I was going to tell the police what I knew, that he wouldn't be hard to find.

I went to the house—saw my set of keys hanging from the door and pocketed them—and found Ellen hanging up the phone in the kitchen. "They're on their way," she said to me.

She came into my arms, and as I held her, I said, "He must have sent them."

Ellen pulled away, looked at me. "What?"

"Conrad," I said. "He sent them."

"No," she said, shaking her head. "He wouldn't."

I moved my hand to Ellen's shoulders. "Ellen," I said firmly, "it all fits. These guys wanted the disc of his book. They were probably prepared to kill us for it. That dead guy in our shed?

At the very least he was prepared to cut off all my fingers to get it."

"No, Jim, it *doesn't* fit," Ellen maintained. "It doesn't make sense."

"Who else but Conrad would want it? He stole that book from that kid, and all these years later, he's still covering his tracks. I wouldn't be surprised if he killed that kid years ago, threw him off the falls, made it look like he killed himself. What choice did he have? How could he have Brett Stockwell going around telling everyone he'd written that book, that Conrad Chase was this huge, fucking fraud?"

"Jim," Ellen said, "you have to listen to me."

"No, you have to listen. I don't know why you keep defending this guy. I know he's your boss, but now it's looking like he's a killer, too. If he didn't kill the Langleys, then he sent those two to do it. And when he found out there was still a disc with that book on it, he sent them here to get it."

"I gave him the disc," Ellen said.

I looked at her. I couldn't process what she'd said to me. "What?"

"The disc. The one you gave to Natalie Bondurant. I asked for it back from her today, I told her she didn't have to worry about it anymore. And I gave it to Conrad. I met him at lunch."

"I don't understand. Why would you do such a thing? Why would you do that without talking to me about it first?"

"Jim, he's not a killer. He's an arrogant asshole, I'll grant you that. But he's not a killer. He couldn't have sent those two men here tonight. He had no reason to. He has the disc."

My head already hurt. Now it was getting much worse.

"This isn't making any sense at all," I said.

And then Ellen, who had been looking in the general direction of the back door, screamed.

I whirled around, saw the shadow of someone standing there. A man, a big man.

As he came into the light, I saw that it was Drew.

He opened the door. "Sorry, didn't

mean to scare you," he said. He looked at me. "I decided you were right. I came back. I'll tell the police what happened."

TWENTY-EIGHT

In another minute, we heard the sirens.

The ambulance was far too late for Mortie. Drew stood by the door to the shed, watching uncomfortably as the paramedics assessed Mortie's condition. Once they'd determined he was, in fact, dead, they made no attempts to move him.

By the time Barry Duckworth arrived, there were half a dozen cop cars on the scene. I figured it wouldn't be long before the TV news crews arrived. At least they wouldn't have to ask for directions. It would be the second time in a week that they'd been to this part of Promise Falls.

Ellen put on a large pot of coffee. It wasn't so much that she wanted to be the best host a crime scene ever had.

She just needed to keep busy. I guessed it was a good thing that she'd already decided to pour out her booze.

Drew and I came back from watching the paramedics' examination of Mortie, sat down at the kitchen table. Ellen was looking in the fridge and the freezer, trying to find any treats to put out. "Don't worry about it," I said. "Coffee's good."

"Bingo!" Ellen said. She pulled out, from the farthest reaches of the freezer, a frozen cake. It was like an archeological discovery.

"It's good you came back," I said to Drew.

"We'll see," he said as Barry appeared in the doorway.

First, we gave him the *Reader's Digest* version of what had transpired. When Barry understood that one of our attackers was still at large, he asked Drew, who'd chased the man and seen him get into his car, for a description of the vehicle. Something GM, he said. A Buick, or a Pontiac. Four doors, white. Some mud splattered around the wheel wells. Barry phoned it in so police throughout the Promise Falls area could be watching for it.

Barry took a seat at the kitchen table, accepted Ellen's offer of coffee and a piece of frozen cake, and asked us to lay it out for him.

I told him my end of the story. The two men showing up, tying me up in the shed, taping my fingers to the hedge trimmer. Ellen told her half, about the dark-haired man bursting into the house, tying her to a chair and leaving her there. Then, later, bringing her out to the shed when I'd demanded to know that she was okay.

That brought us to Drew.

"Where do I know you from?" Barry asked, looking at him warily.

"I robbed a bank," Drew said matter-of-factly.

"Son of a bitch, that's who you are," Barry said.

"Five years ago," Drew added. "The one at Saratoga and Main."

"That didn't go very well," Barry said.

"If by not going very well, you mean I got caught as I was walking out the door, yeah, that's right. I spent a little too long in there, someone hit the silent alarm, and you guys were waiting for me when I walked out."

Barry nodded. "I don't know that you were cut out for that line of work."

"No."

"And you're out now?"

"About six weeks," he said. "Mr. Cutter here gave me a job cutting grass."

"Well, isn't that nice of him," Barry said, glancing at me. "And what were you doing out here tonight?"

"I'd busted one of Mr. Cutter's mowers and was dropping by to fix it before we started out for work again tomorrow."

Barry looked at me for confirmation. I nodded.

Ellen and I both told Barry what happened after Drew arrived. How he'd seen the dark-haired one take Ellen from the house to the shed, then seen the predicament I was in. How, when Ellen managed to unplug the hedge trimmer, the one whose name I knew to be Mortie lunged for her, and then Drew came in and hit him with the shovel he'd taken from the back of my truck.

"He saved our lives, Barry," I said.

"These guys," Barry said, "you ever see either of them before?"

We explained that we'd only gotten a look at Mortie, and only since he'd been dead, but we didn't know him. And neither Ellen nor I had any idea who the other guy was. "But he had a tattoo," I said. "On his arm. A knife. And he appeared to have dark hair."

"That sound right to you?" Barry asked Ellen. She nodded. "You didn't hear his name at all?"

"Mortie was smart enough not to say it out loud," I said.

"Maybe he wasn't planning to kill you," Barry said. "Otherwise, why be careful about that?"

"I don't know," I said.

"And you say they were here for a disc?"

"Of a book. I told you about this before but you weren't interested," I reminded him. "It was a copy of a book that was on a computer owned by Brett Stockwell, a student of Conrad Chase's years ago, when he was still a professor and not Thackeray's president."

Barry was scribbling things in his notebook. "And this disc would be interesting why, again?"

"Because Conrad later published a book that was pretty much that book."

Barry frowned. "So what are you saying here? The president of Thackeray College sent a couple of thugs to torture you and get that disc and maybe kill you, too?"

"No," Ellen said. "He's not saying that. That wouldn't make any sense because Conrad already has the disc. I gave it to him earlier today."

I gave her another puzzled look and shook my head.

A uniformed officer came into the kitchen to speak with Barry. "We checked the dead guy for ID," he told the detective. "Nothing on him but some cash in his pants pocket. Quite a bit of it, too. Looks like a couple grand."

"Okay," he said, and the officer went back outside. Barry looked up from his notebook. "So who the hell else would want this disc, then? Who else knew you had it, who might still think you had it?"

"I don't know," I said. "Conrad's wife, Illeana, suspected I had it, but if Conrad knew we didn't have it, it stands to reason she knew, too."

"Anyone else?"

I tried to think. Penny had said she might have mentioned the existence of the book on a computer Derek had found, but had she mentioned a disc? I didn't think so.

Barry made some more notes, then put down his pen so he could work his fork through his slice of frozen cake, shove it into his mouth. "You know, Jim, I've known you a long time, and you're a pretty good guy, with a pretty good head on your shoulders, but honestly, this is really getting way out there."

"Barry," Ellen said, "don't you think it's possible that these men who came here tonight are the same ones who killed the Langleys?"

Barry put down his fork. "I don't know, Ellen."

"Whatever the reason, whatever they

were looking for, isn't it a bit much to think that what happened here tonight isn't related to what happened at the Langleys' a few nights ago?"

Barry slowly finished chewing the cake in his mouth and swallowed.

"The Langleys get murdered, a computer goes missing, and then a few nights later, two men terrorize us, wanting a disc related to that computer. Doesn't that tell you something?"

"I see where you're going with this, Ellen," Barry said.

"Our son—Derek—he certainly didn't have anything to do with this tonight," my wife told him. "He's in jail. And he wouldn't exactly send someone to torture his parents. He didn't have any more to do with what happened here than he did with what happened at the Langleys'. Barry, you have to let Derek go. He's innocent."

Something flashed in Barry's eyes, like maybe he knew it, too. I hoped he wasn't the kind of person to sacrifice the life of an innocent to protect his reputation. The arrest of our son was a feather in Barry's cap for a couple of days there, and plucking it out was going to be embarrassing.

"We'll see, Ellen," he said noncommittally. "You know that there's more to Derek's relationship with the Langleys than meets the eye."

We were all silent for a moment, until Ellen leaned in close to Barry, looked him in the eye, and said, "He didn't do it, and you know it. You know it in your heart."

Barry pushed the plate away from himself. "I want to talk to all three of you individually." He looked at Drew. "You first."

He took Drew outside with him.

Ellen said, "A bank robber?"

"My lawn company doesn't yet have an advanced screening process for new hires," I said.

"No no," Ellen said. "I'm not second-guessing you on that. I just, I don't know, I don't think I ever met a bank robber before."

"I don't much care at this point if he's the Boston Strangler," I said. "I just hope Barry doesn't do anything stupid and charge him." I got up, leaned against the fridge, feeling exhausted. The attack on us by our two visitors would have been enough to knock the wind out of me, but the questions surrounding everything that had happened were equally draining.

Some of them needed to be directed at my wife.

"Ellen," I said, "why'd you give the disc to Conrad?"

"I thought it was the right thing to do, for reasons that are hard to explain."

"Sometimes," I said, "I wonder if you still feel something for him."

Her eyes looked tired, and almost sad. "You don't get it, do you?"

"What?"

"I despise that man." She paused. "More than you'll ever know."

"Then why are you helping him? Don't you understand what's going on here? Can't you connect the dots? Don't you see what he's done?"

"You're just seeing what you want to see," Ellen said.

"No, you're turning a blind eye," I shot back. "Even if Conrad didn't send those goons to get us tonight, he's involved. Somehow, he got wind of the fact that a computer, belonging to his student, the one he stole a book from, had resurfaced. He realized what was on it, and either went over to the Langley house himself or sent someone there to get it. And it all went horribly wrong, and they all ended up dead."

"No," Ellen said. "He already had the computer."

"What?"

"He told me. Earlier, on the Friday that the Langleys were murdered, Albert Langley called him."

"Wait a minute. Langley gave him the computer?"

"Adam told his father about the computer he and Derek were messing around with, what they'd found on it. Albert immediately recognized what it was, knew the book, knew it was the same as Conrad's. So he called Conrad, told him about it, and Conrad came by Albert's office and took it away. He was Conrad's lawyer. And his friend. From way back."

I moved away from the fridge, walked

slowly to the sink and back again, rubbing my forehead.

"He told you this?" I asked.

"Yes."

"You believe him?"

Ellen paused. "Yes."

"God, this is totally . . . this is completely fucking with my head," I said. "But if those guys who came here tonight didn't know Conrad had the disc, then they must not have known the night they went to the Langleys' that he already had the computer, too."

Ellen said, "I don't know. And I don't care about any of that. It doesn't mean anything to me. All I care about now is getting Derek out of jail. I want him out, and then I want to put all this behind us. I don't care about that goddamn book, I don't care about Conrad, I don't give a shit about any of it. None of it matters as long as Derek's in jail."

I approached her, slowly at first, then put my arms around her. "I know," I said. "I know."

But there were still questions. So maybe Conrad didn't have anything to do with what had happened here tonight. And maybe he didn't have anything to do with the murder of the Langleys.

But there was still the matter of his book. And who wrote it.

And if it was Brett Stockwell, and if Conrad wanted to steal his book, how, unless he'd made some deal to pay the boy off, could he allow the boy to live and expect to get away with it?

Once Barry was done with interviewing Drew, he spent some time with Ellen in the living room. That left me and Drew alone in the kitchen.

"So," I said, smiling, standing by the counter, "a bank robber."

"I wasn't very good at it," Drew said. "My first holdup, I blew it."

"Why'd you do it?"

"I needed money," he said, looking at me like I was some kind of an idiot. "I had a child to support."

I recalled his comment, that he didn't have kids anymore. Rather than pursue this, I asked, "How'd it go with Detective Duckworth?"

He shrugged, happened to glance up at the clock on the kitchen wall. It was nearly midnight. "We still workin' tomorrow?" he asked.

I smiled tiredly. "How about I pick you up at nine instead of eight?"

"That's okay," he said. "If they don't take me in."

I wanted to say something encouraging, but I had no idea how his talk with Barry had gone.

He said to me, "You could have just said you killed him. The cops would've believed you without even thinking. But not me. Not with a record." He frowned. "I was starting to think maybe you're actually an okay person."

If I'd made a bad impression when I'd first met Drew, I wasn't sure how I'd done it. And besides, was that what you had to do to qualify as an okay guy in Drew's book? Claim to kill someone when you hadn't?

Wasn't that a lot for Drew to ask of me, even if he had saved my life? And Ellen's? Maybe it wasn't. The thing was, I might have done it if I'd thought the police would buy the story. But there was still Mortie's accomplice out there somewhere, and no matter how disreputable he might be, his version of events could end up undercutting mine.

It seemed better to stick with the truth. I just hoped it didn't end up getting Drew screwed.

Finally, Barry and I had some one-on-one time, but we ended up covering the same ground again, and if Barry had found any inconsistencies in our stories, he wasn't letting on.

The last thing I said to him was, "They won't charge him, will they? Ellen and I'd probably be dead now if Drew hadn't shown up."

Barry shook his head slowly, as if to say no. But all he said was, "How's your hand?"

There were marks where my fingers had been jammed into the teeth of the hedge trimmer, but the skin hadn't been broken. "Okay," I said.

"You were damn lucky."

"Yeah," I said. "I've got horseshoes up my ass."

*   *   *

We walked back into the kitchen together. Ellen and Drew were outside on
the deck, talking. A different uniformed
officer, who was holding something
down at his side, out of view, sidled
past them and came into the kitchen.

"Detective," he said, and presented
Barry with a plastic evidence bag.
There was a gun inside it.

"A Glock 19," Barry said. "Nine mill.
The Langleys were killed with a nine-
millimeter weapon."

I felt my own eyebrows go up.

"Where'd you find it?" Barry asked
the cop.

"Alongside the lane, just by the
grass. We've marked the spot."

"What's going on?" I asked. "You
saying this is the gun that killed the
Langleys?"

Barry shook his head. "Nobody's
saying that. Not yet. If it's the same
gun, it's made an amazing reappear-
ance. Every square inch around here
was searched after the Langleys were
killed." He told the cop to keep the re-

covered gun out of sight, and called Drew in.

"Yeah?" he said.

"You said you followed the second guy?"

"Yeah, but he had a head start, I couldn't catch him. I'm strong, but I'm not a good runner."

"You notice anything funny when he got to the car, whether he dropped anything?"

Drew thought. "He was just getting in and the door was closing, then he went to open it again, but I was getting close, and he closed it and backed up like crazy, kicking up gravel and everything."

"Come show me exactly where the car was," Barry said.

We all walked up the lane together, Barry and Drew and the cop who'd brought in the gun in the lead, me and Ellen following.

"Okay," Drew said. "It was dark, like now, but the car was parked just up here, about three car lengths in from the road, you know?"

Barry was nodding. The cop had a

big flashlight and was shining it ahead. Drew pointed out to the highway. "I had to leave my car up there because I couldn't get past it."

I squinted into the darkness where Drew was pointing, saw a car up there, looked like an older Ford Taurus, maybe a Mercury Sable.

Drew stopped walking. "I think it was right about here."

"And the car," Barry said. "It was nose in?"

"That's right."

"So when our dead guy's buddy got in, it would have been over here, on the right side of the lane." The cop shone his light in that area.

"Yup," said Drew. The cop's light had picked up a small flag that I was guessing had been used to mark where the gun was found. "What's that?" Drew asked.

Barry said, "That's where our friend dropped his gun. Son of a bitch."

TWENTY-NINE

The police weren't done with us until nearly one in the morning, and ordinarily I might consider that a bit late to call someone, but when Ellen suggested getting in touch with Natalie Bondurant to tell her about what had happened, and how these recent events might help Derek, I said, "Do it."

If Natalie was upset at our having disturbed her, she gave no indication. "I want to know what evidence they get out of that gun," she said. "Pronto."

Despite what we'd been through, we slept better that night than we might have expected. I think we were able to sleep because we felt, for the first time since Derek's arrest, that there was hope.

"I'm all over this today," Ellen said at

breakfast. "I'm going down to see Natalie, I'm going to see if I can get in to talk to Derek."

I felt comforted, seeing Drew standing at the curb outside his mother's house when I turned down his street. Clearly, Barry had not changed his mind through the night, and Drew had not been taken into custody.

"Hey," I said as he climbed into the truck.

"Morning," he said.

"How are you?" I asked.

"Tired," he said. "Later, that detective? I was getting in my car to go and he asked all his questions all over again. A couple of times."

"Things okay?"

"I think he was finally satisfied that we were all telling the truth."

"You okay otherwise?" It seemed a somewhat foolish question. He'd killed someone the night before. Even though his actions had been justified, taking the life of another person, it certainly wasn't the sort of thing I'd be able to shake off.

"I wondered if you'd actually come this morning," he said.

"Why?"

"Because of my record," Drew said. "Because you found out I'd been in prison."

"I'd be a real asshole, after what you did for me and Ellen last night, to bail on you."

He nodded, stared straight ahead beyond the windshield. "How about you?" he asked. "You okay?"

"Yeah," I said. I felt a need to try to connect with Drew, to draw him out more. I sensed this sadness in him. "It can't be easy, coming out of jail, starting over again."

Drew nodded. "It's kind of like being born. You're thrown into the world, not really ready. No job, no money, no way to get around."

"At least there's your mom."

Another nod. "Yeah. And I ran into an old buddy, guy named Lyle, he's letting me borrow a car. You can't manage without a car."

I said, "You mentioned last night that

you'd had a kid. That you needed money."

"Yeah," he said.

"But not anymore? Was it a custody thing?"

"No," he said. "Died."

What do you say? "That's rough" was the best I could think to come up with. "I can't imagine, losing a child. When did it happen?"

"Not that long ago. Another few weeks she'd have been eighteen. It's with me all the time. I figure it always will be."

"What about her mother?"

Drew shook his head. "Not on the scene. Not for a long time. She was a flake. She fucked off years ago."

"So when you were in prison, who looked after her? Your mother?"

He glanced at me. "Yeah. My mother. That's why now, with her getting older, I feel I owe it to her to help her out."

"Sure," I said. I waited a beat. "What happened?"

"Huh?"

"To your daughter?"

Drew pushed his tongue around inside his cheek. Finally, he said, "She got sick. She didn't get help from people when she needed it."

"Doctors," I said. "They missed something?" He shrugged. He didn't want to talk about it. I guessed that it was too painful to do so, and that my questions had become too personal. "Sorry, man," I said, and dropped it.

Our first house of the day belonged to Walter Burgess, Brett Stockwell's retired high school English teacher. It was my first time here since he'd asked me to take on his property.

He came out to greet me, while his companion, Trey Watson, watched us through the screen door.

"Hello," Burgess said. "Anything you need to know from me before you get started?"

"Not really," I said. "Just if you have any requests."

"Just watch out for the tomato plants up against the house around back. Trey'll have a fit if something happens to them."

"Don't worry."

He cleared his throat, like he was

working up to something. "A lot's happened to your family since you dropped by the other day."

"Yeah," I said. Certainly Derek's situation was well known. The incident at our house the night before hadn't quite become common knowledge yet.

"I'm sorry for your troubles," he said. "When you were here before, you were asking about Brett. You said there was a book. On an old computer of his."

"That's right."

"Did you sort that all out?"

"Not really."

Burgess nodded. "That was pretty much it, though? What was on the computer?"

"I don't know, exactly," I said. "I never actually saw it. What makes you ask?"

He shook his head like it didn't really matter. "Trey, he was just curious, that's all. So I thought I would ask. But it's nothing."

Something twigged in the back of my mind. Something Derek had said in passing when he first told me that he'd noticed the computer was missing from

Adam's room, and what was on it. He'd said there'd been letters to some teacher Brett had had back in high school.

"Letters," I said.

"Pardon?" Burgess said.

"There were letters on the computer. To a teacher."

Burgess took a breath. "Were they to me? What did they say?"

"I don't know. You think they were to you?"

He ran his tongue over his lips nervously. "It's possible. He wrote a few to me back then. They were . . . he seemed a bit infatuated with me, if you want to know the truth." He shook his head, trying to dismiss the whole thing. "I'm sure it wouldn't have mattered anyway. Trey worries about these sorts of things. It hardly matters now. It's not like I have a job to lose anymore." He licked his lips again. "If you should happen to run across them, would you let me know?"

"I'll keep my eye out," I said.

He thanked me and went back into the house. I went over to Drew, mentioned to him about the tomato plants, and we got started. I took the tractor, cut the front and back yards, while Drew tackled the tight areas with the mower.

When we were done and packing things away, I thought Walter Burgess might come back out again, even if to say nothing more than he was happy with the job, but the front door never opened. Drew and I got in the truck.

"What's their story?" Drew asked as we pulled away from the curb.

"What do you mean?"

"Well, I could tell they were a couple of pansies, and I don't have anything against that."

"Sure."

"But they were really going at it in there."

"Go on."

"I'd stopped the trimmer for a few seconds, had to get some more line out of it, and you were far enough away on the Deere, in the backyard, I think, so you weren't making that much of a racket, and the two of them were bickering away in there like all get-out."

"Really," I said, turning the A/C fan up a notch. "About what?"

"At first, it was just random shit, how the one, not the one who came out and said hello to us, but the other one, he was going on about the tomato plants and whether we'd been warned about them or not, and then they started getting into other shit, and then the one with the plants said, 'Maybe you'd be happier with some of your boy toys instead of me.' And something like 'You can't be too careful, these things can come back and bite you in the ass.'"

"He said that?"

"Yeah."

"So what did Walter—the one who came out and saw us—what did Walter have to say about that?"

"He said the other guy was overreacting, then he told him to go fuck himself."

I fiddled a little more with the A/C. "Everybody's got a lot of shit on their plate," I said.

"Yeah," said Drew. "No kidding."

*   *   *

We were pulling up to our second prop-erty of the day when my cell rang. I wasn't expecting to hear any news from Ellen this early, but you never knew. I flipped open the phone without looking to see who was calling.

"Hello?" I said.

"Has something *else* happened be-tween you and Lance?" a man asked. It took me a second to realize the mayor was on the other end.

"What are you talking about, Randy?" I said.

"Look, you two guys, you need to cut this shit out," the mayor shouted into the phone. "He came back to work late yesterday after he got his face stitched, said he was okay to drive, but then last night, he's supposed to run me up to some fucking fund-raising thing at the hospital and he doesn't show. And he hasn't shown up this morning."

"So why you calling me, Randy? You asking me to drop what I'm doing and drive you around today? I can pick you up in my truck, but you'll have to ride in the back with the tractor."

"Always a fucking comedian," he

said. "I just want to know if you know where he is. I've called his house, his cell, called a couple of other people who know him, nobody's seen him."

"Why would you think I'd know?"

"I wanted to know whether you'd had another run-in with him. If you punched his ticket, let me know and I can stop expecting him."

"I didn't punch his ticket, Randy," I said.

"So you haven't seen him? Not since you paid him a visit yesterday?"

"That's right," I said. Unless that had been him the night before, working with Mortie. But I didn't think it was Lance then, and I didn't think it was Lance now. Besides, those dots didn't connect, did they? And if that dark-haired guy had been Lance, wouldn't he have found some excuse to kick the shit out of me? Me, tied to a chair, unable to fight back? Lance wouldn't have been able to resist a target like that any more than I would have, had the roles been reversed.

"This isn't like Lance," Mayor Finley said. "I mean, he's an asshole, I know that, but he's generally a reliable ass-hole."

"I wish I could help you, Randy," I said. "But I've got work to do."

"Where are you?"

"What?"

"In your truck. Right now. Where are you?"

"I'm on the north side. On Bethune."

"Shit, that's not far from where Lance lives. Drop by his place, see if he's there."

"Randy, are you kidding me?"

"You know where he lives, right?"

I did. When we both worked for Finley, I'd occasionally pick him up or drop him off with the mayor's Grand Marquis.

"Forget it, Randy. Send some other errand boy."

"Now you listen up, Cutter. You waltzed into city hall yesterday and assaulted a municipal employee. And to the best of my knowledge, no one called the cops on you. Not me, not even Lance. So there's a favor you owe me. On top of that, if that dumb fuck passed out last night because of some

sort of delayed concussion or something, thanks to you, then—"

"Fine," I said. "I'll drop by his place.
But if he's there and blows my brains
out, I'm gonna be pissed with you."

"Thanks. Call me."

The mayor hung up. More than two
years since I'd left his employ, and it
seemed as though I'd had more conversations with him the last week than
I'd had working for him on a daily basis.

"What are we doing?" Drew asked.

"Making a stop along the way," I
said.

I turned right off Bethune onto
Raven, climbed it to Mountainside,
hung a left. Lance lived on the second
floor of a two-story apartment, ac-
cessed by an outside stairwell. I pulled
the truck and trailer up to the curb, noticed Lance's Mustang in the alleyway.

"Hey," I said to Drew, "that look anything like the car you saw that guy drive
off in last night?"

He seemed surprised to be asked,
then said, "No. It wasn't like that. I told
the cop. It was a Buick or something, a
four-door."

I'd forgotten. "Right," I said. "I'll be right back." I got out, climbed the steps to the apartment door, banged on it.

I tried peering through the door's window, but there was a curtain in the way. I banged again, then spotted a doorbell button and leaned on it. I wasn't raising anyone.

I came back down the stairs, got out my cell, phoned Randy back.

"The car's here, but he's not answering," I said.

"Did you try the door?" he asked.

"No," I said. "I did not try the door. I'm not barging in there. Lance'd love that, me busting down the door to his place. He's probably in there with a shotgun."

"Jesus, Cutter, the way your mind works."

"Randy, do you have any idea what the last twenty-four hours have been like for me?"

"No," he said. "What? Something happen?"

I just shook my head. "I'll tell you all about it sometime. After you lose your bid for Congress, have some time on your hands. Then—"

"Excuse me."

There was a short Chinese man in a flowered shirt and shorts standing next to me. I said, "Huh?"

"Were you just upstairs?" he said, pointing up to Lance's apartment.

"Yeah," I said. "Well, no. I knocked but no one's home."

"Something's leaking up there," the little man said. "I live below. Something's coming through the floor."

Into the phone, I said to Randall Finley, "Hang on." Then, to the short man, "Show me."

He led me into the unit directly below Lance's and pointed to the ceiling. There was a dark circle, about four inches in diameter.

"Not there yesterday," the man said.

"You got a chair or something I can stand on?" I asked him.

He brought a stepstool from the kitchen and opened it up under the spot. "Whatever it is," he said, "landlord's going to have to pay to get it fixed. I called him, left a message, then you show up. I don't want a spot on my ceiling like that. Looks like hell."

"You hear anything funny up there?" I asked him, mounting the stool.

"I was out last night," he said. He smiled. "Dancing. I watch those TV shows, I decide I want to learn to dance."

"Great," I said. I reached up, touched the spot with the tip of my index finger. I brought it up close to my eye, lightly rubbed it with my thumb, felt the texture.

"What is it?" the man asked. "Is it oil?"

"No," I said. "It's not oil." I put the cell phone to my ear again. "You still there, Randy?"

"Yeah. What the fuck, you forget about me?"

"Randy, you better send the cops over. Might want to think about looking for another driver while you're at it."

THIRTY

This was no death by watering can.

"One shot," said Barry. "Right through the heart, looks like."

"Fuck me," said the mayor.

Randall Finley and Barry Duckworth were looking down at Lance, who lay facedown on the floor, dressed in nothing more than a pair of boxers and a white T-shirt. I got a good look at his arms. No tattoos. The blood had pooled under him and gradually soaked through the floorboards and down to the unit below.

I was hanging back by the door. I'd seen a dead body recently, so Lance's corpse was no novelty.

Barry told the uniformed cops hanging around to start knocking on doors. The man downstairs might not have heard anything, but someone else might have.

"If someone did hear a shot," I said, "why didn't they call the police?"

Barry gave me a tired look. "Nobody ever calls the cops when they hear one shot. They go, hey, what was that? Listen for a second shot, when that doesn't happen, they think, must have been a car, they go back to watching TV."

That did sound like the world we lived in.

"You got any idea who might have done this?" Barry asked me.

"No," I said. "But it won't be long before you find out he and I weren't getting along. We'd had a couple of run-ins this week. One of them at city hall."

"That a fact?" Barry asked.

"Yeah," I said.

"I seem to be running into you all the time now. That seem odd to you?"

"A bit."

"You hang around, okay?"

"Sure. I'm just going down to my truck."

I'd already spoken to Drew once, after I'd concluded it was blood leaking down through the floor into the apartment below, told him we were going to be stuck here awhile. When I went down to see him again, he was leaning up against the truck.

"What's going on?" he asked.

I told him.

"I'm starting to think you're bad luck to be around," Drew said. There wasn't a hint of irony in his voice.

The mayor walked over to where Drew and I were standing. He spoke directly to me, didn't so much as nod in Drew's direction. People skills.

"Can I talk to you a minute?" he said.

I walked with him a few yards down the sidewalk. "This is a hell of a thing," he said.

"Yeah," I said. "Imagine, someone not taking a liking to Lance."

"Oh shit, Cutter," Randy said. "If being an asshole was all it took to get yourself killed, you and I would have been dead long ago."

I agreed with half of that.

"Barry brought me up to speed on what happened at your place last night," he said. "Ellen, she's okay?" His concern seemed nearly genuine.

"Yes," I said.

"Those guys, you think they were out to kill you?"

"I wouldn't be surprised," I said.

"All that, plus your boy still in jail," Randy said. "When it rains, it fucking pours, isn't that what they say?"

"What did you want to talk to me about, Randy?" I asked.

"I need a driver," he said bluntly.

"You've got others on the city payroll who already filled in when Lance was off," I said. "Get one of them."

"I want you to come back and work for me," he said.

"I don't get it," I said. "You know I don't respect you. I punched you in the goddamn nose."

"I had that coming," he said. "I was going through a bad spell."

Randall Finley's life was one long bad spell.

"The thing is, I think that's what I like about you," he said. "You're solid, and you don't take any shit. I need more than a fucking driver. You help keep me in line. If that'd been you with me last week, when I went to that unwed mothers' place and made an ass of myself, you'd have found a way to get me back in the car before I did too much damage. Lance, he wasn't so good at that kind of thing. He just kissed my ass and did what I told him to do. He didn't know how to keep me from crossing the line."

"I wasn't always successful that way, either," I said. "That night, with that girl, that was an ugly scene, Randy. She was a child."

"But see, there's a perfect example. It was Lance who set that up. He'd had a go at her himself, I'm guessing. See, you'd never have arranged that for me in the first place. You've got, whaddya call them, standards. And morals. Lance indulged my weaknesses, where you know how to keep them in check."

"So you need a keeper," I said. "Not a driver."

Randy grinned. "If it makes you happy to think of it that way."

"I hope that kid sorted herself out."

"Who?" the mayor asked.

I sighed. "The one you kicked in the face when she bit your dick."

"Look, Cutter," he said, waving his hand dismissively, "the thing is, I learned a valuable lesson that night. I stopped messing with hookers. You see what I'm talking about? You taught me that lesson. I mean, I was pissed with you, about the nose and all, but you made me see the error of my ways. I'm grateful to you."

I couldn't help but laugh. "You sure are in the right line of work, Randy. You can lay it on thicker than anybody."

He grinned. "I like you, Cutter, even though you hate my guts. I'll pay you twice what I used to. Council'd never approve it, but I can find the money someplace. That's probably a hell of a lot more than you're making pushing a fucking mower."

That gave me pause. I didn't know how long Derek's legal problems might continue. And even if they didn't go on long, Natalie Bondurant was going to cost us a good chunk of change regardless. The lawn business was okay, but it wouldn't pay as well as my old salary doubled.

"Let me get back to you," I said.

Randy flashed me a huge smile, made a fist, and tapped me on the shoulder. "We'll talk later."

"Yeah," I said. "You need time to grieve."

He punched me again in the shoulder. "You're a pistol, that's what you are."

Part of me didn't want to be bothered, but I couldn't help but think about Lance, and why he was dead. I couldn't see any way that he might be mixed up in the murder of the Langleys or the missing computer.

I felt a headache coming on when Barry came down to talk to me. Again, I was dragged away from Drew so that I could be spoken to privately.

"What are you doing with that guy?" Barry asked me, tipping his head in the direction of my new employee.

"He was in the right place at the right time, more than once," I said. "You ever

think things happen for a reason? I
didn't used to, now I'm not so sure. I
had an accident out front of his
mother's house, he helped me out, I
found out he needed work and I gave
him some."

"He robbed a bank," Barry said.

"So you said. I'm not planning to get
him to do my taxes or make my de-
posits."

Barry shrugged. "Your call." He
cleared his throat, a signal that he was
about to switch gears. "Tell me about
this little spat you had with Lance," he
said.

"The other day, the mayor took me
for a drive, and when we got back,
Lance was pushing my buttons and my
elbow found its way into his stomach.
He got back at me a couple of days
later. Hid behind my trailer when I was
out on a job, sucker punched me, left
me rolled up in a ball on the street. And
then I returned the favor while he was
reading the sports pages."

"You two never did get along."

"No."

"We found somebody lives next door

says she heard something yesterday, late afternoon, just before six. She was getting ready to watch the news, heard a shot, didn't hear another, didn't think another thing about it."

"Just like you said," I said.

"I suppose you can account for your whereabouts at that time?" Barry asked.

"I've got a witness who can put me at my place right about then," I said.

"Not the dead guy I found in your shed, I hope."

"No, he came later. One of your cops. The one you had babysitting the house. He was leaving about that time, packing it in, talked to me on the way out."

Barry nodded. "Well, there you go." I thought he was done, and then he said, "That lady, watching the news. She did more than most people. She actually got up, went to her door, and opened it to stick her head out, just to be sure."

"But she didn't hear the second shot, so she sat back down."

"Yeah, pretty much. But she thought

she heard a man's voice. Thought she heard him say one word."

I waited.

"She heard someone say 'shame.'"

I let the word bounce around inside my head for a second. I thought back to what Natalie Bondurant had told us after she'd spent some time interviewing our son.

"Derek," I said. "That's what he heard someone say, in the Langley house."

"I know," Barry said.

I ran my hand over the top of my head. "Barry, there's so much going on, I can't keep it all straight."

"You and me both," he said. He said I was free to go and turned to walk away, then stopped and looked back. "There might be some good news about your son today," he said.

I started to open my mouth to ask, but Barry held up his hand. "I got nothing else to tell you."

"Then let me ask you about something else," I said, closing the distance between us. "There'd be a report somewhere, wouldn't there, about Brett

Stockwell taking a header off Promise Falls?"

"Ten years ago?"

"Yeah."

"I suppose so."

"I'd like to see it."

Barry studied me for a couple of seconds. "Let me see what I can do."

THIRTY-ONE

We still managed to get another yard in before lunch. Drew threw himself into his work. I couldn't help thinking that if he'd put the same energy into robbing banks as he did into cutting yards, he'd have a shitload of money tucked away someplace by now. I was going to phone Ellen about Lance, but decided she didn't need any more news to distract her from dealing with Natalie Bondurant, and getting our son sprung from jail.

For lunch, we drove back down by the river, just down from the falls, even got the same picnic table.

"So that was the mayor," Drew said, taking a drink from his water bottle. "Finley."

"Yeah," I said.

"And you used to work for him."

"I did. Not a period I'm particularly proud of, but we all have to do things sometimes that we don't much care for. The thing is," and the words were catching in my throat as I tried to say them, "he wants me to come back and work for him again, now that his regular guy is dead. And the truth is, I could use the money."

"So . . ." Drew looked at me. Here it was, his second day on the job, and it was looking like he was about to be laid off. And after all he'd done to save his boss's life. And his boss's wife's life.

"Look, I haven't made up my mind yet," I said.

Drew bit into his sandwich. "It's okay," he said. "Whatever you decide."

"Ellen won't believe it," I said. "If I go back and work for him, it'd have to be temporary, that's for sure. Until he found someone else to replace Lance."

"So Lance was his driver?"

"Yeah. He'd been with the mayor's office a long time, doing the same thing I did, before I quit."

"Why'd you quit?"

I took a deep breath. "There were lots of things. But they all came to a head one night. Things got a bit out of hand."

"What do you mean?"

"Let's just say that marriage is not all that sacred an institution for this guy, and the thing is, to a degree, if you want to fool around behind your wife's back, that's none of my business, you know? I don't have to like it, but then I'm not the morality police, either. But Jesus, when it's a kid . . ."

Drew picked up on that right away. "A kid?"

"You know, a street kid. I looked at her ID. Even if he didn't know for sure, he could have guessed she was under-age, there was no excuse. Listen," I said, recalling that I was supposed to keep my former boss's indiscretions to myself, "I shouldn't even be talking about this. It's over. Maybe, I don't know, he's not as big an asshole now as he was then."

Drew said, "So you just quit?"

"After I'd punched him in the nose, I kind of had to."

"So this kid, she was hooking?"

I nodded. "I gave her my name and number, told her to get in touch with me, but she never did."

"But you knew who she was," Drew said. "You'd seen her ID."

"Yeah," I said.

"You never tried to track her down, help her get her life back on track?" Drew asked.

"No," I said. "I didn't do that."

I felt Drew's eyes on me. "I remember her name," I said. "Sherry. Sherry Underwood."

"And you're going to go work for that man again?" Drew asked. "A man like that?"

"Maybe people change," I said, although I didn't believe, in my heart, that Randall Finley was really any different today than he was back then. Maybe just more careful. "You've changed, haven't you? You tried to rob a bank. Would you do that today?"

Drew thought about the question. "Maybe," he said.

The fact was, if I went back to work for Randy, I'd be doing it for my son. To pay for Derek's lawyer. I'd have driven Satan himself to work if it meant I'd be able to help my boy.

We were nearly wrapping up for the day. We were hot and sweaty and matted with grit. My cell rang.

"Something's happening," Ellen said. "Natalie just called and told me to meet her at the courthouse. Get here as fast as you can."

I dropped Drew off at his mother's house, then booted it downtown. He'd been pretty quiet the rest of the afternoon, at least during those moments when we weren't using any of the equipment. Once in the town's center, I had to circle the block three times until I found a spot long enough to accommodate the truck and trailer.

I looked a mess, but from the sound of Ellen's voice, this was not the time to go home and take a shower. I found her and Natalie Bondurant near the front entrance to the courthouse. Ellen gave me a quick once-over, smiled, and said, "You've got a twig stuck to your neck." She reached out and plucked it off.

I liked that she was smiling.

"They're dropping the charges," Natalie said. "They're kicking him loose."

"Oh my God," I said and threw my arms around Ellen. We held on to each other as Natalie continued.

"The case was already falling apart," she said. "They might have had enough to go to trial, but they knew they'd never win. What clinched it was the gun."

"The gun?" I asked.

"The one found at your place last night. They ran a ballistics check on it and determined it was the same weapon that was used on the Langleys."

"Jesus," I said, taking my arms from around Ellen. "So those two, Mortie what's-his-name and his buddy, they killed Albert and Adam and Donna."

"Well, that's yet to be proved," Natalie said. "But that's the gun they left behind. It's difficult to build a case against your son when he's sitting in jail and the gun he supposedly used ends up in the hands of those two. Not that there isn't a way it couldn't have happened, but the cops would have to connect the dots, and there aren't any dots to connect."

Ellen gripped my arm.

Natalie continued, "It also means those men who came to your house are now being linked to those two earlier homicides in Promise Falls. These guys were on quite a tear."

"And Lance," I said.

"Lance?" said Ellen.

"He's dead. He was found shot in his apartment this morning."

Ellen looked ashen. "Oh God, I didn't even know."

"A neighbor heard someone say 'shame' after the shot went off. Just like what Derek heard somebody say when he was hiding in the Langleys' basement. I'll bet, when they take that slug out of Lance, they're going to find that the same gun killed him as well."

"Why?" Ellen said. "What's the connection?"

"I don't know," I said. "I don't even know whether I care anymore."

"One of them," Ellen said, "is still out there. The one with the dark hair."

Natalie nodded. "And when the police find him, maybe some of these questions will get answered."

"What about Derek?" I asked. "When will we see him?"

"They're bringing him up now," Natalie said.

And then, as if on cue, he appeared. He was being escorted by a court official, wearing the same clothes he'd been arrested in, and the moment he saw us he ran. Ellen got ahead of me and took him in her arms first, and I ended up hugging both of them together, and everyone was crying, and we held on to one another like that for a very long time.

We offered to take him out for dinner. To Preston's, the best steak house in Promise Falls. But all Derek wanted was to go home, and it was just as well, since I needed to get into a shower. Turned out that was what he wanted as well, and he stood under it so long that by the time I had mine there was only cold water left.

I didn't complain. There probably wasn't enough hot water in the world to wash the prison experience off him.

We ordered two large pizzas to be delivered to the house, and spent the evening together in the kitchen, talking and laughing and crying, and if there had ever been a moment when we felt closer as a family, I could not remember it. We felt reborn, like our lives had been handed back to us. We were whole again.

"It's going to be different now," I said to Derek.

"I know," he said. "I gotta stop messing up."

"I don't mean that," I said. "I mean that we have to be straight with one another."

"Okay," he said. "I will."

"If you're in trouble," I said, "you have to come to me and your mother. Right away. When it happens. No more secrets." I glanced at Ellen. "Right?"

Ellen blinked. "Yes," she said. "That's right. No more secrets."

*   *   *

A cop came to the door, told us he'd been asked by Detective Duckworth to take a drive by our house every half hour or so. Mortie's buddy was still out there someplace, after all, and might decide to come back.

I asked him whether he wanted a slice of pizza.

"Anchovies?" the cop asked.

"No."

"Okay."

Back at the table, picking away at pizza crust, I said to my family, "Randy asked me to work for him again."

"What?" said Ellen. "Randy?"

"Yeah," I said. I grimaced. "There's an opening."

"I thought you hated that guy," Derek said.

"I'm not exactly the president of his fan club. But we could use the extra money. At least for the short term. Once we pay off the legal bills, then I can tell Randy he has to get somebody else. A month or two, whatever it takes."

"What about the business?" Derek said. "You going to pack it in? What about my job? I'll have to find something else for the rest of the summer."

"Here's what I was thinking," I said to him. "You run the business. You know how to do everything. You know the clients—we got a new one, but you don't have to worry about the Putnam place. They dropped us."

"Why?" Derek asked.

"Don't worry about it. But you know the drill."

"I can't do it all alone. It's too much for one person."

"I know. Drew can help. The two of you can do it."

"Drew?" Derek said. "The one who killed the guy in the shed?"

We had filled him in on the things that had happened while he'd been away, and how they had led to the charges against him being dismissed.

"Yeah, that Drew," I said, thinking suddenly that maybe it wasn't such a good idea. Derek might have qualms about pairing up with someone who was capable of that, even if the man's actions had saved his parents' lives.

But Derek said, "Cool. Sure."

I called Randy. "Here's the deal," I said. "You can have me for a few weeks, till I've paid off Natalie. So I'm already putting in my notice. That should give you enough time to find someone else you can live with for the long term."

"I knew you'd say yes," he said. "You know why?"

I had to ask. "Why, Randy?"

"Because when you're with me, you're always being reminded of how much better a person you are."

The son of a bitch was generally a stranger to the truth, but he seemed to be onto something there.

Derek spoke briefly on the phone with Penny, but her parents cut the call short. I gave them the benefit of the doubt and concluded they didn't still believe our son was guilty of murder. They just didn't want their daughter hanging out with a boy who'd figured out how to secure a makeout pad for a week.

We had ice cream around ten, and then Derek said he wanted to go to bed. He'd hardly slept since his arrest. He'd told us only a little about what it was like living in the Promise Falls jail. Those days were clearly not something he wanted to relive at the moment. Maybe some other time.

When we turned out the lights that night, we felt as though we might be seeing some light at the end of the proverbial tunnel.

Funny how wrong you can be about these things.

THIRTY-TWO

Technically speaking," I told Derek before we headed out Monday—we'd spent Sunday catching our breath and doing as little as possible—to pick up Drew, "you're the boss. It's your dad's truck and equipment, you're the boss's son. But don't go telling Drew what to do or anything. You're a kid—a smart kid, getting smarter every day—but you're a kid, and ordering an older guy like that around, it gets kind of awkward. Do you get what I'm saying?"

"Yeah," said Derek. "Don't be an asshole."

"Bingo," I said. "Mom and I will take the car, you follow us in the truck, once we've got Drew and I've introduced you, your mom's going to drop me off down at city hall."

"I can't believe you're really going back to work for him," Derek said. "I mean, I'm not saying whether you should or not, I'm just surprised."

"Me too," I said. "But you do what you have to do."

"I can pay you back," Derek said. "I'll work for free, that'll save some money. It was my fault. Being in the house. That's what got me into trouble. You and Mom shouldn't have to pay for my stupidity."

"Get in the truck," I said.

Ellen and I got in her Mazda, Ellen behind the wheel, and I gave her directions that led us to Drew, standing on the curb in his usual spot. Ellen pulled over, I got out and waited for Derek to pull over, get out and join us.

"My son," I said. "Drew, this is Derek; Derek, this is Drew."

They shook hands.

"I'd have called and explained, but I realized I didn't even have your number," I said.

"And I don't have a cell," Drew said. "Not really money for it in my budget at the moment." To Derek, he said, "So, you're out. Congratulations."

"I'm going to spend the next few weeks working for the mayor's office." I couldn't bring myself to actually say Randy's name, not after Drew's judgmental comments the day before. "Derek's going to fill in for me in the meantime. He knows the drill, the customers, all that stuff."

"Okay," Drew said.

"So, I've gotta take off," I said. "Talk to you at the end of the day," I said to Derek, gave him a hug he wasn't too embarrassed to receive, then walked back to the car. Ellen slipped out, gave Derek a hug of her own, then settled back in behind the wheel.

The last thing I heard was Derek saying to Drew, "So, like, my dad says you robbed a bank."

Maybe I should have given him just a little more advice.

I was dressed a little differently for work today. Black dress slacks, black shoes, off-white dress shirt, gray sports jacket.

I had a tie rolled up and tucked into my pocket for emergencies, but given that the heat was still with us, I was going to try to get away with an open collar.

I had forgotten that there's a lot of sitting around in this job, and that was how I spent most of my morning. I got caught up on news with some of the office staff, who were both sympathetic and congratulatory about our home situation.

Shortly after lunch, Randy said we had just a few items on the agenda for the afternoon. He was trying to keep his schedule light, since tomorrow was his news conference, where he intended to officially announce that he was running for Congress.

The first thing on today's schedule was a car dealership opening, where the mayor cut a ribbon and ate some cake and glad-handed and had his picture taken pretending to close a door on his hand. I hung out by the Grand Marquis, preferring to keep as far away from this sort of stuff as possible, although I did score a free barbecued hot dog.

After that, we were off to the Swanson House, the place where single mothers and their babies could find support and a place to live. This was the mayor's second stop here since barging in unannounced that night the week before. He'd already cleaned the rug he threw up on, but now he was there to present the home's manager, Gillian Metcalfe, with a check for five thousand dollars. I was pretty sure the city came up with more than five thousand a year for Swanson House—it was probably more in the range of fifty or a hundred grand—but if you handed it all over at once, that tended to limit the number of photo ops. Better ten to twenty stops with a five-thousand-dollar check each time.

Randy was visibly pissed as we walked up the sidewalk to Swanson House. "I don't see any media," he said. "You see any fucking media?"

I did not. There were no TV vans, no cars with the logo of the local newspaper plastered to the door. Could it be that the mayor handing over a measly five grand to the single mothers' residence wasn't particularly newsworthy?

I could recall times in my previous stint with Randall Finley when, if he showed up at a scheduled event that was clearly going to have less of a publicity payoff than anticipated, he walked. He'd been invited one time to a high school graduation ceremony, but when he arrived and learned from school officials that he wasn't sitting on the stage as the students came up to receive their diplomas, but instead in the front row, where he would not be on view 100 percent of the time by the parents in attendance, he bolted.

"I gave up two other events that would give me better exposure than this one, now that you've got me sitting down with the regular people," he told the astonished head of student services. "If you're not putting me on the stage here, I can probably still catch one of them."

At the time, I sidled up to him and whispered, "People will never forget this if you blow them off."

And he'd said to me, "And where were you mayor, exactly?"

But Randy wasn't going to pull any of that kind of shit with Gillian Metcalfe. She had media savvy. Dumping the Swanson House's soiled carpet on the steps of town hall was evidence of that. So even if no one from the press showed, Randy was going to make sure she was happy, or at least as happy as he was likely to make her with a five-thousand-dollar check. If Gillian was smart, and she was, she'd give that check a limited-enough look of approval to guarantee there'd be another one before too long.

While the mayor was shaking her hand and trying to make small talk as she smiled under duress, I wandered down to the house kitchen, which was about twice the size of one in a standard home. There were two stoves, two oversized fridges, a couple of microwaves, loads of counter space, as well as half a dozen high chairs and plastic bibs scattered about. I could hear one, possibly two, small babies crying upstairs, but the child sitting in one of the high chairs in the kitchen was looking very content as his mother fed him a gooey white mixture I took to be pablum.

"Hey," I said, trying not to intrude, but not wanting to be rude, either.

The baby's mother glanced at me, flashed me a smile, but she had to focus on getting the tiny plastic spoon into the mouth of her baby, who looked about ten months old, I guessed.

There was something about the mother that made me look at her more closely. Twenty years old, maybe, but there was still a chance she was in her teens. Dirty blond hair that hung to her shoulders, brown eyes, a stud so small I almost missed it in her nose. A couple of forehead zits, pale skin, no lipstick, a sharp cleft in her chin.

I was trying to place her, almost certain I'd seen her before somewhere. Her outfit—track pants and sweatshirt—was wrong. This wasn't the getup I'd seen her in before.

"Your baby's beautiful," I said, moving closer.

The young woman beamed. "Thank you. His name is Sean."

"Hey, Sean," I said. Pablum squirted back out of his mouth and dropped onto the high chair tray. He glanced down, stuck his hand in it.

"And I'm Linda," the mother said.

"Linda, hi," I said. I extended a hand. "I'm Jim. Jim Cutter."

We shook hands. Bits of baby food stuck to my palm.

"Hi, Jim," she said. "So, you work for the mayor?"

On her way into the kitchen with the baby, she'd seen Randy chatting up Metcalfe.

"I drive him around," I said. "Actually, this is my first day in a couple of years, working for him. I'm sort of filling in. His other driver, he's kind of unavailable."

"He came in here last week and threw up," Linda said. "Not the driver, the mayor."

"So I heard. It's kind of his specialty."

"Throwing up?"

"Well, making an ass of himself. He has a wide repertoire of techniques at his disposal."

Linda smiled, got some more pablum on the spoon. "Yeah, no kidding."

The way she said it suggested she had some familiarity with the mayor's leadership style.

"You look like you want to ask me something," Linda said. "You want to know why I'm here, why I haven't got a husband."

It was true, I was about to ask her something. But not that. "I don't think that would be any of my business," I said.

"It's okay," she said. "This guy, Eric, he got me pregnant, and I think maybe he would have married me, but he got sent to Iraq, and I was thinking that when he got back, he'd be a father to this boy, even if he didn't actually want to marry me, but then he got killed."

"I'm sorry."

"He was in a helicopter, and it went down."

"I'm sorry," I said again.

"It's a stupid war," Linda said.

"That's what a lot of people think," I said.

"So I didn't have a job or any money,

and they're letting me and my baby stay here until I get myself back on my feet, you know?"

"Sure." I paused. "You're right, I was going to ask you something, though, but not that. Something else."

"Oh yeah?"

"You look familiar to me. I feel as though we've met before somewhere."

She looked away from Sean long enough to study my face, then went back to the feeding. "Yeah, I might have met you once," she said. "It's possible. I've met a lot of people." She hesitated. "A lot of men."

Then I remembered. She was the girl standing outside the room, in the hallway, the night I found Randall Finley with the underage hooker. Linda, I'd assumed, was earning her money the same way as Sherry Underwood, at least that was what the tight top, short skirt, and heels had suggested to me at the time.

"You used to . . . I mean, I seem to remember that you . . ." How did one put this to a young mother feeding her baby?

"Fucked guys for money? Don't worry," she said, nodding at Sean. "He can barely say 'Mommy' yet." She studied me again. "But I don't think I ever did you."

"No," I said. "You didn't." I sat down at the table so she wouldn't have to crane her neck up to look at me. "So you managed to get off the street."

"Yeah," she said, then gestured around her. "I moved up to this. A home for knocked-up teens."

I smiled. "Don't put yourself down."

"I've been a screwup most of my life," she said. "But I really want to get it together, especially now." Her cheeks swelled with pride as she looked at her baby. "I'd like to finish high school and go to college."

"What would you like to do?" I asked.

"I'd kind of like to get into journalism," she said. "I've seen a lot of shit, ways people live that they shouldn't have to, that people should be writing more about. I don't think most people really care about street kids or what happens to them. Believe me, I know what I'm talking about. I'd like to try and change that."

"Good for you," I said, trying hard not to sound patronizing, because I meant it. For a moment neither of us said anything. Finally, I said, "You knew a girl named Sherry, didn't you?"

"Sherry?"

"Sherry Underwood," I said. "Back then, when you were, what do you call it, a working girl?"

"Hooker," Linda said.

I smiled. "Hooker. Back then, you hung out with her? Worked together?"

She thought back. "Yeah. Sherry. Shit, haven't thought of her in a while. She was a couple of years younger than me. Kind of young to be out there, but what are you going to do, right? You need to eat."

"So you knew her."

"A little."

"Do you know what ever happened to her?" I asked.

"Why?" Linda asked.

I hesitated. How to explain. "Well," I said, "I was around one night, when she was in a bit of trouble. She should have gone to a hospital. She'd gotten kicked in the nose. I tried to talk her into going to see a doctor but she wouldn't do it."

"Oh yeah," said Linda. "I remember that. You were there." She glanced out the kitchen door. "So was that guy out there handing over the check."

My eyebrows went up. "You remember him?"

"You'd be surprised how many people I remember. Some more important than him. Anyway, I can tell you why she wouldn't have gone to the hospital. You sit there all night, you lose a lot of money, plus it's not like we had any kind of health plan, you know?"

"Sure. She still around? Is Sherry still working the street?"

"I don't know," Linda said. "I got out of that before she did. So our paths didn't cross that much. But I saw her one time, not long after I got knocked up, downtown, in Kelly's?" Another downtown diner. "She didn't look so good."

"What do you mean?'

"I don't know," Linda said. "She was

looking really rough. She was, like, sixteen or seventeen, looked like a hundred. Some kids, they handle the street okay, but others, it wears them down, they get into drugs, meth sometimes. Or they get AIDS or something like that." She said it very matter-of-factly.

"So things weren't going that well for her," I said. "You think she still hangs out down there?"

Linda was using a damp cloth to clean Sean's face. "Like, I kind of doubt it," she said. "Given how she looked last time I saw her, unless someone got to her and helped her get her life back on track, she's a goner."

"Dead? You think she's dead?"

Linda shrugged. "Shit, who knows? Unless she managed to turn her life around on her own, which is not very likely. I mean, come on, what are the odds anyone else is going to take the time to help some dumb street kid get her life back in order? It's like I said, most people, they really don't want to deal with people like us."

THIRTY-THREE

Mayor Finley popped his head into the kitchen, looking for me. "Hey, let's roll," he said, without so much as a glance at Linda and her baby, just like when I had Drew standing next to me outside of Lance's place. If Randy didn't need to speak to you, didn't need to know who you were, he didn't see any need to acknowledge your existence.

Back in the car, he said, "Okay, so we might as well go back to the office. I got a committee meeting at two, then at three-thirty I got this tree planting at a school."

"Sounds nice," I said.

"Fucking pain in the ass," he said. "Every goddamn school in the city is on this green kick, you know? They make the kids stop bringing plastic bags to school, they think they've solved global warming. Then their mommies come pick them up after school in their fucking Hummers."

Once in a while, Randy actually had an insight that was valid.

He said, "So, who you think did it?"

I had been thinking about Derek and Drew, wondering how their first day working together was shaping up, how Derek's second day out of jail was going. "Huh?" I said.

"Lance. Who offed Lance?"

"I don't know," I said.

"I'm thinking, jealous husband? Dope dealer? Some pimp he tried to get out of paying? Gambling debts, maybe? Or what about this?" He leaned forward in his seat, all conspiratorial, like there was someone else in the car with us. "Maybe a gay lover."

"I don't know," I said again.

Finley settled back in his seat. "The thing is, despite all the time we spent together, I didn't really know all that much about him."

"Why do you think that is?" I asked.

In my rearview mirror, I saw him shrug.

"I guess I really didn't give a shit," he said. "To be honest with you, Cutter, other people's lives, they don't really interest me that much."

There was a campaign slogan in there somewhere, I thought. My cell rang.

"It's Barry," the police detective said. "You want to grab a coffee?"

"I've got a bit of a window this afternoon. Mayor doesn't have to go out till about three to plant a tree." I'd been thinking about Kelly's, where Linda said she'd last seen Sherry Underwood. It was close to city hall. I mentioned it to Barry.

"Half an hour," he said.

By the time I'd dropped Randy off and parked the car in the underground garage, it was time to meet with Barry. He was already in a booth, and there were coffees and slices of cherry pie on both sides of the table. He hadn't touched his pie yet.

I sat down.

"What's this?" I said, looking at the pie.

"Peace offering," Barry said.

"There's no whipped cream," I said.

Barry raised his hand, snapped his fingers. The waitress came over and Barry said, "Could you bury this in Cool Whip or something, please?"

She took the plate away and was back in under thirty seconds, the pie now largely obscured by white fluffiness.

"How's that?" Barry said.

"Better."

"I'm sorry about your son. It made sense at the time. He was in the house, he lied about being there, and I don't know what, but there was something funny going on between your boy and Mrs. Langley."

I said nothing.

"But that earring," he said. "They never managed to get a DNA trace off it. That, and those guys coming to your place, the gun. The case fell apart. I was doing my job, Jim. But I called it wrong."

He was looking me square in the eye.

"If it had been me you tossed in jail by mistake," I said, "I'd forgive you immediately. But it was my son. It's going to take longer."

Barry nodded. "I accept that." He paused. "So you're back working for Randy. I didn't see that coming. What, does he want his nose broken again?"

"I never actually broke it," I said.

"Ha! So, you admit it."

I rolled my eyes. "I have legal bills to pay, Barry. That's why I'm working for him."

Barry had the decency to blush. "Okay."

"I've promised him a month or so. That's it."

Barry nodded, and said, "Tell me again, this thing about the book and Conrad."

I laid it all out for him, slowly. How the guys who'd attacked me and Ellen wanted the copy of the disc Derek had found. So I'd thought it only made sense that they were the ones who'd come to the Langley house, to take away the computer Derek was given by Agnes Stockwell.

Except I'd since learned that the day the Langleys were killed, Albert Langley had given the computer to Conrad Chase. At least, I was thinking, that was what Conrad had told Ellen. Albert knew that what was on its hard drive would be of interest to Conrad, and he should have sole possession of it.

"So maybe the Langleys weren't killed because of the computer," Barry said. "It wasn't there."

"Well, Ellen and I were nearly killed because of the disc, and we didn't have it," I pointed out.

Barry put some pie into his mouth. "So if those guys had it wrong thinking you had the disc, they could have been wrong thinking the Langleys had the computer."

"Maybe."

"How do you know Albert Langley gave Conrad the computer?"

"Conrad told Ellen. When she gave him the disc."

Barry chewed his pie very slowly. "But Conrad could have been lying. Maybe he actually acquired the computer *after* the Langleys were murdered. Or"—he swallowed his pie—

"Ellen is lying when she says Conrad told her he already had the computer."

"You think Ellen lied to me?"

"I'm not saying I think that, I'm merely raising it as a possibility. Listen, I love your wife. Her French toast is amazing. If I could get my wife to leave, get Ellen to come live with me, I'd be a happy man."

"I thought you loved your wife."

"I do. But she can't make French toast worth shit."

"Jeez, Barry, I think you're off base here, about Ellen lying to me."

"I'm just thinking out loud. Okay, let's assume Conrad told her. But he didn't have to have told her the truth. Let me ask you this: Who knew there was a copy of this so-called book on a disc?"

"Me, Ellen, and Derek, of course. Maybe his girlfriend Penny. Maybe her parents. Conrad figured it out, and there's Illeana."

"The onetime actress. Did you ever see her in *Messed Up*?"

"No," I said.

"Only thing she ever made during her short career that got her any attention, and that was mostly because she showed her tits. You can rent it at Blockbuster."

"I'll pass," I said, eating through the whipped cream so that I could find my pie.

"What do you make of this Illeana?" Barry asked.

"A wolverine," I said.

"Only met her once or twice, at things out at Thackeray. But she and her husband don't want to talk to me. Too far down the food chain."

"Cut grass for a living and see what happens."

"Yeah, okay. So the reason I ask about her is, we got an ID off the dead guy in your shed, who your new buddy Drew put down, and his name was Morton DeLuca. From New York. And while we haven't found his partner yet, we suspect he might be a guy named Lester Tiffin. They work together a lot, or so the NYPD tell us."

"Tiffin?" I said.

"Yeah."

"Illeana's last name is Tiff."

"Yeah, I know that. She shortened it."

"This guy, is he related to her?" I asked. "An ex-husband, a brother, or something?" I tried to put it together. "She brought in hired help—family—to get the disc back? Didn't know Conrad already had it?"

"You're getting ahead of me here. I'm going out there today to talk to them, to Conrad and Illeana. Not a word about this Tiffin guy to anyone, hear me? I probably shouldn't even have mentioned it, but I've kind of fucked you around of late."

"No shit. That'll be fun, interviewing the college president and his wife."

"That's why I get the big bucks," Barry said, washing his pie down with coffee. He reached for a napkin from the chrome dispenser, but there were so many jammed in there it shredded when he took it out. "Shit," he said, and pulled out a handful. He dabbed at the corners of his mouth.

"I looked up the Brett Stockwell thing," he said. "That kid who went over the falls. Like you asked."

"Okay." I was surprised he remembered.

"Not that much in it. He fell, hit his head on the rocks below, snapped his neck, would have died instantly."

"But it was ruled a suicide."

"There was no note, if that's what you're asking. But there were no obvious signs of foul play, either. No one saw anything or heard anything. They think it happened in the evening, maybe not that many people around here, although the walkway over the falls is a pretty popular spot for joggers and cyclists and what have you. A lot of interviews were conducted, with his mother, teachers, even Chase, and it seemed like maybe he was a bit of a troubled kid. Intense, moody. And creative. That doesn't necessarily mean suicide, but some of the indicators were there."

"Was there anything in the report that says he couldn't have been thrown over the railing, pushed over?"

"No. I suppose it could have happened that way, but there's nothing that specifically rules out aliens coming down and tossing him over, either."

"So that's it," I said.

"Pretty much."

"What? There was something else?"

"There were fibers, just a few, on the railing. There are these concrete pillars spaced out along the bridge over the falls, then metal railings between them. On one of the concrete pillars, there were a few threads."

"From what?"

"A shirt, a blouse, something. But it didn't match anything the Stockwell boy was wearing. But those fibers could have been there awhile. Nothing to suggest there's anything connecting the two."

I thought a moment, then said, "Here's how it looks to me, Barry. Conrad Chase read that kid's book. Was really impressed with it. Realized the kid was a literary genius in the making. So maybe he offered to buy it off him, so he could pass it off as his own. Or maybe he decided to steal it outright. Either way, the Stockwell kid must have objected, or if he didn't even know what Conrad had done, he was going to be pissed when the book came out and he saw that it was his. So Conrad had to deal with that situation. He had to kill Brett Stockwell. I think he threw that kid over the falls. I think he killed him. I don't know what he had to do with the Langleys, but it seems pretty likely that this all has something to do with those two goons coming to our house the other night. But the thing I'm most sure of is, he killed Brett."

"Be nearly impossible to prove," Barry said. "Even if you're right, that he ripped off the kid's book, and that could be proven somehow, it wouldn't be evidence that he threw Brett over the falls. The best you could hope for is that, if the business with the book came out, he'd be ruined profession-ally."

That would be something, at least.

"Hey," I said, switching gears again. "If I was trying to find some sad-case kid from a couple of years ago, she'd have been around fifteen at the time, working the street, where would I go?"

"You got a name?"

"Sherry Underwood."

Barry wrote it down in his notebook. "What's she to you?"

I pondered a moment. "That's hard to say. She's someone I think I let down." Barry looked at me. "Getting Derek back, getting him out of jail, I don't know. I feel like we came so close to losing him, got him back from the brink. I wonder if it's too late to do that for someone else."

Barry studied me a moment longer, then said, "I'll check the name out later if I get a chance. I love doing all this legwork for you. In the meantime, you could try the Willows." I'd heard the name, but wasn't sure what it was. Barry said, "A drop-in shelter for kids, on Lambton. There's a guy there, Art, ask for him, tell him I sent you. What's this about, really?"

I gave Barry half a smile. "It's about how the mayor got punched in the nose."

Lambton Street wasn't that far a walk from the diner, so I decided to hoof it. The Willows was settled in between a store that sold T-shirts and posters to the younger crowd, and a shop run by a Korean woman that sold thousands of different kinds of beads for people who wanted to make their own jewelry.

Half a dozen kids were milling around on the sidewalk outside the Willows. A couple of them were dressed all in black, their dark hair streaked with flashes of pink and purple, their lips and eyebrows adorned with silver studs and loops. The others didn't appear to have adopted any actual uniform. It looked more as if they'd left home with nothing but the clothes on their backs. Ripped jeans, T-shirts, sneakers. One of the girls was standing on the sidewalk in bare feet. The one thing they seemed to have in common was an air of abandonment, that they were here because no one else wanted to take them in.

I went inside. There were about ten cafeteria-style tables set up, a couple of pinball machines, a video game, a bulletin board plastered with notes about places where one could sleep for the night or find short-term work. There was an opening in the back wall where kitchen workers could hand food through.

There was also a raised counter to one side, a kind of rundown hotel check-in, and it was there that I spotted a man probably in his forties leaning over some paperwork. He had almost no hair on his head, but at least two days' worth of growth on his face, and even before he spoke there seemed a sense of weariness about him.

"Excuse me," I said. He looked at me, still hunched over, resting on his elbows. "I'm looking for Art."

"You found him," he said. "What's the matter? Kids blocking the sidewalk?"

"No. Barry Duckworth said you might be able to help me."

He sat up straight. "You a cop?"

"No. I'm trying to find out what happened to a young girl. She might have come to a place like this."

Art said, "Let me guess. You're trying to find your daughter."

I shook my head. "No. Not mine. Somebody else's."

"You a detective? Trying to find somebody's kid?"

"No," I said, getting annoyed. "It's not that at all. This is someone I ran into a couple of years ago, someone I tried to help, but maybe I didn't try hard enough."

"You got a name?"

"Sherry. Sherry Underwood."

He nodded right away. I expected him to have to think about the name for a while. "Yeah, sure, I remember her."

"She comes to this shelter?"

"She did, for a while. But then she was gone. Someone's here for a while, then they take off. Happens all the time. No one exactly gets their mail sent here."

"What do you know about her?"

"Listen," he said. "I run this place to help these kids out, not rat them out to parents and others who fucked them over and turned their backs on them."

"It's not like that. I just needed to know."

"I can tell you this much. She had a mother who was useless and a father who wasn't there and she gave old guys blowjobs and let them fuck her so she'd have money to eat, and when I last saw her she was high, which is how these kids pass a lot of their time, because if you had to live like they do you'd want to be high a lot of the time, too. I'd love to be able to tell you her story's unique, but it's not. What else can I do for you?"

"Do you know what happened to her after she stopped coming here?"

"She married a prince and lived happily ever after," Art said. "Look, I don't know, and good luck trying to find her. I've got a staff of four, a constant parade of heartbreak, and we do the best we can."

"Sure," I said. "How about any of the men who might have been her customers? Do you know who any of them might have been? You ever see any of them around here?"

"If she'd ever tried to run her hooking operation out of here, we'd have kicked her out. But I'd see her in here after, sometimes, counting her money, writing stuff down in her little notepad."

I was pretty sure I knew that notepad. I'd written down my name and number in that notepad.

THIRTY-FOUR

The mayor planted his tree, nearly putting the spade of his shovel through the foot of a seven-year-old, and on the drive back to city hall said, "Big day tomorrow."

"Yeah," I said.

"I'm keeping my schedule pretty clear through the day. A couple things in the morning, but they're in the building, then I'm leaving the afternoon wide open, getting ready for my announcement in the evening. You okay to work tomorrow night?"

"Your wish is my command," I said.

"You know," Randall Finley said, "when you've already told your boss you're going to quit on him first chance you get, it gives you a lot of fucking latitude, doesn't it?"

"Works for me," I said.

Because he had nothing else on for tonight, Randy said I might as well take the Grand Marquis home with me. Saved calling Ellen for a lift, or seeing whether Derek could pick me up with the truck if he and Drew were done for the day.

As I was coming out of the underground parking, there was a thin, silver-haired woman standing there, and when she saw me behind the wheel, she flagged me down. Powering down the window, I recognized her as Elizabeth Hunt, Conrad Chase's literary agent. Who'd met up with him after the Langley funeral.

"Mr. Cutter," she said. "I'm so glad I was able to catch you. I was told I might find you at city hall."

"You're looking for me?"

"I wonder," she said, almost apologetically, "if I might have a moment of your time."

I was blocking the ramp and there was no obvious place to pull over, so I motioned for her to come around to the passenger side and hop in. She walked around the front of the car and got in next to me.

"I'll just pull ahead," I said.

"Oh, just drive around the block a couple of times," Elizabeth Hunt said. "Then you can drop me off right where you found me."

"Sure."

"So you're working for the mayor now. I understand from Conrad that's a job you used to have."

"At one time," I said. "You're still here. I saw you at the funeral, but figured you'd have gone back to New York by now."

"I'm still staying at my place on the lake. This is supposed to be a bit of a holiday, but Conrad's found a way to make it a busman's holiday," she said, and then smiled awkwardly. "He's nearly finished with his manuscript and he's a bit anxious as he nears the end of the process. I don't know whether you know a lot about writers—I'm sure you do from your wife—but sometimes they need a bit of hand-holding."

That was a bit hard to picture with Conrad, but I let it go.

"And I just wanted to say, I hope you and your wife are all right, after that horrible incident out at your house the other night," she said.

I glanced over at her. "Yes," I said. "We're fine."

"And your son, the charges have all been dropped."

I nodded, made a right turn.

"You must be wondering what the hell I want," she said.

"I figure you'll get to it," I said.

"First of all, I have to tell you, I'm here because Conrad asked me," she said. "I told him, 'Conrad, don't worry about this,' but he can be very persistent. And a bit of a pain in the ass." She sniffed.

I had no idea where this was going, but decided I'd just drive.

"Conrad thinks very highly of you," Elizabeth said. "He has a great deal of respect for you."

I looked over at Elizabeth. "You gotta be kidding me."

"Evidently, your opinion's important to him." There was something in her voice that suggested she was as surprised as I was.

I shook my head. "He has odd ways of showing it."

"He says you don't believe he wrote his first book," she said bluntly.

When she didn't say anything, I guessed she expected me to respond. "That's right."

"So why's that?"

"He didn't tell you?"

"No."

"Then I don't see any reason to get into it. Let's just say yeah, he's right, I don't think he wrote it."

"That's a very serious allegation," Elizabeth said.

"So sue me."

"There's a lot of buzz about his new book. It's not very helpful, tossing around allegations that the man is a fraud."

I shrugged. "You really think anyone's going to listen to a grass-cutting chauffeur?"

"Maybe not."

"Ms. Hunt," I said, growing weary and wanting to get home to see how Derek's first day on the job with Drew had gone, "cut to the chase, no pun intended."

"He wants you to read his new book," she said. "You and your wife, Ellen, but you in particular."

I glanced over at her again. "He mentioned something about that. I thought he was kidding."

"He's not. I think he feels he has to prove something to you. He wants you to read it, and then, I guess, you'll believe that he wrote *A Missing Part,* too."

"I'm sure he did write this book, and I don't care."

Elizabeth Hunt sighed. At that moment, I felt some sympathy for her. It wasn't her fault Conrad Chase was an asshole. "I could make the book available to you on disc, I could e-mail it to you, or I could give you an actual paper copy of the manuscript."

"I'm not interested," I said.

"All right then," she said. "I asked."

I flashed her a smile. "You can tell him you gave it your best shot."

We rode along in silence for a moment. I was heading back to the ramp where she'd first spotted me.

She said, "You really despise him, don't you? You think he's a fraud?"

I thought about that as I steered the car over to the curb. "I think he's worse than a fraud," I said. "I think he's a killer."

Elizabeth Hunt blinked. She had nothing to say. We were back where we'd started from. She unbuckled her seatbelt and got out.

"He doesn't talk much," Derek said over a dinner of baked chicken and rice. "I mean, Drew's a good guy and all, and he's a really good worker, like, I could hardly keep up with him, but he doesn't have a whole lot to say."

"I've noticed," I said. "I don't think he's a very happy guy."

"I thought we'd have lots in common," Derek said, "because we've both done time."

"Derek!" Ellen said. "You have not *done time.*"

"I was in jail," he said. "Not for as long as Drew, but I was there."

"You were never convicted of anything," Ellen told him. "Drew was. That's a big difference. He did something wrong. You didn't."

"Yes I did," Derek said. "I did plenty wrong."

"I don't want to talk about this anymore," Ellen said. I couldn't have agreed more.

"I asked him about what it was like, killing that guy, the one who scared you the other night," Derek said.

"Jesus, Derek," I said. "Don't ask him stuff like that. He's probably having a hard time dealing with it."

We were all quiet for a moment, until Ellen asked, "What did he say?"

"He didn't really say anything," Derek said. "He just asked me a question instead, what it was like, being in the Langley house when they all got killed."

If Derek could ask difficult questions, I suppose Drew was entitled to do the same.

"And what did you say?" Ellen asked.

"I said I'd probably have nightmares about it for the rest of my life."

Ellen reached out and grabbed Derek's arm and squeezed. I was about to do the same, but the phone had started ringing.

We'd been pretty much ignoring the home phone the last few days, not eager to talk to reporters, or endure abusive comments from the nutbars of Promise Falls who knew how to block their caller ID. But now that all the charges against Derek had been dropped, and that fact was becoming increasingly known, we weren't quite so anxious every time we picked up the receiver.

"Hello?" I said.

"It's Barry."

"Hi," I said. I didn't want to say his name out loud, expecting it would spark angry scowls from Ellen, if not Derek as well.

"You and Ellen busy?" he asked.

"Just finishing up dinner," I said.

"I need you to come into the station. Got somebody for you to have a look at in a lineup."

"Who?"

"Maybe the partner of that guy who ended up dead in your shed. How's an hour?"

"We'll be there," I said.

I hung up and told Ellen. She went white. The idea of being anywhere near the other man involved in the attack on us, even if there was a sheet of one-way glass separating us from him, filled her with dread.

"I don't know if I can do it," she said.

"It'll be okay. It'll be like on TV. He won't be able to see us. We'll just be able to see him."

"He wore that mask the whole time," she said.

"But they can get him to say a few words," I said. "We heard him talk plenty. And there was the tattoo on his arm."

Ellen nodded. I leaned in, kissed her on the neck. "It'll be okay. I'm gonna jump into the shower, put on some fresh clothes."

"Sure," she said. "I'll clean up here."

As I was about to step into the shower, I heard the phone again, but someone grabbed it after the first ring, so I got in and let the water rain down on me for a good five minutes. When I got out, the bathroom was filled with steam, the mirror clouded over. I used a towel to make a clear spot on the glass and took a look at myself. My face was still bruised from my run-in with the late Lance, there were bags under my eyes, and my cheekbones seemed more prominent than they had two weeks ago.

"You," I said, "need a vacation."

On the way to the station, I said to Ellen, "Who phoned?"

"Fucking telemarketer," she said. "Windows."

Barry met us at the station entrance, led us down a hallway, up some stairs, talking the whole way.

"Cops in New York picked him up for us, shipped him back up here for you to have a look at."

"Who is it?" Ellen asked. "What's his name?"

"I'd rather not say anything at this point," Barry said. "I'd like you to view the lineup cold."

Barry had already told me that they were interested in a partner of Mortie's by the name of Lester Tiffin, believed to be related to Conrad's wife, Illeana Tiff. I had not, as yet, shared this information with Ellen. I was worried that throwing this kind of unsubstantiated detail into the conversation might be like tossing a stick of dynamite into a campfire.

We were taken into a room that really was like the one in the movies, one wall a sheet of glass that looked out on a mini-stage wide enough to hold half a dozen people. Barry was in the room, as well as another, unidentified man in a well-tailored suit. A lawyer, I was betting.

Barry grabbed a phone handset hanging from the wall and said to someone in another room, "Showtime."

Six men walked into the room on the other side of the glass. All white, all with dark hair, all around six feet tall. Three had short-sleeved shirts on, three had sleeves that went down to their wrists.

"Face forward," someone barked at them.

"Have a close look," Barry said to us.

I scanned the faces of all six men and recognized no one. "You know he was wearing a mask," I said. "A stocking mask."

"I know," Barry said. "I thought we'd get them all to say a few words for you."

Ellen nodded. "That might help."

"What would you like them to say?" Barry asked.

"Have them say," I said, " 'This mask is so fucking hot.' "

Barry grinned, nodded, picked up the handset, and repeated my instructions.

In turn, each of the six men said, "This mask is so fucking hot."

There was something about the way the fourth man, who was wearing his shirtsleeves down to his wrists, said it.

"That guy," I said.

Ellen said, "Maybe, I'm not sure." The guy in the suit made a snorting noise.

"Would it be possible," I asked, "for all of them to put on stocking masks?" The suit looked at me like I was an idiot. "All I was thinking was, there might be something familiar in the way their faces get mashed down."

The suit said, "That's ridiculous. Everyone up there will look like the suspect, including my client. I'll make laughingstocks of all of you all the way to Albany."

Barry said, "I don't think that'll fly, Jim."

I nodded. "What about their arms? The other man, he had a tattoo of a knife on his arm. His right arm."

Barry spoke into the handset and then a voice on the other side of the glass instructed the men wearing long sleeves to roll them up.

The fourth guy, the one whose voice sounded familiar, was very slow about it.

"Let's go," someone barked at him.

He rolled up the sleeve, and once it was past his elbow the tip of the knife appeared. He rolled it up farther, exposing more of the blue blade, then the handle.

"That's it," I said, my pulse quickening. "That's the tattoo I saw on the guy."

Barry said to Ellen, "You recognize it?"

Ellen shook her head slowly, and said, "No."

I whirled around. "What?"

"I don't recognize it."

"What are you talking about? You were with him even more than I was. He went back into the house to get you, he brought you out to the shed."

"It was dark," she said. "And I was so scared, I don't know."

Barry sidled up next to Ellen and whispered, "He's denying everything, we haven't got anyone who can put him with his pal Mortie, so if you can't—"

"Detective Duckworth, something you'd like to share with the class?" the suit asked.

"Ellen," I persisted, "how could you not recognize—"

"I think we're done here," said the suit. "It's clear the woman can't make any kind of ID, Detective Duckworth."

"Ellen, are you sure that's not the guy?" Barry asked. "Jim recognizes the tattoo."

"No," she said. "It's all wrong. That's not how I remember it at all. It was much longer, and skinnier. It went down below his elbow."

"Ellen," I said, trying to control my voice, "what the hell are you doing?"

The suit, heading for the door, said, "I'll expect you to be releasing my client momentarily." And then he was gone.

I was still looking at Ellen, but she couldn't look me in the eye.

THIRTY-FIVE

Once we were out in the parking lot, I grabbed Ellen by the arm and forced her to look at me. "What the fuck just happened in there?"

Darkness had fallen in the time we'd been in the police station, but I could see, by the glow of the parking lot lights, the tears on Ellen's cheeks. She was struggling to free herself from my grip. "Leave me alone!"

"The fuck I will! You let that guy walk! He and his buddy nearly took off my fucking fingers! They probably were going to kill us!"

"Stop it!"

"You have any idea who that was?" I couldn't stop myself from shouting. "I do. My guess is that was Lester Tiffin. And you know who the fuck Lester Tiffin is? He's related to Illeana. A brother, maybe. A hood from New York. She didn't exactly come from the best of families before she landed in Hollywood and finally ended up with your Conrad."

"Don't call him that. He's not *my* Conrad."

"Who called tonight when I was taking a shower? Illeana? Conrad?"

"It was a mistake!" Ellen shouted. "The whole thing was a mistake!"

"What?" I said. "What was a mistake?"

"Them coming to the house. Coming for the disc. It was all a stupid mistake."

"Is that what you call it? When someone tapes your hand to a hedge trimmer? A fucking boo-boo?"

"You okay over there?" It was a cop, approaching us across the tarmac. "Ma'am, are you all right?"

I released my grip, dropped my arm to my side.

"It's okay," Ellen said. "Everything's okay, Officer."

He stood there a moment, making

sure, then turned and walked over to a patrol car.

"I want to know what the hell's going on," I said.

"It was him," she said quietly.

"In there? In that lineup? That was the guy? You recognized him?"

"At least his arm. And it sure sounded like him."

"You know he's going to get away with this. What he did to us. You can sleep at night knowing he's walking around free?"

"He won't bother us again," Ellen said. "I'm sure of it."

"Oh," I said. "Well, that's good to know. I'll sleep soundly tonight." I shook my head in disgust. "Ellen, don't you get it? Those two, the one Drew killed, and that guy you just let walk, there's every reason to believe they killed the Langleys."

"No," she said. "I'm sure they didn't."

"You're *sure*?"

"I mean, I'm pretty sure," she said, sniffing. "I need a tissue," she said.

I found an unused one in my pocket and handed it to her. We stood there a moment, not talking, while Ellen blew her nose, dabbed the tears from around her eyes.

"Conrad phoned," she said. "It was Illeana's idea. She didn't know I'd given Conrad the disc. She called her brother, Lester—"

"Get in the car," I said.

"What?"

"Get in the goddamn car."

She did as she was told. I got behind the wheel of the Mazda and sped out of the lot, the tires squealing as I rounded the corner and headed in the direction of Thackeray College.

The president lived in a grand house that always put me in mind of Wayne Manor of *Batman* fame. Maybe not quite as big, but imposing. The kind of house that said, *I live here and you don't.*

I drove up the semicircular driveway so quickly I nearly swerved onto the well-manicured lawn. I hit the brakes at the front-door steps. Ellen threw her hands forward toward the dashboard. We hadn't said a word on the drive over. Ellen knew where we had to be going, and she must have realized there was little she could say to get me to change my mind.

I was prepared to drag her out of the car, but she had her door open before I got around to her side and was mounting the steps alongside me. Before I could bang on the door or storm right in, Conrad-style, it opened.

The man stood there before us.

"Illeana and I have been expecting you," he said. "Please, come in."

All the way over, I'd been picturing myself bursting in, guns ablazin', but his manner threw me off my game. So Ellen and I went through the door and were led into the expansive living room.

Illeana was standing there, and she looked shaken. Her eyes were bloodshot, her usually perfect hair unkempt, and there was a large glass of what appeared to be scotch in her hand.

"Ellen, Jim," she said. But she didn't approach. She was frightened. Of us, or Conrad, or both.

"Her brother's lawyer just phoned," Conrad said. "Lester's being released."

Looking at Ellen, he said, "Thank you very much."

Ellen said nothing.

Then Conrad turned to his wife and said, "Tell them."

"Conrad, wouldn't it be better if you told them what—"

Then, suddenly booming like thunder, Conrad shouted, "Tell them! Tell them what you did, you stupid cunt!"

If I hadn't been paying attention before, I was now.

Illeana, the ice in her drink clinking from her trembling, said, "I'm so sorry. I don't know what I was thinking. I was just . . . I was just trying to protect my husband."

Ellen and I waited. Ellen, I suspected, already knew the basic story.

"When I heard you arguing," she said to me, "with Conrad, when we came out to your place, about this disc, I couldn't stop worrying about it. I wondered what was on it, whether there was any truth to the fact that it was Conrad's book. No matter how his book got on that disc, I thought it might damage him, especially with his new book coming out and—"

"Get to it," Conrad said.

"And then I came out to see you, to ask you for it, this disc, and you refused to give it to me. So then I decided to find another way to get it back." She looked away a moment, took a drink of her scotch. "I need to sit down," she said, and deposited herself into one of half a dozen overstuffed, velvety chairs that dotted the room. "I called my brother. He . . . he knows, and has friends who know, how to handle things like this. He said he and his friend Mortie could come up from New York and get the disc from you."

"Jesus Christ," I said.

"They weren't supposed to hurt you," she said. "They were just supposed to scare you. He said if anyone could get you to tell them where the disc was, it was Mortie."

I said, holding up the fingers of my right hand, "If my wife hadn't pulled the plug in time, I wouldn't have any of these."

Illeana said, "I'm so sorry."

"Sorry?" I said.

"She didn't know," Conrad said. "She didn't know that Ellen had given me the disc earlier in the day. She'd gotten it back from your lawyer."

"Conrad had no idea I was doing this," Illeana said. "Not until that detective, Mr. Duckworth, not until he came out here and asked about my brother, that he was known to hang out with Mortie DeLuca, the one your friend killed in your garage." Another tear ran down her cheek. "Oh my God, I never dreamed someone would end up dead because of this."

I must have looked stupefied. I know that was pretty much how I felt. "So what, we're supposed to forget all about this? Because why? Because we're all such good friends? Because my wife works for you?" I looked at Conrad. "You put in a call to her, tell her not to identify the suspect, Illeana's fucking brother goes free?"

"It's not quite that simple," Conrad said.

"Fuck this," I said. "I'm telling Barry all about this. Everything." I pointed a finger at Illeana. "You got that guy killed. Not that he's any fucking loss. But it was you, when you decided to bring your brother into this, when you decided to stick your nose in, that's when you got that guy killed."

"Please, Jim," Ellen said. "Let Conrad explain about—"

I waved Ellen off. I wasn't done with Conrad and Illeana. "And I guess you'd have me believe that this has nothing to do with the Langleys."

"It doesn't," Illeana said. "It has absolutely nothing to do with them, I swear."

"Really? Then how do you explain the gun? The gun they found by your brother's car, the one he dropped getting back in when he was being chased by Drew?"

Illeana, red-eyed, glanced at her husband and back at me. "I didn't know anything about a gun."

"It must have already been there," Conrad said.

"No," I said. "The property had been searched before."

"That's not possible," Illeana said.

"Lester, he couldn't have had anything to do with that. Nothing. Maybe, I don't know, maybe the person who killed the Langleys sold him that gun, or gave it to him."

I stared at her. "And who might that have been, Illeana? Would that have been you? Did you know all about this other book, the one on Brett Stockwell's computer, from earlier on? Was it you who wanted to get that computer out of the Langley house before it incriminated your husband?"

"No, that's impossible," Conrad said. "Albert had called me about it earlier that day. I picked it up. It wasn't in their house that night, when they were killed."

"This is all horseshit," I said. "But I don't need to sort it all out. Barry can do that."

"Jim," Conrad said, taking a step toward me, trying to sound reasonable, almost kindly, "I understand that you want to bring the police into this. If I were you, I'd want to call Barry, tell him everything, make sure that Illeana's brother is brought to justice, punished for what he and his friend did to you and Ellen."

I waited.

"Illeana," he said, and glanced contemptuously at his wife, "has done a lot to try to distance herself from her past, from the kinds of people she grew up with, from her own family, many of whom are not what you might call upstanding cit—"

"Hey," she started to object.

"Shut up!" he bellowed again, his face suddenly flushing. He took a moment and continued. "But sometimes she can't stop herself, and she calls on those people when she gets in a jam, as she did this week."

"I don't know what this—"

Conrad cut me off. "Hear me out, Jim. I know you won't believe this, but I'm telling this to you as a friend. Because I care about you and Ellen."

I bit my tongue.

"The people behind Mortie and Lester, these are not good people. They're not . . . rational people. They're not very happy about what happened to Mortie. They're not very happy with your new friend Drew. And they weren't very happy to think that Ellen here might have identified Illeana's brother in that lineup tonight. But their unhappiness has been mitigated by Ellen's failure to do so."

Ellen said, "I would have told you this if you'd given me a chance."

Conrad looked down at the floor briefly, as though shamed by what he was having to tell me. "It was made very clear to me and Illeana that we should pass on to you the message that if you didn't let this drop, right now, they couldn't guarantee your safety."

"What?" I said, feeling the hackles rise. "They're threatening us? Trying to intimidate us, to keep our mouths shut?"

Conrad nodded. "Yes."

"Well, for fuck's sake, if that's what they think—"

"Jim," Conrad said, keeping his voice very even, "I don't like this any better than you do, but you don't understand these people like I do. I need to lay this out for you. If you go ahead with this, you have to know the risks you're taking. On behalf of yourself, and others. Drew, certainly. He killed one of their family. And Ellen. And Derek. Pursue this, you're turning them all into targets."

"Jesus Christ," I said.

"Let it go, and they'll call it even."

I looked at Illeana. "Who are you?"

She didn't say anything, but there was something in her eyes. While I'd seen moments where Conrad's anger had frightened her, there was also this look that said, *Don't mess with me, don't mess with my people.*

Conrad said, "While Mortie did die, and they might normally want some retribution for that, they also appreciate the gravity of the situation you were in. They're also mindful of the bad judgment Illeana exercised. They would be grateful to see this all end here."

"Grateful," I said.

Ellen reached out and touched my arm. "We're dropping this. We've been through enough. I know how wrong it seems to you, to let Illeana's brother get away with this, but we have to do it. For ourselves. For Drew. But most of all, for Derek. If something happened to him, I could never forgive myself."

"Why didn't you just tell me?" I asked. "On the way to the lineup?"

"I was afraid you'd try to talk me out of it, or that you'd tell Barry. That your pride, your fucking sense of justice, would get in the way of common sense. I don't like keeping quiet about this any more than you do, but I'll do it if it makes us safe. Because it's over. This thing with the disc and trying to get it back, it's all over."

Nobody said anything for a minute or so. I suddenly felt very tired. I walked across the room and rested my arm on the fireplace mantel, steadying myself. I stood there a moment, looking at the cold ashes in the fireplace, still there from last winter.

"Fine," I said.

Ellen came over and put a hand on my back. "Thank you."

"Yes," Conrad said. "Thank you." He took a step toward me and said, "Really, Jim, thank you." He cleared his throat. "I wonder if I might have a moment to speak with you, privately."

"Huh?"

"Come with me, to my study," he said.

I followed him down a carpeted hallway and into his sanctuary, a room lined with bookshelves and dominated by a large oak desk in the center that was stacked with papers, a computer off to one side.

He grabbed one of the two leather chairs that faced the desk, indicated for me to take the other one. I sat down.

"Again, thank you," he said. "The fact is, there could have been other repercussions had Ellen identified Lester. Not as serious as those I intimated, but damaging just the same."

For a second, I don't know why, the note he'd written to my wife, the one I'd found in her purse, came into my head, and I saw a flash of my wife's thighs wrapped around his head.

"There are things you don't understand," Conrad Chase said. "Things that could have an impact on you, and Ellen, if everything comes out."

"What do you mean, if everything comes out?"

He cleared his throat, looked down at his pants, picked off a piece of lint, and let it fall to the carpet.

"I know you don't believe this, Jim, but I like you," Conrad said. "I hope that when Elizabeth came to see you, she conveyed that. The fact is, you've really rattled me these last few days with your accusations and insinuations. So I unburdened myself to Elizabeth, had her approach you since I wasn't having much luck on my own. And I gather she didn't have that much luck, either."

I said nothing.

"The thing is, and I fear this is going to sound insincere or patronizing, but running Thackeray these last few years, I've had the opportunity to meet governors and senators and even a couple of presidents. Plus, at the annual festival Ellen puts together, I've met some of the greatest literary minds in the country. Quite a few of them have had some very flattering things to say about me. They think I'm a writer of great talent. But you, Jim, you consider me to be a fraud."

I wondered what I would do with a watering can if I had one just then.

"The thing is, you're a bright guy. A lot brighter than you let on sometimes, I think. And you're an artist. I think you understand something of the creative process." He smiled ruefully. "You don't believe I wrote *A Missing Part.* There aren't many people around privy to the story surrounding Brett Stockwell's computer, so there aren't many people to question the veracity of my authorship in the first place. You're a very select group."

"I'm honored," I said.

"That's why I tried to get Elizabeth to persuade you to read my new book." He reached over the desk and patted a stack of paper about three inches thick. "This is it. I wanted you to realize, I *can* write a book."

"Even if you wrote that pile there," I said, "it doesn't change anything about the first book."

Conrad's lips went in and out for a moment. "Yes, well. Let's say, for the sake of argument, just a little flight of fancy here, but let's suppose there were something to your suspicions about my first book. What if this book is designed to make up for that? Wouldn't that be worth something?"

Again, I was at a loss for words.

"This is the wrong time to ask you again if you'd read it. A lot's happened, you certainly don't owe me any favors at the moment."

"When do you think that might change, Conrad?"

He chuckled. "Good point."

"Here's an idea for a book," I said. "Why don't you do one about a college president who's so fucking self-consumed, even after he's acknowledged that his wife nearly got a guy killed, he still thinks the guy would like to read his book."

Conrad nodded slowly. "Well, I thought it was worth a shot. Perhaps Ellen will read it. I'll drop it by sometime."

"Yeah, that'd be great." I ran a hand over my face, took a breath. Now I had a question. "What did you do with the computer, Conrad?"

"I took out the hard drive, smashed it

to bits with a sledgehammer, took a drive out to Saratoga Lake, rented a boat, and dropped it in the middle of the lake."

There was something about the forthright way he told me that I almost admired. "Did you look at what was on it before you did all that?" I asked.

"Briefly."

"Did you notice anything else in there? Some letters, for example?"

Conrad cocked his head and eyed me curiously. "Letters?"

"Yeah."

"No, I didn't notice. Why?"

I waved my hand at him. "Doesn't matter now."

He settled into his chair, tented his fingers before his chin. "You're a decent guy, Jim, and I understand your view of me," he said. "And you have every right to be angry at—to be appalled by—what happened to you and Ellen. You were terrorized. What my wife, Illeana, put into motion, it's unforgivable. But there's a reason why I asked Ellen not to identify Illeana's brother Lester when he went into that lineup. To expose what Illeana did, and her motives, no matter how misguided and unnecessary, runs the risk of subjecting me to greater scrutiny, and ultimately, that's going to reflect on Ellen." Another pause. "And that will have an impact on you. And your son."

"I don't know what you're getting at," I said.

Conrad leaned in closer to me. "You need to talk to your wife," he said.

THIRTY-SIX

I need to tell it from the beginning," Ellen said, sitting at our kitchen table.

When I'd come out of Conrad's study, I'd headed straight for Ellen, said nothing more than "Let's go," and drove home with barely a word between us. When we got inside, Derek was sitting in the living room. MTV was on the tube, but he appeared to be fast asleep. Cutting grass all day in the sun will do that to you.

I gave him a nudge.

He woke with a start. "What? Where am—oh, okay." He scratched his head.

"Hey, buddy," I said. "Your mom and I need to talk. Why don't you hit the sack?"

"Yeah, sure." Groggily, and with great effort, he made his way upstairs. When

we heard his door close, we found ourselves in the kitchen, standing, moving
from counter to fridge to table, as
though circling each other.

"Let's sit down," I said, and we each
took a seat at the kitchen table. "Conrad said I should talk to you. That you
had some things you needed to tell me.
Other things, not about what Illeana
did."

"I don't quite know what you mean,"
she said. "Things I had to tell you about
what?"

"About everything," I said. "About
how all this got started. He wasn't exactly specific." I paused.

Ellen took in a long breath and when
she exhaled she seemed to tremble. "I
suppose it's time," she said. "It's always
has been, really. I've wanted to talk to
you about this so many times, but never
felt I could. Maybe, because talking
about it wouldn't change anything, except it would probably change your impression of me." She laughed quietly to
herself. "Or maybe not. Maybe your last
impression was formed when you found
out about me and Conrad."

"I got past that," I said.

"No, you didn't," she said.

"It was a long time ago."

"It doesn't matter. I hurt you, and you've never healed. And what I have to tell you now, I don't know whether it will make things better or worse between us. It's why I've held off telling you."

"I need to know what's going on," I said.

And that was when she said she needed to start at the beginning.

"When I got the job here," she said, "and we made the move from Albany, they paired me up with Conrad pretty much from the beginning."

"I know," I said. Like maybe I'd forgotten.

"We—you and I—were going through a bit of a rough patch then," Ellen said. "I'm not blaming you. It was me, too. I was throwing myself into my work, you were depressed about yours. Your art, the lousy security jobs."

"What does that have to do with—"

"Just let me tell this," Ellen said. "It's hard." She took a long breath. "Conrad advised me, offered input on who we should try to get for the festival. He read a wide cross section of stuff, from the very literary to so-called popular fiction. And so did I, although I didn't bring a Ph.D. in English literature to the table. But together, we were able to come up with a list of people we wanted to bring to the festival, and once we'd settled on the ones we hoped to attract, we started approaching them, or at least the people who represented them."

I still didn't know what this had to do with anything, but I listened.

"That was how Conrad got to know Elizabeth Hunt. She represented a wide range of people, from the oh-so-literary to that guy who wrote about the serial killer who collected the hearts of his victims. The one they made a movie out of? Anyway, they kind of hit it off, and she said to Conrad, if he ever wrote anything, he should definitely show it to her.

"And the truth is, he'd been working on something. For years. The Big Novel." She said the words like they had quotes around them. "And as I got to know him better, I realized that his project, this book that meant so much to him, was going nowhere."

"Aw," I said.

Ellen's head snapped up. "I can't tell this if that's what you're going to do."

Admonished, I shut up.

"He was feeling under a lot of pressure to produce something, to make his mark as a member of the Thackeray faculty. Others had been published, not that they'd had bestsellers or anything, but they'd written academic works that had been well received within the community. They had something to show for themselves. But Conrad didn't want to produce some essay that would be read by fifty people and then tucked away on a library shelf. He wanted to do more than that." She took a breath. "And then he met Brett Stockwell."

"His student."

"That's right. A promising, gifted student. Gay, and troubled, moody, and mature beyond his years. Certainly where his writing ability was concerned. Conrad, who normally didn't have a good thing to say about any of his students—who felt so much above them—talked about him all the time."

"Let me guess. Brett showed him the novel he was working on."

"He wasn't just working on it. He'd finished it. He wanted Conrad to read it, tell him what he thought about it." She shook her head and looked downward again. "He worshipped Conrad. He desperately wanted to know what his favorite professor thought of his novel. He so looked up to him."

"And Conrad betrayed him," I said.

Ellen gave me the look again. The one that said shut the fuck up and let her tell it.

"So Brett gave him this book to read. He told him he'd been working on it for months, hadn't shown it to anyone else, hadn't had the nerve to even tell anyone else what it was he'd been working on. Conrad was very skeptical at first, because, even though he regarded Brett as a fine student, he doubted he had the stuff to write a novel at his age, at least a good one. Brett had the book on a disc, which he gave Conrad, and which Conrad read on his own computer. And he was blown away by it. It was a strong piece of work, satirical, provocative, funny. It was vastly superior to the book Conrad had been struggling to write for years."

Ellen stopped. "I need a drink," she said.

She got up, opened the fridge, and I expected her to pull out a bottle of wine. I figured that, after pouring out what she'd had the other day, she'd had a change of heart and replenished her supply.

But she brought out a bottle of Fruitopia and held it up to me, asking, without asking, if I wanted one. I nodded.

Ellen sat back down, uncapped the bottle, poured it into two glasses, and continued. "The thing was, Brett's book was similar in subject matter to the one Conrad had been working on. I mean, not the exact same idea by any means, about a man who wakes up one day and finds his entire sexual identity has been changed, but it was a satire of contemporary sexual attitudes, and I think when Conrad read the book, he somehow convinced himself that this was the book he'd been trying to write all along, that in many ways he and Brett were on the same wavelength. Conrad wanted a professional opinion at this point. He wanted to know whether he was alone in thinking it was brilliant. So he sent the book to Elizabeth Hunt."

"Did he tell her who'd written it?"

"No. He didn't say anything at all."

"Do you have any idea what he was thinking at the time? When he sent it to Elizabeth? Was he thinking, if she loves it and can get it published, I'll be able to take credit for launching Brett Stockwell's career? Or was he thinking, if she loves it, I'll tell her it's mine?"

"I don't know what he was thinking. I don't even know whether he knew. There had to be something going on in the back of his mind. Maybe part of him was hoping Elizabeth would say the book was terrible, that it was unpublishable, because that would have been the end of it. He wouldn't have to think about it anymore."

"But that's not what Elizabeth said, is it?"

"No," Ellen said. "She said it was brilliant. That it still needed a lot of work, but it was brilliant. She said she wanted to try to sell it, that she wanted to represent the author. And she asked Conrad, 'Who's the author? Are you the author?' To this day, I think, he can't believe he said yes."

"How do you know all this?" I asked.

"That was when . . ." And Ellen's voice trailed off.

"When you were sleeping together," I said. She said nothing. "He was sharing all this with you, these developments."

"Up until the time that Elizabeth reported back that the book should be published. He stopped talking about it then."

"Conrad didn't want to admit to you what he was contemplating doing."

"No. I know he met with Brett. I'd come to see Conrad about something, to his office, and the door was slightly ajar and I could hear that he was having a meeting with a student. So I just hung around outside, waiting for them to finish, and then I realized that he was talking to Brett, about his book."

"What did Conrad say?" I asked.

"Conrad told him the book was not very good."

"You're kidding."

"He told him it was amateurish, unbelievable, clichéd. He piled on every negative adjective he could think of."

Of all the things I'd known, and imagined, Conrad to have done, this seemed the worst. Trying to put aside my own issues briefly, it struck me that what Conrad had done to Brett, in that moment, was a far greater betrayal of trust than sleeping with my wife.

"I watched Brett come out of that office, his laptop slung over his shoulder, and he was absolutely destroyed," Ellen said. "There were tears running down his cheeks. Can you imagine it? You hand over your book—your life—to this man you hold in such high regard, whose opinion means everything to you, and you get completely crushed. And maybe, *maybe,* you could defend something like what Conrad did if the book really stunk, that there was no sense misleading a kid into thinking he had talent when he didn't, the whole Simon Cowell approach, but the thing was, Conrad was lying."

Brett's sadness, his overwhelming disappointment, reached through nearly a decade to take hold of me.

"I can't believe anyone could do that," I said.

"I confronted Conrad, told him I'd heard everything, asked him what the hell he was doing, that I knew he loved the book. And he was totally taken aback, flustered, grasping for an explanation. He said the book had its moments, but it was not *that* good, that the kid wasn't going to make it as a writer if everyone went gaga over everything he did, and I realized at that moment what a horrible mistake I had made, what a despicable person Conrad Chase was, and I hated myself for involving myself with him, for betraying you."

I said nothing.

"I asked Conrad what he was up to, why he'd say what he did when I knew that Elizabeth had thought the book showed so much promise. I asked him if he had any idea what he'd done to that boy, to Brett, how he'd left his office looking like he was ready to kill himself."

It was like a lightbulb went on. "Oh my God," I said. "So all this time that I've been thinking Conrad killed that kid, he really did commit suicide. Although, in a way, Conrad did kill him. By lying to him, by telling him his book was a piece of shit. That's what drove Brett over the edge, what drove him to jump off Promise Falls."

"No," Ellen said quietly. "That's not what happened. That's not what happened at all."

"So, wait a second," I said. "So I *am* right. Conrad did kill him. He pushed Brett over the falls so he could get away with stealing his book."

"No," Ellen said again. "That's not what happened, either."

THIRTY-SEVEN

I don't get it," I said.

Ellen reached out and touched my arm, and said, "Just let me tell the rest of it, okay?"

"Go ahead," I said.

"I asked Conrad what he was up to, why he was telling Brett his book was crap when I knew he thought it was brilliant. And I knew Elizabeth had read it and liked it, and then it hit me, what he was planning to do. So I asked him whether he was planning to pass off Brett's book as his own."

"What did he say?"

"About what you would expect. He was offended, outraged, said I was losing my mind. But I kept pressing him, and finally he starts hedging a bit, says he wasn't going to rip off the book. But maybe he could make some sort of deal with him. Tell Brett that because he was so young, just a student, no publisher would ever look at his stuff, but if he fronted the book for him, he could help him get published, and they could share the royalties. Or maybe he could buy the idea from Brett, make him a cash offer now, get him to sign something, relinquishing the property. He was spouting all kinds of nonsense, but I could see it in his eyes, that he'd made up his mind that he wanted this kid's book, that it was his ticket to finally getting some recognition at Thackeray.

"I pressed him on what he'd told Elizabeth. Had he told her, I asked him, that Brett was the author of the book, and he said, not exactly. I told him I couldn't believe that he was even considering something like this, especially after telling Brett his book was no good. The fact that Conrad would do this, it made me wonder . . ."

"Wonder what?" I asked.

"I just . . . I just wasn't sure."

"Were you thinking then that Conrad might actually kill him?"

"I don't know. I don't think so. I don't know what I was thinking. But then he came out from around his desk, he came right up to me and said, 'Don't screw this up for me, Ellen.' He was holding me by the shoulders, and he looked so, I don't know, it was as though something had come over him. He just had this look. It scared me."

I'd seen that look that day in the shed, when I confronted him with the news of the missing computer, and what was on it. And I'd seen it earlier this evening, when he'd gotten so angry at Illeana.

"But he didn't scare me so much that I wasn't prepared to do something about it," she said, and shook her head sadly. "If only I'd just left it alone."

"What?" I said. "What did you do?"

She put her hands over her face, like she was steeling herself for the rest of what she had to tell.

"I got in touch with Brett. All the students have these cubbyholes, so I left him a note, told him to meet me down-

town the following night, at Kelly's."
Where I'd had pie with Barry, where
single mom Linda had last seen Sherry
Underwood. "I was thinking we should
meet off campus, where it was less
likely we'd be seen. I said in my note it
was really important that I talk to him
about his book. He barely knew who I
was, just that I'd been working with
Conrad. We'd said hello a couple of
times, but that was it. But I felt I knew
this kid because Conrad had spoken
about him so often, and when I saw
him walk out of that office, humiliated
and destroyed, I couldn't stop thinking
about him. I felt, because I'd been having a relationship with Conrad, that
somehow I was complicit, and I hated
that feeling."

"So you met?"

"I went to Kelly's at nine, not knowing
whether he'd show up or not, not even
sure he'd seen my note. But about five
after, he came in, carrying a small
backpack and his laptop, and I waved
because I wasn't positive he'd connect
me to the name on the note, but I didn't

have to, he knew who I was, and he sat down across from me in the booth.

"He looked terrible. He was such a sweet kid. Frail looking, as if a strong wind would carry him away, you know?" Now she was beginning to tear up. "He was such an innocent. I mean, the way he wrote, he was so mature, but he was still a babe in the woods, you know?"

Softly, I said, "Go on."

"He took out my note, put it on the table, asked me how I knew about his book. And I told him that Conrad was a friend of mine"—she didn't look at me when she said it—"and he'd told me about the book, about how good it was."

"That must have surprised him."

"Yeah, it did. He said, 'Well, he sure didn't tell me anything like that. He told me the book was a pile of shit.' I told him it *wasn't* a pile of shit. He said I hadn't read it, that I didn't know what I was talking about, and I told him that someone who did know what was good, a literary agent from New York, was very impressed with it. He was dumbfounded. 'How did some New York agent get my book?' he wanted to know. And I told him Conrad had given it to Elizabeth Hunt to read."

"He must not have known what to make of that," I said.

"He kept saying he didn't get it. Why would Conrad crap all over his book if he actually liked it, and had shown it to an agent? And then it was like a switch got flipped, and he looked at me, his mouth half hanging open, like he'd figured it out but couldn't bring himself to say the words."

"You said them for him."

"I said to him, 'Brett, I think Conrad wants to pass your book off as his own.' And then he started to argue with me, he said that was impossible. He said Conrad Chase was his favorite professor, the best professor he'd ever had, there was no way he'd do something like that. I asked him whether Conrad had proposed any sort of arrangement with him, maybe to help him write the finished version, a sharing of royalties, anything like that, because I thought, okay, I'll at least give Conrad

the benefit of the doubt, he had mentioned those things to me. But Brett
said no, Professor Chase hadn't dis-
cussed any of those things with him."

"The son of a bitch," I said. This time,
Ellen didn't give me a look to shut up.

"Yeah," she said. "But Brett kept
saying I must be wrong, that Conrad
wouldn't betray his trust. The whole
reason he'd shown the book to Conrad
was because he trusted him, trusted
his judgment. But the longer we sat
there, the more Brett started to realize
he'd made a huge mistake, started to
accept that what I was telling him was
the truth."

"At least," I said, "he knew that his
book wasn't bad. That those things
Conrad had told him, that he was lying,
that he had his own agenda."

Ellen nodded, half shrugged. "Yeah,
but it didn't seem to matter. He was so
crushed, he couldn't see the good
news in all of this. He started to cry,
and then he just started pouring his
heart out to me, about how his father
had died the year before, how it was
just him and his mother, how he was so

mixed up, that he was gay, that he couldn't tell his mother about it, and how he thought he'd found in Conrad someone he could trust and talk to."

"Jesus," I said.

"And what I wanted to say, but didn't, was that I felt some of that, too. That I'd been sucked in by Conrad, as well, by his personality, his supposed confidence, his intellect, and that I'd made a terrible mistake. That I'd put my marriage at risk for someone this shallow, this self-centered, this monstrous."

"Would it have made you feel better," I asked, "if you'd put your marriage at risk for someone better?"

She bit her lip as she looked at me. "I deserve that." She wiped away some tears from the corners of her eyes, and continued. "I told Brett he couldn't let Conrad get away with this. He had to tell others about his book, maybe even send a copy to Elizabeth Hunt. I'd vouch for him, I said. I asked him who else had read the book, and he put his arm around his laptop like it was an infant, and said no one. He'd given Conrad a copy of the book on disc, but no one else."

"So there was only one other copy," I said. "On the laptop?"

"That's what I thought at the time. But when you told me about what Derek and Adam had found on that computer, from Brett's mother's house, that was the first time I realized he must have had a copy of it on his home computer as well. And it was the first Conrad ever realized there was another copy of the book around."

"And yet," I said, "you've helped him. You gave him the disc. You've helped him cover up for this. I don't understand."

"I'm nearly done," Ellen said. She rested her head in her hands a moment before continuing. "Brett wasn't angry about what Conrad had done to him. He was too hurt to be angry. He said everybody was just out to fuck him over. That was the story of his life. He said he didn't give a shit about his fucking book, Conrad could have it for all he fucking cared. Nothing mattered anymore, he said. And he got up suddenly and left Kelly's."

"What did you do?"

"First, I didn't know what to think. He was so upset, I didn't know whether it was better to leave him alone or go after him. I decided to go after him, in case he decided to do anything foolish."

"What, did you think he might kill himself?"

"I didn't really think about that. I was just worried about him. So I got up and ran after him, and when I got out of the diner I didn't know which way he'd gone, then I caught sight of him, heading north, where the road goes over the falls."

"Okay."

"I ran after him, called out to him, but he was ignoring me, really hunkered down. So I kept running, and caught up to him, on the bridge, about halfway across, I grabbed his arm and told him to stop."

"And he did?"

"Yeah, he looked at me, and it was pretty dark there by then, but I could see that he'd been crying pretty hard. There wasn't anyone around, no one walking on the bridge, hardly any traffic. I asked Brett if he was okay, wanted to reassure myself that he wasn't going to do anything crazy, because he'd always struck me as this sensitive, moody kid, you know?"

I waited.

"He said yeah, he was going to do something. He was going to let Conrad get his wish. He could have his fucking book. Brett said he didn't give a shit anymore. And he slid the strap of his laptop case off his shoulder and took a step toward the railing, and I could see what he was going to do. He was going to throw his computer into Promise Falls."

"What?"

"I shouted at him, 'No, don't!' I told him that the laptop was his proof. Of course, I realize now, he still had proof, on his computer at home. I guess this was just an angry gesture, a way of expressing how betrayed he felt. But I didn't know that, I was telling him he was the one who'd written the book, that he couldn't get rid of the laptop, but he wasn't listening to me, and I was thinking, he can't do that, he can't let Conrad get away with this, and as he let go of the strap, and the computer went over the railing, I went for it."

I think I was holding my breath at about this point.

"I reached out beyond the railing for the strap, and I thought I had it, I just touched it, but it slipped from my hand, and dropped onto that ledge that runs along the side of the bridge, on the other side of the railing. The strap had caught on a bolt, the laptop was hanging there."

"Jesus Christ," I said.

"I was trying to reach for it through the railing, but Brett was walking away, he said he didn't give a shit, but I was determined to get the computer. So I tried reaching over the railing instead of through it, and I still couldn't reach it, so I swung a leg over."

"No," I said, as if I could stop her now, years later, from doing something so dangerous.

"I thought if I could stand on the

ledge, hold on to the railing with one hand, I could crouch down and grab the strap."

I was slowly shaking my head with belated worry.

"I got it, and wrapped it around my wrist, and somehow, as I was trying to stand back up, I slipped a bit, my foot went off the edge, my head dropped below the top of the railing, and I guess I screamed. That's when Brett, who'd nearly walked off the bridge by this point, turned around, saw what I was doing, and started running back."

"Go on."

"I had the laptop strap tight around my wrist, but the computer had dropped down below the ledge and caught on something, so I couldn't move my arm up, couldn't stand up, and was barely holding on to one of the railing posts with my other hand. Brett saw the fix I was in, he was shouting 'Hang on! Hang on!' while he was swinging his legs over the railing to help me, but he did it too fast, and when his feet landed on the ledge, he lost his balance."

Ellen stopped. With her elbows on the table, she made a cradle for her face with her hands and began to sob.

"Ellen," I said. I shifted my chair closer, put a hand on her shoulder. "Ellen," I said again.

"You see, he went to reach for me, to help me, almost instinctively. But he hadn't taken a moment to steady himself. And then I saw it in his eyes, as he realized he was teetering in the direction of the falls," she wept. "He tried to reach out for the railing, and he almost had ahold of it, but he was such a slight boy, he had such small hands."

Ellen looked away for a moment. "But the momentum was carrying him away. He couldn't get a grip. And then he was gone." She looked at me with her red, puffy eyes. "And you know what?"

"What?"

"He never even made a sound. He just slipped away into the roar of the water. I never heard him hit the bottom."

THIRTY-EIGHT

Somehow, I pulled myself back onto the bridge," Ellen said. "I think I must have been in some sort of shock, I don't know. I still had the laptop. I looked down, hoping for some sign of Brett, but there was nothing. I ran to the end of the bridge, where there's that set of stairs that goes all the way to the bottom?"

She looked at me and I nodded. I knew the stairs.

"I ran down there as fast as I could, looked all along the water's edge, and I knew in my heart that no one could survive a fall like that. Not with all the rocks at the bottom of the falls. And then I thought I saw Brett, part of him, his back and one of his legs, on a rock, the water falling down on him, and I knew he was dead."

She stopped. "I'd done such a horrible thing."

"You were trying to do the right thing," I said. "What happened was an accident, plain and simple. You did do the right thing, warning him about Conrad, what he was going to do. For all you know, Conrad was planning to do him in himself. Maybe, if you hadn't followed Brett out to the bridge, he might have taken his own life. Thrown himself off along with the laptop."

"If I hadn't followed him, I think he'd still be alive."

I would have said more to try to assuage Ellen's feelings of guilt, but I sensed there was still more to the story. "What happened after?" I asked.

"I didn't know who else to go to," she said, "except Conrad."

"You should have come to me," I said.

"God, I wanted to," Ellen said, her eyes pleading. "But where would I have started? You didn't know, at this point, that I had been . . . seeing Conrad. To tell you about this would have meant, ultimately, confessing to everything, and, Jim . . ." She reached out and touched my arm. "I didn't have it in me."

I nodded.

"But I felt I had to tell someone, and that had to be Conrad, because what I'd done, I'd done because of him—not *for* him—but because of what he was going to do. I'd fucked it all up royally, but I was angry at him, I wanted him to share the blame, because he was the one who'd set this in motion. I went to his house. He had a place just outside the college where he lived alone, not the house he has now, of course. I just walked in through the front door and found him at the kitchen table, marking papers. I threw the laptop right in front of him, and he said, 'What the hell is this?'

"I told him what had happened. How I'd tried to warn Brett, told him how his professor had betrayed him, and Conrad was getting red in the face, like he was going to explode. And then I told him what had happened, how Brett had tried to throw his own computer over the railing, how I'd gone after it, nearly falling to my death, how Brett had died trying to save me."

"And his reaction to all that?"

"When I got to the part where Brett was dead, Conrad suddenly changed. He went into this kind of dead calm. He asked me if I was kidding. He asked me if that computer was Brett's, whether it had Brett's book on it. I assumed so, but hadn't actually checked, so Conrad took it out of the pouch and opened it up and had a look and he didn't say anything, but I could tell he was scrolling through something, and he was nodding, and then he closed the laptop. And all he said was, 'I'll look after this.'"

"He knew then he could get away with ripping it off."

"I knew that's what he was thinking. And I told him so. I said, 'If you get that published under your name, I'll let the world know what you've done.' And he said to me, he grinned, he flashed me that fucking grin of his, and said, 'And shall I tell the world how I got all the existing copies of this book? Shall I tell the world how it is that the actual, so-called writer of this book is unavailable to claim authorship? Shall I tell the world how you pushed him off Promise Falls, how you did it for me?'"

"He couldn't have expected people to believe that."

"That's what I told him. I said, 'Go ahead and try that story, but I think people are going to believe me when I lay everything out for them. And then he said, 'What will they think when they find out you left the scene? Left Brett Stockwell to die without calling the police?'"

I must have made a face. "That wasn't going to look good for you."

"I know. But even that I thought I could explain. That I was in shock, which I was. I'd nearly died myself. I'd take my chances, at any rate. I knew that what Conrad had on me was potentially damaging. I could accuse him of stealing that kid's book, but he could turn around and say he'd never meant to do that, that I'd acted on my own on his behalf—"

"Like Illeana did," I said.

"Yeah, a bit like that. His story would be that I'd pushed Brett Stockwell off that bridge as a gift to him, so he could steal the book and get away with it."

"It's far-fetched, but someone might have believed it."

"I was so confused," Ellen said. "I was scared. And I was ashamed. I was afraid that if people believed Conrad's story, what would that do to me? To us? And our son? We'd all be dragged into it." She shook her head resignedly. "Coming forward, exposing Conrad, it would have meant you finding out that we'd had an affair. It was over by the time you found that note, but by that time it was too late to come forward, to tell the truth about what Conrad had done. My silence had the effect of confirming his version of events."

Ellen reached out and touched my arm. "I love you," she said. "I love you now and I loved you then. I stayed quiet, hoping you'd never find out about any of it."

I got up, walked around the kitchen,

braced myself against the kitchen counter, looking down into the sink. "So all these things I've been trying to do these last few days, to show what Conrad had done, you sabotaged them," I said, "because it would find its way back to both of us. You didn't want me talking to him, you wanted to do that yourself. You got the disc back from Derek's lawyer and gave it to him."

"More or less."

"And Albert Langley, he must have known what Conrad had done years ago, to have tipped him to the computer Derek and Adam were messing around with."

"Yeah, Conrad confessed his sins to Albert. Not out of guilt, but to cover his ass, in case of any unexpected developments. When the book was about to come out, he started getting paranoid, went to Albert to talk it over, wanted to know if someone should accuse him of plagiarism, what were his options? Could he sue? He swore Albert to secrecy, which he didn't exactly have to do, with Albert being his lawyer and all. Albert told him to ride it out."

"And Albert must have known that the only other person who knew was you," I said.

"I suppose," Ellen said. "All these years, Conrad and I, we've had this sick hold on each other. When his book came out and the reviews were fabulous, and it made him rich, I had to smile through the whole thing. I wanted to quit, leave Thackeray, get away from him, but he said he wanted me to stay here, that I was doing a good job, that we could put this behind us. I think he was afraid that if I ever left, got out from under this thumb, I'd find the courage to expose him. He said I'd never get a job anywhere else, that he knew people. Maybe he couldn't write his own book, but I believed he could make up some lies to tell anyone else I might want to work for."

Ellen took a breath, then, "Anyway, Conrad never told Illeana what he'd done, about Brett and the book, so when she got wind of something this week, that you were supposedly trying to destroy her husband's reputation, it didn't much matter to her at that point whether it was true or not. She just didn't want it coming out and ruining her perfect life with the college president. And so she got her brother and another goon to get that disc back. When Conrad found out, he went mad, couldn't believe what she'd done, and he called me, spelled it all out for me, said if I identified her brother in the lineup, not only would things unravel, but that Illeana's people were very dangerous. He told me they'd kill Derek if they had to."

"Jesus, what a mess." I sat back down at the table, took her hands in mine. "If I'd been you, I'd have done the same thing. I wouldn't have fingered Illeana's brother. Better to cut our losses now."

"You remember what I said the other day?" Ellen asked. "When Derek was arrested, when he was in jail, and I said we were being punished? It was for the terrible things I've done, for letting that boy die."

I squeezed her hands. "No," I said. "No."

What I couldn't bring myself to say was, if we were being punished for that kind of thing, then I was going to have to shoulder some of the blame as well.

THIRTY-NINE

I spoke to Derek as he was getting in the truck the next morning, about to head off to pick up Drew and cut lawns for the day.

"Hey," I said.

"It's gonna be another hot one," Derek said.

"Are you okay with this, back to work this soon, with Drew, without me? Because I was thinking, maybe it's a mistake, throwing you back into things so fast, turning the business over to you, after all you've been through, being in jail and all."

"It's okay," Derek said. "I think, like, maybe it's the best thing. It gets my mind off stuff, you know?"

"Sure," I said. "That's what I was hoping."

"How about you? What's it like, driving that dickhead around again?"

I laughed. "It's okay. I don't know whether I've changed, or Randy has, but he's not bothering me the way he used to. He's still an asshole, no question, but I'm not letting him get under my skin. Maybe because he knows he's only got me for a short while. I think you've got the better deal, working with Drew."

"Yeah," Derek said. "I'm trying not to be a jerk with him, like asking him any more about robbing banks or anything. I kind of just let him be, you know? I'm trying not to be too pushy."

"That's probably best," I said.

"But the guy can really work. I can barely keep up with him." He paused. "I better shove off."

I don't know whether it hit us both at the same time to do this, but we threw our arms around each other, gave each other a couple of pats on the back, and then he got in the truck and was gone.

As I watched the truck head up past the Langley house, it occurred to me that despite all the revelations of the last twenty-four hours, all the secrets revealed, I still didn't know anything more about what had happened in that house the other night than I did before.

Ellen came outside a moment later, ready to go to Thackeray.

I put my hands along the tops of her arms and said, "You remember when we first learned about the Langleys being killed, you were ready to move away from here. Well, now I am, but for all sorts of different reasons. You've got a great résumé, you should be able to find work almost anywhere. Wherever you can find something, I'll find something."

"I don't know," Ellen said.

"Conrad has no hold over you anymore. If anyone's holding the trump card now, it's you. For what Illeana had done to us. Because you didn't identify her brother."

"I got to thinking in the middle of the night," Ellen said. "About the gun."

"The gun?"

"The one they found that night, when

Mortie and Illeana's brother Lester came to see us, right by the car Lester was driving. If that really was the gun that was used to kill the Langleys, what if . . ."

"What if what?"

"What if, somehow, I let Lester and his buddy get away with that? What if, to protect all these secrets, what if that means the Langleys' killers go free?"

"But it sounded to me like Illeana didn't bring her brother into this until after she heard me talking to Conrad about the missing computer, and the disc Derek had. And that was well after the Langleys had been killed."

"That's true."

"Maybe Drew was mistaken, thinking he saw Lester drop the gun out of the car. It was dark, we were all pretty rattled."

Ellen thought a moment. "God, I hope I did the right thing, at the lineup. You wake up in the morning, you start seeing things differently."

"Let's try things the way they are now," I said. "We lay low, we ride this out."

"I don't know," Ellen said softly. "I don't know what to do." She looked into my eyes. "Maybe you're right. We should start over. Someplace else."

I took her into my arms. "Let's talk about it tonight."

"Okay," she said, and while holding me continued, "Everywhere I look, I'm reminded of tragedies and horrible choices. The Langley house, your shed, Promise Falls, the college. I want to get away from all of it before anything else bad happens."

"Nothing else is going to happen," I said. "Nothing else is going to happen."

There was no rush to head down to city hall. Randall Finley was keeping his schedule pretty light for the day, and those things he did have on it were various committee meetings that were held in the building. So he didn't need my services till later. He was saving up his strength for his big early-evening announcement that he was going to run for Congress.

I figured I would head in about mid-day, maybe take a run out to the Wal-cott Hotel, on the west side of town, where Finley's campaign strategists had hired a hall and were decorating the place with streamers and signs and laying out booze and snacks.

So I was able to do something I rarely do around the house, which was putter about, drink some coffee, take my time reading the paper. But of course, whenever such an opportunity presents itself, something usually comes along to ruin it.

This time, it was Barry's unmarked car coming down the lane. It wasn't possible to view Barry Duckworth's ar-rival without feeling apprehensive. I was walking across the grass as he was getting out of his car. "Hey," I said.

"Hey," he replied.

"Is this going to be bad news?" I asked.

He shrugged. "Just in the neighbor-hood."

"You're never just in the neighbor-hood."

"How you doin' today?"

"It's been a long week, Barry. For you, too, I suppose."

"That was quite something last night," he said. He had to be referring, of course, to Ellen's failure to identify Lester Tiffin at the lineup. "I figured, once she saw that tattoo, we'd have that thing nailed."

I just shrugged. Maybe Ellen was going to change her story, but it needed to come from her, not from me.

He shook his head sadly. "I don't know, Jim. I think something's going on. I think if the two of you aren't covering up for somebody, then at least Ellen is. And that's not very helpful to me."

"Sorry, Barry. Some of the things you did to us in the last week weren't very helpful, either."

He let out a long sigh. "I don't want to get into a pissing match with you, Jim. I just want to figure out what the fuck is going on. Three people get killed up the lane here, you and Ellen get terrorized by a couple of thugs, your old buddy Lance ends up dead. That's a lotta shit, and I can't help but think it's all connected."

"What about the gun?" I asked him. "The one that was found just up there."

"Yeah, it was used to kill the Langleys."

"Did it have Lester Tiffin's fingerprints on it?"

Barry just looked at me. It was as good as saying no.

"Is it possible," I said, "that that gun had been out there all this time, that somehow your guys missed finding it when they were searching the property after the Langleys were killed?"

"Not possible," Barry said.

"I remember reading about this case," I said, "up in Canada, they were searching the house of this serial killer. They sent in a team and tore the house apart looking for evidence, pulled up the floorboards, took off drywall, didn't find a thing. Then, the killer's lawyer waltzes in after the search is done and, based on a tip from his client, pulls out a videotape from behind an overhead light fixture. The guy videotaped his killings."

"You're making a point?" Barry said.

"I'm just saying, even the best cops sometimes miss stuff."

Barry was still shaking his head. "If that's true, and that gun had been sitting there since the Langleys got killed, tell me how it managed to get itself over to Lance's place and shoot him."

I said, "Oh."

"Yeah, oh. Same weapon. Pretty neat trick, wouldn't you say?"

"Yeah," I said.

"I'm not done with this thing, and I'm going to get to the bottom of it whether you and your wife want to cooperate or not."

"I got it," I said.

"And despite the fact I think you're holding out on me, I've done you another favor."

"What?"

"You asked me to check out that name. That girl. Sherry Underwood."

"Right," I said. "You did that?"

"I did. She's dead. She died about a month ago. In the hospital."

"What happened to her?"

Barry shrugged. "Sick. Drug abuse,

HIV, malnutrition, the whole shooting match. Died of heart failure."

I felt my shoulders sagging. "Oh," I said. "She was just a kid."

"Welcome to my world," Barry said. He got back into his car, put down the window, and said, "Don't jerk me around, Jim."

I drove the mayor's Grand Marquis into town around one. There was a boxful of pamphlets and press kits that needed to go out to the Walcott, so I volunteered to do that. Not because I wanted to help with his campaign, but because I needed something to do. And I was still getting paid by the hour. Randy didn't need to be taken any-place until late afternoon, when he was going to pop into a Rotary Club dinner and say a few words before going to his press conference.

I opened up a press kit and glanced through a copy of the mayor's prepared speech. It was a cobbling together of every platitude, cliché, and empty promise ever uttered by an aspiring politician. Finley would probably do well with it. There were a few shots at special interest groups, unions in particular, which would play well to Randall Finley's constituency, but they were a bit held back compared to things he'd said about Promise Falls's municipal workers over the years, whom he had often characterized as, basically, dog fuckers. But now that he was running for Congress, Randy must have felt he couldn't totally alienate organized labor. You could say a few negative things about a working guy's union, but still count on his support so long as you made your opponent look like a Commie-loving pansy.

There were half a dozen people out at the Walcott getting things ready, and they tried to rope me into putting up streamers, but I begged off, saying the mayor wanted me downtown, ready to take him anywhere at a moment's notice. Taping up streamers demanded a level of enthusiasm I could not bring to bear.

I took the Grand Marquis to the car wash, then headed back to city hall and parked out front. I read the paper till around five, when Randy got into the backseat so I could drive him to the Rotary event.

"So, Randy," I said, "you nervous about tonight?"

"What do I have to be nervous about?" he asked. "They're going to eat me up."

As I was pulling up to the Holiday Inn, and Randy was waiting for me to run around and open the door for him, my cell rang. "I'll see you in there in a minute," I said, forcing him to open the door on his own. He could use the exercise, I figured.

"Hi," Ellen said. "You heard from Derek?"

"No," I said, glancing at the clock on the dash. It was 5:05 p.m. "Why would I hear from Derek?"

"No reason," she said. "He's just usually back here before five. I wondered if he was running late or anything. He didn't leave a message, so I thought maybe he'd been in touch with you."

"Nope," I said, feeling only slightly uneasy. "Didn't you call him?"

"I tried his cell but it went straight to message."

"Maybe he's in a bad area, or forgot to charge it up," I said. "I wouldn't worry. Look, we honored our side of the deal with Illeana's people. I'm sure everything's okay. I've gotta go into the Holiday Inn. Randy's doing the Rotary before his other thing."

"Okay, talk to you later."

Randy wasn't having dinner with the Rotarians, but offering some greetings before they sat down to theirs. It was a kind of pre-announcement announcement. A few jokes, a bit of electioneering, and when he took questions from the audience he dodged the ones about his political intentions with "I think you'll have the answer to that question in a couple of hours."

He got a nice round of applause. Not quite as enthusiastic as he was hoping for, though. "The fuck was their problem?" he said, walking down the hall with me back to the car. "I thought I killed in there."

"Tough room," I said, and this time, feeling generous, I opened the car door for him.

He was settling into the back when my cell rang again. "Still no sign of him," Ellen said. I could hear the edge in her voice.

I looked at the clock again. It was six. "Still no luck with his cell?"

"Nothing."

"You know what the job's like," I said, trying to be positive. "There's any number of things that could hold them up. Tractor breaks down, they run out of gas, and if they're running the machinery, Derek's not going to be able to hear the phone anyway."

"I know. I just, I don't know. What if those people, what if they changed their mind? What if they still want revenge for what Drew did?"

"Have you got the phone book there?"

"Hang on . . . Okay, I've got it."

"Look up Lockus. That's Drew's last name. He hasn't got a cell, but his mother must have a phone. Try the house, see if Derek's already dropped him off."

"Just a sec . . . There's no Lockus," she said.

"The house is on Stonywood," I said.

"There's nothing."

"Well, shit. So his mother's name is either different from his, or she's got an unlisted number."

"Hey, Cutter," the mayor said from the backseat. "We going to just sit here or what?"

I held up my hand, asking for silence. I was trying to think what day it was, then said, "Okay, I know the houses they'd be hitting today, the ones Derek and I would do in the afternoon. I'll swing by them, see if they're there, and I'll get back to you."

"Thanks," Ellen said.

I closed the phone, turned to Randy, and said, "What have you got between now and seven?"

"Jeez, Cutter, I was thinking maybe I'd find someone, get me a blowjob. What do you think I want to do? Let's go back to the office, I'm gonna have a stiff drink, then we'll head over to the

Walcott around ten to seven, make my big entrance."

"I've got to do a couple of things. Why don't you just sit back and relax and I'll give you a tour of Promise Falls."

"What is this, Cutter? A joke?"

"Randy, just chill out. It's important. My son hasn't shown up."

Randall Finley sighed. "So what? He's probably jumping some teenage pussy. Isn't that what happens when guys get released from jail?"

I already had the car in drive and was heading in the opposite direction of downtown. We tried to organize our clients by neighborhood, do the north side one day, the south another, and so forth, instead of crisscrossing Promise Falls every day. This particular day, we did properties mostly in the northeast.

"Cutter, honestly," Finley said. But there was more resignation than anger in his voice, so it looked as though he was going to indulge me.

I sped past the four clients we had in that part of the town, and I didn't need to knock on anyone's door to see if the work had been done. I could see for myself. All the yards had been cut, the edges neatly trimmed, the driveways blown free of clippings.

I called Ellen again. "Anything?"

"No," she said.

"Did you try calling Penny?" I hated to suggest it, knowing Ellen wouldn't get a warm reception if she called the Tucker house and got Penny's mother or father.

"Already did it," Ellen said. "I got Penny. Derek's not there."

"I'll stay on it as long as I can," I said, and ended the call.

"This kid of yours," Randy said. "He's starting to strike me as some sort of a problem child, you know? You thought about getting him counseling or anything like that?"

I ignored him.

Maybe Derek and Drew had gone for a drink after work. Derek was too young for a bar, but there was no reason they couldn't have popped into a fast-food place, or a Dairy Queen, for something to help cool them down after a hot day.

But why wasn't he answering his phone?

I was worried. Not panicked, but definitely worried. But there was one other stop I needed to make before I started sounding any alarms.

"Hey, Cutter," Randy said from the backseat, "it's nearly six-twenty. I'm at least gonna want to take a piss before this thing at the Walcott."

"One more stop," I said, turning the town car around and heading back in the direction we'd just come from. "Just hold your horses. It's not like they're going to start without you. You walk in a couple minutes late, it'll just build the suspense."

"That's probably true," Finley mused.

I tried not to think about what sort of trouble Derek and Drew might have stumbled into. But if they were being stalked by the kind of people who thought nothing of taping your fingers into a hedge trimmer, then—

No, better not to think too long on that.

The only thing left to check that I could think of was to go by Drew's house, see if he'd already been dropped off. If he had, that would mean, presumably, that Derek was somewhere between Drew's place and ours.

Or that something had happened to Derek between Drew's place and ours.

I parked out front of the house on Stonywood, still half hidden by tall shrubs that hugged the sidewalk.

"Two minutes," I said to Randy, and was out of the Grand Marquis before he could object. I left the motor running so he could enjoy the A/C.

I trotted up the walkway between the hedges, mounted the steps to the front door, and rang the bell. After ten seconds or so, I leaned on the buzzer again. Now I could hear footsteps inside the house, approaching the door.

It opened wide, and there was a man standing there. Not Drew, but a silver-haired man in his fifties, glasses, a white shirt and nicely pressed tan slacks, slippers. He had a folded newspaper in his hand.

"May I help you?" he asked quietly.

I was a bit surprised to see this man and not Drew's mother. Hadn't Drew said his father had passed away? Maybe an uncle. But I was also pretty sure Drew had mentioned that he was looking after his mother on his own.

"I was looking for Drew," I said.

"Who's that again?" the man said.

"Drew," I repeated. Maybe he was hard of hearing.

"Drew?" he said. "No Drew here."

"No no," I said. "This is the house. I'm looking for Drew Lockus. He lives here, with his mother."

"Don't think so," the man said. "My name's Harley, and I live here alone. My wife, she passed away a few years ago."

I took a step back, looked at the house, said, "Big guy? Could be a football player? Short hair?"

"Oh yeah," Harley said. "That sounds like the fella that's been standing out here on the sidewalk every morning, waiting for some lawn service truck to pick him up. That the guy you're looking for?"

FORTY

What's with you?" Randy asked, putting down his window as I walked slowly back to the town car. "You look like you've seen a ghost."

I had a very bad feeling. Something was very, very wrong.

"The fuck?" the mayor said. "Hello? Earth to Cutter!"

"Shut up, Randy," I said.

"What?"

"Shut the fuck up for a minute." I stood there by the car, thinking, trying to put it together. If Drew didn't live here, if this wasn't his house . . .

I thought back to the times I'd dropped him off. How I'd see him in my rearview mirror, standing on the sidewalk, watching me leave. How I'd never seen him go in or come out of that house. How the very first time I'd seen him, he'd been using the hedges to shield himself.

I felt my knees weaken when it hit me.

Drew had been following me.

Telling me he lived there, with his mother, it was all bullshit, so I wouldn't realize he'd been following me.

But if he was meeting me here every day, then he had to get here some-how—

"Where you going?" Randy called to me. I was running up to the corner of Stonywood and Pine. The house Drew had claimed to live in was on the corner. I glanced both ways up Pine, no cars on the street, except two lots down there was an old blue Ford Taurus, the paint faded, rust around the wheel wells, parked at the curb. I remembered Drew pointing to a car like that at the end of our drive the night Ellen and I had been attacked. I ran up to the car, tried the door, but it was locked. The windows were all up and I peered inside. There was the usual junk. Fast-food containers and to-go coffee cups, plastic and paper bags. Also a small spiral-topped notebook and a crudely folded map of what appeared to be Promise Falls.

I wanted to see the car's registration.

I tried all four doors on the Taurus, and when I found them all locked, I looked for something to break a window. The closest driveway had some decorative stones in the garden, each about the size of a grapefruit. I reached down for one, pulled it out of the topsoil, and smashed in the front passenger door window.

I was expecting alarms to go off, but this Taurus model was evidently too old to have an anti-theft system, or if it did have one, it no longer worked. I cleared enough glass away to unlock and open the door, then reached down to the glove box and opened it. There was a tattered owner's manual, some pens, old maps, a packet of tissues. I found a small plastic folder, opened it up, and found the registration.

The car was in the name of a Lyle Nadeau. Shit. I'd just broken into a stranger's car.

Then I remembered something Drew had told me during one of our lunches, that an old friend named Lyle had lent him a car. A guy just out of jail wouldn't be able to buy a vehicle, register and insure it. I felt my initial hunch was right. Drew was driving here each day to be picked up, to maintain the fiction that he lived in this neighborhood and hadn't been following me.

I looked at the stuff in the console. A Promise Falls map, various locations circled.

Including the area of my house.

My hand touched the small notebook, and there was something about it that tugged at my memory. I flipped through the pages. There were all manner of things written down in it. Shopping lists, lists of things to do, what appeared to be license plate numbers, columns of figures, initials and phone numbers.

I kept flipping until I came to the page I was now dreading, and expecting. And there it was. My name. My phone number. In my handwriting. Placed there the night I found Randy

Finley in a hotel room with an underage hooker.

What had Drew said? He'd had a child, a daughter, but not anymore.

Sherry Underwood.

I was holding her notebook.

A dozen questions were bouncing around in my head, but these were the ones forcing their way to the front of the line:

Where was Drew now? Where was Derek? And what the hell had I done, sending my son to work with him?

The mayor was coming around the corner, huffing and puffing. "Do you know what time it is?" he asked, tapping the face of his watch. "Do you have any fucking idea?"

I reached into my jacket for my cell phone, but before I could flip it open and call Ellen, it went off. I glanced at the display. Home calling.

I put the phone to my ear. "Ellen," I said. "Is Derek home? Have you seen him?"

"Jim," Ellen said, her voice very sedate, as though she was forcing herself to be calm. "Drew would like to speak with you."

There was some fumbling as Ellen handed over the phone.

"Jim?" It was Drew Lockus.

"Drew, what the hell is going on?"

"Hey, Jim," he said tiredly. "I'm really sorry about all this."

"Sorry about what, Drew?"

"You seem like an okay guy, you know, for the most part? Even though you let my girl down."

"Drew, what's going on at my house?"

"I was going to do this yesterday, but I had to find another gun. I had to leave the other one at your place the other night. An opportunity kind of presented itself."

The gun in the grass, next to where Lester Tiffin had been parked. Drew had left us with the impression that he was not going to stick around and talk to the cops, but then he'd come back. He must have gone up to his car, grabbed the gun that killed the Lang-leys, Lance, and those other two whose names I couldn't remember at the moment, and dropped it where the police could find it. Let the police start sniffing around the two men who'd terrorized us, hang the Langley thing on them.

"Drew," I said again, trying to keep my voice calm, even if I wasn't, "what's going on at my house right now?"

"I'm just here with Derek and Ellen. We're just hanging out."

"That's great," I said evenly. "So what's the deal with the gun?"

"Well, that's what I'm going to use to shoot them if you don't help me out."

"Are Ellen and Derek okay, Drew?"

"Oh yeah," he said casually. "Everyone's fine. We're just sitting at the kitchen table. I was kinda filling them in on everything, and I was apologizing to Derek for putting him through what I put him through the other night."

"At the Langleys'," I said.

I felt as though someone had touched an icicle to my neck. The memory of what I'd worried about before. That someone had gotten the wrong house.

"That was a huge mistake," Drew said. "The mailbox, I just thought it was your place. I never even noticed the second house, your place, farther on down the lane. I feel terrible about that, honest to God, I really do. That was an awful thing that happened to them, especially the boy, what was his name? To Adam. They didn't deserve that, but sometimes things happen the way they happen."

"Yes," I said. "A terrible thing."

"I mean, even if it had been the right house? If I'd gone to your house, like I meant to in the first place, I wouldn't have wanted to kill your wife and your boy. But I didn't have much choice at their place, because they were witnesses, you know, and I wasn't done doing what I had to do."

"Sure, Drew," I said. "I get what you're saying."

"I didn't even know until a couple of days later that I'd screwed it all up. When I heard about it on the news, I felt bad. Because Mr. Langley, he wasn't in the notebook."

"Sherry's notebook," I said.

"Yeah, right. You know the one I'm talking about?"

"I have it with me now, Drew. I went by your place, trying to find you. Except it wasn't your place."

"No," he said, sounding regretful. "I don't really live there. And my mom, she died years ago. That was a fib. I'd been following you around, after I screwed the other thing up. I had to think of something fast when you saw me. You pissed about that?"

"No, Drew, it's no big deal. Listen, would you mind if I talked to Ellen for a second?"

"In a minute, Jim. I haven't even told you what I want you to do."

Randy Finley tugged at my sleeve, pointed again to his wristwatch. "Hello?" he said. "Could you chitchat a little later? I got this date with Congress. Remember that?"

"Is that him?" Drew asked.

"Is that who?" I said.

"The mayor."

"Yes," I said.

"Okay, that's good, because he's what I need your help with."

"What is it you want, Drew?"

"You know what he did, don't you?

Between what Sherry told me, before she died, and what Lance told me before I killed him, and what you told me from when you worked for him, I figured out that he was one of the ones. One of the ones who killed my daughter. They all killed my daughter, you know. All the men who used her, who paid her for sex."

"I see your point, Drew."

"But I don't think you were one of them, even though your name was in the book. I did at first. Then, after I got to know you, I figured you wrote down your number so Sherry could call you for help, right? And that was a nice gesture, but it turned out to be kind of meaningless, didn't it? An empty gesture. You should have done more, Jim. You were there, weren't you, when the mayor was doing it to her. And yet you didn't get her help right then and there, like you should have. You should have done something to that man, called the police, had him arrested, helped my little girl. I mean, you're a decent person, and even you did nothing. I'll bet Sherry never got closer to getting help than she got when she ran into you."

"What about you, Drew? What were you doing?"

"What?" For the first time, he sounded angry. "Where was I? I was in fucking jail! That's where I was! Counting every fucking day till I got out, so I could help my little girl! Her mother, she was nothing but a useless bitch, you know that? She never did anything to help Sherry, never gave her a goddamn thing but a last name because she wouldn't marry me. She was a drunk, she was a drug addict. She could be dead now for all I know and I hope she is. I did my best by Sherry. I tried, I swear to God I tried, even went so far as to rob a fucking bank to try to get some money to raise her right. And you know what happened then. I got sent away, and there was nobody to look after her. No one to guide her, no one to point her in the right direction. All I could hope for was that there'd be some people out there, some people with some sense of fucking decency, who'd help her until I could get out and do it myself. And maybe you came the closest of anybody, but you didn't do enough."

"But you came to kill me because you thought I was a customer," I said.

"Yeah," he said, his voice softer now. "But then, when I screwed up and got the wrong house, I decided to take it a little slower, to watch you first, and then you offered me a job, and I got to know you a bit, right? And decided, maybe I wouldn't kill you. At least I'd think about it first, you know? But the others in that book, Sherry's customers, they all had it coming."

"Like Lance," I said. "And there were two others, a few weeks ago."

"And there are more in the book I haven't got to," he said. "I might not get to all of them." I could hear the regret and resignation, the tiredness, in his voice. "I don't know how much longer I can do this."

"You should turn yourself in," I said. "Get yourself a lawyer. You've got a good case, Drew. These men, they all did terrible things to your little girl."

"What little girl?" the mayor asked. "What the fuck are you talking about?"

"The one I want," Drew said, "is the man you're with. But I don't think I want to kill him. I think I want to do something to him that's even worse than that."

"What, Drew? What is it you want?"

"This is the night, right?"

"What night?"

"The night where he tells everyone he's going to run for something, not be the mayor anymore. Something big. Derek was telling me all about it."

"Yeah," I said.

"And it's soon, right?"

"Pretty soon."

"You tell the mayor that when he goes onto the stage, he has to tell everyone that he had sex with a girl. An innocent, underage girl. A girl who was selling herself to get by, and that he took advantage of that fact. He has to tell everyone what he did."

"That's going to be a tall order, Drew," I said. "I don't know that he's going to go along with that."

"You've got one of those phones, right? That can take little movies?"

"Yeah. It can do that. In short doses."

"You take a picture of him, making that speech, with all the people there. He has to tell them that he hired a little girl, she was only a child, that he hired a girl to have sex with him. If he doesn't do that, I'm afraid I'm going to have to kill your boy, Jim. I'm going to kill your boy, and I'm going to kill your wife. I really hate to, honest I do, but I will, if the mayor doesn't do what I say, and the two of you don't come here after. You do that, and I won't hurt your family. But don't go thinking about calling the police. I see any police show up around here, I hear anybody coming close to this house, and I'll kill them right away, whether the mayor does what he's supposed to do or not. Do you get what I'm saying, Jim?"

"I hear you, Drew."

"You talk it over with him and give me a call back." And then Drew hung up the phone.

I closed mine.

"Jesus Christ on skates, you were on

there for a fucking hour," the mayor said. "You're going to make me late to my own announcement. What was that all about, anyway?"

I turned to Randy and said, "You're going to have to make some changes to your speech."

FORTY-ONE

Mayor Randall Finley said: "You. Are out. Of your fucking. Mind."

"That's what he wants," I told him, both of us standing outside the town car, the engine still running. "He says if you don't do it, he's going to kill Ellen and Derek."

"Oh, come on, Cutter!" the mayor said. "Has it occurred to you that he's probably going to do that anyway? And that my saying a bunch of lies isn't going to make any difference? Jesus, Cutter, I've got a reputation to think about here."

I grabbed him by the lapels of his thousand-dollar suit and threw him up against the side of the car. "Randy, I don't think you've fully grasped the seriousness of the situation. And if it's any comfort, you won't have to tell any lies at all. You'll be telling the truth."

"I didn't know," he said, shaking his head like a little boy. "I swear I didn't know."

"Don't give me this shit," I said. "The minute I walked in there, I could tell she was a child."

"I didn't force her to do anything," the mayor protested. "I didn't force her to choose that line of work."

"That's right," I said, moving my face an inch away from his. "You're totally blameless. You're just an innocent consumer."

"It was Lance," he said, spittle forming at the corner of his mouth. "It was his fault. He's the one set it up. He said he knew this girl, she was great, so I let him handle it. You see what I mean? How I was always better off with you handling everything? You'd never have booked her for me. You should never have let Lance do that."

"It's always someone else's fault, isn't it?" I said, still holding him, my nose up to his. "Because you don't know how to control your impulses, and the rest of us should realize that, so if we don't stop you, we're the ones who're to blame."

"I'm just saying, that's all," he squeaked.

"Because you couldn't keep your dick in your pants, because you thought nothing of fucking around with teenage hookers, I'm in one fuck of a situation right now. There's a guy with a gun holding my wife and my son hostage. Things have a way of coming back and biting you in the ass, Randy, and now they're biting me, too. That girl's father, you know how many people he's killed so far, by my count? Six. Not counting the guy he killed in front of me a couple of nights ago. If you don't go into that hall tonight and tell everybody what he wants you to tell them, he's not just going to kill my family. He's going to kill you, too. The only thing is, Randy, he'll have to beat me to it."

"Okay, okay, okay," Randy said. "Let me think, let me think." He glanced at his watch. He was due at his own function in fifteen minutes. "Maybe there's a way I can make this work. . . . You know, the whole Jimmy Swaggart thing, confess my sins . . . Shit, it'll never work."

His cell phone rang. I moved back enough to allow him room to reach into his jacket.

"Hello?" he said. "Yeah. . . . Right. . . . I know. . . . We're on our way. . . . Right. . . . See you soon." He put the phone away. "They're having shit fits that we're not there yet."

"They're going to be in for quite the surprise," I said, backing away, opening the door, grabbing Randy by the arm and throwing him into the back-seat.

Once I was behind the wheel, he said, "You know what this is, don't you? This is kidnapping!"

"Randy," I said, "I'm taking you to your own goddamn press conference. But I am issuing a death threat. If you don't do what this guy wants, and my family ends up dead, I swear to God, I will kill you."

I threw the car into drive and tromped on the gas. Randy, who was leaning forward to tell me something, was thrown back into his seat so hard I caught a glimpse of his shoes in the rearview mirror.

As Drew had instructed, I called the house.

Ellen answered. "Hello," she said.

"It's me. How you holding up?"

"We've been better. He's right here, he wants to talk to you."

Then Drew's voice. "What did he say?"

"We're heading to the press conference now. I've explained to the mayor what he has to do."

"That's great, Jim. I really appreciate it."

Like I'd just offered to let him borrow my car.

"Jim, I'd like to talk to the mayor," Drew said.

"Sure thing." I held the phone away from my head, looked at Randy in the mirror, and said, "He wants to talk to you."

"Christ, no, I don't want to talk to him," Randy said.

"Take the phone, Randy," I said.

He reached over the seat and took it

from my hand. "Hello?" he said. "Yes, it is. . . . Uh-huh. . . . Of course, I can understand how you might feel that way. . . . I'm afraid I was unaware of that. . . . Well, let me put this to you, sir. What sort of father lets his daughter get into that line of work?"

I couldn't make out the words, but I could hear Drew shouting at that point.

Randy, backpedaling, said, "Okay, okay, okay. I'm sorry. You're right, perhaps that was a bit out of line. . . . Yes, well . . . Okay." And he handed the phone back to me.

I put it to my ear. "Yeah?"

"He's an asshole," Drew said.

"You see, Drew?" I said. "There are things we can agree on. I'd like to talk to my wife again."

"I don't know, Jim. I think it's better you just get done what you have to get done."

"Drew," I said, "if the mayor does what you want him to do, does that settle things? You going to do to him what you've done to the others?"

There was a long pause at the other end of the line.

"Drew?"

"I want to talk to him after. I want you to bring him here. I want him to explain himself to me face-to-face."

Then Drew ended the call, without promising he wouldn't kill Randy, and without promising he wouldn't kill me. The only ones he'd promised to spare, if he got what he wanted, were Ellen and Derek.

"What did he say to that?" Randy asked.

"Your performance better be a good one," I said. "What'd he say to you?"

Randy was quiet, then, "He said a bunch of stuff. Told me I should be ashamed of myself. Seems to me there's plenty of shame to go around. He's the one got sent to jail, didn't look out for his daughter."

I wondered if Randy would ever get it.

When we pulled up out front of the Walcott, Maxine Woodrow, Randy Finley's campaign strategist, was standing there, waiting. She looked liked she was about to have a heart attack.

If she hadn't had one yet, she surely had one coming.

The moment the Grand Marquis stopped, she had the mayor's door open and said, "We were all getting so worried about you! We're all ready to start!"

She took the mayor by the elbow and started leading him into the hotel. I left the car sitting there and followed them inside. As we rounded a corner and headed to where the convention hall was located, we could hear upbeat music—"Don't Stop (Thinking About Tomorrow)" by Fleetwood Mac, it sounded like—and people talking. As Randy entered the room, the eyes of about fifty supporters were on him and cheers went up.

"Randy! Randy!" they chanted.

There were a couple of local news crews there as well. The lights on their cameras came on, and suddenly Randy was bathed in white light. He held his hand up, shielding his eyes, but waved at the same time. The son of a bitch was actually smiling. Adoration, even when it's coming only moments before total humiliation, was impossible for him not to enjoy.

"Everyone's so excited!" I heard Maxine shout above the chanting.

"Yeah, well, me too!" Randy said.

"Randy! Randy!"

I stayed close to him. Normally, I'd hang back, grab something to eat. I was, after all, just the driver. But this time I wasn't letting him out of my sight. I was barely going to let him out of arm's reach. I didn't trust him to do the right thing once he got to that podium.

The supporters were waving signs in the air. There was *Finley for Congress* and *Finally, a Man Like Finley* and *Finley First!* Music was pulsing through the speakers, the kind of stuff you hear at sporting events to get the crowd going. It wasn't all that big an event, and wisely, Maxine had not booked that big a room. Rule number one in politics: Always book a room that's too small.

Maxine was approaching the microphone, holding up her hands to get everyone to settle down. She blew into the mike and a raspy blast shook the room. "Is this on? Can you hear me?"

A number of people shouted yes. "Well," she said, "it is my extreme pleasure to be able to introduce to you this evening a man who has served you so proudly for many years now as your mayor, a man who's always put the constituent first, a man who knows what the people need and is willing to fight for them to get it, our man of the hour, Randall Finley!"

The crowd applauded. The mayor mounted the three steps to the raised platform on which the podium stood, gave Maxine a hug, and positioned himself by the mike. He looked down at the first row, saw his wife, Jane, sitting there, and gave her a wave. He must have decided that wasn't enough, because he walked back off the stage, down to where his wife was seated, leaned over and embraced her. He put his arms around her, pressed his cheek to hers and kissed her. He also took a moment to whisper something in her ear. Maybe something along the lines of "Get ready."

Then he was back on the stage, something close to a spring in his step, and looking at him, you'd never have had an inkling.

I stood off to the side of the small stage, no more than ten feet away, my phone out. I'd bought this gadget to take video of customers' yards when they wanted landscaping done, but never got much more out of it than two-minute snatches. I'd have to make that work.

"Good evening, good evening!" Randy said. "Thank you for that won-derful welcome. It's really terrific to be here. It's truly an honor. We are on the threshold of exciting times!"

"Exciting" wasn't the word I would have chosen.

"As you know," he continued, "I've always tried to do my best for you as mayor of Promise Falls, but I've been doing a lot of thinking lately, and the skills I've brought to bear on a local level, I would like to apply on a national level."

There was some murmuring in the crowd, some applause, then people

whispering "shh" so Randy could continue.

"This nation is in a terrible mess," he
said. "It's in an economic tailspin, it's
being eaten away by a pervasive moral
decay."

He had that right.

I hadn't hit the record button on my
phone yet. Nothing Randy had said so
far stood a chance of rescuing my family. Or saving his ass, either.

"This nation needs to be put back on
the right path, and I believe that if you
send me to Congress, I can help put it
back on that path. I am the person for
that job." He paused, giving the room a
chance to cheer and applaud. Everyone obliged.

"And there are a number of reasons
why I may be," he said, "the perfect
person for this assignment. I know
what it means to be on the right path,
and I know what it means to have
strayed from it."

I held up the phone, got ready.

"As you know, I speak my mind, I've
gained a bit of a reputation for doing

things to excess occasionally. I've had to pay to clean a few rugs in my time."

That brought laughter.

"I think a real leader needs to have done a few things wrong in his life to know how to get things right," he said. "My father, God rest his soul, was a wise, decent man, and he used to say to me, 'Randy, you show me a man who's made no mistakes along the way and I'll show you a man who hasn't gotten anywhere.' He was the kind of man who knew that to embrace life, to accept its challenges, meant making mistakes, because without mistakes there are no accomplishments. If it weren't for mistakes, and failures, how would we be able to measure our successes?"

He was taking the long way there, but he seemed to be going in the right direction. Maxine Woodrow whispered in my ear, "He's gone off text. What's he doing?"

I held up my hand to shush her. Randy glanced over, locked eyes with me, and I felt him sending me a message. Something along the lines of *If*

*this is what you want, you're going to
get it, and then some.*

I started recording.

Randy looked back at the crowd and
continued, "There are many different
kinds of mistakes. You design a bridge,
you make a mistake in the engineering,
that can result in catastrophe. You
overthrow a dictator with the best of intentions, to eradicate his weapons of
mass destruction, and they turn out not
to be there, well, there are conse-
quences to those kinds of mistakes in
judgment.

"But I want to talk to you about a different kind of mistake today. A mistake
of the heart. A mistake of the soul."

There wasn't a person in that room
not listening to every word Randall Finley had to say.

"My wonderful wife, Jane, is here today," Randy said, looking down at her.
Jane Finley, fiftyish, plump, black hair
piled on top of her head into something
that looked like a bird's nest, blushed.
She had in her lap a copy of the prepared speech, and if she'd been read-

ing along she must have been as puzzled as Maxine.

"A lot of you know Jane, and you know how she's always been there for me, how she's stood by me, sometimes through very dark times, often when I didn't deserve her support. I'm not an easy man to stand by. I live to excess. I am a man of appetites. And far too often I've indulged those appetites without thought to how my actions might affect others."

"What the hell is he doing?" Maxine whispered into my ear again. I ignored her and kept holding up the phone.

"I don't have to tell you people," the mayor said, "the kind of scrutiny public figures live under. Some politicians and celebrities will tell you it's terrible, that they want to be left alone, that their private lives are nobody's business. Well, I'm not so sure about that. I think, when you vote for me, when you trust me to make decisions on your behalf, you're entitled to know what kind of a man I am. My values, what I stand for, what I believe in. Like when I've accomplished great things, like the new hospital wing

I pushed through this past term, with its state-of-the-art burn unit, or the grant I delivered only yesterday to Swanson House to help young women whose lives haven't gotten off to the perfect start they might have hoped for.

"But you're also entitled to know about the less than great things I've done, because how can you trust me if you don't know everything there is to know about me?"

My phone stopped recording. I set it up to start again.

The crowd could feel Randy getting closer to something, and judging by their rapt expressions, the suspense was killing them. I knew what was coming, and I was feeling the suspense, too.

"So here I am before you tonight, announcing my intentions to represent you in the nation's capital, to do greater good than I have ever done before, but I also stand before you tonight to tell you about a period of darkness in my life, a darkness I was able to emerge from only through my own personal commitment to be a better man.

"What I have to tell you I've never revealed before, not even to my wife, because I'm not proud of it. I allowed my baser instincts to control me, I surrendered to a power greater than greed or alcohol. It was lust. I was unfaithful. But I was more than that. There was an occasion when I availed myself of the services of a sex worker, and as if that was not bad enough, I subsequently learned that this person was underage."

There was a collective gasp in the room. Jane Finley looked decidedly unwell. Maxine said, "Oh my God."

"I exploited this young woman in a way that shames not only me but all men everywhere. Not a day goes by that I'm not tormented by my contribution to this woman's life of degradation. I have done detestable things. I have hurt people. But what good is a man if he cannot learn from his misdeeds? If a man cannot be redeemed, even a man such as myself, then what point is there in going on? If I knew in my heart that my past misdeeds made it impossible for me to do good in the future, I'd end it all right now, right here, on this stage.

But that's not what I believe. I believe I have the ability to make this nation safer, and stronger, and more committed to the values that have made it the greatest country on the face of the earth, and that's why tonight, I stand before you, a humbled man, a man with many faults, but still a man with a dream, a man who is asking you for your support so that I may take my fight to Washington to make this country everything it should be!"

At first, silence. And then, a smattering of applause.

"I know you're shocked by what I've told you," he said, "and you're entitled to be. You're entitled to judge me. And some of you will judge me harshly. I certainly deserve it. But I would ask any of you here tonight who has not strayed, who has not sinned, who has not had a dark moment in his or her life, to come up on this stage right now and strike me down."

He paused, and we all waited for someone to rise to the challenge. No one took the bait.

After waiting an appropriate time,

Randy finished up. "Let my challengers make of this what they will. Will they be as honest with you as I've been tonight? Are they willing to lay bare their sins for others to judge? If there's someone else out there willing to be more open with you than I have been tonight, then not only will he deserve your vote, he'll have mine as well, because that's the kind of man that I am, faults and all!"

This time, a bit more than a mere smattering of applause.

"I know that this room is filled with good people. I know each and every one of you wishes you could go back in time and change at least one thing, one thing that you wish you could undo, a time when you hurt someone close to you, a time maybe when you were deceitful, a time maybe when you broke the law even though you knew better, and believe me, if I had such a time machine, I'd be putting so many miles on it it'd be out of warranty in no time."

No applause, but actually a few chuckles.

"But no matter what you've done,

what mistakes you may have made, I will represent you. I will be there for you, just as I've always been there for you in the past. And I'm going to be there for you in the future, because my name is Randall Finley, and if you make the decision not to give up on me, I swear to God I will never give up on you!"

Real applause this time, slowly spreading across the room.

"I thank you!" he said, waving his arms. "God bless you all!"

Now nearly everyone was applauding, and about half the room was on its feet. Someone shouted, "Give 'em hell, Randy!"

Maxine looked like she'd swallowed a frog.

"Thank you!" Randy said over the applause. "Good night!"

They were still applauding as he strode off the stage, pausing long enough to whisper in my ear, "Put that in your cock and smoke it."

FORTY-TWO

So whaddya think?" the mayor said, getting into the back of the Grand Marquis. "You know what I think? I think I've still got it."

I got behind the wheel, turned the ignition, kept quiet.

"What?" he said from the backseat. "You got nothing to say?"

"You're something else, Randy."

He settled back into his seat. "Take me home, Cutter," he said.

"We're not quite done, Randy," I said.

"What are you talking about? I said the thing. You got a picture of me saying it, right? On your phone? Isn't that what this psycho wants? Can't you just send that from your phone to his phone or something? You don't even have to go out to your place. Guy sees that, he lets them go, he goes home, this whole thing is over."

I feared it wasn't going to be that simple. And given that Randy's admission had not exactly resulted in his total humiliation, I wasn't sure how Drew was going to react to his speech once he saw it.

"He wants to meet with you," I said. "Face-to-face."

"No fucking way," Randy said, and I thought, when I caught a look at him in the mirror, that I saw some fear there.

"He still has my family, Randy," I said.

"Look, Cutter, I'm not unsympathetic." I glanced at him again in the mirror. "But I really think this is a matter between you and him, you know? Did I or did I not do my thing? Didn't I do what you asked? And even though I did my best to spin this thing in my direction, you think my little speech isn't going to end up on CNN? Those lefty bastards, that son of a bitch Wolf Blitzer, you wait, they'll only see the negative in what I said."

Within the hour, I figured.

"No, I think I'll just have you take me home," he said. "I'm going to have to talk to Jane. I figured it was best, let Maxine take her home, give her some time to cool off, you know. I've caused her a lot of shit but nothing quite like this, nothing this public. All my other stunts, as long as they weren't happening under her nose, she could more or less deal with them. But this . . ."

"Randy, I know you think this is one hundred percent about you, but maybe I haven't made myself clear enough about—"

Randy's cell phone rang. He had the phone out and to his ear in a second. "Yeah, honey, hi," he said. Mrs. Finley, evidently. "Whoa, whoa, hang on a second. . . . There's a lot more to this than meets the eye. . . . No, I haven't lost my mind. . . . It's a long story, I'll explain it all later, but Jesus Christ, honey, this is actually a kind of life-and-death situation here and when you know the whole story you'll understand. . . . Was it true? Okay, some of what I said, I embellished a bit, but the God's honest truth is I was coerced, honey. Like I said, it's complicated. You go home, take a couple of those pills the doctor gave you to settle your nerves. . . . That's right. I'll see you soon." He flipped the phone shut. "I hope you're happy," he said. "The sooner I get home, the better, get this all sorted out."

"Not yet, Randy. We're going back to my place. This guy wants to talk to you. He wants to give you a piece of his mind. Maybe, considering that he lost a daughter, you could give him that much."

"No thanks," he said. I could see, in my mirror, he still had the phone in his hand. "Time to bring the cops into this. Let them sort it out. I already confessed my sins, so I don't see what the fuck there is to lose now, you know? What's Barry's number? He can bring in a SWAT team or whatever it is they do, get a sniper, aim through a window, take him out, stupid bastard'll finally get what's coming to him."

I thought about what Drew had said, that if he saw any police moving in on the house, he'd kill Ellen and Derek.

When I saw Randy flip his phone

open, I hit the brakes and nosed the car into the curb. I was out the door in a second, had Randy's open, leaned in across the empty seat and grabbed for the phone in his hand.

"Jesus, Cutter, knock it off!" he shouted as we wrestled.

Once I had the phone, I withdrew from the backseat, slammed the door, and pitched the gadget as far as I could into an empty lot.

"Goddamn it, Cutter!" Randy shouted, opening his door. "I can't do it! I can't face that guy! The son of a bitch'll kill me! You know he will!"

I shoved him back into the car and was ready to slam the door but he kicked it back open again. I dove into the backseat, on top of him, grabbed him by the lapels of his jacket.

I dragged him across the seat, Randy flailing at me the whole way, and when I had him on the other side of the car I lifted him up and slammed him up against the window. The back of his head hit the glass hard and all of a sudden he stopped squirming and struggling. His eyelids fluttered.

Christ, I thought, *I've killed him.*

But he was doing some low-level moaning, and was at least conscious enough to reach a hand to the back of his head to feel his wound as he slid down into the upholstery.

Confident that Randy was not going to make a run for it in the next minute or so, I got out of the backseat and settled in again behind the wheel.

As I put the town car in drive, a very bad feeling washed over me. I knew that not only was it very likely I was delivering Randall Finley into the hands of his executioner, I was delivering myself as well.

But I'd sensed that Drew was being straight when he told me he'd spare Ellen and Derek if I did what he asked.

If I had to sacrifice Randy's life, and my own, to save my wife and son, then that was what I was going to have to do.

I was pulling into my own driveway when Randy fully realized where he was. He sat bolt upright in the back, looked out the window, saw the Langley house.

"Goddamn it, Cutter," he said.

My pickup and trailer were parked in the lane only a short ways down from the road, so we were going to have to walk in. Maybe that had been Drew's plan, to have Derek block the driveway to allow Drew plenty of time to see anyone, cops in particular, approaching the place.

"How's your head?" I asked, stopping the car and turning around in the seat.

Randy rubbed it. "You goddamn son of a bitch, you attacked me," he said.

"You're able to form complete sentences," I said, "so it doesn't sound like you sustained any brain damage."

"I can't go in there," he said.

"You're going in there," I told him.

"Okay, okay," Randy said, doing what he did best, which was try to put a good spin on the situation. "Okay, let me just think for a minute."

I waited.

"Let's say I meet with this guy, I talk to him, I persuade him to give himself up. That'll look good, right? Congressional candidate gets killer to surrender. That would work."

"That sounds good, Randy," I said.

"I pulled it off back there, right?" he asked, referring to his recent speech. "Maybe I can do it again." But his voice lacked confidence this time.

"You're the man, Randy," I said.

"And if I can do that, maybe get this guy to surrender, the press won't be so inclined to put a negative spin on that other stuff." He ran his hand nervously over his mouth. "And it gets better."

"What do you mean?"

"This girl, this guy's daughter? The hooker?"

"Yeah," I said.

"Well, she's dead, right? She got sick and died? Isn't that what you told me?"

"That's right."

"That's good news, right? It's not like she's going to be able to give details of when we hooked up. You know what else? Everything I said in my speech, I can just deny the whole thing. Who's to say otherwise? I just say I was forced, I had to make that statement, that I was doing it to save your wife and kid. Even if this nutjob gets out of this alive, it's just hearsay, right? What his daughter told him? Well, that's not going to stand up in court, am I right? And then Lance, he's no longer around, either, so he's not going to be able to say shit about this."

Randy was turning into a blathering idiot.

"This could actually work to my advantage. People see this guy, me, willing to jeopardize his career to save his driver's family. That's going to play very well, don't you think?"

"You're forgetting there's one other witness, Randy," I said.

He appeared baffled. "Who's that?"

"Me," I said. "Remember, I was there? When you were with Sherry Underwood? She bit your dick? I punched you in the nose?"

I saw his face come close to a grin. "Oh, I'm not worried about you, Cutter. I already got your promise to be discreet. You forget about that?"

I said nothing.

"I got an idea," Randy said. "Why

don't you go in first, sound him out, show him your little phone video, get a sense of what he's thinking, then come back out here and fill me in."

By that time, Randy would have thumbed a ride back into Promise Falls.

"I don't think so," I said.

I decided to do my job properly now, and went round and opened the door for Randy, real respectful. But he sat there until I reached in and grabbed the back of his jacket by the neck.

"Okay, okay!" he said as I dragged him out. Once he was on the gravel, I saw him glance back at the highway, at the occasional car and truck racing past. I knew what he had on his mind. Run up there, flag someone down.

"Don't even think about it," I said.

I grabbed hold of him again, pushed him ahead of me, my house just a few yards ahead of us.

I hoped that, when I next came back out of this house, it wasn't in a box.

FORTY-THREE

I mounted the steps of the front porch, holding on to Randy by the arm, and knocked on my own front door.

I shouted, "It's me, Drew! It's Jim Cutter! I'm here with the mayor!"

I heard the deadbolt turn back, and the door opened. It was Derek. "Hey, Dad," he said. He looked okay, if frightened. I stepped into the room, saw Ellen sitting in a chair across from the television, and Drew, in the doorway to the kitchen, a gun in his hand.

"Hey," he said, raising the weapon in the general direction of Randy and myself. "Both of you, keep your hands up in the air."

We did as we were asked. He approached, and tentatively, in a half-crouching position so his own body and gun were as far away from us as possible, he patted both of us down to see whether either of us was carrying a weapon.

Satisfied that we were not, he moved several feet away and said, "You got it?"

I took the phone, which he'd already patted over, from my jacket pocket. "Yeah," I said. "It's in a couple of bits, and I'm sure the eleven o'clock news is going to have it, too."

"Show it to me," he said.

I handed the phone to Derek. It always took me forever to figure out how to access data that was already in the phone, even basic numbers. While my son fiddled with it, I said to Ellen, "How you doing, hon?"

She gave me a very weak smile. "Been better."

"Are you hurt?"

She shook her head. She nodded toward Derek and said, "We're okay." She didn't say it, but there was an implied "so far" at the end of her sentence.

"Okay, I think I've got it here," Derek said, looking at the phone.

"Hand it to me," Drew said, reaching out with his free hand. But Derek was still fiddling.

And I thought, did I have a plan? I realized I did not. I was hoping Drew would be a man of his word, although I also knew that might be a lot to expect from someone who'd been on a killing spree. Maybe it was naive to believe that if I delivered the mayor to him, and the video of his speech, he'd honor his promise and let Ellen and Derek go. There'd been something in his voice, when we'd spoken on the phone, that suggested to me that he was at the end of this. I tried to tell myself he was done taking vengeance on those who had used and abused his daughter, that maybe he didn't much care what happened to him now.

And maybe, once again, I was talking out of my ass. A man who didn't care what happened could be doubly dangerous.

I was looking for opportunities. Ways that I might be able to get the jump on Drew. Or distract him. There were, in the room now, four of us and one of him.

Of course, he was the only one who was armed.

But I was standing not far from the fireplace, where the poker I'd grabbed the night I'd found Derek and Penny on the back deck was hanging.

Derek said, "There, got it." And he handed the phone to Drew, who snatched it away from him.

He was looking at the small screen, his eyes darting back and forth between what was on the phone and the rest of us in the room.

"How do you turn this up?" he asked.

"The little thing," Derek said, "on the side there."

Drew couldn't figure it out, so Derek, tentatively, approached and showed him how to do it, then stepped back. Now we could all hear Randy's voice coming from the phone. "This looks like the middle of a speech," Drew said.

"It is," I said. "I tried to catch the parts that mattered."

Drew looked very agitated, waiting for Randy's confession, trying to keep an eye on us. Derek was looking very antsy, his eyes jumping, his fists opening and closing. He looked as though he was getting ready to spring. I tried to catch his eye, tell him to take it easy. The last thing I wanted was Derek getting shot, trying to be a hero.

I shifted a little closer to the hanging poker.

From my phone: ". . . I think, when you vote for me, when you trust me to make decisions on your behalf, you're entitled to know what kind of a man I am. . . ." Drew nodded, didn't take his eyes off the tiny screen. Then: "I also stand before you tonight to tell you about a period of darkness in my life. . . ."

Drew's eyes kept darting between us and the screen. He was worried we were going to try to jump him.

". . . I was unfaithful. But I was more than that. There was an occasion when I availed myself of the services of a sex worker, and as if that was not bad enough, I subsequently learned that this person was underage."

"Okay," said Drew. "We're getting to it."

"... I have done detestable things. I have hurt people. But what good is a man if he cannot learn from his misdeeds. ..."

And then Drew was watching the part where Randy started turning the oil tanker on a dime, making virtue out of peccadilloes. A few seconds later I could hear the applause coming out of the phone, and by the time someone shouted "Give 'em hell, Randy!" Drew was shaking his head very slowly. He looked at Randy. "They like you. You told them you'd had sex with a young girl and they applauded you." He was dumbfounded.

Randy did something I'd rarely seen him do. He went red with embarrassment.

Drew looked back at the phone one last time, as though the gadget itself were the object of his contempt, flipped it shut, then, suddenly, flung it hard at the living room window, shattering it. Ellen jumped. Drew, turning on all of us, his voice full of exasperation, asked, "What's wrong with those people? How could they . . . how could they cheer a man like that on after he admitted something like that?"

None of us had an answer for that.

To Drew, Randy said, "Look, pal, I did what you wanted. I said what you wanted me to say. I came here of my own free will to meet you face-to-face. I can't help it if the crowd didn't react the way you wanted them to."

"You son of a bitch," Drew said, his gun hand trembling. While he glowered at Randy, I positioned myself in front of the fireplace poker.

A line of sweat ran down Randy's temple.

"Drew," I said softly, "the mayor here may have come out of this smelling like a rose right now, but that won't last. His opponents will seize on that admission. Eventually, it'll ruin him."

"Sure," said Randy. "I'm toast."

"I don't know," Drew said. "This isn't how I thought it would go."

"Yeah, well, this isn't exactly how I expected to be spending my evening either," Randy said, trying to smile.

Here he was, trying to win some sympathy from Drew. I couldn't recall ever seeing him this desperate.

"What, am I supposed to feel sorry for you?" Drew asked.

I reached behind me for the poker, and was wrong in thinking it was a move I could handle deftly. It clinked against the iron stand as I moved it, and Drew turned and trained his gun on me.

"What was that?" he demanded.

"Nothing," I said.

"Show me what's in your hand."

I displayed the poker and Drew clenched his teeth. "Drop that and go stand over there," he said, motioning to the bookcase.

"Sure," I said, letting the poker clang to the floor. "No problem." I caught the desperate, hopeless look in Ellen's eyes at that moment. I shifted over and parked myself by the books.

Turning his attention back to the mayor, Drew said, "I should feel sorry for you, *you,* a guy who screws teenage girls?"

"Look, pal," Randy said. "There's a

few things you need to understand. First of all, I had no idea your daughter was that young. She looked a lot older, you need to know that from the get-go. I would never have entered into any arrangement with her knowing she was as young as she was. I have certain lines that I won't cross."

Drew stared at him.

"Secondly, I never approached her directly. That was handled by an associate of mine, a Mr. Lance Garrick. I'm guessing maybe you already know him, right? He should never have set that up, and I want to say, listen, Lance deserved what he got. I can't see where anyone would blame you for what you did there." He forced a laugh. "More than once, I felt like shooting him myself."

Drew kept looking at him, wondering where he was going with this. I didn't have any real idea either. I glanced at Ellen. When I looked over her way, something on the bookshelf caught my eye.

Resting on top of a row of books, inches below the next shelf, was a lawn-cutting blade from the tractor. I'd set it there when I'd come back into the house the other day and found Ellen staring out the window at the Langley house.

"The thing is," Randy said, "there's a lot of blame to go around here, and let's face it, you own a bit of that yourself." His tone wasn't totally argumentative. He seemed to be trying to make a point with Drew, but I thought it was a risky one.

"Randy," I said.

"Wouldn't you agree?" the mayor persisted. "Huh, Drew?"

Drew said, "All I know is, of all the men who took advantage of my daughter, who helped to put her into the ground, there wasn't one who should have known better more than you."

Randy didn't say anything.

"I was with her when she died," Drew said. "I got released just in time to be with her. I was there with her nearly every minute of her last week. She told me about all the mistakes she made, how much she wished I could have been there through the bad times. And

I found her book, her little notebook. She wrote down everything. Phone numbers, names, license plates. Most men, they didn't give their real names, but with the other information, I was able to piece things together. I'd call a number, get hold of a guy, tell him I wanted to hire him for a job, anything to get a face-to-face with him, you know? Then sound him out, maybe ask him if he knew where I could hire a girl for some fun. Gradually, I found out who some of the sick fucks who used her were. I told her, before she died, that I was going to make it all up to her. I promised her. But I didn't track you down through that book. But I found your buddy Lance. He did your dirty work for you. He set things up for you. He told me everything before he died."

"Listen, pal—"

Drew cut Randy off. "You killed her! You and all the others! You might as well have gotten a gun and shot her yourself. Maybe that would have been better. At least it would have been quicker, you bastard!"

"Jesus," Randy said. "Look, I've done

what you wanted. I told the people what you wanted me to say. I came out here so you could give me shit. So we're good, right? You're not going to kill me."

"Yes," Drew said. "I am."

The mayor's cheeks, so red earlier, were quickly draining of color. "Hey, come on. A deal's a deal."

"And not just you," Drew said. He looked over at me. "You too, Jim."

"No," Ellen whispered.

"Come on, man," said Derek.

I was just thinking about how I could reach up and grab the blade, but stopped when Drew turned his attention to me. "I know you don't think I did enough where Sherry is concerned," I said. "And I'm sorry about that. I really am. I'll always regret it."

"Not for a whole lot longer," Drew said.

"What would you have done, Drew? Just tell me. Suppose the roles had been reversed. I've got a daughter, her life's gone off the rails, and you happen to bump into her. She's a total stranger to you. But you see she's in trouble, she's made some bad choices. So you give her your name and number, tell her if she wants help you're available. And she doesn't want that help. What would you do?"

Drew's eyes appeared to sparkle for a moment, and then I realized they were moist, that he was trying to hold back tears.

"You were her only chance," he whispered. "You were what I prayed for while I sat in prison. That someone would see the trouble she was in, and help her, until I got out and could do it myself. But it didn't happen. And by the time I got out, it was too late."

I glanced again at Ellen, her eyes wide with fear. Then at Derek, wide-eyed as well, but not with fear exactly. Like he was looking for an opening, an opportunity. If someone in the room could provide some momentary distraction, anything, just engage him in conversation for a second, Drew would look away, and maybe that would give me just enough time to grab the tractor blade, attack him with it, use it like a machete or something.

I might end up getting shot, but if I

could manage to inflict a little damage, I might be able to save my wife and son.

It was Randy who stepped in. "I'll tell you this much," he said, and Drew looked his way. "You're right to think you could have expected more of him, but me, come on, everybody knows what I'm like, so—"

Everything after that happened very fast.

I swiveled around, wrapped my hand around the heavy steel blade. I'd yet to sharpen it out in the shed. The edges were blunt and rounded. But at a foot and a half in length, it would still do a lot of damage if I could hit Drew with it.

Drew, even though he'd been distracted by the mayor, spotted that I was up to something, because he'd snapped his head around to look at me, coming at him with the blade, and now his gun was up, and there was a loud noise, like a cannon going off, and I felt something hit my shoulder and knock me back up against the bookcase.

Ellen screamed. Derek yelled, "Dad!"

The blade went flying out of my hand and hit the wall.

With all this sudden commotion, no one, Drew in particular, heard the steps on the front porch, so it was a shock to everyone when the front door flew open and Conrad Chase, clutching a small, shallow box in his hands, came into the room.

Drew, gun still extended, whirled around, bug-eyed.

Conrad barely had a chance to say "Jesus! What the hell's going—" before Drew shot him in the head.

As Conrad was jerked backward, the box flew from his hands and opened in midair, hundreds of pages of manuscript spilling onto the floor.

That was when Derek launched himself across the room, like he was jumping from one part of the high school roof to another, flying across the coffee table. He was completely off the ground when he collided with Drew, who seemed momentarily stunned not only by the two shots he'd just fired, but by the pages fluttering all over the place.

Drew's gun arm went high, and another shot went off. Bits of plaster fell from the ceiling.

Derek was neither big enough nor strong enough to keep Drew down. He was a big man, and there was no way Derek was going to hold him down by himself. Even though my shoulder was searing with pain, I bolted four steps across the room and fell onto Drew, grabbing at the wrist that held the gun and slamming it to the floor. Derek had hold of his other arm, but Drew was still trying to use it to get at me, dragging Derek across his body.

I kept both hands on Drew's wrist while Derek tried to sneak in a punch to Drew's gut, then his face, but he wasn't having much impact. Out of the corner of my eye I saw the mayor on the far side of the room, watching what was transpiring like it was some cockfight for his entertainment.

In that glance, I failed to spot Ellen. Where the hell was Ellen?

And then there was a loud *whack,* and Drew stopped thrashing about. Very tentatively, I let go of his wrist, rolled over onto my knees, and saw Ellen with the poker in her hands. And Drew's head covered in blood.

Conrad lay, bloody and unmoving and undoubtedly dead, in the open front doorway.

Trying to catch my breath, I got to my feet, reached over and gave my son a pat on the shoulder, then took a look at the blood seeping through my shirt over my left shoulder where Drew's bullet had grazed me.

Randy, filled with renewed confidence now that the threat in the room had been neutralized, stood over Drew Lockus and, pointing a finger accusingly, said, "Maybe if you'd been a better father in the first place, none of this shit ever would have happened!"

This time, when I punched him in the nose, I broke the fucker.

FORTY-FOUR

We were sitting in the car, Ellen and I, parked across the street from a house where I did regular yard work.

We'd only just pulled up to the curb, so I hadn't turned the engine off yet, and we were still feeling the benefits of the air-conditioning in Ellen's little Mazda. I was in the passenger seat, taking a break from driving while my shoulder healed. Ellen, sitting behind the wheel, had one hand resting on the wheel, the other on the door handle.

"So," she said, looking straight ahead.

"Yeah," I said.

A lot had happened in the last few days since Conrad Chase had died in our house. Famous writers turned college presidents tended to garner a lot of attention when their lives ended as violently as Conrad's had.

In the moments since then, when we weren't answering Barry's questions, or avoiding the six o'clock news team, Ellen and I had been doing a lot of talking. About small things, about big things. About where we'd been and where we were going.

The time seemed to be right to make some changes.

My job driving Mayor Randall Finley, had, not surprisingly, come to a rather abrupt end, once again. I hadn't promised to work long for him anyway, so losing the gig prematurely wasn't that big a deal. And I still had the lawn-cutting business. For now.

The thing was, Randy's job appeared to be in a bit of jeopardy, too. He'd managed to wow the crowd at the official announcement of his bid for Congress, and had the distinction of being the only politician in history known to have, in the same speech, outlined his ambitions while also admitting to sex with an underage hooker. As he'd predicted, his speech had not only made it to CNN and every other news network on the planet, it was a consistent favorite on YouTube.

And the Promise Falls town council had lawyers working overtime, studying the town's constitution, attempting to determine whether there was some way they could impeach Randy. Although the mayor had not yet abandoned his congressional bid—Randy was the eternal optimist—it appeared that even if he never made it to Washington, he was at least going to experience some of its procedures.

He made some noise about charging me with assault for punching him in the nose a second time. When I had a moment to speak with him privately after what had happened at the house, I said, "Then our deal is off? I have your blessing to be indiscreet, and disclose all the details of your time with Sherry Underwood, how you not only screwed her, but hit her as well?"

So we were back where we'd started from. As much trouble as he was in, he was grateful not to have an eyewitness to his evening with Sherry Underwood.

He was right about one thing: ultimately, it came down to his version of the story versus a hearsay tale from Drew Lockus, a man who'd just been on a killing spree and who lacked a lot in the credibility department. As it turned out, Linda, the single mother who had been waiting in the hall for her friend Sherry the night she'd had her meeting with Randy, had never actually set eyes on the mayor.

But even if all the details of the mayor's bad behavior failed to come out, I had a feeling he was pretty much finished, at least politically. A guy could only be that reckless for so long before it finally caught up with him.

When we'd had our brief chat about my oath of silence, I had asked him, should his political career go into the toilet, whether he was any good with a Weed Eater. I mentioned that, with my shoulder all bandaged up after getting shot, Derek and I could probably use another hand.

Drew was charged in the murders of the Langleys and Lance Garrick, as well as Edgar Winsome and Peter

Knight, the two other men Drew had been led to by piecing together the information in Sherry's notebook. The police still had no interest in charging Drew in the death of Mortie, the man who'd come, along with Illeana's brother Lester, to terrorize me and Ellen that night in the shed.

For that act, we were, curiously, still in his debt.

After the pages that had scattered across our living room had been collected, I actually read the first couple of chapters of Conrad's book. It was about a news photographer whose most famous, Pulitzer Prize–winning shot, of a man's execution in Afghanistan at the hands of the Taliban, turns out to be the work of another photographer who'd failed to get out of the country alive.

I didn't read the whole thing, but it didn't come across to me as some kind of veiled confession. It seemed to me Conrad was merely milking his own experience for material. It struck me that what Conrad was really doing was ripping off Brett Stockwell a second time. The first time, he'd stolen the boy's novel. The second time, he'd exploited the boy's misfortune to write another.

Ellen, whose contacts in the publishing world are much better than a landscaper's, hears that the book has been deemed unreadable. That, however, does not necessarily make it unpublishable. Time will tell whether Conrad has a posthumous bestseller.

"You remember what I said a while back," Ellen said, tipping her head back onto the headrest.

"Which thing?" I said.

"When Derek was in jail, about how we were being punished for things we'd done," she said.

"I remember. You still feel that way?"

"Look at what we've done, between the two of us," she said. "How horribly wrong good intentions can go. I tried to help Brett Stockwell, and it backfired, destroyed people's lives. You scribbled your name in a book, gave a girl a number to call if she wanted help . . ."

"And the Langleys ended up dead," I said. "Because Drew went to the wrong house to seek revenge."

We both thought about that for a moment. I wondered whether Ellen was thinking what I was thinking, that maybe we were cursed or something.

"Where will we go?" she said finally. "After I go in there"—she jerked her thumb at the house—"and do my thing."

"I don't know," I said. "Maybe no place. Maybe there's no point. You can leave a place behind, but your secrets will just follow you. Maybe the best thing to do is stay put and ride it out."

"I don't want to wake up another day and see the Langley house."

She had a point there.

"What about Derek?" she asked. "You think he's going to be okay?"

"He'll manage. He's tougher than we give him credit for."

Ellen powered down the windows, killed the engine. "You saw what he did this morning, didn't you?"

"What?" I said as hot, humid air rushed into the car.

"He took one of your paintings, that one you did of the Berkshires, from the shed and put it on the wall in his room."

"You're kidding."

"No."

Decorating his cell, I thought.

"He saved our lives," I said. "When Drew was distracted by Conrad."

Ellen reached over and held my hand, gave it a squeeze. "I'm going to send my résumé to a whole bunch of public relations agencies. All over the country. And if I can't get something from that, I'll try something else."

"I'm sure wherever it is, there'll be grass to cut," I said.

"Do something else," Ellen said. "You could teach art. Work in a gallery. Go back to painting."

"We'll see."

Ellen took a deep breath, exhaled slowly, preparing herself.

"You ready?" I asked her.

She glanced at me and tried to smile. "As ready as I'll ever be, I guess."

"You're sure?" I asked.

"Yeah," she said.

"Because there's going to be a lot of fallout from this. For you. For Conrad's estate, his publisher, a whole lot of people."

"Sometimes, even if it takes ten

years to get around to it, you have to do the right thing," Ellen said, and got out of the car.

Together, we walked up to Agnes Stockwell's door to tell her that she needn't feel guilty any longer, that her son, Brett, did not kill himself, that he was an acclaimed and published author, that he had died trying to save my wife's life.

ACKNOWLEDGMENTS

All I did was write this thing. A number of others made it happen.

In the U.S., many thanks to Irwyn Applebaum, Nita Taublib, Danielle Perez, and everyone else at Bantam Dell. I'd also like to thank everyone at Orion in the U.K., in particular my editor, Bill Massey.

And to my agent, Helen Heller, way to go.

ABOUT THE AUTHOR

Linwood Barclay is a former columnist for the *Toronto Star*. He is the author of several critically acclaimed novels, including *No Time for Goodbye* and *Stone Rain*. He lives near Toronto with his wife and has two grown children. His website is www.linwoodbarclay.com.